Summer and Snow

Summer and Snow

Magic in Myth Book 2

J.S. Alexandria

SHADOW RAIN PUBLISHING

Summer and Snow is an 18+ romance novel that contains adult themes and graphic scenes. Content warnings include: graphic sex, violence, kidnapping, torture, foul language, and parental death (off-page).

Elements of this story are inspired by Asian, European, and some Native American cultures. While we attempted to accurately capture the spirit of these rich and varied cultures, there is an element of fiction embedded within these pages. This book is not intended to be interpreted as a literal or informational text, nor is it meant to be representative of these diverse cultures.

THE ALLMANNER DISTRICT
EAS MANOR
FARMLAND
MARKET SQUARE
TITAN'S FEN RESIDENCES
L'EL HEIGHTS
BARRACKS
GUARDHOUSE & GATE
DARK ARTS MARKET
TITAN'S FEN
MARKET DISTRICT
IN THE GREATER WORLD
GERMANY
FRANCE
CZECHIA
THE BLACK FOREST
FAERLOCH
AUSTRIA
DANI'S HOUSE

NORTH TO THE WITCH'S SAFEHOUSE
THE CITY OF
FAERLOCH
MAPPED
IN THE PRESENT AGE
MADDIE'S HOUSE
NORTHERN SUBURBS
EXPRESSWAY
RIVERSIDE DISTRICT
HERN MS
HOUSE TRICT
BUSINESS DISTRICT
KING STREET VET CLINIC
HIGH RISE DISTRICT
KARI & JIAN'S HOUSE
MELISANDE MARTIAL ARTS
ROGER'S CONDOMINIUMS
UNIVERSITY DISTRICT
EASTERN DISTRICT
PUB DISTRICT
THE DEN
SOUTHSIDE RESIDENCES
THE LOCH RIVER
SOUTHERN SUBURBS
EXPRESSWAY

To us.
Again.

If the endless dream guides your restless spirit, seize it! Raise your flag and stand tall!

Chapter   One

CROWN PRINCE

... their skill in empathy magic became widely known early on, and is one of the many reasons House Titania rose to such prominence. It was Queen Dyanthe Titania who is credited with the origin of the 'Golden Rule,' strictly followed by members of the House for generations, until the Malady made...

– Gherald Schmidt, Faerloch Historical Archives

Slate Melisande, crown prince of the fae, was a fucking creep.

Winter was wrapping its icy fingers around the city of Faerloch, Germany. The first snow dusted the bare trees, the sidewalks, and the tops of buildings. The cold didn't bother him much—a light performance jacket with the collar turned up and a black knit cap protected him from most of the chill.

His fae blood wasn't as easily susceptible to the elements as a mortal's.

He cocked his head, picking apart the complex sounds of the city to tune into one sound in particular.

A Vespa. A GTS Super model, to be precise.

He braced his hands on the edge of the building, leaning over the parapet as the sleek white scooter came zipping down the street. Its rider wore a visored helmet, white like the bike, with a long red braid streaming out from under it, whipping through the air like an angry cat's tail. Slate watched with sharp eyes as the Vespa's tiny engine revved before shooting forward through a crowded intersection, weaving expertly through traffic. He tracked the bike as it took a sharp turn down another street and screamed through a newly turned red light, making his heart clog up into his throat. Her reckless driving habits, so at odds with her personality, would send him into an early grave.

Slate took two steps back and fell into a portal he'd tossed down, skipping over to another building down the street, tracking the Vespa across the city.

He shouldn't be following her.

His ex-girlfriend. Daniella O'Callaghan.

He'd tempered the heady desire to see her for *months*. Half a year had gone by since the last time he'd spoken to her. He knew she was alright, knew she'd been spending more time with her friends—including Kari—and working her normal night hours at the vet clinic. None of his uncle's ilk had shown interest in pursuing her after that fateful night almost six months ago.

Slate could still feel the fire in his bones from when the Faerie Dust Glamour had been ripped from his marrow. Could still taste the blood in his mouth. Hear the arena exploding. Sometimes he even woke up in the middle of the night, drenched in sweat, thinking his own magic was swallowing him into the void—

Slate sucked in a deep, frigid breath, cutting off his thoughts as he returned his focus to the white Vespa.

He'd gone to see Dani once, at the very end of summer. He'd spied her outside the vet clinic where she worked, less than a month after the whole fiasco at the arena. Staying in the city had been difficult for him then—his ability to shield himself against the emotions of others had been absolute shit, as had his ability to maintain a glamour. Around mortals, who rarely shielded themselves, it had been like drowning in a crowded room of screaming people. But he'd wanted to ascertain for himself that she was alright.

He'd caught only a glimpse of her, a moment that had felt like an eternity as much as a blink.

He'd seen her. She hadn't seen him.

He'd resisted the urge to see her again.

Until now.

He had no right to even speak to her, let alone see her. He'd broken up with her. Totally. Completely.

He hadn't fucking wanted to.

But he had.

He'd needed to keep her safe. To take the Silver Valley's attention off her. It was part of the reason why he kept his distance for so many months. Though, Slate's advisors had a working theory that Zeyphar didn't hunt Dani because of the narrative Zeyphar spun for the faerfolk—that Slate was a prince in distress and needed to be redeemed from the rebels. Kidnapping Slate's friends would be counterproductive to that narrative.

And he wouldn't be surprised if Roger had precautions in place.

Either way, he'd stayed away from her out of an abundance of caution. Last thing he needed on his conscience was to drag her back into the crosshairs of the Silver Valley Council.

But the need to see her was crippling. He *wanted* to see her. He *wanted* to mend the gaping, painful wedge between them, caused by a maniacal fae king and an exploding arena, but his life was infinitely more complex now than it had been. He tried to lean into the idea that she was better off without him. Other days, missing her was a suffocating ache in his lungs.

Slate portal-skipped several more times, navigating the upper reaches of the cityscape like a shadow. He paused on the fire escape of some derelict building, catching his balance effortlessly as the iron structure shifted and groaned under his weight. Fingerless gloves protected most of his hands from the iron, but he relished the small burn to his fingertips nonetheless; pain had become a welcome distraction from the emptiness of missing Dani. He had a feeling his father knew it too, considering how willing he was to run Slate through vigorous martial arts drills.

Not the healthiest way to deal, but throwing himself into training was a coping mechanism he was long familiar with.

The Vespa stopped at a traffic light. He watched as she flipped the visor, leaning back on the seat. Even from up high, his fae vision caught the details of her face; creamy skin bespeckled with freckles and those unique eyes of hers—brilliant summer green with flecks of hazel and gold—before the light changed, and she tapped the visor back down.

Despite the brisk air, he was close enough to catch her scent—the faintest taste of sunshine and grassy meadows, all things warm and green. The desperation of missing her steamrolled him, crippling him until drawing a full breath was difficult at best.

He *really* shouldn't be following her.

It had started innocently enough. As the weather turned cooler, he'd finally strengthened his mental shields, meaning he'd been able to come to Faerloch more and for longer periods. His visits to the city proper to test the strength of his shields—and because he'd missed the rich vibrancy that was Faerloch—had quickly become less about testing himself.

Those innocent visits had brought him closer and closer to a certain animal hospital.

One day he'd gotten it into his head to simply... check on Dani. See how she was doing, just a little peek. And despite the rational part of him that argued he shouldn't even open that door for himself... he hadn't been able to resist.

That had been a week ago. A week since he'd waited for her to leave work. A week since he'd gotten his first glimpse of her in months. A week since he'd followed her home to make sure she was safe, then debated calling her.

He hadn't. Obviously.

And now, a week later.... he was here.

Stalking her. He was self-aware enough to recognize the lunacy of it.

Dani slowed to a stop outside some swanky cafe along the Loch River. Slate perched himself on the roof of a ritzy condominium across the street. In the distance, he could see the red *torii* marking the pedestrian bridge into the Eastern District, his home.

She took off her helmet and buckled it to the bars along the back. Then she unbraided her hair and shook out the strands before taking a couple of pieces near her face and securing them back with a little clip. Slate checked his mental shields—woven like fine filaments of ice and frost, delicate but stronger than steel at the moment—before he reached out with his magic. No more intrusive than soft snow against a frozen earth, he listened at the threshold of her emotional grid. She was high from the drive but nervous. No... more than nervous. Anxious. And there was a touch of... guilt.

Beneath those superficial emotions of the moment was a swirl of complicated feelings; sadness, loneliness, and a hint of fear. Not fear for her life, but a different kind. A heavier, slow-simmer kind.

Those base emotions had been present when he'd touched her with his magic last week as well. Had she always felt like that, deep down inside, even before the Championship Fight? Was that her default setting?

The thought made his heart tighten.

Fuck, the longing to go to her was a powerful whisper in his ear. It would be the work of a moment to portal to the corner, walk around it, and greet her right there on the street.

A panic thrummed against his ribs, warring with the intense desire to close the distance between them. He couldn't... he couldn't do that. He didn't think he'd recover properly if he saw fear in her eyes at the sight of him.

"My lord."

Slate nearly jumped out of his skin. He whirled around and found two fae soldiers standing on the roof with him.

A glamour concealed their pointed ears, and the pair had done their best to dress like mortals, but with their all-black attire, they looked more like hitmen. Their expressions were less than pleased as he faced them, but that was pretty standard when their charge slipped away from them two hours ago.

Frankly, he'd been expecting them sooner.

Ghosting his escorts had become a bit of a game for him in the last couple of weeks. For the first few months he'd been with the fae, he'd tolerated the constant presence of two or three guards everywhere he went. His sudden deep dive into the fae and what these people were capable of had opened his eyes to the fact that, while he wasn't exactly a slouch, even his heavy experiences in martial arts and fighting were little match against as formidable a foe as one Zeyphar Titania. Or Zeyphar's own personal entourage of highly trained fae soldiers.

Soldiers who had approached him on more than one occasion since the summer. Slate had barely walked away from one such encounter and had spent weeks under lock and key in the fae village of Titan's Fen for his safety.

But as his confidence in his own abilities soared, he found himself less tolerant of being followed all the time.

It was a conversation he'd had *frequently* with his 'keepers' at Titan's Fen—Kallen, Saida, and Galyn.

"Guess hide and seek is over for the day, huh, boys?" Slate swallowed his startled heart and leaned his hips against the low partition along the edge of the roof. He crossed his arms across his chest and tipped his head over his shoulder to watch the street. Dani was straddling her bike, texting. His heart skipped a beat as his mind jumped back to the near-constant communication they'd once had. Endless flirting, sassy quips.

He missed that the most—the ease of everything between them. It had been effortless to talk, to flirt, to touch, as if they'd been doing it for years instead of just months. He'd been magnetized to her from the start, and most days, he still felt a little lost without her.

"My lord, it is unwise for you to disappear—" one of the soldiers began.

Slate waved his hand, not taking his eyes off the street. "You know I don't need an escort, Basyl. And stop calling me that." It was a battle he was going to have to give up; no matter how many times he asked, the fae from Titan's Fen still ended up calling him 'my lord' or 'your grace'. Worse when they called him by his *title*: Prince Zlaet.

Mortifying.

Slate angled his head to glance at the guard. Basyl had gone still—the unnatural stillness of the fae—then his shoulders dropped in a visual sigh. He tipped his head forward as he said, "I'd not forgive myself if something were to happen to you."

All sense of royal proprietary vanished, much to Slate's relief. He had danced with Basyl many times in the training ring, both of them kicking the shit out of each other. Same with the other guard here with him today—Shea. He'd found the best way to get beyond formalities with the fae was to bleed together.

"Obviously I'm fine..." Slate's words drifted off as his attention shifted back to the street. He frowned as Dani's head snapped up, and a smile lit up her face. He followed her gaze down the street, turning to brace his hands on the half-wall partition.

His breath froze in his lungs.

"My lord?"

He hadn't noticed Basyl and Shea shifting closer to him, both of them angling to follow his gaze with their own.

A man approached Dani. She slid off the bike and walked the short distance to greet him. Slate's pulse jumped when the man leaned in and kissed both of Dani's cheeks, then said something to her with a hand at the small of her back as he guided her into the cafe.

Ice pricked at Slate's fingertips, pricked the inside of his mind.

Was she...?

He jumped into a portal and skipped himself down between the buildings. He popped out behind a dumpster and peered around it to see he had a narrow view through the windows of the cafe across the street. Enough that he could spy Dani's vibrant red hair as she stood chatting with the man from the street, waiting in line by the counter. He watched as they ordered, grabbed their beverages, then headed for a table together.

It was an intimate corner table, and the scene was so familiar it threw Slate for a minute. A different cafe. A different season. A different man.

Same woman.

She was on a date. Unmistakably so. The casual shift to her shoulders, the way she leaned forward in her seat, listening intently, fingers ceaseless on her cup. Her back was to him, giving him a good view of her date. With his sharp vision, he could see her date watching her with a mixed sense of adoration and cautious excitement, and when Slate listened at the door of the guy's mind, he *felt* the man's attraction toward her.

That ice migrated up his hands, crackling along the inside of his mind. She was on a date.

A *date*.

Anger punched him behind his eyes, sharpening his senses. His skin thrummed with energy, twisting up between his blood and his bones.

It quickly fizzled out, spiraling into something far more potent and far more crippling—hurt.

What date number was it? Five? Seven? *Ten?*

His... she was...

He should leave.

Through the large glass window, he saw her tilt her head back as her shoulders shook a little, and he caught the corner of a smile on her lips as she laughed. The man offered her a grin, a flush across his face, as though he didn't quite know what to make of her.

Slate didn't fault him for that—Dani was extraordinary.

He pushed off the wall. A part of him wanted to linger, to see where this date went. He was self-aware enough to know he'd seen enough, though, and he knew staying would only drive that hurt deeper into his heart. He turned toward the back of the alley and threw down a portal.

He didn't look back.

Within the space of a heartbeat, the alley was once more empty, nothing but whorls of snow and dust in his wake.

Slate appeared on the ancient stone bridge just outside of Titan's Fen. He didn't bother waiting for his two guards; he took a moment to orient himself amidst the murky shadows of the Forest of L'el before striding across the bridge.

The image of Dani sitting at that little cafe table was burned into his mind.

Logically, he knew he had no grounds to be jealous or bitter. He'd broken up with her. Intentionally. He couldn't expect her to wait around for six whole months. In fact, he had no business hoping she'd wait at all.

Beyond the stone bridge, the ward surrounding Titan's Fen shimmered over his skin. A large crenelated wall with parapets set into a steep mountain pass appeared out of nothingness. Weapons lowered when the guards recognized who was approaching the entrance to the town.

The gate opened. Guards nodded in greeting to him, some of them pressing a palm to their sternum in a more formal gesture. Slate didn't respond. Head down, hands tucked into his pockets, his sneakers ate ground with steady, purposeful strides. He could portal once he was past the complex triple ward that protected Titan's Fen, but he considered walking the entire distance—the rhythm of his feet against the ground was almost numbing.

An icy numbness against the raw burn of jealousy and bitterness he had no right to feel over Dani.

She deserved better. She deserved safety. She deserved to not have to look over her shoulder because of him. He wanted that for her.

He couldn't have it both ways—he couldn't have her and also guarantee her safety.

But staying away from her was difficult at best. An undeniable truth lay between them, a single word that shook the already unsteady foundation of everything they were, everything they weren't, and everything they could be.

Mayts.

She was his *mayt.*

The fae believed *mayts* were coveted and special; people destined to be together, two halves of the same whole. Slate believed it too. He *knew* something was different about Dani; they orbited each other differently, as if they'd danced not once, but thousands of times before. It was the number one reason why he kept going back to see her, the reason he struggled to let her go.

If he was honest, he didn't know how to go back to her, even if he did drum up the courage. How was he supposed to pick up the broken pieces? Long gone was the martial arts instructor she'd chosen to go on ten dates with. He'd been broken down and remade into something different—a fae prince, a warrior, heir apparent to the fae crown, an inheritance dumped on him with the death of his mother a few years ago. He'd been thrust into a war he didn't start, but was sure as shit expected to finish. He was surrounded by fae who were a mixed bag of devoted loyalty and hostile skepticism, constantly on edge due to the looming threat of his unstable uncle. His life was a mess.

He couldn't expect her to want that.

Some days, *he* didn't want it.

As soon as Slate passed through the final ward, he portaled his way to his private suites in Eas Manor, only to find them occupied.

"Slipped your escort again, I hear."

Slate paused, eyeing the fae male who stood in the sitting room of his suites. Heathered purple eyes stared back, steady and even.

Irritatingly calm, like always. One day he wanted to see what Lieutenant Kallen Ewyt looked like when he was shaken up.

"That was fast. Isn't it considered bad form for folk to barge into the *Titania's* space?" Slate strode across the room, tugging off his knit cap and gloves and running his fingers along his hair, smoothing the long, dark ponytail. "Or gossip about him?" He gave the fae male a pointed look as he peeled out of his light performance jacket.

Kallen shrugged, completely unbothered. He returned Slate's look with one of his own. "Your escorts reporting to me isn't gossip. It's their job. It's *my* job to keep you safe, and I take that job *very* seriously."

"We both know I don't need the escort," Slate countered, rolling his eyes.

"Where did you go?" Kallen's voice was suspiciously casual.

"None of your business," Slate snapped, mood fouling at the memory.

"Make it my business then." Kallen followed Slate into his bedroom, taking Slate's snark in stride.

Fair enough, Slate supposed. Kallen was used to being on the receiving end of his temper.

Slate slammed his wardrobe shut a little too hard, and weighed the merits of simply kicking the lieutenant out. Then again, the fae male had the power to trap Slate in the village by reconfiguring the inner ward perimeter.

Something he'd done before.

"I went into the city proper," Slate finally admitted, swallowing his heart as his mind pulled up the image of Dani letting that man kiss both her cheeks. "I... went to check on someone. And I didn't need company."

He peered over his shoulder to see Kallen watching him. The male slowly nodded. "You went to see your female."

It wasn't a question.

Slate tugged open a drawer and yanked out a tank top and a pair of cotton martial arts pants. "Yep." His one-sided obsession with Dani wasn't a carefully guarded secret. Fae were curious beings by nature, so most of the people he counted as his friends knew about her.

Including Kallen.

"I'm assuming it did not go according to your plan."

"Ah... no."

Not that he'd had a *plan*, really. Slate tugged off his shirt and slipped into the tank top, revealing the intricate magical tattoos that covered the entirety of his arms from wrists to shoulders. They extended down his entire torso, in fact, from collarbone to hip bone, front and back. A never-ending scroll of Japanese, Chinese, and Korean calligraphy inked directly into his skin, different sizes and characters. They culminated into a complex enchantment that helped him control his new magic, courtesy of Jian.

"I mean... no. Just..." Slate's voice sounded strained in his own ears. "She was out with someone else."

Kallen's brows rose. "Someone else?"

"Yeah."

Kallen made a musing sound in the back of his throat. "Would *someone else* be another suitor?"

"Yeah. Probably."

Talking about it felt like pressing an iron knife into his lungs. Slate fell silent, stripping out of his jeans and changing into the cotton pants. He had an appointment to get his ass kicked by Guard Captain Saida this afternoon. He was looking forward to it in a macabre, self-sabotaging kind of way. He needed a distraction from all the thoughts crowding his brain.

Dani was *his*. He'd marked her. His *mayt*. And yet... the writing had been there, all over the wall of that cafe. She had moved on.

Maybe it was better this way, as horrible and painful as it sounded.

"And you are choosing to follow her around without her knowledge because...?"

"I told you, I was just checking on her."

Kallen nodded slowly. "I see." He thumbed the sleeve of his shirt casually. "I was under the impression you no longer had any intention to *mayt* with her."

Slate's head jerked up. "What? No! I mean—listen, it's not like that." He checked his petulant, defensive tone and took a breath. "I broke up with her. We're done. She's allowed to date other people and shit." How was he supposed to parse his feelings into neat words to be understood?

It didn't matter. It didn't matter how he felt, because she had moved on. Which was fine. Totally fine. It was better this way. Goddess only knew how many times a few of his casual friends here at Titan's Fen had tried to coerce him into dating someone else.

Fuck, even Jian had innocently mentioned the idea of him dating other people. Or implied it. Or maybe Slate had thought he'd implied it.

They'd had *words* after that.

Kallen gave a half-shrug. "Then why are you following her?"

"I told you already. I was just checking on her."

"Checking on her would be as simple as asking one of the twins about her well-being."

Slate said nothing. A prickle of icy shame tickled the back of his throat, shooting down into the space around his heart and squeezing the organ hard.

"It's been a while, has it not? Half a year, yes?" Kallen pressed.

"Something like that," Slate muttered casually, as if he didn't know exactly to the day how long it'd been.

"Are you planning to speak to her yourself?"

"I don't..." he swallowed the wobble in his voice, "I don't know." He twisted a stray piece of dark hair near his face. "Everything's different. I'm not the same person I was before."

"And that would bother her?"

"*Fae* bother her, for some reason."

Kallen frowned, crossing his arms over his chest as he leaned against the wall. "She is your *mayt*. She might not yet choose it, but the soul cannot resist the call of its other half. Fae may bother her, but *you* will not."

"Yeah, well, look around us, Kallen," Slate growled. "I'm the king of the fucking fae. Or gonna be, probably. If we all live long enough. Who would want this? No offense," he added quickly.

Kallen gave him a sardonic little grin. "My lord, *none* of us chose this life, I can assure you. Our current situation was thrust upon us by Zeyphar, same as you." His heather eyes narrowed. "You are afraid she won't choose you."

"Wouldn't you be?" He was both ill and positively violent at the idea of her getting close to someone else. And yet... his heart and his mind waffled. Kallen was right. He was afraid. Afraid she'd reject him. Afraid she wouldn't. Afraid he'd put a target on her back. Afraid he might have already. Afraid of letting her go. Afraid of her moving on.

The fae male studied him for a long moment with an unreadable expression. And mind. Kallen's emotions were locked up tighter than a nun's virginity. Slate guessed not even Zeyphar himself could get through Kallen's impressive mental shields.

"The Goddess often brings us together with people who will make a lasting impact on us, whether it is for a moment or a lifetime," Kallen mused in a quiet voice. "Nothing happens by coincidence. There is a reason you have found your *mayt* at the same time as you have returned to your throne when a war of succession is imminent." Kallen pushed off the wall and headed for the door. "If you cannot trust yourself, throw your trust at the Goddess. She will guide you."

Slate frowned at the back of Kallen's head. "You sure you're a soldier and not an Acolyte or whatever?"

Kallen looked over his shoulder to pin him with a knowing look. "Stop slipping your escort."

CHAPTER — TWO

INTENTIONS

... a singular full moon, one of Her sacred symbols. The soul is inevitably drawn to its other half, thus, the refusal of a mayt-bond—and the inevitable fading of the mark itself—is rare...

– Gherald Schmidt, Faerloch Historical Archives

The day was mild, the sun baking the earth despite the season. Around him, melting snow and icicles made a concert of music; a melody of drips and sloshes as cars, bicycles, and pedestrians alike plowed through the chilly puddles.

For the millionth time, Slate told himself he needed to stop following Dani across the city. It was unsustainable. He couldn't continue to follow her around like a shade.

Kallen's words from two days prior stung him.

He'd once again ghosted his escorts, and now he perched on the edge of the flat roof of a ritzy townhouse on the outskirts of the Business District, facing the backyard, his form glamoured from view. Abutting the yard was the backyard of another townhouse that had long been converted into a vet clinic. Even in the fading daylight, he had a compelling view of Dani as she played with some of the dogs for an evening outing. He was close enough that he could hear her voice.

It was a rub along his skin; an ache, a longing.

Nothing happens by coincidence.

Maybe he did need to just... let go of the obsessive what-ifs and just approach her. Find a little bit of external trust in whatever forces drew them together in the first place. Trust that everything would work out exactly as it should.

She was his *mayt*. That had to count for *something*.

What would she say to him? How would she react? How would *he* react? Maybe he should run this whole idea by Kari first, to get a better bead on Dani's headspace. He'd avoided asking Kari anything more in-depth than a simple check-in on Dani's well-being. He hadn't wanted to know if Dani missed him.

Or worse, if she didn't.

Would she even care if he came back?

The little insecure part of him was vehement in its icy insistence that she wouldn't care—she was dating other people. *He'd broken up with her.*

"Full of surprises, as usual, *Slate Melisande*," a dry voice said from behind him. "From mortal to fae to prince and now... *stalker*. Quite the progression."

Slate nearly fell off the roof, his heart jacking into his skull. He scrambled, getting his feet under him, and whipped around.

In the shadows cast by the access door, Slate made out the profile of a tall, lithe male leaning casually against the wall with his hands in his pockets. Nothing about him screamed remarkable—shoulder-length mahogany hair pulled neatly away from his sharp face and secured at his nape, brown eyes, and a fair complexion. He was dressed immaculately in gray slacks, a matching vest, and a crisp white shirt. Plain, perhaps, and yet...

The male's aura thrummed against him like a deep echo. Resounding and endless, like peering over the edge of the abyss and being unable to see the bottom. Deep. Unknown. Shadows and sin and danger.

And death.

It wasn't a safe feeling, for sure, but Slate's heart resumed an even rhythm and the goosebumps along his skin receded. This male wasn't his *friend*, but he certainly wasn't an *enemy* either.

Yet.

Slate swallowed, clearing the jitters from his throat. "Roger."

The vampire pushed off from the wall and slid on a pair of slender sunglasses he pulled from a vest pocket. Shadows seemed to cling to him even as he stepped away from them, moving with a gait that was a little too smooth to be human as he approached Slate. The hairs on the back of Slate's neck rose in a primitive response, and he kept his eyes locked on the male's every move. Tension continued to vibrate in his muscles—alert and aware that no matter what kind of magic he'd unlocked in his bones, he was several millennia behind this vampire in terms of not only strength, speed, and magic, but also killing experience.

Roger stopped beside him, slender hands back in his pockets now, and he cocked his head as he eyed the scene below. Without a word, he arched one slender brow at Slate, who had the grace to flush.

"It's not what you think." The growled words leaped from Slate's mouth before he could censor them.

That brow rose impossibly higher.

He checked the urge to lash out at the vampire and instead focused his eyes on the red-headed female below them. "I'm just checking on her," Slate finally murmured. Dani's light laughter echoed up to them, and some of the wild tension inside him eased.

The hairs on the back of his neck twitched, and he knew Roger was still watching him. He kept his gaze locked on Dani, who was trying to retrieve a tennis ball from an unwilling golden retriever.

"Indeed..." the vampire drawled, somehow managing to make his smooth-as-honey voice dry as paper. But he said nothing else, simply studying Slate like he was some bug that might need to be squished.

"What?" he snapped at the male, a bit of that tension bursting, and he barely kept himself from strangling Roger when the male's thin lips curled into a smirk.

"Why now, after nearly six months?" Roger's tone was neutral, seemingly friendly, but Slate picked up on the edge buried beneath.

Razor-sharp. Deadly.

"You don't know that I haven't checked on her before—"

"Try me."

Slate snapped his mouth shut and zipped his eyes back to the front. It was very likely Roger knew everyone and every*thing*, all the way down to the tiniest cockroach, that approached Daniella. Not that Slate had any hard and fast facts to back that up, but he did know Roger had a level of affection for Dani that rivaled Slate's own. And with the vampire's ability to work the shadows, it was unlikely *anything* suspicious got past Roger.

Including Slate's little stalking-floaty-dance he'd been playing lately.

Silence fell, and Slate's heart clenched as Dani ushered the dogs back into the kennels that lined the side of the narrow backyard. She would go inside soon, and out of his field of vision.

But not out of his head. Or his heart. Or his fucking dreams.

"What are your intentions?" Sharp eyes tinged with red cut to him. "While I appreciate you intentionally distancing yourself from Daniella for her safety, this... spying you are doing seems counterproductive to the message you left for her this summer and your subsequent disappearance. Surely you are intelligent enough to consider how your reappearance will impact her well-being."

Gone was the attempt at amiability; Roger's voice remained soft, but it was sharper now. Slate barely curbed the desire to bare his teeth at the vampire and tell him to fuck off. Like he owed some explanation to this male. Roger was *not* his friend.

But... he *was* Dani's friend. Slate hadn't forgotten the last encounter he'd had with the vampire—the thinly veiled threats.

"You are something that is not as it seems."

"If you hurt her..."

Well, he had a feeling he'd gone past that, if he was being honest with himself. He couldn't exactly blame Roger for his concern.

Fuck, how could he explain his intentions when *he* didn't even know what they were?

He opened his mouth to speak, not quite sure what was going to come out, but Roger spoke instead. "I have allowed you to spy on her for long enough. If you wish to continue seeing her, you must confront her face-to-face. I will not allow further breaches of her privacy."

"I wasn't *spying*—" Slate growled.

"You watch her in secret. That, by its definition, is to spy." Another slight raise of that eyebrow, so condescending, so patronizing. Slate's ire spiked a little more. "Besides," Roger continued. The weight of the vampire's stare shifted away from him. "You cannot hide your presence from Selene."

With a blink, Slate followed Roger's gaze to the roof across from them. Even from this distance, he spotted the two luminous orbs trained on him. A better man than Slate would've wavered under the female griffin's intense, unblinking stare. Slate could nearly taste how incensed Sellie was with him. She sat predator-still, with only her head visible above the edge of the roof, which is why he hadn't noticed her before.

"Well, shit," Slate growled.

Baka. He should've known better—he *did* know better. No fae glamour worked on griffins. And after the shit that had happened over the summer, Sellie would never leave Dani's side.

The fact that Roger had to point out such an obvious oversight to him, like he was a *child*, just spiked his irritation. His fingers curled into his palms as a stab of shame twisted in his chest. It wasn't his intention to spy on her.

But that's sure as shit what it looked like. To the vampire. And now to Sellie.

"Selene will not tolerate spying. And neither will I." Roger's voice was level and even, but still razor-sharp. "Consider carefully your intentions."

"I don't have to explain myself to you, vampire," Slate snapped.

Roger's answer was a smile as cold as ice. A smile that could instill nightmares in small children and grown men alike. New instincts had Slate feeding some empathy magic toward the vampire, a thin attempt to see past that look and into the emotions underneath. He came upon a black mental shield, solid and insurmountable. Slate backed off immediately, not remotely interested in knowing what lay beyond those black shields.

Hell, most likely.

"Certainly not," Roger murmured, voice smoother than silk sheets. "But one way or another, you *will* have to explain yourself to Daniella. You should be less consumed with following her like a lost puppy and more focused on explaining to her why you ended a relationship with your *mayt*."

All the blood drained right out of his head at Roger's targeted quip, fast enough that it was only with a firm grip on his self-control that he didn't sway on the spot. Roger was watching him carefully.

"Does... does she know?" Slate sucked in a slow breath he hoped looked more casual than he felt.

"If she does, it was not from me," came the mild response. It was no accident Slate's magic could just now pick up subtle threads of fury unfurling off the vampire. Shadows curled around the male, and even through the dark tint of the sunglasses, Slate peeped a hint of red in the vampire's eyes.

Unspoken were the words: *she should hear it from* you.

Roger was angry, and he definitely wanted Slate to know it.

"I'd greatly appreciate it if you didn't tell her," Slate said tightly, swallowing his own emotions in a vain attempt to sound unbothered by the whole *mayt* mess.

When he was, in fact, very bothered.

"I scent no claiming on your end, which leads me to believe you do not possess a *mayt*-mark. Hers will fade in short order, and soon, it will not matter."

It will not matter.

It was like someone sucked the air right out of his lungs. He didn't know what to do about Dani, he didn't know his own next steps, but having everything they shared together reduced to something that would soon *not matter*?

No.

No.

"Would you stop me, if I went to go talk to her right now?" It came out more desperate than he cared to casually admit.

Roger turned his head and Slate followed his gaze. Both of them watched as Dani stowed the animal toys in a bin before heading inside. A hollowness opened in his chest when she disappeared into the building. Once again out of sight. Out of reach. Across the painful gap that existed between them.

"As I said, I will deny her nothing, not even you." A whisper of words from the vampire.

It was not a reflection on the vampire's feelings toward Slate, but rather a need to provide Daniella with whatever she desired, be it good or bad for her.

In more ways than one, Slate suddenly felt like he was standing on a precipice. He idly wondered if Roger wasn't here to give him a little... shove over the edge.

Silence fell between them, tense and swelling.

Roger turned on his heel, his movements silent, and strolled back toward the ever-deepening shadows behind them. "A word of caution, princeling."

Slate bristled at the word, watching the narrow line of Roger's retreating form.

"It would be unwise for you to force another such conversation between us in regards to spying on Daniella." Roger paused, and when he glanced over his shoulder at Slate, the sunglasses were gone. Blood-red eyes locked with his. "The next one will not be so gracious."

Translation: *Get your shit together, Melisande.*

His skin tightened at the deadly implication. Slate scowled, opening his mouth for a retort, but by the time a proper one popped into his mind, the deep, long shadows had already swallowed up the vampire.

TWO CHOICES

... contingent upon a period of confinement in Thule spanning the remainder of what mortals deemed 'The Dark Age,' during which penance would be extracted. The vampire Marius' whereabouts thereafter remains unknown, though rumors suggest...

– Gherald Schmidt, Faerloch Historical Archives

"So," Karisi Meho drawled from where she was carefully measuring tea leaves into a teapot. "How was your *date* the other day?"

The curvy bombshell of a woman only stood as high as Dani's brow, but appearances were deceiving when it came to this half-Japanese, half-Korean female. She moved with far too much grace as she brought the antique teapot over to the low table in the center of the room. Muscles rippled under the smooth flesh of Kari's thick thighs as she folded her legs beneath her to kneel on the floor pillow opposite Dani, her sports shorts clinging provocatively to her generous hips.

Without even trying, Kari was undeniably sensual. Dani wondered how much of that had to do with being one of the elusive *kitsune*—a fox demon—from the Eastern-based Mystic branch of magic.

Dani watched as Kari poured tea into two mugs, and took hers when Kari nudged it toward her. "It was fine." Dani smiled at Kari, bringing her mug up to blow across the steamy surface.

Kari tossed her long rose-gold hair over one shoulder and propped her elbows on the table on either side of her tea, gunmetal gray eyes sparkling with devilish delight. "Just fine?"

Dani's smile wavered a bit, but she tugged it back up and sipped at the hot tea. "Yeah. It went well." And it had. Derrick had been polite, gracious, attentive...

So why did she feel like her words were an effort to convince herself as much as they were for Kari? It's not like she should feel *guilty* about dating or anything. She was completely single, with zero obligations to stay that way.

Kari shifted her weight to the side, cocking her head as she studied Dani, the gesture fox-like and observant. Kari finally picked up her neglected tea and took a dainty sip of it. She set the mug down, folded her arms on the table before her, and pegged Dani with a look.

"You aren't going to ask him for a second date." It wasn't a question.

"I might. I mean..." Dani sighed through her nose and let her cheerful smile fade, looking at her tea. "I feel like I should. At least give it a try."

Kari scoffed lightly. "Not all men are worth ten dates."

Dani's spine stiffened, shoulders tensing. She sipped her tea, willing her muscles to relax.

"What date number?" he asked roughly, kissing down her neck, tasting her skin.

"I... I don't... six, I think..." A pitched moan escaped her as he scratched his teeth gently along her left shoulder.

She suddenly wanted to vomit at the idea of sharing skin with someone else. Absently, her fingers brushed the fading scar on her neck as she sucked in a slow breath.

Unfortunately, Kari missed nothing. Her expression softened, irking Dani instantly—she didn't like being pitied.

"There are plenty of other fish in the sea, *tori-chan,*" Kari offered with a smile. Dani wasn't sure when Kari had started calling her 'little bird' in Japanese, but right now the term seemed to baldly fit how much she wished she could fly away from this conversation. She was sure Kari saw that too, but the woman didn't let up. "I see the people that watch you in the pub. You'd have a line of willing suitors out the door if you wanted."

"I think you're confusing me with you," Dani said with a little laugh, eager to shift the conversation.

Kari's lips curled up sensually, but her expression told Dani she wanted to push the conversation more, so Dani hurried to say, "How did things go with that were-tiger from two nights ago?"

There was a beat of silence, and Dani found herself praying to the Goddess that Kari took the bait. The *kitsune* regarded her with a knowing look, and Dani tensed.

"She was a great fuck," Kari finally said with a wicked glint in her eyes, and Dani relaxed. "Stamina for *days*, you know?"

"Are you going to see her again?" Dani asked, far more comfortable talking about Kari's sex life than her own.

And Kari's sex life was wild enough that Dani had no doubt the authors of the Kama Sutra could learn a thing or two.

So she asked questions and guided the conversation away from the topic Dani was not ready to talk about.

Dating. Not dating. But mostly… *Slate.*

In fact, she was beginning to wonder if she was *ever* going to be ready.

"I should probably head out," Dani said a little over an hour later, eyeing the clock on the wall. "I have some errands to run before work."

Kari glanced back over her shoulder from where she was rinsing out their tea mugs at the sink. "That's fine, I have to get some shit done at the studio before class tonight."

Dani's gut clenched at the word *studio.* Once, she might have asked for details, but talking about the martial arts studio made her think of the absent *master* of said studio. She wondered if one day it wouldn't matter. If one day, she could go and watch Kari teach a class without her stomach shriveling up at the memories associated with the place.

How was it possible that the absence of one person could make a place feel like such a void?

"Good luck," Dani said with a smile, getting to her feet. Kari's response was a smirk and a wink.

Dani saw herself to the door—having come and gone so many times over the last few months had made her real familiar with the place. She slipped her boots on in the foyer, called out a last goodbye to Kari's father Joon, who was working in the basement, and slid open the Japanese-style front door.

Dani's breath abandoned her as she came to an abrupt halt.

There, leaning against the low stone wall that separated the small front lawn from the street, was a figure she'd seen hundreds of times in her dreams. Time screeched to a standstill, and her heart clenched painfully.

Slate.

It was him. *Really* him. In the flesh.

Surely she was dreaming. It couldn't be—

His gaze clashed with her own, and the entire world faded away. Nothing existed for that split second of time except for the male before her.

High cheekbones slashed beneath large, bright sapphire eyes that were distinctly almond-shaped, with thick dark hair pulled back from a tanned face into a messy bun, revealing the silver hair shorn short at the sides of his head. Her fingers twitched helplessly with the instinct to brush back some of the dark strands that had escaped his tie.

He was the same, and yet... not.

He was her Slate, but with a cloak of power around him that even her weak magical senses picked up on. His heartfire—that inner heat Dani sensed in all animals and Lorefolk alike—was a campfire compared to the smoke and embers it had been before, like it was for most mortals. His features had become sharper, and new muscle filled out his clothing. Beyond that, there was something almost predatory about him, more animal than man.

No, more *fae*.

Slate was fae.

Prince of the fae. This man—male—before her wasn't the same person she'd tangled in the sheets with this summer. Slate before had been someone you didn't want to cross in a dark alley. This one was someone you didn't want to cross *period*.

Unbidden, fear sent a shiver of ice sluicing through her veins.

"Hi." Slate broke the silence first.

His voice was a jolt through her, husky and oh-so-familiar. That cold fear retreated at the sound, and suddenly it was harder to see the *other* in him and easier to see the familiar. How could the ice of fear withstand the warmth that came with the memories of his voice? Of nights spent with his hands on her skin and his lips at her ear...

She swallowed her suddenly dry throat. "Hi."

Slate pushed off from the wall and linked his hands behind his back, rocking on his heels. "So... uh... how–how are you?" he asked, his voice rough and uneven.

A flare of anger sparked in her chest, burning away the fear for a heartbeat.

Wait a minute. *How are you?*

Like nothing happened? Like he didn't leave her alone with little more than a voicemail? For six *entire* months?

His heartfire flared—so miniscule, she'd not have noticed if she wasn't already tuned into it, and her anger stumbled.

Magic.

Was he using magic, right this moment? That instinctual fear swelled back up, warring with her heart.

It's Slate... her heart whispered. *It's Slate, it's alright. You're safe.*

But her gut seemed to be having hearing problems as a clammy sweat broke out across her palms. She curled her fingers in and tucked them behind her, a mirror to his own stance. He was still staring at her, and she realized she hadn't answered him yet. "I—" She had to clear her voice, but it still came out strained. "I'm fine."

Fine. Her mantra lately... everything was *fine*.

"That's good," he said with an attempt at a smile, and though it was forced, it still punched her right through her ribs.

He was here.

All of a sudden, the fact he was the prince of the fae became so much less daunting. Less important, in the grand scheme of things.

Because he was *back*.

He came back.

Had he come back for her?

No. She shut that train of thought down *hard* because he'd broken up with her. There was no reason he'd come back for her. Her skin was suddenly too tight across her entire body. The tension stretched between them, tight as a rubber band at the threshold of breaking.

She had two choices: walk right past him and get on her Vespa... or talk to him.

"How are you?" she repeated his mundane question back to him, the fear inside her turning to lead at the thought of not hearing him speak at least once more, despite her anger, despite her hurt, despite... well, everything.

"Same. Fine." His hand came up, along with a spike in his heartfire, and she felt a *pressure* from the heat of that fire. A familiar pressure that was burned in her mind, one that brought up an image of Kat's smiling face as she was led away, terror in her blue-gray eyes at odds with her dreamy expression. Two hands, one large and masculine, the other slender, female, with talon-like nails, perched on her best friend's slender shoulders as that same pressure beat at Dani's 11-year-old senses.

Fae magic.

Her stomach dropped out from under her and her fingernails dug into her palms as panic crawled up her throat. *Fae, fae, fae.*

He skated his hand over his hair and down the back of his neck, a hint of color brightening his cheekbones.

It was a visual slap of familiarity that helped to ground her and clear her thoughts. His eyes jumped away from her face, then back.

"I... ah..." He let out a nervous laugh, and it was so very Slate that she found herself leaning forward, as if her body subconsciously needed to close the space between them.

She was getting emotional whiplash from the constant ping-pong between fear and... longing? Anger? Heartache? She didn't even know, could barely decipher her feelings right now.

Slate cleared his throat with a lopsided grin that hit her right in her chest. "I've been wanting to come find you for a while."

"Have you? After breaking up with me and vanishing for six months?" Was that bitterness in her tone? She tried to shove it down, tried to pull up the cheerful smile she was so accustomed to wearing these days, but her muscles wouldn't cooperate.

Her words caused his shoulders to tighten, and he looked away, his long fingers twisting around a stray piece of hair by his face, and Dani recognized it as one of his nervous gestures. He dropped his hand, gaze jumping back to hers. "Yeah. I just... wanted to check on you, I guess."

The words didn't process fast enough.

Check on her.

Check on her?

After he broke up with her and disappeared for six months?

Six months. It had been half a year; at this point, he'd been out of her life longer than he'd been in it.

Not that it felt that way, sometimes.

Before seeing his face, she might have said she was moving on. She hadn't cried over him in weeks. Her pulse no longer jumped whenever she got a message or a phone call. It had been on her mind just this morning that maybe she wouldn't need to take the detour to Kari's house to avoid going past Melisande Martial Arts.

She'd taken the detour, but *still.*

Now... looking at his face, hearing the sound of his voice... she realized she'd just grown accustomed to the gaping hole he'd blown through her life and the ache he'd left behind. And now that hole yawned in front of her, threatening to drown her again, until her ribs felt too small to contain her heart, competing against the bitter taste of betrayal and resentment tightening her throat.

How dare he come back after so long to make her hurt again. How dare he just *abandon* her for six months, then stroll back in like he had the *right* to check on her.

Just to check on her.

Not because he wanted to see her, or he had missed her, or...

She gave herself a mental shake. He didn't want her, didn't want to be with her, and she needed to remember that.

She forced her feet to move, taking a step away from Kari's doorway. "I have to go," she told him, hoping her voice sounded steadier to him than it did to her own ears. She moved before she could stop herself, gaining momentum until she was striding past him, eyes locked on the pavement in front of her feet.

As she passed him, his heartfire flared once more, making the icicles of fear inside her renew their pricks against her insides. Her breath caught at the sensation that had haunted her dreams for over a decade. That quickly, he went from the man who made her heart flutter to a strange fae male with more power than he knew what to do with. It wasn't rational, but every instinct inside her screamed for her not to turn her back to this predator or his magic. The hair on the back of her neck rose, and she could feel him watching her.

And still, she forced herself to move.

Yet when she made it past him, the distress of having a predator at her back faded with each step, to be replaced with a sense of rising panic and desperation. Her heart was begging her not to walk away from Slate, even as her self-preservation instincts urged her to *run*.

Dani barely managed to slip a leg over her bike to straddle it.

"Dani."

Her name on his lips stirred a myriad of feelings inside her. Some instinctual part of her, call it female intuition, knew precisely what he was going to say. She was both desperate to hear it and yet terrified in the same breath. She didn't want to look at him, knew her defenses would crumble at the sight of him.

"Wait."

The single word undid her. Sucking in a breath, she turned her head and found him watching her, standing exactly in the same spot.

"Can..." he faltered, but he never took his eyes from her, like he was starved for the sight of her. It made warmth bloom around the chill in her belly. "Can I... I dunno, can I see you again? Like, for real? Get coffee or something?”

There was so much yearning in his voice, which made no sense when *he* was the one who ended things. He could have come back any time.

But it was still there, plain across his face, and despite her anger, her heart clenched in her chest as her fingers white-knuckled the handlebars. It was hard to think clearly through the distraction of that bright heart-fire within him, hard to think clearly when half of her was terrified of his magic while the other half wanted to run to him.

She swallowed hard.

He was fae. And he'd broken her heart with a single phone call then shredded it with his absence. What if he did that again?

Suddenly, that was far more terrifying than even the presence of his inner flame. So much so that she forgot how to breathe.

“No,” she choked out, the words tumbling from her on the razor's edge of that fear.

She kicked her Vespa into gear and shot out of the small driveway, heart in her throat and ice in her veins.

She didn't look back.

Roger was holding a hobgoblin by his ankle when the shadows whispered in his ear. His hackles rose, and he sucked in a slow breath through his nose to calm the bloodlust licking at his heels.

“It seems today is your lucky day, Günther. I have places to be.” Roger dropped the lorebeing, and watched as he scrambled back to the piles of alleyway trash that was his most recent home, cowering from the vampire with a hand over his throat. “Don't worry,” Roger assured him with a deliberate smile that had the male's yellow-brown eyes widening in visible terror. “We can continue our conversation later.”

Roger's nose wrinkled at the fresh smell of urine, and he curled his lip in disgust as he stepped away from the pathetic being at his feet. The shadows welcomed him into their cool embrace, pulling him away from the stench of fear and garbage.

Fresh air replaced the filthy air of the alleyway, and Roger pulled a pair of sunglasses from his pocket. He slid them over his face as he stepped away from the shadows and into the sunlight that bathed the roof of a three-story apartment building in the Eastern District. Shadows clung after him, offering a modicum of protection from the ball of fire in the sky, though his skin still smarted painfully.

Younger vampires would already be ash, but there were advantages to being old as dirt.

His long legs ate up the distance to the low wall that ran along the perimeter of the roof, and his gaze locked on a head of red hair down below the moment she came into view.

Roger paused, slinking back a step, letting his shadows writhe and curl around him as they obscured him from view. It allowed him to watch the scene unfolding below him with perfect clarity.

Allowed him to see Daniella's face as she came face-to-face with one Slate Melisande.

Emotions flared and skittered in her eyes, as readable to him as any book, and his muscles tensed.

His mind traced back six months, to that summer night when Karisi had brought this woman to him, shaken and bleeding. To the first moment he saw that small mark on her neck, the one that was as glaringly obvious to him as the cut that had leaked her sweet-smelling blood.

Both had infuriated him, for similar yet different reasons.

That mark was a target, a bullseye for forces that would seek to harm her. And the bloody slice in her flesh had been a vivid preview of it. Luckily, the Silver Valley fae seemed to be reluctant to approach Daniella after he and Loraine made it known throughout the city that to bother her was to incur their wrath. Roger suspected Zeyphar wasn't willing to risk that until he was more certain about getting his nephew within grasp.

The bite mark on her neck also meant the beginning of an inevitable path… one that caused the darkness inside him to roil and thrash. It tasted bitter with resentment, and a hint of… fear.

Emotions Roger was unaccustomed to feeling.

And yet since that first smile Daniella had offered him back in London all those years ago, there have been many *feelings* he'd long forgotten about. *Emotion.* Life.

That's what Daniella was to him, and he would savage anyone who took that light from him.

The mark was a threat... because who was Slate Melisande, recently a *mortal*, to protect her from the dangers that would follow that mark? Roger was to leave the safety of his light to some *faeling* with too big a head on his shoulders?

The darkness bucked, whispering of blood, destruction, *mayhem*. Just as it had when Daniella had been before him six months prior, vulnerable and lost, and the darkness had pushed, whispered to *take*, take before he lost his chance.

It was like a bucket of frigid water over his head. Roger closed his eyes, pulling back from the lip of the roof, teeth bared in a silent snarl as he forced the darkness down inside him. Down into a pit so deep inside him, he didn't know yet how it hadn't swallowed him up.

Now that he knew Slate was confronting her, and not spying on her, he had no right to continue to watch, lest he become no better than the princeling he'd pointed his finger at.

But Daniella's expression as she faced Slate for the first time in six months lingered even as Roger pulled back toward the blessed shadows behind him. He hesitated a moment, half of him already deep within the shadows, and looked back toward the edge of the roof.

His chest felt tight, his heart heavy.

He had one last thought before he let the shadows take him away: *I wonder if she knows how much she's in love with him...*

CHAPTER — FOUR

NEEDS AND HAPPINESS

... when it became clear the Goddess may not have sentenced the clan to their fate. However, due to the fact that the curse's magic seemed to be tied exclusively to Mhaeve and her wild magic, and not to the Goddess, and with no living relative known, the Oíche Gearlach clan...

— Gherald Schmidt, Faerloch Historical Archives

Dash nipped at her fingers, and Dani realized she'd been brushing the same spot on his fur for over five minutes.

All while staring at the wall and failing miserably to keep her thoughts... empty.

Instead, one word seemed to be echoing inside her empty skull like a relentless drumbeat: *No.*

Slate wanted to see her again, and she'd told him... *No.*

It was only yesterday she'd uttered that word, but it already felt like weeks and months had passed. She alternated between congratulating herself for excising toxicity from her life, and wallowing in an overwhelming panic that she'd made a terrible mistake. And that panic was getting difficult to ignore when her heart kept insisting that nothing about Slate had ever been *toxic*.

Dani had worked entirely too long on compartmentalizing her feelings since Slate left. Organizing them into neat, carefully labeled spaces in her mind and heart—panic here, longing over there. With each passing hour, no, each *minute*, it became harder to view this entire situation through that neat, careful lens now that she'd seen him again. He brought back all the shades of gray when she'd been trying to keep things black and white. Panic kept blending with the longing, anger kept spiking alongside happiness, until she could no longer discern where each emotion originally started.

It was getting harder to ignore the taste in her mouth that said she was lying to herself.

Because no matter how much she wanted to deny it... she wanted to see him, too.

But she was scared to see him. Just thinking about it made her throat close and her stomach clench. Trying to stuff her emotions back into their labeled spaces gave her a ghost of a headache along her temples.

Part of her didn't want to stuff everything back, because that small part of her heart whispered that while Slate made everything messy, it was an intense, happy kind of mess. He was *her* mess.

The sound of a knock echoed through her quiet house, followed by the creak of the door to the garage opening and shutting. "Thank you, Sellie... Dani? Hello? *Tadaima...*" A faint, mellifluous voice called from the hall, and Dash wiggled in her lap until Dani lifted her hands. The russet fox slipped from Dani's lap like liquid fire, slinking low across the floor as he sniffed furiously toward the direction of the voice.

"In here," Dani answered, setting aside the brush she'd been using on Dash, who was now crouched by the hallway, ready to pounce on whoever appeared.

Faint footsteps sounded before Kari came into view, full lips curled in a wicked grin. She gasped in faux surprise at the fox, who abandoned his stealthy crouch as he lunged at the curvy woman. Kari laughed, smoothly avoiding his pounce, and the little fox flounced into the ground in front of her to writhe excitedly.

"Dash! Hello, handsome. You protecting your mama?" she cooed lovingly.

Dash zipped back and forth in front of Kari, gekkering and chattering in excitement and smug satisfaction for defending his home. Kari laughed again, and Dani finally cracked a smile. "Hey, Kari."

Gray eyes flashed to hers, and Dani, like the coward she was, slipped her gaze away, afraid of what those keen fox eyes would see. Instead, she picked up the brush again and beckoned to Dash with it. "Come back here, I wasn't finished."

The fox wound himself around Kari's ankles once more before he yipped and bound toward Dani. He hopped back into her lap and curled up contentedly. Smoothing the brush over his russet fur, Dani kept her attention on the fox in her lap as Kari drifted further into the living room. "I wasn't expecting you this morning," Dani commented.

While it wasn't uncommon for Kari to drop by—she was one of the few people keyed into the ward around Dani's house—they'd only seen each other yesterday. Dani had a sinking feeling she knew what this visit was about, and her stomach tightened. Every part of her wanted to avoid talking about *him*. "Did you want to go get a drink at the Den after—"

"I know you talked to Slate yesterday when you left," Kari interrupted, raising a brow as she stared at Dani, hands planted on her hips.

Dani nearly fumbled the brush, heart slamming against her chest and robbing her of breath.

Kari let her purse slip from her shoulder to plop it onto the ground by the couch. "Babe, I'm going to try and say this as gently as I can... but you've been avoiding the 'S' word for six months now. At some point, we have to talk about where the two of you stand. Jian and I can't continue to tiptoe around you both. That's not the healthiest way to go about life—avoiding all the things that make you uncomfortable."

Dani's chest tightened, and she flashed back to Maddie's words that day on the roof six months ago, the day she'd decided to go find Slate, only to discover he'd left. *You can have a life, or you can have a life led by fear. Make your choice.*

And she had. At that moment, on that rooftop a lifetime ago, she'd chosen to face her fears.

But he'd broken up with her and left, and instead of overcoming her fears, she'd stuffed them back down, and they'd grown bigger, more daunting.

All the courage Maddie had helped her dredge up had withered under the crushing knowledge that Slate hadn't wanted to be with her.

So much so that he'd left for half a year.

Dani managed a numb nod, eyes trained on Dash in her lap, and Kari folded her legs beneath her on the other end of the couch. A tense, weighted silence fell, and Dani flipped her eyes up briefly to catch Kari studying her.

The *kitsune* offered her a lopsided smile. "I just..." Kari started, then tilted a single shoulder in a half-shrug. "It just kills me to do nothing, you know? The both of you just kill me..." Her tone shifted to something that sounded like an apology. "But I can't let you just brush this one aside, girl. Unless you plan to just up and leave and stop being friends with me and Jian..."

"No." Dani shook her head. "No. You two are my friends."

"Then we need to talk about what the hell is going to happen between you and Slate." Kari's eyes dipped predator-quick to Dani's neck, and Dani had to fight the urge to run her fingers over the scar on her left shoulder.

Kari was right, of course. It was unfair of her to expect the twins would continue to tiptoe around the subject of Slate, even if Dani hadn't asked them to. They were too observant *not* to notice how any mention of him triggered a myriad of uncomfortable emotions. And maybe for the first few months, she'd needed that distance, some sense of normalcy. But now... now it was just a toxic habit and frankly, she was growing *tired* of constantly running away from what she wanted in favor of some contrived routine of *safety.*

"Nothing is going to happen. He broke up with me, Kari. He made it very clear he wanted nothing to do with me," Dani said stiffly, staring down at where she was rhythmically brushing Dash's fur.

I'm done. We're done. I can't see you anymore. I'm sorry I dragged you into all this.

Silence was her answer, for long enough that she had no choice but to look at Kari. The *kitsune* was watching her with an unreadable expression, sitting stiller than Dani had ever seen her be.

"Is that really what you think?" Kari asked, her voice painfully quiet.

"I..." Dani's simmering anger slipped at that tone, at the shuttered expression on Kari's face. "Kari, I heard his voicemail. I've listened to it more times than I can count. He said—"

"Dani." Kari leaned forward, holding Dani's gaze. "I need you to take a moment and think past the hurt, and yes, I know his voicemail hurt you. You have every right to be upset. But take a moment and *think*. It couldn't have escaped you that Slate was head over heels for you."

Dani's brows crashed together, a different kind of panic wriggling to life inside her. Panic that Kari was about to take away the anger she'd held onto with a clawing grip, because it was far easier to handle than the hurt of being abandoned.

"Why would someone who is crazy about you break up with you?" Kari asked in a gentle voice, one that prodded at Dani's bruised heart.

Tears stung Dani's eyes, and she blinked them away as she shook her head, lips pressed tightly together.

"He was trying to protect you from his lunatic uncle."

Dani's eyes closed as those words punched her right through the chest. Words that had been spoken before to her, long ago, when she'd still been wallowing. Roger and Maddie had been over, and Roger had suggested as much in an effort to make her feel better. For a while, she'd clung to the idea, giving herself hope that Slate hadn't just abandoned her for no reason.

But when days had turned into weeks, and weeks into months, it had become a hollow hope that had turned to bitterness in her chest. What was the good of protecting her if his actions wrecked her on the inside? What good was a physically safe body if her heart was withering like a plant denied sunlight?

"So what, his uncle is gone now? The threat has vanished?" Dani asked, voice thick and echoing with that bitterness that had festered inside her. She opened her eyes and pegged Kari with a glare, which she knew was unfair, but she had so many emotions roiling inside her.

Kari raised a brow, and Dani forced herself to take a breath, looking away from Kari's knowing stare. "Zeyphar is still a threat, but..."

Dani waited a beat for Kari to finish. "But what, Kari?" Dani prompted.

Kari sighed. "He misses you, *tori-chan*. He thought he was doing right by you, staying away, but he misses you. Desperately." She shrugged, and her words caused Dani's heart to flip inside her chest.

The traitorous organ became a fluttering mess inside her as more of that hope slipped past the barricade of anger she'd erected. But hope was dangerous and capable of causing Dani untold harm if Slate had no intention of staying.

He misses you.

"He... he said he just wanted to check on me," Dani whispered, and her voice sounded brittle to her ears.

"And you believed him?" Kari asked with a smirk. "*Kami* above, Dani. Slate is the worst at lying."

Can I see you again? Like, for real?

Dani drew in a long breath as more of that hope slithered past her emotional defenses. It caused panic inside her to flare and had her instinctively wanting to shore up those defenses.

"I... Kari, I can't go through this again. I can't... I can't handle it if he leaves again." Her lower lip trembled, and Dash nipped gently at her fingertips, a low whine coming from his small body. Impressions of comfort filtered into her mind, impressions of being petted, of a full bowl of food, the sight of Dash's favorite toy.

No cry. Stupid male. You have us, came the imperious voice of Sellie. Despite the fact the griffin was likely curled up in her nest in the garage, she was highly sensitive to Dani's emotions.

Sellie's words, crisp and clear in her mind in a way only the most intelligent of creatures could manage, made the corners of her lips twitch upward. As far as Sellie was concerned, Slate wasn't worth Dani's time or emotional consideration.

Kari's expression narrowed, and once more, her attention dipped to the scar on Dani's shoulder. "He won't leave you again."

It was a firm, confident statement, and Dani almost wanted to believe it for the truth. *Kitsune* were renowned for knowing a great many things about the world, after all.

Could she believe it?

"You can't know that." This time, Dani lifted her hand and brushed her fingertips over her shoulder, feeling the raised texture of the white scar that never healed correctly. The gesture soothed her a little, taking her blood pressure down a few notches.

Kari looked like she wanted to say more, but she pressed her lips together in a thin line. "Then you just have to follow your intuition on this one," Kari said with a little shrug. "Either you see him again... or you walk away."

Walk away?

Dani's breath snagged, a wholly different kind of panic blooming into life in her chest.

"Walk away... from Slate," she repeated numbly, staring at Kari.

"Yes. Like, if you decide you're done and you need to wash your hands of him... *kami* knows I don't like messy men." Kari shrugged again. "And Slate's life is messy now."

Dani swallowed hard, throat suddenly dry. Wash her hands of Slate... as in... completely sever all ties to him?

That felt so wrong, she couldn't breathe for a second. It made her realize she'd still harbored a hope of seeing him again, of *being* with him again. Being around Kari, and occasionally Jian, it had been a whisper in the back of her mind that through them, she would see Slate again. Even if he broke up with her, even if she'd convinced herself he didn't want her, she'd still had that *hope*.

Kari's gaze drifted away from her, surveying the living room. "No one will judge you... least of all him," she continued. "He gets it, you know? He can barely handle his own life some days." Kari's lips curled into a smile, but it lost all its sharp, devious edges. "He's a mess too, honestly. But he can't just walk away from the fae stuff. I'm not sure what demons you've got from your past, or if that has anything to do with it at all, but I know *everyone* will understand if you don't want a fae prince for a boyfriend. We get it, if that life has too much risk."

Dani's thoughts and emotions twisted into a knot, sliding this way and that in no discernable order with every word Kari spoke. But her mess of thoughts slowed at one word: *Boyfriend.*

Was that what Slate had been to her? Some... boyfriend? *Boyfriend* seemed woefully inadequate, which was why the prospect of opening her heart to him was so utterly terrifying. He could crush it to a point she might never recover from, the way she hadn't really recovered from the death of her parents, or the loss of Katarina, her childhood best friend. Already, he'd dug a hole inside her she'd been spending the better part of six months trying to backfill.

But that terrifying power he held over her heart was also the same reason why she couldn't just walk away. If he'd just been some *boyfriend* to her, it would be easy to believe he wasn't worth all of the trouble that came along with him, that she could just forget him.

But she couldn't.

And therein lay the biggest problem. Slate wasn't just some human male who had broken her heart. He was fae, a race that had haunted her nightmares since they'd taken Katarina from her, then kidnapped her after the death of her parents.

Worse, he was a fae *prince.*

"Is he different?" The words sprung from her lips of their own volition.

Kari's brows drew together, head tilting. "Different how?"

"Different. Like. You know. The magic and the... *faeness.*" The image of Zeyphar, from that night in the arena, filled her mind.

So cold.

So cruel.

"He's still the same. Temperamental and impulsive," Kari offered with a rueful smile and a shake of her head. "Still loves his martial arts movies and fighting and doing stupid shit with Jian. But I won't lie to you, he's got a lot of magic. He's definitely more dangerous than he used to be."

That made Dani's skin prickle. "Dangerous how?"

Another long assessment came from the *kitsune,* her lush lips pressed together as her storm cloud eyes scanned Dani's face. "These are questions you should ask him, *tori-chan.* If information is what you need, he will happily tell you anything and everything you want to know."

Which would require facing him again. Dani blew out a breath, looking back to where Dash was now bathing her free hand with his long tongue.

"When I say dangerous, babe, you know he would never be dangerous to you, right?" Kari asked gently, leaning toward Dani to catch her eye. "He would never hurt you."

Did she know that? She had known, before the fighting ring exploded around her, that Slate would never hurt her. But what about fae Slate?

She didn't know, and honestly, even if Kari told her every detail she wanted to know about Slate's new magic, would it really reassure her? Would simple words be enough to assuage her fears?

No. Which meant she was back to those two choices. Walk away from Slate, or face him.

Walking away from Slate might save her from pain and fear, but walking away forever would shred her heart.

If it was going to hurt either way, she might as well have his kisses, his wicked humor, his charming smile, and his endless sass. If she was going to come out bleeding no matter what choice she made... she'd rather be on the side that meant she could have Slate again, even if it was for just a short while.

"I mean, I know I'm biased, obviously," Kari continued, as if the silence between them was too heavy to bear. There was a hint of panic in her voice, like she'd backed herself into a corner and she wasn't quite sure how to get out of it. "It's no secret how I want this to end up, but you need to know that Jian and I will support—"

"I need to see him." The words exploded from Dani's lips, a burst of sound that had clawed its way from her heart and up through her throat.

"—you in whatever decision—" Kari's mouth snapped shut, and she blinked. "What?"

"I need to see Slate... in person, I think. I don't... I don't want to talk about this over the phone. Where can I find him?" Dani watched Kari's face go from shock to confusion to pleasantly surprised, watched as Kari's mouth curled into a rare smile of delight, as opposed to her normally wicked or sensuous ones.

"Really?"

Dani answered Kari's smile with one of her own, feeling *lighter* all of a sudden. "Yes, really. Can you...will you help me?"

Kari cocked her head to the side, eyes unfocused, and Dani knew she was communicating with her twin. "Jian says Slate has an afternoon class to teach in the studio, plenty of time before you have to work. He started teaching the odd class here and there about two weeks ago," Kari added when she caught sight of Dani's surprised face.

Feeling *lighter* became feeling *light-headed,* and Dani gripped the hot mug between her hands to combat the sudden dizziness. Kari was watching her carefully, so Dani offered her a tight nod, even as her heart did somersaults above the now-smaller knot of ice in her belly. She was going to see *Slate*.

And it was hard to tell, but maybe the part of her that was over the moon about it was a *little* bit bigger than the part of her that was scared out of her mind.

"This is amazing!" Kari screamed from behind her, and the female's fingers tightened on Dani's leather jacket as Selene pitched sharply to the left.

Dani cracked a smile, glancing back to see the *kitsune* had her head tilted back, eyes closed, and her long rose-gold hair streamed out behind her, snapping in the wind. Sellie's voice drifted through her mind with a distinctly disgruntled impression from the griffin: *She is loud...* and the impression changed to a reluctant admission. *Good bottom.*

Dani smiled, running her fingers through the fur-and-feather mixture at Sellie's neck. *You mean she has a good seat. She's not uncomfortable to carry.*

Mid-flight, Sellie cocked her snowy-owl head in inquiry. *Big word. Uncomfort.. able...*

You'll get it, Dani assured her. When Dani had made it clear she was going to see Slate in the Eastern District with Kari, Sellie had *insisted* on carrying them. She'd been imperious, but beneath it, Dani could tell she felt responsible for not being there six months ago at the Championship match.

When the arena, and Dani's life, had blown up in her face.

Now she focused on the mental sound of the griffin's voice, the impressions of haughty displeasure or curious delight as they passed over the city. It was something to focus on, instead of the way her body kept flashing between hot and cold as she considered what she was about to do.

She was about to jump from a cliff and hoped Slate would catch her.

And she prayed he'd understand there might be some tree branches in the way.

Sellie pitched again, and from behind her, Kari's voice came close to her ear. "There's Ebisu's garden."

Dani's stomach did a little flip against her intestines, and she angled her head to peer down toward the growing sight of a lush flower and vegetable garden that flourished on the roof of the apartment above Melisande Martial Arts.

Roof gardens weren't terribly unusual in the city, but Ebisu's was undoubtedly unique. For starters, it was winter, but someone must have forgotten to tell the plants under Ebisu's care. The flowers seemed fuller, more colorful, and the vegetables that came from it? Dani had personal experience with how flavorful they were, and she knew it was all because of the sheer number of faeries who inhabited it. They adored the garden itself as much as they loved its caretaker.

Dani's heart tightened in her chest when she spied the southwest corner of the rooftop; the nest that Sellie had slowly built in the two-or-so months that Dani and Slate 'dated' was still there.

Had the faeries maintained it... or had Ebisu?

Or... or had Slate?

Sellie let out a croon of pleasure as she beat her white-speckled wings once more before setting down gracefully in her nest. Kari and Dani were sliding off her when the griffin was accosted by small, slender bodies, iridescent wings shimmering in the sunlight as they darted excitedly around her head. Dani could hear their whispers in Faerish as they chattered happily at the griffin who patiently listened, despite her distinct *im*patience with most beings.

Dani made it all of two steps from Sellie's nest when she froze. Froze as fear welled up and seized control of her limbs, her lungs, making it hard to breathe. Fear of facing a fae, and even greater, the somewhat irrational fear of rejection.

Kari had made it clear Slate was still crazy for her, but that insidious what-if continued to whisper at the back of her mind.

She was distantly aware that Kari had stopped and was watching her. Kari reached out and gently placed a hand on the small of her back. "Dani?"

Kari's touch and the concern in her voice snapped through Dani's paralysis, and she jerked her head to the side to find the woman watching her, no smile this time. Calm radiated from her, a sense of serene determination, projected for Dani's benefit, no doubt.

"You want to come down, or should I tell him to come find you here?"

"I... yes." Dani jerked her head. *Do not chicken out*, she scolded herself. "Tell him I'm here."

"Oh, babe, he already knows you're here. But I'll have him come up here to you." The *kitsune* shot her a quick smile before she strolled over to the roof access door.

There was another soft croon from behind, and Dani felt warmth, encouragement, and a firm impression that Sellie would take her away from here in an instant, if she wanted. It helped loosen her shoulders, calm her racing pulse. She took a deep breath, and finally managed to make her feet move, to get them to take her to the long wide bench that separated the vegetable garden from the flowers.

She sat, facing the access door, and tangled her fingers together in her lap. Her heart pounded in her ears and her palms were sweaty, but despite her trepidation, a burgeoning excitement was simmering in her blood. It was like a part of her could sense Slate's proximity, and was whispering to her:

Finally.

CHAPTER FIVE

ONE HUNDRED PERCENT REAL

... the human population had exceeded expectations, and conflict was imminent. In the ensuing discussion, which lasted several years, it became increasingly obvious a resolution would not be found. This resulted in the Fae Civil War, which spanned...

– Gherald Schmidt, Faerloch Historical Archives

No.

That one word had shattered Slate's entire life, had blown him open so far and wide he wasn't certain he'd ever recover all the scattered pieces. That one word still rang in his ears a day later.

No.

A familiar numbness had settled over him, a defense mechanism against the jagged pain inside him, all because of that one fucking word.

Slate stitched enough of his pieces back together solely because he had to be somewhat functional today, his ingrained sense of duty and responsibility motivating him. He'd committed to teaching a martial arts class later.

So here he was, trying to get a playtime session in with Jian before his class. Focusing, however, was proving to be a challenge.

He felt fragile, like a bomb—any slight aggravation would set him off.

"Your footwork is sloppy today."

A vibration shook up Slate's spine at the idle comment. He barely checked the impulse to snarl at the male sitting in the waiting room, tipping his chair back on two legs, book in one hand.

"Don't you have somewhere *more important* to be?" He didn't *need* an escort when he was within the confines of the Eastern District. The ward protected him from his uncle's malevolent forces as long as he stayed within it.

Kallen licked his fingertip and idly turned the page of his book. "You slipped your escort four times in two weeks. I assure you, my lord, I have *nowhere* more important to be at the present moment."

"Then come out here and spar with me, instead of yapping your fucking trap out there."

"I am content with my novel."

Slate did snarl this time, pulling a dark chuckle out of his best friend opposite him. He zipped his gaze to Jian's. "Shut up."

Jian held up his hands in surrender, a grin still lining his face, pinching his thundercloud-gray eyes with a devilish humor identical to his twin's. "I didn't say anything."

Slate snatched the paddles out of Jian's hands, every movement jerky. "Gimme those."

They worked on a few kicking combinations, the act of holding paddles so innate that it freed up Slate's mind for other thoughts.

Like Dani, driving away on her bike, zipping out of sight, out of his life.

No.

He'd chosen. He'd taken Roger's—albeit threatening—advice, and he'd chosen. Chosen to step off the sidelines and get back into the game.

He'd whiffed it. Hard.

The sound of snapping paddles filled the growing tension of the silence. Slate could feel Jian's probing curiosity coupled with an intense flavor of *need*. Slate translated it as Jian's save-the-world complex; he wanted to fix whatever he was vibing off Slate.

"You wanna talk about what's bothering you?" Jian finally asked.

Slate said nothing. He didn't have words to describe what he was feeling. Angry. Hurt. Scared. He knew he deserved to feel like shit, since it was his doing, his fault. He'd broken up with her, but still.

His best friend studied him for a heartbeat, then returned to his kicking combination. Slate passively noted that Jian's fighting skill had grown exponentially in the last few months—his training with Slate and the fae warriors was starting to show in the lines of muscle on his body, and in his confidence and skill. It was a startling observation because Jian didn't like to fight.

Sure, he was a martial artist, but even more than Kari, Jian preferred brains over brawn. He was more willing to talk his way out of a situation than throw hands.

"I saw Dani yesterday..." Slate confessed, the words popping out as his temper fizzled down, snuffed out like a candle flame in favor of a sharper, more painful emotion—hurt. His insides trembled with it.

He almost hated that he understood why she didn't want to see him.

"I figured. Your *chi* and magic are all chaotic." Jian held his hands out for the paddles. Slate handed them over. "Wanna watch my patterns?"

"Of course." Anything to take his mind off the pressing hurt that threatened to consume him. Air was suddenly a scarce commodity.

"So what happened?" Jian asked, settling into the ready-position for the lowest-ranking black belt set of patterns. "How'd it go?" He started walking through the movements, solid and stable. Like everything Jian did in life, his patterns were steady, with perfect technique and a flawless foundation. He wasn't explosively powerful like Slate or flexible and graceful like Kari, but he was unfailingly steady.

The world needed more steady people. Slate needed Jian's steadiness.

"I just... met her outside your house," Slate said, pacing around Jian, half his mind watching his friend's pattern, the other half reliving his brief yet painful encounter with Dani. "Nothing really happened. I just... said hi."

Jian paused mid-transition, cocking a russet brow. "You *just* said hi?"

"Yeah." Slate bristled. "That's polite, saying hi to someone."

"Yeah, like a friend. Or an acquaintance. Not your ex-girlfriend who you've been studiously avoiding for six months but can't stop thinking ab—"

"I had my *reasons*."

Ramping, ramping... that trembling inside him was ratcheting up to a shaking, vibrating his bones. The tattoos visible on his forearms pulsed, the glow of them shifting from a light henna to a deep mahogany. They were absorbing extra magic; magic his body produced but couldn't absorb into his bones fast enough, courtesy of the fae glamour that had fucked up his magical development.

The color change was not missed by his best friend's sharp eyes. Jian's gaze flickered to the tattoos before snapping back to Slate's face. "Did you apologize?"

The air sucked right out of his lungs. "No..." he said. "I didn't."

"She deserves one, you know." Each word was carefully articulated. "She deserves an explanation—"

"What would I even say to her, Jian?" The words exploded from him on a gusty release of breath. "'*Sorry my life is a fucking shitshow, I broke up with you to protect you from my crazy fucking uncle*'?" Which wasn't the *entire* truth, and it tasted like dirt in his mouth.

The truth was he was afraid.

His life had fallen apart on him in a matter of hours that one night after the arena exploded, and he'd done the best he could with the situation he'd had. Breaking up with her had been the cleanest way to protect her, but it was also because he'd been afraid to face her. To see the panic in her eyes when she looked at him, knowing she was especially scared of the fae.

He hadn't known about the *mayt* thing. He'd convinced himself that she was the one thing he couldn't have. Ever. He hadn't known that fate had other plans for them that would make this entire situation messy and uncomfortable. He'd wanted to protect her from the fae.

God, Jian was right. She deserved a real fucking explanation, and he had no idea where to even start with it.

Instead, this whole break-up thing had festered between them like an infection. Empty words left unsaid.

"Listen." Jian held up his hands, and all pretense for working on patterns and foundations halted. "You don't have to explain it to me. I *know*. And until maybe a month ago, I would've told you to stay away from her, because you needed to focus on *yourself*. And if I'd thought you could go see her and have that conversation? I would've told you to do that too." Something tragic and knowing skittered across his face. "No one likes to be kept in the dark, man."

The sour taste of guilt echoed from a long-buried chamber in Jian's emotional grid. Guilt and fear, before the emotions were sucked away, disappearing behind Jian's impressive mental shields. He had a feeling Jian still felt guilty about keeping *him* in the dark about him and Kari.

Slate tugged his own magic back; he'd learned that while his best friend kept a lot of emotion on the surface of his mind, Jian had many secrets too. Secrets he wasn't even willing to share with Slate. Only Kari and the gods themselves knew what was behind Jian's mental shields.

Slate watched as Jian started his pattern work again, mind whirling. Shame swirled through him, beating relentlessly against his already thrumming insides. It sat hot and heavy inside him, like poison in his lungs. He swallowed hard.

"Maybe I should—" His throat choked a little around the words, his brain and heart catching up with his mouth and short-circuiting. "Maybe I should just give it up. Give *her* up."

She was better off without him. Was this what the rest of his forever would look like? An aching gap in his life that had once been illuminated by sunshine and summer?

Should he go after her?

No, because there was a deep part of him that was resistant to pulling her into all his shit. There was no stuffing his life back into its once-mortal box.

"She is your *mayt*, Zlaet," Kallen quipped.

Both men turned to glance at the fae male, still in his chair, still reading his book.

"Gee, I didn't notice," Slate growled. He'd nearly forgotten the lieutenant was still there.

Kallen's eyes shifted from his book and settled on Slate, steady and unflinching. "That plays a factor. You followed her like a shade because the soul finds it difficult to resist the call of its other half—"

The slight heat of embarrassment warmed Slate's cheekbones.

"—and she is likely similarly inclined. Not even you have the reservoir of self-control to *give her up* on a whim. Whether it is tomorrow, next year, or a decade from now, *mayts* almost always choose each other."

His mind snagged on two words: *almost always.*

"Your attempt to protect her is noble—"

"That's a word for it," Jian muttered.

"Fuck you," Slate snarled.

"—but in the end, she will find her way back to you. She will choose you. Have faith in that." Kallen tipped his shoulder in a slight shrug.

Slate shook his head. "It's an illusion of choice, stolen by fate."

"Sometimes it is a choice. Sometimes it is fate. Something your *tatkyr* has said to you before, yes?"

"She's not gonna choose to have a fae prince with a crazy uncle as her fucking boyfriend," Slate said, the words scathing and acerbic to disguise the catch in his throat.

Kallen returned his gaze to his novel, once again turning a page. "You do not know that. Perhaps Tanyiel-*tana* would enjoy being a queen consort. You would have to ask her."

Slate nearly choked on his own breath. He didn't even want to *touch* that idea. The idea of having Dani as... as a queen... as *his* queen... it was so far out of the scope of his current reality it bordered on mythical.

"I think..." Jian hedged, and Slate slid his gaze back to his best friend. "I think whatever you choose to do from here, you *need* to be one hundred percent real with her. An apology. An explanation. Something. You need to clear the air."

Slate nodded, unsure of what to say.

"Listen." Jian turned and shucked off his uniform top, folding it carefully and dumping it on top of his gear bag. "I'm done. I have some clients to see this afternoon. But." Slate spied a sly smile, there and gone. Slate frowned. "Kari's coming over, and she's bringing you a gift. It'll definitely cheer you up."

Slate rolled his eyes, heading into the office. He recognized Jian's wicked mischief and comment for what it was—a distraction tactic. He was grateful for it. It gave him a leg to stand on amidst the sea of numbness inside him.. "I don't need another porn magazine."

Jian's laugh was full and deep. "It's not that, promise. It's better."

Something about his tone pinged a warning in Slate's head. He poked his dark head out of the office door and narrowed his eyes at Jian for several heartbeats. His best friend gave nothing away beyond a subtle hint of devilish mischief, maybe a bud of trembling excitement.

"Then... what is it?" he hedged slowly.

"A woman," Jian's tone was light and airy. "A real one."

His entire body seized up. He didn't move for several long, agonizing moments as his brain filtered what Jian said and extrapolated what it meant.

Kari was—but Dani had—

"No..." Barely a thread of sound. He hardly dared to breathe, his lungs stuck somewhere between inhaling and exhaling.

"Yes."

He stared at Jian, daring him to lie to him. Not a whisper of untruth danced in his eyes—only a mild sense of knowing and meddling delight.

There was a distant thump. All three of them glanced toward the roof. Then, the slamming of the access door echoed from above them, and Slate's magic picked up on *her*—the scent of fresh green meadows, of rolling hills and sunshine—

He threw out a hand, gripping the doorframe hard, suddenly weak at the knees.

He heard the light footsteps on the stairs, and his blood pressure spiked. Adrenaline shot through him as a body rounded the corner.

It was Kari.

Disappointment clashed with exasperation—his magic would have known if it had been Dani coming down the stairs, but he was too much of a mess to process straight. Kari opened her mouth to speak, but she shut it and grinned at him, pure fox witch.

"I meddled a little..." she said by way of greeting. "Sorry." She didn't sound sorry at all. "She's waiting for you—"

Strength returned to his limbs, like pins and needles, and he was eating up the distance, striding past Kari as she laughed at him. Down the hall. Up the stairs. Through his apartment. Up more stairs. Pounding. Fast. Everything was pounding.

He paused at the access door to the roof. A piece of steel separated them. He could feel her clearly on the other side; a wavering, tentative excitement to her, a bubble of intense, skin-flushing fear. Slate managed to pull himself inward, focus his attention on himself.

He... he had this one moment.

One shot.

He sucked in his aura, trying to keep the output low, less fae, more human, and mustered a few deep breaths in a vain attempt to calm his racing heart. It was a desperate bid to not look as though he'd just run up the stairs. He smoothed a hand over his hair, down his tank top...

And slowly, he pushed open the door.

Slate's eyes zeroed in on Dani immediately; she was perched on the bench by the pumpkin patch, hands clenched together tightly in her lap, spine ramrod straight.

The winter sun turned her hair into living fire, and her emerald eyes jumped to his face as he stepped out onto the roof. He felt the flush of chaotic emotion race through her before he tugged his own magic back, fortifying his mental shields to the best of his nascent ability. He couldn't... he couldn't handle both their emotions at the same time. Call it self-preservation, but he was about to implode all on his own.

It was impossible to string his thoughts together to form coherent words. Any sort of mental preparation vanished. It didn't matter how or why she came back. All he understood was the pull in his very marrow toward her. The rest of the world could burn down around him, and he wouldn't care.

The access door slammed shut like a gunshot. The moment the ringing silence faded, a low hiss echoed from the corner of the garden—feral and fierce. The hairs stood on the back of his neck as his heart leaped into his throat. There, perched in the nest his father had lovingly helped maintain for the last six months, was Selene. Pale blue eyes narrowed. Feathers puffed up. A low hiss rumbled from her fur-feathered chest, punctuated with several clicks of her beak that managed to sound haughty as well as pissed.

Made her sad. Cry a lot. Bad man.

Words like a cool night wind filtered into his mind. Slate stared at the griffin for a moment, processing the fact that she actually *spoke* to him before the actual words themselves filtered through his addled brain.

Bad was woefully inadequate to how he felt about the entire situation, but it was also a rather succinct summary.

He dragged his attention to Dani, noting the stiff way she sat on the bench. Everything about her was tight, from the cut of her shoulders, to the lines around her eyes. Like a stone statue that might crumble if he touched her.

He hated that.

Slate sucked in a breath, willing words to form, willing *anything* to come out of his mouth, even if it was something stupid.

Apologize, Melisande. Say something. Say sorry.

"Dani. I—" But the words stopped halfway between his heart and his mouth. Her eyes held him completely hostage as they limned silver for the barest of heartbeats. She drew in a shaking breath.

"Why?"

The soft word echoed loudly in the space between them, more breath than voice, but it shot him right in the chest.

Why. Why. Why.

Did he even know why? Why anything?

"Why?" he repeated back to her, something to fill the empty, tense space breathing between them.

"You broke up with me, and..." her voice cracked. She pulled in another breath, "... and left me for half a *year.*"

Even without his magic, her words were such a raw, aching hurt that they cut him right to the quick. He couldn't breathe for a moment, everything north of his sternum seizing tight with a familiar, painful emotion.

Guilt.

"I know..." he replied hoarsely, attempting words around the raw ache in his throat. "I know I did."

She watched him, blinking back her tears that had yet to fall as her fingers curled into little fists in her lap. The silence once again stretched taut and thin between them. He couldn't even think clearly, consumed by the fact she was right in front of him and everything was somehow both right and wrong all at once, and it was confusing and painful. Right in that she was here and yet... wrong because this wasn't how it was ever supposed to be with them.

Not like this.

A single tear overflowed the rest and tracked a lonely line down her freckled cheeks.

It wrecked him, to see her sitting all alone on that bench. Her body was strained and tense, as if her hurt and anger were physical weights dragging her down, and she was doing whatever possible to keep her head above water.

She was drowning.

And it was his fault.

He closed the distance between them. Step by step, slow at first, a part of him hesitant to rush her. She tensed, the shaking in her shoulders stilling as she watched him.

Once he was close enough, he dropped to one knee in front of her, bringing them nearly eye level. He gently propped his hands on the bench on either side of her thighs, but he was careful not to touch her, careful to watch for signs that he should back the fuck off.

"Daniella," he said, voice hardly above a whisper, "you have to know... I didn't want... it was the hardest thing I've ever done."

"Don't say that..."

"I thought about you every single fucking day. I never stopped wanting you. I would literally *dream* about you."

She covered her face with both her hands, muffling a staggering sob.

His heart squeezed painfully in his chest, and the instinct to touch her, to reach for her, was nearly overwhelming. It took every ounce of his will to keep his hands to himself.

"Don't say that," she repeated, her tone harsher despite being muffled by her hands.

Slate's brows crashed together as his heart lurched in his chest at the agonized fury in her voice. "It's the truth—"

"You can't say that. You can't just come back here after six months and say stuff like that. You *left* me! With *no* explanation!" Her voice cracked again, and her hands slipped down her face until she glared at him over her fingertips, misery and anger alike swimming in those tears.

Her words slapped him, and he recoiled a bit, unable to shut down his magic as her anger and grief beat at him in hot and cold waves. "I know… I fucked up."

"I watched you almost die and then you just… left." Tears clogged her voice. She swallowed hard and covered her face with her hands again. "Everyone said you were fine, that you'd be back… and then… and then you never came back."

There was a raw vulnerability ghosting around the edges of her words, a heartbroken rasp that disguised itself as anger. It punctured him, piercing straight through his lungs and filling him with the sour taste of guilt. He'd thought—at the time—he'd been making all the right calls exactly the right way.

But he'd still fucked up. Just… ripped them both apart, ripped her apart, and neither one of them ever truly recovered properly.

"I know… you have every right to be pissed at me. Shit, I'd be pissed at me. I *am* pissed at me."

She sniffled, face still cradled in her hands. A long, tense silence pulled thin between them. It ratcheted through him, filling him with a bubbling, quaking anxiety to populate the empty air with words and explanations and apologies and feelings.

Slowly, he reached toward her and gently touched the back of her hand with his fingertip. She started, dropping her hands enough that he could see her face again.

"I… what I did, I did to protect you," he began, the words edging out of him in an awkward roll, gaining more and more momentum as he went. "I thought it would be safer for you. Everything fell apart so fast and I just thought... it would be safer for you if I broke it off. That maybe the fae would leave you alone if I didn't have any contact with you anymore."

She drew in a wobbly breath and swiped the heels of her hands across her face, wiping away the tears. She took a breath... and another. He forced himself to wait, to live in the silence, tamping down the desire to jump back in and offer her more apologies and explanations.

"You couldn't tell me that yourself?" She broke the silence in a hoarse whisper. "You couldn't give me a choice?"

She watched him, eyes wide. It was a struggle to keep his magic from reaching out, to get a bead on her emotions, but a part of him didn't want to know what she was feeling.

"I was scared," he finally admitted, rubbing at the back of his neck, gaze skittering away from hers. Looking at the garden but seeing nothing. "Of everything. Of what was happening, what I am, what you'd think. And I didn't wanna drag you into the middle of this. I didn't wanna potentially involve you in something dangerous."

"Is your life dangerous?" she asked, and he heard a pained note in her voice.

He brought his gaze back to hers. He swallowed hard and nodded. Once. "Sometimes. It's definitely... stressful."

Another silence stretched in the space between them; the intensity of this moment haunting the edges of that tension. Slate actively tugged his own aura in closer. The tattoos visible along his arms and his collarbone pulsed a little, and he noticed the way her gaze shot to them, lingering, studying.

"Why now, then?" Dani finally asked in a whisper, gaze tracking over the magical ink on his arms. "Have you resolved things with your uncle?"

"Umm. No." He shook his head.

Her gaze flipped back to his, searching his face as her slender brows grew together. "Then... what's changed? Why now, after six months?" The anger was leaking from her voice, leaving only hurt behind.

It was somehow worse than her fury, like razors over his skin.

How was he supposed to explain this one? *I physically cannot stay away from you anymore. It hurts me. I miss you. You are* mine.

"Because I'm selfish," he said, replacing his hand on the bench, soaking in her closeness. He didn't dare touch her again. But it was alright, for the moment. Simply being close to her satisfied the touch hunger inside him that had grown worse each day he'd been away from her. "I'm selfish and I'm not ready to find out what it feels like for you to move on. I saw you go on that date the other day—"

Her eyes widened, something like guilt chasing across her face.

"—and I felt some way about it that I'm not particularly proud of. And everything is still really fucked up in my life, but a lot is different now too, and I'm different. I'm stronger, and God fucking help anyone who tries to come after you because I will kill them."

If possible, her eyes grew even wider, her lips parting. A tension shimmered across her shoulders, and her eyes darted over him, as if she were visually assessing the creature before her, re-evaluating him. Wariness simmered in her gaze.

"That was aggressive, I'm sorry," he said in a rush, backpedaling immediately.

Her silence felt like a million years long as he held his breath. Finally, her shoulders relaxed a pinch. "It's... it's okay. You've always been a bit hot-headed, even before."

He offered her a wicked grin, small but sharp. "My most charming trait, honestly."

She almost smiled at that. Almost.

"But..." He rocked back from her, releasing the bench and showing her his arms. "I'm... not dangerous to you anymore. I've settled into whatever this version of me is, with the magic and shit. I'm not as explosive as I was six months ago. Jian helped; these tattoos are like Kari's. They help absorb extra magic my body can't absorb. Otherwise, I could...." he trailed off.

A beat of quiet fell again. "Could?" Dani prompted.

He didn't want to say it, but he had to be honest with her. "I could detonate."

Her eyes dropped to the curls of scripted ink, color leaching from her face. "Why would you detonate from your own magic?" Distress tinged her voice.

She hadn't seen him, the night after the arena, when his magic nearly overwhelmed him and sucked him into the void. He was alive solely because of Jian.

His skin felt too tight, the instinct to relieve her of her distress a powerful urge. "It's a side effect from the glamour. My body didn't mature with my magic, so it can't adjust to all of it running through me now. Jian says my body will equalize eventually, but for now, I need the tattoos to give the magic somewhere to go." He shrugged, as if he wasn't still slightly bothered by the fact he could go nuclear again if not for Jian. "I have more magic than my body knows what to do with right now."

Dani stared at him, horror edging into the myriad of emotions on her face. "Your magic is dangerous to you?"

"Not really, thanks to Jian," Slate assured her, deciding now was not the time to mention he technically could overload the tattoos too, if he wasn't careful.

Her gaze tracked over the whorls of ink again. Silence swelled between them once more, and he jumped into it this time, unable to wait.

"I'm sorry," he blurted. He sucked in a breath, watching her face. "I shouldn't have... I should've found you sooner, given you some kinda explanation... but I just..." He shook his head, caught up in the what-ifs and the acute disappointment in himself. That shame still coated his throat; every swallow painful. "Just... I'm sorry," he settled on, feeling stupid and raw and torn open. He sucked in a silent, shaking breath deep into his quaking lungs. "That's... that's all. I'm sorry."

HOLDING GROUND

... Trials, in which those with Wild Magic were targeted and persecuted by a nameless zealot group. It is unknown if one of the High Fae Noble Houses orchestrated the Trials, but it ultimately led to...

- Gherald Schmidt, Faerloch Historical Archives

I'm sorry.

Words she didn't know she needed to hear until they punched right past her lingering anger. Dani sucked in a breath, gaze drawn from those unusual pulsing tattoos to find him staring at her, raw and real and unguarded. His sapphire eyes were pools of pain, panic, and a wild desperation that had her heart pounding against her ribs.

She didn't know if a single apology could make up for the months of painful loneliness he'd subjected her to. And yet, staring at him now, with such open vulnerability, she felt herself softening, more of that anger slipping away. It would be a pointless battle to hold onto it.

Firstly, her anger was a candle compared to the bonfire of gnawing loneliness for him that clawed at her, urging her to reach for him now and damn the past. Secondly, holding onto that anger would only poison things between them.

She would have to decide right now, because if she wanted to be with him again, she couldn't allow the anger to remain, to fester and rot what could be between them. Moreover, she knew it could become a weapon she could wield against him, hold over his head in revenge for leaving her the way he had.

But Dani had never been the type of person to hold on to grudges, with the one exception being toward those who hurt animals.

He had messed up, but he was sorry; the pain and desperation that was festering inside her was reflected plain on his face. He would do anything she asked of him to earn her forgiveness.

Frankly, she didn't want to be angry anyway.

Dani let out a slow breath, and dipped her chin in a nod, watching him intently. Her voice was hoarse when she whispered, "I accept your apology."

A visible shudder ran through Slate, and his hands returned to either side of her legs as he braced himself against the bench once more, but he didn't touch her. The pressure of his heartfire expanded in a sudden flare of magic use, and she stiffened at the reminder of the faeness inside him.

The other hurdle between them, one not as easily put to rest as her anger.

Dani breathed through the cold prickling of her scalp and skin, forcing herself to stare at Slate, to study the face that had been haunting her dreams. She wasn't sure, but he might have noticed her stiffness, because his heartfire banked, and Slate stilled—unnaturally so, the way Roger often did, and his brows furrowed slightly.

As if holding his breath, he stared at her, a hint of hope brightening the desperation in his face as he watched her process. "Dani?" he whispered gently.

"Give me a second," Dani murmured, centering herself on the familiar angles of his jaw, the unusual silvery hair cut short on the sides of his temples, on his wintery scent.

There were new angles to him, a hardness of muscle and of life that had shaped his face and his body in new ways. The tattoos were a visceral reminder of the changes to his body, but they were also foreign to her, symbols and characters that had nothing to do with her nightmares. She could see the faeness in him, but she could also see *him*.

She knew, by the way he had already started to rock away from her, that he didn't want to make her uncomfortable, didn't want to scare her, and it hit her that if he could excise his faeness for her, he would. He would deny a part of his very being for her comfort.

A trickle of shame wriggled in past the fright constricting her chest like a balloon, piercing the tightness until she deflated. His whole world had been up-ended, his very existence changed in a fundamental, biological way, and rather than her comfort him, he was comforting *her*, taking care of *her*.

It was entirely possible he had been as scared of himself as she was scared of the fae in him, but unlike her, he couldn't exactly walk away from who or what he was.

It triggered something inside her that was as undeniable to her as breathing; a need to care, to soothe. It was the same, and yet different, from that undeniable urge to soothe a frightened animal. It was simply a part of who she was, but with him, the urge was overwhelming, like a primal part of herself was tuned to him, and him alone, and his distress brought it alive in a new way.

Dani's hands flashed out, fingers wrapping around Slate's wrists as he released the bench to prevent him from putting more space between them. He was trying to let her process, but she'd had enough distance from him.

Slate's gaze dropped to her hands before jumping back to her face. Slowly, he replaced his hands on the bench, and Dani's breath clouded in the space between them. "I want to try."

Slate was predator-still, watching her with caution. "Try what?"

She jerked her chin toward him. "Try... you. Us." She shrugged, trying to ignore how her insides were trying to force their way up her throat. "I'm not... I don't want to walk away. I want to try *us* again and see where we go."

"Where do you wanna go?" His voice was a breath of sound.

She opened her mouth to respond, then shut it. The words got stuck in the tangle of organs blocking her airway. *Go where?*

Where the happily ever after is.

She didn't know how to say that, though. Didn't know how to explain that where she wanted to go—where she hoped *they* could go—was through a thicket of fear. She didn't know what it was going to look like. Feel like. But Goddess above, she really *did* want to try.

"I'm not sure yet," she settled on.

A beat of silence passed before he nodded, and out of the corner of her eye, she saw his fingers tighten on the edge of the bench knuckle-white, before he released it with a silent breath. His tattoos pulsed, turning a darker shade, a shimmer that was entirely magical.

Fear threatened to choke her, but she stubbornly refused to concede to it. Slate was *not* the fae who had stolen her best friend from her. She just needed her brain to intercede before her instincts poured ice through her body.

"Maybe we can just kinda... back up a little?" she continued, swallowing the ice until she could breathe again. Her fingers loosened on his wrists, but she didn't release him entirely. "I think I need information. I need you to... to talk to me." She floundered, gaze sliding from his as she sucked in another breath. "I need to know what's happening so I can understand."

He was already nodding. "Everything. I'll tell you anything and everything you need to know."

"Explain it all to me like I'm four years old."

His mouth twitched into a smile. "Absolutely. I can do that."

"Alright. I'd like that."

He nodded again. Yet another beat of silence passed between them, his wrists flexing under her touch, as if he wanted to touch her, but he held himself still, staring at her with a joy tainted by uncertainty. He gently tugged his wrists free, sitting back from her, and the emotions that punched through her at that small retreat made the fear of his faeness pale in comparison.

He'd put only a few inches between them, but her soul cried out: *Don't leave me.*

Something in her snapped.

In a wave of courage that tasted like winter and storms, she surged forward, her knees hitting the ground as she flung her arms around his neck and buried her face in the crook of his shoulder. A tremor rippled through her, the relief at the contact overwhelming her senses, like she was a plant starved of sunlight suddenly thrust onto a sunny ledge.

His body was harder than she remembered, corded with more muscles, but his scent, the *feel* of him... it was like a balm to her soul, and she was crying again. Unlike before, these tears felt like a release, like poison leaching from her. Each drop left her lighter as they drained away her anxiety, panic, fear, and—most of all—her loneliness.

STARTING OVER

... even the rare half-fae—sometimes known as demi-fae—have been recorded to live for hundreds of years...

- Gherald Schmidt, Faerloch Historical Archives

Slate sucked in a breath of surprise, skin coming alive at the abrupt contact. His heart dove into his stomach, before coming back up to lodge in his throat. He froze, brain and body alike short-circuiting at the riot of sensations her touch ignited.

It felt both stunningly relieving and alarmingly overwhelming all at once.

Touch-starved. It was a phrase that was thrown around casually among the fae. Physical touch was commonplace; more casual and open, and even fae healers staunchly proclaimed that the lack of physical touch manifested symptoms in fae, not unlike an illness.

It wasn't a concept Slate truly grasped until this moment *right now.*

His frozen body waged an internal sensory war for all of two heart-beats. He had to actively force himself to slow down, to not crush her, as he wrapped his arms around her and held her against him. He braced himself for rejection, for her to push him away, but she only leaned harder into him.

He swallowed his suddenly dry throat. He shifted carefully, dropping his raised knee to the ground and leaning back on his heels, holding her to him. One of his hands slid up her back until he rested his palm against the nape of her neck, the position as natural as breathing. It was a struggle not to bury his face in her neck, right over that little scar he prayed was still there, and inhale the scent of her into his lungs.

He didn't want to push too hard and overwhelm her. Still, a powerful need to crush her body into his bulldozed through him, followed swiftly by the insane impulse to strip her naked right here on the roof and run his hands over every living inch of her.

He needed to know she was real, that she was safe, needed to remind his starved senses what she felt like, wanted to absorb her vitality, and let it soothe his frayed soul. He felt her release a hard, shaking breath, and his next inhale brought forth a sharp scent of brine.

Why was she crying? Did he make her cry?

Of course he did.

Pure male panic blazed through him, and he tensed, fighting the urge to tighten his hold. *Fuck fuck fuck.*

Dani made a small sound, a stifled sob, and the sound of it tore him open.

Powerless. Here he was, a fae prince with ample magical reservoirs and decades of fighting skill, taken out at the knees by the one woman he'd literally trade his beating heart for. Despite the negative way she'd reacted before, her tears spurred him to reach with his magic, to listen to her emotions. He had no idea how she was able to tell when he was flexing his empathy magic, but he'd worry about that later.

Her emotions were an ocean of anxiety and stress—twin to his own—but swirling in the maelstrom was panic, fear, and the overwhelming agony of *loneliness*.

Slate pulled his magic back, pulled everything in tighter to himself as his own feelings jammed up his throat. He'd done that. He'd made her feel that loneliness.

And he was lonely, too.

Neither one of them spoke for several long minutes. The scent of her tears faded, leaving behind the damning evidence of wetness against his neck. The rhythm of her breathing stuttered, recovering from the crying, and a bolt of guilt stabbed him in the chest.

Slate Melisande, if you hurt her? I will be back...

Well, he supposed he could add that to the list of things he'd fucked up.

Dani sucked in a breath, and she pulled back. It took an amazing amount of discipline to let her take the distance, to lose the warmth and pressure of her body. He didn't take his hands off her, though, settling his hands on her knees, nestled between his.

"I'm so tired of crying," she said with an injection of faux laughter, wiping her cheeks with the edge of her sleeve. "My eyes itch for hours afterward."

"I'm sorry..." he said, the nauseating taste of guilt in the pit of his stomach.

Dani gave a little shake of her head, but she offered him a watery smile. He took it in like a fresh breath of air.

He leaned down slightly, sharing breathing space with her and catching her eyes. He offered her a half smile in response. "You know, Roger's gonna kill me if you keep showing up here and crying. He doesn't need another reason to dislike me." He injected as much teasing into his tone as he could, trying to keep it light.

She let out a chuckle, this one less watery than the last, and it eased some of the tightness in his chest. She sucked in another steadying breath. "He wouldn't kill you. He's more of the 'torture-you-infinitely' type of guy."

"That's... definitely worse."

Another ribbon of laughter from her as she finished scrubbing at her face. "He wouldn't. He's all talk, really."

Slate's brows shot up, and her smile became a little more genuine, the corners of her lips twitching up.

"Seriously. I've only seen him hurt two or three people in my entire life."

That was a glorious underestimation of Roger, but she seemed to believe it for truth, and he wasn't about to pull the curtain back for her.

"Besides, Roger will mind his own business," she said with a hint of tartness. It was such a welcoming reminder of her usually sunny, fiery self that he couldn't stop himself; he slipped a hand along her cheek. A shot of emotion punched through him—this one belonging to himself—as her head tipped slightly, leaning into his touch.

Slate recognized that emotion as *love* before he buried it deep behind his mental shields. He didn't want to risk projecting to her, didn't want her to see that yet. Not when his little bird had just returned to his palm.

"Listen..." He swallowed hard, swallowing the catch in his voice as he dropped his hand from her cheek, but he couldn't give up touching her, so he placed his hand on her knee. "I need you to know how real I am when I say that I'm sorry. Truly, I—"

A finger over his lips stopped him, and another ghost of a smile from her. "While I appreciate the groveling," her voice was soft, "you don't need to convince me. You said you're sorry, and you've never been a good liar." She crinkled her nose at him. It wasn't a criticism, but it wasn't praise either. Just a piece of reluctant truth.

Her finger was a distraction, his entire being was suddenly focused on that point of contact. He was unreasonably disappointed when she pulled back. Stifling it, he offered her a smile of his own—a little sharp one, with a wicked pinch around the edges. "That's true. Secrets and bullshit aren't exactly my specialty."

A silence drifted between them, curling like the mists of their shared breaths.

"Do you..." he started. Once again, he swallowed everything down hard. "Do you... can you forgive me, Dani?"

Dani's eyes slid away, down to where his hands rested on her knees. Slowly, she covered his hands with hers, the softness of her skin sending a shiver down his spine. "I'm not angry with you anymore." She flipped her eyes up to meet his. "I think forgiveness is the next natural step. I don't know if I can say I've forgiven you so quickly, but so long as you don't plan on disappearing on me again, I'll get there."

Not exactly what he wanted to hear, but it was enough. Enough to know he had a chance to earn her forgiveness. He didn't need his magic to read in her expression that he'd hurt her. And it was a wound on his own heart, one that pulsed along a powerful need to rectify said hurt. "That's fair," he said, trying to keep the tightness from his voice.

He was disappointed, but a larger part of him was willing to do, say, and be anything in order to gain her forgiveness. Even as a part of him whispered that it was okay if she never did. Because he'd fucked it up pretty bad, and him ghosting her for six months didn't deserve to be forgiven.

"But," she added softly. "I said I want to try, and I mean that. Like, really try."

"Anything you want." He nodded. "I want what you want."

He'd said the same thing to her a lifetime ago, on a rainy street at the threshold of summer. It rang true still—whatever she wanted, however she wanted it, whatever pace she set, he'd follow. Without hesitation, without condition.

This time, though, it wasn't a carefully crafted lie to be used as an excuse to stay together. It was the whole entire truth.

He saw recognition flash across her face at his words. Her eyes skirted away, and he couldn't help it; he reached with his magic, felt an echo of shame, a sting of guilt and trepidation. His brows pinched together. How much easier would everything be, if Slate was a better liar and they could stand here and cling to the shaky foundation they'd started on?

But if they were truly going to start over, to *try*, he wasn't going to stand on lies this time. He wanted *her*, and that was the long and short of it.

She nibbled on her bottom lip, instantly drawing his attention, but she wouldn't meet his gaze. "I've been working on this whole... *courage* thing." Her eyes flickered to his, then away once more, and the taste of her shame spiked. "I know I was... difficult..."

The need to take that ugly emotion from her, to soothe her hurt, was overwhelming. "No, I definitely win in the 'difficult' department." He offered her a lopsided grin. He had never faulted her for her choices, and he certainly wouldn't start now. If she was truthful in her commitment to *try*, then her cowardice meant nothing in the face of this new bravado. He didn't know what haunted her, what drove these fears, but he couldn't help the prick of pride in him as he watched her wrestle with those demons. "Once you have your own fucking 'magical girl transformation,' we can compare notes on *difficulty*."

Dani blinked at him. "Magical-girl? Are you... did you just make a Sailor Moon reference?" Some of the heavy guilt and shame bled away under a hint of surprised delight. Her lips slowly pulled into a cautious smile.

"*Shh*. Do *not* tell Kari I said that. She hasn't stopped calling me *Sailor Scout Slate* since summer. "

Her smile brightened just a touch more. "You *are* just like Sailor Moon." Amusement danced in her verdant eyes. "Did you sparkle?"

His grin widened, feeling lighter than he had in weeks, *months*. Even if things were still tangled between them, this moment was worth it. This stolen moment with the woman who held his heart—this moment was everything.

"I certainly saw stars, that's for sure. Faerie Prism Power." He offered her the stereotypical two-finger symbol for peace.

She laughed, a real one, and the sound shot through him like a bullet. The desire to kiss her surged through him, but he didn't want to spook her. As it was, he was simply enjoying her nearness as she continued to kneel between his knees. He meant what he'd said—he'd let her set the pace.

She smiled at him, wider now than before. "*Sailor Scout Slate...*" she murmured, laughter in her voice. "I'd pay good money to see you in a Sailor Scout outfit. Pigtails and all."

"*Never*," he breathed in a low growl, but his lips curved in a grin.

She laughed again, and the words jumped out of his mouth before he could censor them. "Maybe we can—do you wanna... date again?"

"Date?" She paused, several emotions flickering through her eyes, the laughter petering out. "Like, ten dates again?"

He nearly choked on his breath. "However many you want."

Her eyes widened; from panic or excitement, he wasn't sure. Maybe a bit of both. She tucked her hair behind her ear, and his gaze flashed to her left shoulder, pulse pounding in his throat at the memory of the *mark*. He wanted to peel the collar of her jacket back, take a peek, see if it was still there. He wanted to thread through her mind again, taste her emotions, but he was cognizant of the subtle winces each time he had so far. It seemed like she could almost *feel* when he used his power—which was an anomaly in and of itself—and it flooded her with panic.

He hated it.

Hated that his magic scared her. Hated that he didn't know *why*.

It was a small reminder that he was still running a lot of defense with this woman, and he had to tread carefully.

She regarded him for a long time. "One," she finally said. "Let's... let's start with one."

He sucked in a tight breath. "Alright." He nodded. "One. I can do that."

"Saturday afternoon. A+ wow factor."

The words brought back unexpected memories, of laughter, of heated skin, and he smiled at her. "I can do that too. A+ wow factor."

CHAPTER   EIGHT

THE NOT-DATE

... and heavy trading of griffin chicks and eggs amongst Faerloch's Dark Market District, where the illegal creature trade thrives despite the efforts of the Silver Grace Coven and their...

- Gherald Schmidt, Faerloch Historical Archives

Unknown

I hope work is going well.

The text came halfway through Dani's shift at work, hours after she'd left Slate on the roof of his building. It was from an unknown number, one she'd deleted from her phone months ago, but she knew who it belonged to.

Shivers puckered her skin even as a flush heated her cheeks.

Slate.

She was on autopilot at the end of her shift as she changed back into her jeans and white t-shirt. Lastly, she pulled on her jacket, that simple text still running through her mind.

Go home? Sellie inquired as Dani slipped on her backpack and waved to the receptionist on the way out.

She didn't answer her friend right away, curling her fingers around the straps of her backpack as she rounded the corner and entered the alley along the side of the clinic. Wintry wind buffeted her face a moment later as Sellie landed before her, wings tucked in tight in the small space. Her luminous eyes inspected Dani with a cocked head.

Dani smiled up at her, running a hand through the soft place where feathers and fur intermingled at her neck, scratching at a favorite spot. Sellie's eyes narrowed suspiciously. *You go see man.* There was distinct displeasure in that tone.

"I shouldn't, right?" Dani whispered to her, not quite sure if she wasn't also speaking to herself. She pulled herself onto Sellie's back, settling in between her wings and burying her fingers in the soft spotted white-and-gray feathers at the base of her proud head.

Stupid idea, Sellie agreed imperiously, and launched herself skyward.

Dani didn't reply as her friend cleared the buildings, rising higher into the night sky. It was almost half past eleven, but it was a Thursday, and the city was still awake. Her eyes snagged on the lights, her ears on the sounds of her beloved city. The tight streets, the historical architecture, the bustling of late-night pedestrians, and yet Dani was still drawn to one flame in the darkness.

Slate.

Sellie made it all of three powerful wingbeats before Dani's fingers tightened in her ruff. She saw the griffin's head twitch, and she barely opened her mouth to speak when Sellie banked suddenly.

Dani tightened her thighs to keep from sliding off, blood pressure spiking as they changed trajectories.

Away from the outer suburbs where Dani's quaint little house rested, and toward the east side of the city, across the Loch River, to the isolated district nestled in the river and farthest from the reaches of the Forest of L'el...

The Eastern District.

"Thank you, my friend..." Dani said around her heart in her throat, leaning forward to run her fingers through Sellie's fur-feathers in a grateful caress.

Sellie didn't respond in her mind, but Dani could hear distinct grumbles, coupled with displeased hissing and small clicks of her beak. She made it a bumpy ride, too, and Dani found herself unable to get too nervous about what she was doing, not if she wanted to avoid freefalling through the air before being plucked out of it by an irate griffin.

She knew from experience that it wasn't pleasant.

Sellie wasn't quiet when she landed on the roof. Her wings gusted flowers and faeries alike, and tiny voices rose in a chorus of irritated chirps and excited squeals. Dani was still chiding the griffin for her entrance when a voice came from behind her, soft and calm.

"The esteem of a lady, once lost, is so difficult to regain, *ne*, Dani-*san*?"

Dani whipped around, spine to Sellie's flank, and found Ebisu Melisande kneeling amidst a patch of mint and thyme. One hand held a pair of garden shears, the other a clump of weeds. A black cat—Dani had almost forgotten Slate's father had a Familiar—sat primly by his side. Above his head, a handful of faeries illuminated the space with faerie lights, small glowing balls in a multitude of colors. She could feel their curious eyes on her, hear their excited whispers.

Two or three of them disappeared, zipping toward the access door, and Dani's eyes barely tracked them before she trained her gaze back to Ebisu. She swallowed hard. "I..." she stammered, trying to calm her racing heart, heat filtering in her cheeks.

"I meant the lady Selene-*sama*, of course." Amusement sparkled in his midnight eyes, and Ebisu calmly set the shears down on a small blanket lined with other gardening tools. He disposed of the weeds, then dusted off his hands with a smile. "It is wonderful to see you again, Dani-*san*." The older man got to his feet, and a part of her passively noticed he seemed more youthful, more alive, than when she'd last seen him six months ago.

"N-nice to see you, Mr. Melisande," Dani offered, feeling pinned. Panic bucked in her chest, and her eyes flickered to the side, one hand going behind her back to tangle in Sellie's fur for comfort. The griffin pressed her flank tighter against Dani's side, a silent show of support.

"I think it's time I go to bed," Ebisu said with a knowing little smile. "Take care, my dear."

With that, Slate's father gave a small bow from his waist, then walked calmly toward the roof access door.

Which exploded outward a moment before he reached it, and spilled out a wide-eyed Slate.

Dani's breath froze in her lungs, warmth and cold going to war under her skin once more. Slate's eyes almost glowed in the low faerie lights as he looked at his father, then over to Dani and Sellie, before wary panic scrawled across his expressive face as he looked back at Ebisu.

Ebisu chuckled, reached up a hand, and patted Slate on the cheek. "Goodnight, *musuko*." He stepped around his son, hands tucked behind his back, and disappeared into the roof-access door, his Familiar at his heels.

Just like that, they were alone.

Well, except for Sellie, who gave a distinctly un-ladylike grumble. *We leave?*

Part of Dani wanted to take her up on that, but it was mostly the coward in her. She straightened her spine and chided herself as Slate turned to face her fully, the roof access door closing behind him.

Sellie gave another little hiss toward Slate before she stalked off toward her nest in the corner. Without the griffin at her back, some of Dani's courage wavered, but it was that cautiously hopeful look in Slate's eyes that made her finally move her feet.

She walked toward him, and he watched her steadily, like he was memorizing every line of her face. Her heart flipped in her chest, warming and melting some of the chill inside her. When a foot separated them, she stopped, and let her backpack slide from her shoulders. It dangled for one precarious moment from slender fingers before she let it thump quietly by her feet.

"I... umm... was hoping we could talk."

Slate blinked, then his smile blew away her uncertainty. "Yeah, sure. Anything you want. Uh... do you... do you wanna come in?" He glanced back behind him, rubbing at the back of his neck.

Go in... go all the way into his apartment? To the kitchen where they'd made dinner that one time?

To his bedroom? Where she'd slept over not once, but twice?

Where they'd had the best sex of her life?

Words jammed in her throat, but Slate breezed on. "We can stay up here too, that's fine." Not a drop of judgment in his voice.

Dani didn't think she was ready for *inside* yet. Being in the garden felt different. Neutral. Like they were in their own world, separate from the reality where his uncle was a crazy king of the fae and her own nightmares held sway over her instead of the other way around.

She nodded. "I'd like that."

"Let me go get us some tea, maybe some blankets, *ne*?" Slate offered.

She jerked her chin in a nod, and when he hesitated, she moved to sit on the bench by the pumpkin patch. He lingered a moment more before he headed for the access door.

Across the roof, Sellie grumbled again, and several faeries giggled.

Dani took the time she was alone to try and address the tangle of emotions in her chest. But they were still a mess by the time Slate was back, a blanket thrown over one bare arm while he carried two steaming mugs. He nudged the door closed with his foot, then brought the tea over to her with an easy grace that reminded her once more of his lineage.

Fae.

It was frightening, but when she looked at his face, it tugged up memories of kisses, laughter, and wicked humor, and of the surprising kindness beneath his temperamental exterior. It made that fright seem smaller, more manageable, as she accepted the mug from him and let the heat of it seep into her stiff fingers.

Slate set his mug on the stone bench, then plucked the blanket from his arm. He offered her a lopsided smile and tucked the blanket around her shoulders in quick, efficient movements.

His scent overwhelmed her senses, sending them into overdrive. She sucked in another gulp of that winter and storm fragrance, and unexpected heat unfurled through her.

He stepped away, scooping up his tea before sitting gingerly on the stone bench next to her.

Dani tugged the blanket closer around her shoulders, hoping the night hid her blush as she glanced sidelong at him. He paused a moment, and she caught the corner of his eye the same as she. He smiled, then shifted deliberately closer, until their shoulders were brushing. "For warmth, of course." His voice was light, and it succeeded in melting more of that ice in her veins.

"Of course," she answered, her lips curling into a smile. She tightened both hands around the mug and took a cautious sip. It was pleasantly scalding, and Dani relished the heat that spread through her as she took a steadying breath.

All of the tangled emotions suddenly seemed unimportant. Less daunting. It stood no chance against the simple pleasure of just... being with Slate, listening to his deep chuckle, feeling the heat of him like a solid wall to her right.

Her eyes snagged on his tattoos again, visible on his arms from the gray t-shirt that stretched across his broad shoulders.

In the dark of the night, they looked almost black, but she'd seen the colors change. Magical tattoos weren't a part of her nightmares, and it seemed like a safe place to start. "Tell me about them." She tipped her chin toward the tattoos.

Slate paused, surveying her face before he glanced at his forearms. When his gaze returned to her face, she sensed his heartfire expand, like the invisible flames had received a fresh gust of oxygen. It made the hairs on the back of her neck stick straight up, but she steeled herself with a sip of tea, stomach tense as her skin tightened over her bones. *Fae magic...*

Slate was watching her closely, awareness haunting his expression, and a bitterness tinged the sapphire of his gaze. Dani spied the tiniest flicker of hurt before he cleared his throat and looked away from her.

"Um, well," he started, voice tight, lips pulling into an attempt at a smile. "It's kinda a long story, actually."

Where was his hurt coming from? Could he tell his magic made her uncomfortable? Her throat tightened a bit, skin prickling. Part of her almost wished she could return to the spring, when everything felt simpler.

"I have time," she assured him, wanting to smooth that hurt from him even if she didn't know how. It was like the sight of his discomfort instantly made her own fears diminish to manageable levels.

"Does this count as a date?" Slate asked with a raised brow, mischief dancing in his eyes. His shoulders remained a bit tense, a hint uncertain, but there was true happiness, true relief, in his gaze.

"Are you saying the nature of your tattoos hinges on whether or not this is a date?"

His smile widened.

She looked away with a small smile. "I didn't think we were counting," she murmured, and, feeling his attention on her, she added, "yet."

She threw the word out like a steak to the wolves and felt her own blood spike in answer. She glanced at him, and Slate's expression had frozen. For the briefest moment, a ravenous hunger flashed in his eyes, gone so fast that it left her breathless. He forced a little laugh. "So, is that a yes?"

"No." She shook her head, both desperate for that hunger and also afraid of it. She had to swallow hard before she could continue. "This is just talking."

And she meant that; the key to getting rid of her discomfort, her fear, was knowledge. Knowing your demons made them less frightening, gave them less power over you. Her fears would be the same, she had decided. "I want to learn about you... about your... magic." It was a struggle to get the word out, and he noticed.

But he didn't comment. He brought his tea to his mouth and took a healthy swallow. "Well, the tattoos are a good start. You gotta admit, they're kinda badass, right?" He grinned at her, wicked and sharp and with so much of Slate's usual confidence that it pulled a startled laugh from her.

His grin widened, and he clenched his fist, flexing his forearm, the muscles thicker now than before he'd left, and rippling with those curling, scripted tattoos that seemed to pulse with magic.

"Yeah... I guess so," she told him, trying to sound unimpressed. But to be honest, they were quite beautiful—thick lines of calligraphy, swirling and curling with both a sharpness and a grace that complimented exactly who Slate was.

They were undeniably *hot* on a male like Slate, but she wasn't going to tell him that. He didn't need his ego stroked.

He chuckled. "You think they're hot."

She blinked, his words echoing her thoughts so accurately that for a panicked moment, she wondered if he could read thoughts.

But that wasn't a fae ability.

... that she knew of.

Slate's smile slipped a fraction, watching her. She pulled in a slow, silent breath for calm, and a long, tense beat pulsed between them.

Slate tugged his smile back up and nudged her with a shoulder. "I can tell when you lie," he murmured, and it took her a whole moment to recognize he was teasing her.

Of course. It was a 'knack' he'd always had, but now they both knew why he was so good at it. *Magic.* And that was... okay. It had always been okay with her, that he could tell when someone lied. It shouldn't change just because she knew it was magic now. It had always been magic.

She refocused on his forearm. While every flare of his heartfire made her nervous, the tattoos were foreign and fascinating to her. She traced a finger over one of the curving lines. His heartfire pulsed. But his scent was in her lungs, his skin under her fingertips and this time, there wasn't any real fear.

Feeling strangely victorious, she let her lips curl into a smile. Slate was still watching her, waiting for her to speak. "Maybe." She shrugged one shoulder, looking away from him with a feigned haughtiness that would've made Selene proud. "But that's for me to know and for you to wonder about."

He chuckled darkly, and her heart skipped a little at the way he was watching her with a mixture of softness and heat.

Reaching for composure, she sipped her tea. "So how do they work?" she continued. "You said Jian did these?"

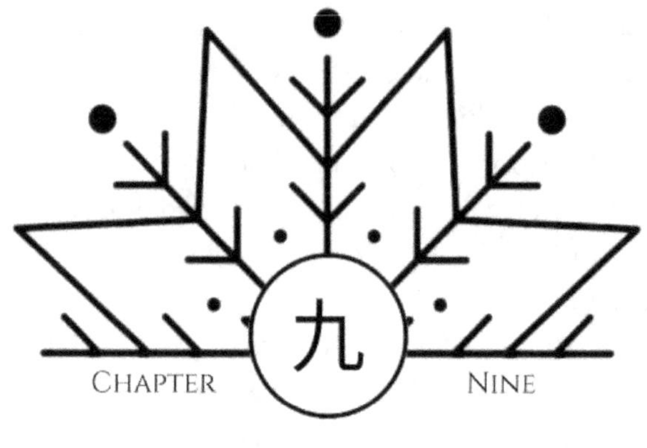

21 QUESTIONS

> *Even amongst mortals, there are speculations that twins carry a unique bond. Amongst Lorekind—or any species carrying significant magic in the blood—twins often result in unpredictable changes or melting of magicks that are amplified between the two siblings to levels...*
>
> *- Gherald Schmidt, Faerloch Historical Archives*

"Yeah. You've seen his tattoos, right? He hides them well," Slate said, hoping he sounded light and casual when his heart was still jammed up his throat. He was still reeling from her abrupt appearance.

He'd expected her to leave when he'd disappeared to make tea, but here she was.

I want to try.

Indeed, it looked like she really *did*, and it caused his heart to squeeze painfully with hope.

"I have..." Dani frowned curiously. "But I didn't realize he did them himself. He's a doctor."

He chuckled. "Yeah, he's definitely a doctor, *but* sometimes enchant-ments involve tattoos, something to permanently anchor an enchant-ment to a person's body. You know Kari's tattoo? The one along her spine?"

Dani nodded. "She said it helps her... govern her magic? She has too much magic for her body and her age, or something like that?"

"Exactly. She was born that way. If Joon-*san* hadn't tattooed a limiter on her when she was little, she might have died. Eventually, her body will adapt and she won't need them. I might keep mine, though. They're cool." He chuckled, glancing at Dani. "These change colors, like a mood ring." He offered her a grin, hoping he wasn't freaking her out too much. "Red is the upper limit."

He didn't miss her quiet, sharp inhale. "What happens after *red*?"

Again, he chose his words carefully. "Well first, white light will skip over my skin. It kinda looks like frost, but it's magic leaking from the tattoos. If I don't burn off the excess—" he hesitated, glancing at her.

"You could detonate..." she murmured, but he noticed her knuckles were white where she gripped her mug.

He let out a breath, looking forward. "That's Jian's theory. I'd rather not find out, though." The real truth was that he probably wouldn't survive a second detonation. His magic would suffocate him, drag him back into the void of icy nothingness and his life energy would simply evaporate. He couldn't bring himself to tell her that though, not now. Being real with her didn't mean he had to overwhelm her with gruesome details.

From the corner of his eye, he could see she was staring at him. He held his breath, feeling the tightness in her shoulders.

"I see..." she finally whispered, voice shaky, and looked at the mug in her hands.

"Yeah... but don't worry, I trust Jian," he assured her, turning his head to smile at her.

She didn't respond, still staring at her tea. It was an effort to keep silent, to give her time to process. He wanted to jump head-first into the silence and explain himself. He wasn't sure what she needed to hear, wasn't sure if what she needed to hear would be synonymous with what was needed for her to *stay*. He had her in his palm again... but he felt like he was treading on thin ice.

Like his little bird could fly away at a moment's notice.

"What... uh, what magic do you have?" She finally asked, and her voice was stronger now. She finally met his gaze, and it felt like a physical caress, even though her expression was shuttered. She seemed... steadier, but he wished emotions translated into thoughts, to learn even a hint of what she was processing.

"Umm... well," he hedged, unsticking his heart from his throat. "I have telekinesis—"

Her breath hitched, and his words died on his tongue as his magic picked up on an aching nostalgia slithering through her emotional grid. "Te–telekinesis?" Her voice was hoarse.

"Uh, yeah, I can move things—"

"I know what it is," she whispered, cutting him off. She bit her lower lip, then glanced at him. "Will you show me?" she asked after a heartbeat.

Some hindbrain instinct inside him didn't want to. Something about the combination of her emotions alarmed him. "Dani, maybe..."

"Please."

It was a whisper, but it rang loudly in his ears, heavy with sorrow and pain. He desperately wanted to know what was going on in her head right now, but she looked like she'd fracture if he pushed.

She watched him, and the set of her jaw spoke of determination, like she was steeling herself. Giving her a short nod, he placed the mug on the ground at their feet.

A breath of concentration... and the cup slid several paces across the roof.

She froze like an animal caught in a trap. He recalled the mug to his feet with shaky control, watching the mixture of panic and sadness that filtered over her face. "I'm sorry." The words were out automatically as he scooped up the cup, and it was an effort not to reach for her, to soothe her physically as well as verbally. "I... I'm sorry. I don't use it much, it's more to augment my fighting—"

"It's okay, don't apologize," she said hurriedly, glazing over him. He didn't miss the way her fingers white-knuckled her own mug, her eyes trained on her tea, a tension lining her shoulders. It wasn't the same panic and fear he'd sensed from her whenever he'd used his magic before—there was far too much sadness in it.

Where was this sadness coming from? The lack of knowledge about her past, about her fears, was maddening.

He was mentally preparing for her to announce her departure when she pulled in a slow breath, and he noticed her shoulders relax a fraction. Licking her lips, she glanced at him, a hint of uncertain apology in her eyes. "Anything else?"

He blanked. "Anything else what?"

"Magic."

"Oh..." He swallowed. "Um. I inherited my mother's gift. I'm one of the lucky ones blessed with empathy." He felt anything but lucky—it was his most problematic magic. Powerful in a different sense than his explosive telekinesis, and far more troublesome.

The color leached from Dani's face, her freckles standing out starkly even in the darkness. "Empathy?" It was a whisper, and he worried she'd shatter the mug with her grip. "What does that entail?" Her voice was a rasp, and tension shot through him.

"Mostly? I feel anything everyone else is feeling... with pinpoint accuracy," he explained. "Well, I have more control now, so I can choose to block people out. But sometimes other people feel what I'm feeling, if I'm sloppy with my control. It's called 'projecting'."

"You... you make people feel things?" There was definitely a tremor to her voice, and an unease slithered through him.

"No, no, it's not like that. I mean, I can, but that's not what I meant."

"But you can?" she asked. "Things they wouldn't feel normally in a given moment?"

Once more, red alarms screamed in his head. He braced himself mentally as he answered her, not wanting to lie, not wanting to keep secrets from her, even if she looked a breath away from passing out. "Depending on how fortified their mind is, yes, I can. Not with any skill or grace yet, but yes."

He'd been told he could turn anyone's mind into his personal playground. Something his mother Aredhel had done with such subtlety and grace, folk claimed she'd been on par with the extinct and mythical Wild Fae, whose magic manipulated the very hearts of all lorefolk.

It was also a magic that Slate had in common with Zeyphar, and that fact alone often left a filthy taste in his mouth. He purposefully didn't work on developing his empathy with the same intensity that he worked on his telekinesis—simply because a part of him didn't want to know what he could do, what he could become with that magic.

A clawing fear choked Dani's mind, enough so that he picked up on it without trying. She sat stone-still, staring at the mug in her hands. Slate waited three heartbeats, waited to see if she would say anything, but she seemed frozen by something he didn't know. Pieces of her began to stitch together in his mind, but he didn't have the space in his head at the moment to analyze it.

Gently, he reached out and plucked the mug from her hands. "Why don't I go refill this?" he said quietly. "And if in the meantime, you decide to go home, my feelings won't be hurt."

Which was a lie, of course, but one he had to stomach. He wanted to offer her a way out, should she decide her nascent courage was failing her at this moment.

Dani's gaze flashed to his, and after a breath, her chin lifted a pinch. "I won't leave."

He offered her a small smile. "Then I'll be right back."

True to her word, she was still there when he returned. The faeries had drifted over to her, dancing around her hair and across her upturned palm. She smiled at them, a ribbon of quiet laughter coloring her voice as she spoke to them and thanked them for the flowers they laid in her hands. But her attention snapped to him the moment the access door shut behind him, watching him as he came closer. This time, the stress that lined her shoulders was marginally softer. She laid the flowers on the bench next to her and took the mug when he offered it, wrapping her fingers around it.

"Thank you," she murmured. She blew across the brim before she took a cautious sip. "I have more questions."

He swallowed his own sip of tea a little too hard. He nodded, buying himself a second to compose his voice. "I have more answers."

He took a seat next to her once more, shoulders brushing. She leaned into him, and the pressure of her next to him felt so right. Her warmth, the scent of her, all of it made focusing a little difficult, but he answered each question. She wanted to know about where he'd been living, what the fae town was like. She asked about his fae friends, if he lived in a castle, and even surprised him when she asked if he could do tricks with his telekinesis. She'd had a faraway look in her eyes when she'd asked, and he'd felt a throb of pain along her emotions.

He was braced for her fear with each answer he gave, but every word seemed to lessen the constant stiffness in her body. She was smiling, and her emotions felt lighter, buoying his hopes to ridiculous and probably unwise levels.

"So you really are a fae prince..." she mused some time later, circling her finger along the rim of her empty tea mug.

He didn't know how to respond to that. Everything north of his heart closed up.

"What's that like?" she continued quietly.

"Awful." The word escaped him before he could censor it, an honest reaction to the one person he didn't ever want to lie to, not when it counted. "Uh..." he backpedaled a little, unsticking his brain. "The *fae* part is manageable. The *prince* part is awful."

A questioning furrow between her brows. He blew out a hard breath and dragged his eyes around the garden, searching the plants and flowers for neat words to describe his life to her. "It's... more responsibility than I ever wanted. The expectations are colossal." He ran a hand over his hair, dragging the tie out, before he twisted a strand by his face, agitation swimming through him. "I don't know who I am most days, honestly."

It was a shot of vulnerability, and he realized what he'd said too late. She was watching him closely, and he sucked his magic back, not wanting to know what she was feeling. Didn't want to burden her with his shit when she had enough on her plate right now.

"But it's alright," he said hurriedly when the silence felt too heavy, and he pulled up a wicked grin to cover his stress.

Dani watched him for another long, agonizing moment, her eyes searching his face. Finally, she scooted a little closer to him and laid her head against his shoulder. He tensed, lungs frozen at the contact as she said, "How are the twins and your father handling the transition?"

"Swimmingly," he replied. He shifted his body a little until they settled into the sweet spot of comfort, even as he debated if he should wrap an arm around her; he decided not to risk it just yet. "My father's taken to Titan's Fen like a fish to water, and Jian's honestly in his element."

They talked of lighter things, simpler things, and he absorbed the feel of her at his side into his soul. He relished every second of contact, every moment where she didn't pull back from him. Eventually, her emotions shifted to something soft yet heavy, a blanket of drowsiness laying thick over her.

Was she...?

Slate fell silent, hardly daring to breathe, let alone move. He focused all his attention on the parts of his body touching hers; his leg, his arm, his shoulder... the pressure of her felt incredible, satiating his starved skin, soaking into him like water soaks into dry soil.

He peeked at her and found she was sleeping against his shoulder.

Gently, no more intrusive than snow on a breeze, he drifted deeper into her emotions, threading his magic through her mind. Her mental shields were thin as rice paper, and even then, they drew back like curtains, granting him subconscious permission to feed into her emotional grid. He balked at the ease of access, backpedaling, a tiny spiral of confused hope ratcheting through him.

It shouldn't have been that easy, even with her sleeping. What did that mean? Did her mind know his magic? Did it have to do with the beginnings of the *mayt*-bond?

Inside, her sleeping mind was calm across the surface, like a lake at midnight; glassy and smooth. It tasted like meadows and sunshine, like the warmth of summer. He dipped a single toe of magic into that lake, peering under the surface. Underneath, a hint of trepidation echoed through her still, coupled with flighty panic. But there was resolve there, and also...

Happiness. A kernel of trust.

He could feel those emotions slipping... slipping... as she fell deeper into sleep, dissipating to be replaced with the sense of nothingness he usually got from sleeping people who hadn't started dreaming yet.

Slate backed up, pulling his magic back. There was no way she knew how open she was to him, and being inside her head without her knowledge felt like a violation of privacy.

To listen at the threshold was one thing... like overhearing a conversation. It was hardly more than an awareness of emotions. But to invite himself into her mind? He couldn't do that.

He swallowed his own emotions, keeping them caged behind his mental shields as he gingerly retreated from her emotional grid. He savored a couple more stolen moments of her presence before he nudged her gently with his shoulder. "Hey, love, are you sleeping?"

"No..." came the automatic, sleepy lie. He chuckled as she sat up and stifled a yawn behind her hand. "I was listening."

"Liar, you were sleeping," he teased her. "You should head home."

Every nerve in his skin rejected that idea, pounding at him to scoop her up and simply dump her in his bed so they could sleep. Sleep near each other. Share space.

She stretched, arms lifting above her head, eyes squinting shut as she hummed. "Alright. Maybe I am tired. What time is it, anyway?"

He checked his watch. "The witching hour. Just after 3 am."

She blinked. "Oh. It *is* late, then." She glanced over her shoulder toward Sellie. Slate followed her gaze. The griffin was dozing too, but one luminous eye slit open, gazing at Dani before shifting minutely to Slate, then back to Dani. Sellie yawned and rose to her feet, arching her back in a tall stretch that made her seem less like a terrifying griffin and more like a house cat. She fluffed her wings, the soft rustle of feathers filling the quiet silence around them.

Slate caught Dani's gaze as she turned back to him. "Thank you," she said. "I think... I needed this."

"Sure." He couldn't help it; he slipped a hand along her jaw in a soft caress, one last fleeting bit of contact. She tipped her face into his hand, and his heart leaped in his chest. "Text me when you get home?" He hoped his words sounded steadier than he felt, warring with the desire to keep her happy and the desire to keep her with him. Maybe one day, they would be the same. To keep her happy would be to keep her with him.

He could only hope.

"I can manage that, I think," came her still-sleepy reply.

Neither one of them moved right away. Her gaze flickered from his eyes to his mouth, faster than the beat of a hummingbird wing, but he felt it like a wrecking ball right to his solar plexus. Oxygen instantly became scarce.

Did he dare?

No, a part of him whispered knowingly. Because a part of him understood that if they started kissing, it would not just *end* with kissing. He'd end up dumping her in his bed, but there would be no sleeping.

And it might just sabotage this small bit of progress they'd made tonight.

So instead, he leaned in and kissed her cheek, a feather-light contact that wasn't nearly enough, but would have to do. "Go home, Daniella." He dropped his hand from her face.

"Okay..." she said. A heartbeat of tension as neither one of them moved. The moment swelled inside him, like a bomb about to blow—

She stood and handed him the blanket. He could hear her erratic breathing, her racing heart. "I'll text you about Saturday," she murmured.

"Okay."

She walked backward, pausing to scoop up her backpack, until she reached blindly behind her and touched Sellie. Wide eyes never left his, but it wasn't fear that bled from her mind and her pores, and the temptation to taste her emotions was overwhelming. But Slate wasn't sure he'd let her leave if he did, so he kept his magic tucked close to him.

"Goodnight," she whispered.

He flashed her a wicked grin. "Goodnight, Daniella."

She was gone with a strong pump of griffin wings and a gust of wind.

CHAPTER TEN

A+ WOW FACTOR

Rowan ultimately succeeded after his death, resulting in the end of the Fae Vampire Wars and the beginning of the Accords talks. However, it also led to the beginning of Marius' downspiral. After a brief disappearance, his rampage throughout Europe lasted for...

- Gherald Schmidt, Faerloch Historical Archives

As the winter wind pulled at her hair, Dani's skin couldn't contain the riot going on inside her.

She was riding a high as wild as the wind right now; she'd spent *hours* with a *fae.*

The *prince* of the fae.

No. Slate.

Slate, whose power had brushed against her on more than one occasion. Each flare of his heartfire had wariness slithering through her as echoes of her nightmares hung in the back of her mind.

But she hadn't run, hadn't even forced space between them. She'd held her ground.

Each time, it had been easier than the last to remember *who* was the source of that power, his proximity a brand against her skin that was impossible to ignore. It had helped that the power had always retreated the moment fear had spiked inside her, as if aware of her discomfort and keen to avoid it.

She suspected it had to do with that new empathy magic of his. A part of her was still reeling from that revelation. Not only did he have the one fae magic she feared the most, but he had telekinesis too.

Katarina had also had telekinesis.

It was what had brought the two girls together, aside from the fact that both of them were bullied. Kat, for her dark skin and kinky hair, and Dani for being the foreign Irish girl whose German had been rough at best. They'd come together because they were ostracized, but they had become inseparable when they'd discovered they each had a magical gift.

But Kat's telekinesis had stood no chance against the fae's empathy magic when they'd taken her. A prisoner trapped in her own body, foreign emotions making her go willingly into her kidnapper's arms.

Empathy magic frightened her more than she was ready to admit, but something else bothered her more right now. Had Slate been using his magic to somehow scale back his *own* feelings in response to hers? Had he picked up on her fear, her discomfort, and altered his actions because of it?

The idea of a Slate who was *less* expressive, *less* readable...

Sure, she was grateful he might try to lessen her fear somehow, but for him to change himself? To somehow pull back on who he was? It made her insides tighten uncomfortably, because the Slate she remembered wore his feelings on both his sleeves, and his face always betrayed him despite his words. He had a terrible poker face.

Was she more bothered by the idea of him using his magic to read her emotions? Or was she more bothered by the idea that he might use that same magic to be less emotive himself?

Was that even how it all worked?

Dani dismissed it for now. There was little sense in dwelling on the logistics when she simply didn't know anything about it. She would simply have to savor the victory of her own courage, savor the lingering heat of Slate's body at her side. It caused a cautious hope to bloom inside her, one that zinged when she considered the taut moment when she'd thought he'd been about to kiss her.

And she hadn't known how much she'd wanted it until he *hadn't*.

As she'd climbed onto Sellie's back, she'd realized she'd wanted his kiss a whole freaking lot. Her muscles had turned to jelly while her skin had tightened over her bones like a vacuum-sealed bag. She'd been on the verge of kissing *him* when her heart had cautioned her for patience, *patience...*

They were stitching back together, mending the frayed tapestry of whatever they were before the summer had blown them apart. And to kiss him then, with so much doubt and uncertainty inside her still... it would cheapen the act.

You can't rush healing, or you might just do more damage...

Words from more than a year ago, spoken by Iliana Harper, the head healer witch in Maddie's coven. Words that had had an entirely different meaning to an entirely different Dani at the time—she had been discussing healing animals, not the daunting task of healing herself.

Especially when at the time, she hadn't even been able to admit she *needed* to heal herself.

You hurt my head, Sellie complained, banking gently to dislodge her from her thoughts. *Time for sleep.*

Dani blinked, leaning over the side of the griffin to see her sleepy suburban neighborhood passing beneath them. She hadn't realized how close she was to home. The sense of loneliness that had wrapped around her the moment she'd stepped backward from Slate suddenly felt... heavier.

No lonely. Me, Dash, vermin... Sellie grumbled, offended. Her massive wings flared, then banked as she brought them down for a gentle landing in front of Dani's garage.

"I thought you were going to stop calling them vermin," Dani teased as she slid off her flank.

Sellie gave no response, only an imperious look that translated into:

Someone like me *should not be cavorting with rats, pigeons, and raccoons.*

Dani chuckled, running her fingers through Sellie's feathers as they walked toward the garage door. Dani punched in the code, and the door slowly rose, clicking along its track until it stopped at the top. "But you call Dash by his name," she reminded the griffin. Sellie continued deeper into the garage to her nest in the back. Dani headed for the door leading inside the house.

Lucky vermin is all, Selllie answered reluctantly, but with a sense of affection for the little fox. Dani hid her smile as she went inside with a quiet "good night" to the griffin.

Roger stared at his phone, disgusted with himself for behaving like some kind of... banal *teenager,* waiting for a text or a phone call.

Daniella had seen Slate last night. For an extended period of time.

His shadows had whispered to him, but he hadn't gone. Hadn't wanted to risk tempting the darkness inside him.

And truly, he had little excuse. After all, she was safe in the Eastern District, warded from those in the Silver Valley due to the *mikos.* Whatever their normal wards were, though, Roger knew the one around the Eastern District was different.

He suspected Ebisu Melisande played a role in its creation.

While he felt assured Daniella was safe from Zeyphar Titania while there, he wasn't entirely convinced she was safe from his nephew. Sure, his instincts told him that the boy loved her, but how was his control? Roger knew what magicks he possessed, knew both could be dangerous gifts for a fae, and the *faeling* had far too much of it, even for one of his mixed heritage. What if he lost control around Daniella?

And *male* empaths...

That darkness inside him hissed, history whispering to him of horrors.

Even beyond magic, what if Slate wasn't careful with that fragile part of Daniella she kept to herself? Daniella was quick to smile and laugh, but he knew there was a hidden sadness deep inside her. Her fears of the fae, of commitment... he wasn't exactly privy to all the facts, but he knew she had significant demons in her closet, ones that went beyond her kidnapping all those years ago. Would Slate take care with those demons, or would he let them out to terrorize her?

Thoughts chased themselves around Roger's head.

Victor would be roaring with laughter if he could see how far Roger had fallen. From the Plague of Darkness to a worried mother-hen with attachment issues over a female that didn't belong to him.

Not anymore...

Hissing at himself now, Roger sat back from the elegant coffee table before him, and swiveled to drape his long body across the chaise lounge that had been custom-made for one of his height, rich with velvet and gold. It matched the other vintage furnishing in his favorite penthouse, one within a building he'd owned for a long time.

He pinched the bridge of his nose, eyes closing as he tilted his head back. *No, Daniella had never belonged to* me... *She belongs to herself, always.*

And yet a dark part of him still whispered: *She belongs to Slate now, is bound to him as she'll never be bound to you. You will lose her light, and I will rise again. We will relish the world once more, drenched in shadows and blood.*

He squelched that thought, pinching it from existence as a chill raced down his spine. The sun was still high in the sky outside his many curtained windows, and he *should* be sleeping. He did not need to sleep often, but his darkness became stronger if he went too many days without. He purged his thoughts with a vicious inner snarl, one that sounded suspiciously like that crooning darkness inside him, that oily snake who loved and hated him in equal measure.

He let out a long breath, slowing his ancient heart until it barely beat at all, seeking the solace of sleep.

His phone vibrated on the table, the sudden sound like a gunshot to his sensitive vampire ears.

That fast, he was sitting once again, facing the low coffee table, staring at the sleek device with its lit screen: *Message from Daniella*.

The phone was in his hand and unlocked in another burst of inhuman speed.

His heart, that ancient rag in his chest, surged and tightened with happiness and dread. She would want to talk about the male, and he would be compelled to help her, unable to deny his light anything she wanted. However, it also meant she was reaching for Roger. The uncomfortable tightness in his bones, the one that tasted like that unfamiliar sense of deep *fear*, eased slightly.

Dani's heart flipped in her chest as she parked her Vespa on the edge of a small car park on Saturday.

Roger and Maddie's words of encouragement from their movie date last night lingered in her mind as she hung her helmet on the handlebar of her bike, pulled off her gloves, and shoved them into her jacket pocket. She brushed her hair back from her face.

Roger's quiet confidence in her, Maddie's playful goading... both had bolstered her, had given her courage when her own was waning.

This was becoming a pattern. The dread that seemed only to ebb when

Slate's face was in front of her. She hesitated a moment at her bike, fingers tightening on her ever-present backpack. The one that had the small illegal handgun in it, loaded with iron bullets.

She considered taking it, the one piece of protection she had against the fae.

The nightmares of her past tugged at her courage, and her fingers spasmed on the strap of her pack. She forced herself to take a breath. She was here to see Slate. *Slate.*

She was safe with him, she reminded herself. She knew that with the same certainty as she knew her own heartbeat. It was all the thinking and hypotheticals that were getting to her.

She left the backpack on the enchanted bike, safe from fast fingers due to her witch wards.

She focused on her surroundings as she stuffed her chilled hands into the pockets of her jacket and started walking. She knew this park. She had come here a few times, but it was completely out of her way on the other side of the city from her house, the Den, or her work. It was a decently sized park, with winter-barren trees dotting the outer perimeter to make room for the giant rink in the center.

An ice rink.

Dani's lips twitched into a smile. A+ wow factor indeed.

"Dani."

The deep, familiar voice wrapped around her like a comforting blanket, easing the trembling of nerves in her chest even as her skin tightened with a mixture of trepidation and excitement.

That fast, all of her mental fretting was swept away on a winter's wind, and she pivoted, turning around to face Slate.

He offered her a grin, emotions like uncertainty and panic skittering away from his eyes to be replaced with a gentle *hunger.*

Not a sexual one—though there was always a little heat in Slate's eyes when he looked at her—but a hunger for the simple sight of her. Like he was drinking in what he saw before him, absorbing the sight of her like it actually sustained him as much as food and drink.

Butterflies erupted in her belly, and her heart hammered against her chest. Heat filtered into her cheeks, and she offered him a small smile in return.

"You're here," he said, relief and happiness in his voice.

He said the words like he hadn't been sure she'd come. It was a sting she knew he didn't intend, but she felt it all the same. Deserved to feel it, after she'd let her fears get the best of her so many times in the past. She didn't exactly have a great track record for commitment.

"You sound surprised." She swallowed the sting, pulling up a teasing smile instead.

He shrugged, but something flickered across his face, and she saw the heartfire inside him swell. Her throat tightened. His grin faltered a little, then his fire banked and she could reach for a silent, steadying breath.

"Sorry..." His voice was a soft murmur, a comfort to a wound he shouldn't have known about.

But he had.

Because he was an empath.

"It's okay," she said quickly, shoving her nerves down. Guilt pricked her heart for how much coddling she was requiring. She needed to be better than this. She *was* better than this. "I'm just getting used to it, that's all. We're trying, right?" She smiled for him, because she wanted his wicked grin back.

He watched her for a heartbeat, like he could see into her soul—and maybe he could, and not just with his magic either—then that smile was back. He gave a little dip of his chin. "Right. Trying."

Dani cleared her throat and jerked a thumb toward the rink. "So... ice skating, huh?"

His grin widened, and he shrugged broad shoulders clothed only in a light jacket. He'd told her to prepare for an outdoor date, so she'd dressed the part. She had on a long-sleeve shirt under her jacket, and thin long underwear beneath her jeans.

"Aren't you going to be cold?" she asked with a raised brow, shifting to fall into step with him as they slowly started toward the rink.

He moved closer until his arm barely brushed her own, but she felt it all the way down to her toes.

"Nah. I don't feel the cold as much anymore. It's a... fae blood thing, I guess." He shrugged, and out of the corner of her eye, she saw him watching her, like he was gauging her reaction to such a casual statement about the fae.

She raised her chin, bringing up a smile. "I bet Sailor Moon doesn't feel the cold either, since she's the princess of the moon, right? Probably pretty cold up there..." The words came from nowhere, barreling past her nerve-wracked brain and coming from that instinctual banter that always just happened between them.

Slate let out a groan, and she glanced over to see him making a face. "Really?" he said. "You really went there?"

And just like that, the awkwardness between them melted. As her lips lifted at the corners, some of the weight in her gut lifted too. "Hey, you started it."

He smacked a hand to his chest in mock offense. "You know, between you and Kari, my pride is taking a hell of a beating." But she saw amusement sparking in his eyes. His happiness called to her own, plucking at her heartstrings. The organ had zero hesitation with Slate, unlike her mind at times.

Maybe she needed to listen to it a little more closely.

"What is pride in the face of your amazing Sailor Scout Slate powers?" Laughter lined her voice.

"You are spending *way* too much time with Kari." Slate grinned at her ruefully, and she felt the brush of his fingers against hers.

Her heart jumped up into her throat, and his hand jerked away, heat filtering into his cheeks, like he'd reached for her hand without thought. Like it was natural for him to hold hands with her while they bantered.

She wanted to grab his hand, wanted his warm palm against hers, but they'd reached the edge of the rink. To Dani's right, a large area had been partitioned off, scattered with benches, and the pavement was topped with a thick rubber mat riddled with holes. People teetered awkwardly over the mat on ice skates as they waddled from the rental kiosk to the edge of the rink.

Some regained their grace, gliding off across the ice like a clumsy duck finding its stride, while others became even more unsteady once they stepped onto the ice.

Slate led the way. He paid for the rentals, figure skates for her and hockey skates for him, and they fell into a surprisingly comfortable silence as they sat side-by-side on one of the benches to put them on.

She kept thinking about his hand, and how she should have reached for him before he'd pulled away. She glanced at his deft fingers as he laced his skates. Sure and strong, with scars crisscrossing his palms and the calluses from years of martial arts. She remembered tracing the lines of his palm with her fingers, her tongue...

Remembered those hands petting every inch of her skin until she was boneless with want.

"Ready?"

His voice jolted her from her thoughts, and her eyes jumped to his face to find him watching her. More than usual, a heat lingered there, and her cheeks warmed. Could he guess the direction of her thoughts? Did emotions reveal that much to someone like him?

She knew absolutely nothing about empaths.

"Yep," she responded and tucked her shoes under the bench. Slate did the same, and she pushed herself to her feet. She wobbled a moment, and Slate's hand was at her elbow, steadying her faster than she could draw breath.

His hand was gone as fast as it had been there, and she missed the heat of it. "Thanks," she murmured, and she wished she could dip into Slate's emotions as easily as he could with hers. Was he as nervous as she was? Fae magic aside, the imbalance of not knowing how he felt while he could read her emotions like a book was a little unsettling.

"Let's do this," he encouraged with a grin, and gestured toward the rink. "Lead the way, love."

Love.

The term of endearment suddenly felt more than what it used to be, and she was frozen for a moment, chest tight. She'd missed that word, said in that voice...

"Unless you're afraid I'll skate circles around you," Slate teased.

"You wish," she replied, finding her voice. She hobbled her way across the rubber mat, then gripped the partition of the rink for stability. Maintaining her grip, she stepped through the small opening and onto the smooth ice, wobbling a second before she caught her balance and glided far enough away to make space for him.

She'd gone ice skating with Maddie and her coven-mates Carrow and Ilie quite a few times, though mostly up by Maddie's place. The witch's substantial property was frequently used by Maddie's coven and sported a small pond where many of their rituals took place.

Knowing she was showing off a bit, Dani angled her skates to pivot herself around in a circle in a smooth move and skated backward a few feet to watch Slate as he stepped onto the ice.

He paused at the threshold, grinning. "I see you've done this before," he called.

She offered him a cheeky smile in return, tugging her gloves out from her pocket and slipping them back on.

His second skate hit the ice, and he pushed away from the wall...

And promptly fell right on his ass when his skates shot out from under him.

Dani gasped, unexpected laughter bursting from her as she hurriedly closed the distance between them. She cut her skates to the side for a quick stop, but Slate was already pushing himself to his feet, laughing.

She blinked at him as he wobbled dangerously, grinning at her, and it hit her like a brick to the face.

Slate might be fae, but he was still... Slate. This mighty warrior prince in her mind, this frightful image she had with his tattoos and the massive power that emanated from him... all of it was insignificant at the outrageously normal fact that he didn't know how to ice skate.

It was so... so *human*.

That frightful image in her head cracked and fractured.

A giggle burst from her. "You took me to an ice rink for a date when you don't know how to skate?"

His grin widened, and held his hands up innocently, before promptly windmilling his arms a bit to keep from falling. "I figured I'd get the hang of it. You wanted A+ wow factor, right? I thought this was more exciting than getting a drink together."

She laughed. "Well, I'm certainly wowed by the fact that you can't skate, so you win."

"Excellent. I like to win." A sharp grin, a wickedness around the edges of his eyes.

Smiling, Dani moved on instinct, reaching for him to slip her gloved hand into his. She didn't know if it came from the urge to steady him or simply to touch him.

He froze, going still enough that it wasn't entirely human, and his fingers squeezed hers as he slowly regained his balance, his eyes never leaving hers. "Thanks..." he whispered, and his voice was hoarse, heavy with emotion that had nothing to do with steadying his balance.

Her throat tightened, and she squeezed his hand back. Offering him a smile, she tugged at him, skating backward a bit and dragging his wobbly form along. He let out a laugh, and the last bit of Dani's trepidation about this date melted away.

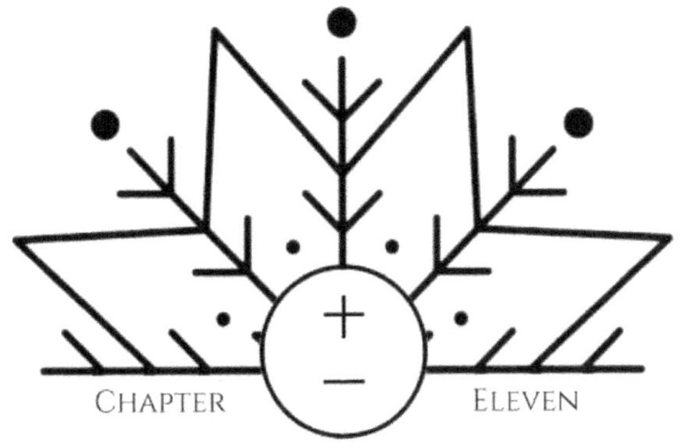

CHAPTER ELEVEN

TWO CRESCENTS, ONE WHOLE

... one that exists within the children of all four Gods. In particular, the fae believe that to find one's mayt is to become whole, and the bite represents two crescent moons joining to form...

- Gherald Schmidt, Faerloch Historical Archives

This was going way better than he'd hoped.

In all honesty, just the fact that she'd shown up had skyrocketed his expectations. They'd texted a little over the last two days, but nothing they'd talked about had given him any firm clue as to whether or not she'd actually show up to the date. He'd told her to dress for an outside date—she'd replied with a simple *okay* and that was it.

She was here. She was laughing. She was *holding his fucking hands...*

He was torn between loving the contact and feeling embarrassed by how much he needed it to keep from ending up on his ass again. He felt like a child learning how to walk for the first time.

He darted his eyes from her face to his feet, watching as he negotiated the blades of the skates against the slick surface of the ice. "This is harder than it looks..." he said lightly, swallowing the hard beat of his heart.

"It's easier when you move faster, like a bicycle." He dragged his gaze up from his feet, finding her watching him. "Going slow tends to make you wobbly." She offered him a small smile, amusement warming her expression.

He flipped his gaze from her face to their surroundings, to the families, parents with their children, other couples on dates, a group of giggling teenage girls falling all over each other. Some glided along with grace and ease, while still others were as wobbly as him. He hadn't felt like such a novice at something in... months. Not since he barreled into Saida's office and demanded to earn his way through her militia.

And promptly got spanked by dozens of fae soldiers.

Dani skated backward a little faster, pulling him along, and when she'd built up a small amount of momentum in him, her fingers slipped free from his with an encouraging grin. Immediately, his balance betrayed him, and he windmilled his arms, legs tensing, and promptly lost his balance. His ass kissed the ice for the second time.

"Are you okay?" she asked, laughter lacing her voice. His magic sensed concerned delight in her emotional grid, and it eased the sting of the fall.

"Yeah. I got it... no, I got it..." he assured her as she came closer, offering her hand. He pushed himself into a crouch, balancing, and slowly pushed himself to his feet. Standing still was easier—he could keep his balance. It was the whole moving part that was challenging.

"You look like you're about to enter the ring with the skates," she observed, a smile crinkling her face, her cheeks rosy from the cold and from laughing. "You gonna start a fight with the ice?"

"I don't start fights, love, I finish them..." he growled, her amusement soothing his frustration as he immediately wobbled with the first attempt at movement. "It's alright... I like a challenge."

Her grid lit up at the same time as the memory of those words assaulted him. Ragged breathing, flushed skin... *I kinda like a challenge.*

The night they'd almost broken their ten-date rule.

Their eyes collided in mutual memory. He could feel the heat inside her mind, and he actively pulled his magic back as her eyes skated from his face to study the ice with great interest. It was far too early in the 're-dating' part of this journey to think about sex, even as his nerves crawled with need at the idea of skating his palms over her naked skin...

Instead, he focused on skating with his feet. He angled his right skate straight, then pushed off with his back one at an angle, digging the edge of the metal skate into the slippery ice. He wobbled... but he slid forward without falling. He brought his back skate forward, pushed off again... less wobbling, more gliding this time.

"Hey! Progress!" She grinned at him, and she closed the distance between them. "You'll be a pro in no time. "

He grinned. "Told you I would."

Her smile was easy, and it tugged at his heartstrings. Her eyes flickered, her smile fading just a hint, but he sensed no trepidation, only a sense of cautious hope. Without hesitation this time, she offered him her hand.

He took it, wishing they weren't both wearing gloves so he could savor the texture of her skin, but beggars couldn't be choosers. Even still, the pressure of her small hand in his lit up his senses. Her smile held a hint of shyness to it, before she tugged him forward.

Half of his attention stayed with the feel of her hand in his, the other half dialed into his feet, focusing on recreating the step, push, glide. She picked up her pace, forcing him to go faster, forcing his feet to glide longer over the ice with each step. Within a few minutes, he'd gotten the rhythm of it.

They talked of lighter topics and gossiped in low voices about the other people in the rink, feeding Slate's secret love of people-watching. He visibly saw her relax, and she taught him a few tricks for skating she'd picked up from her witch friends.

And laughed when he ate ice a few more times.

It was so... *easy*. And he wasn't talking about skating. *Them*. It had always been easy—the talking, the banter, the rhythm in which they moved together; synchronized and effortless.

Fuck, he missed it. To the point of pain.

There were large speakers on either side of the rink playing Christmas music. Dani broke away, angling her skates to pivot herself around until she was skating backward, facing Slate.

"What do you do for Christmas?" she asked

"Christmas?" He cocked his head at her. "Uh… nothing, really. It's not a big holiday in the Eastern District, not like New Year's is. Dad and I usually spend it with the twins. Joon-*san* cooks dinner, sometimes there are presents…" He caught up to her, rotating and attempting to skate backward with her, matching her grace within a stride or two. "What do you do? For Christmas."

"I go over to Maddie's every year on Christmas Eve. We decorate the tree, cook a lot of food, bake *Christstollen*. I spoil her twins, Leo and Sara. Tony gets a little drunk." She gave him a cheeky grin. "He *actually* smiles, you know."

"He does not."

She laughed. "He does! And laughs! And by evening, there are a bunch of witches at her house and everyone's feeling the mulled wine by then, singing carols. Usually, there's a bonfire, spit roasts, and ice skating. And presents, of course. It's usually a crazy week because I go to their Winter Solstice celebration as well." She broke away to show off with a wide figure eight, before coming back to his side. "It's good fun."

Slate grinned. "Sounds it."

A moment of silence passed between them as they glided along. "Is Joon going to be cooking for you again this year?" she asked.

He glanced at her face, before darting his gaze away. His magic wove gently along her emotions, feeling her out. "Not sure yet. There's a big celebration coming up in—in Titan's Fen… for the solstice."

It was also his birthday, but he didn't say anything. As it was, he could taste her apprehension spike at the name of the town. He didn't plan to make a huge deal out of his birthday anyway, and mentioning it to her now felt like he would be forcing her to acknowledge something positive when she already seemed uncomfortable. "So yeah, putting a lot of energy there for that. I'm required to be there."

He left it at that. He didn't want to talk about it more than was absolutely necessary. He could sense some discomfort from her, but none of the sour fear that made his skin tighten. Still, he wasn't willing to risk it, so... he held back a little. Thought more carefully before he spoke; a difficult endeavor for him because he always seemed to lose control of his words around her.

It had taken him weeks upon months to stop fantasizing about going back to his boring mortal existence. He was still learning how to talk about himself as a fae, how to behave, how to present himself. He was finally getting used to it...

But the echo of fear he'd occasionally felt from her the last few days dug up all those fantasies again. Made him wish he could turn back time to when life was simpler between them. Change how things between them had... ended.

Ended?

His mind balked. It *wasn't*, though. It wasn't over.

She watched him, and he sucked his magic back in, not wanting to know what she was feeling as she assessed him. But like a moth to a flame, his empathy magic reached out toward her mind anyway.

He sensed a slight discomfort, and some sort of... confused uncertainty, as if she didn't know quite how to feel about him bringing up fae business so casually.

He decided to change the subject, and the conversation shifted as easily as a spring wind, onto easier topics. Eventually, Slate suggested they go grab something hot to drink from the heated tent along the edge of the rink. Something tickled his senses as Dani voiced her agreement, and his attention shifted minutely.

It was routine for him now to spread out his senses and his empathy magic when he was out in public, like little feelers that would alert him of trouble before trouble found him. Like listening to a thousand conversations in a crowded room, and picking up the sound of your own name being said. And something pricked the barest edges of his feelers, growing stronger with each second.

His skin tightened with anxiety when he recognized the distinct emotional grids of two of his soldiers. He'd snuck away again, hoping this time he wouldn't be found out, because he'd told Kallen he was staying in the Eastern District. And he didn't need an escort in his own district. He'd been positive he could buy himself a few hours alone before his private babysitter service found him.

He'd been wrong.

He didn't know if he'd tipped his hand, or if it had something to do with the way she could sense magic, but visible anxiety crawled over her. She didn't say anything, but her eyes flickered before she cast a quick look around. Her emotional grid shifted, taking on a tinge of nervous restlessness that reminded him all too much of an animal on alert for predators. Her gaze jumped to his with a guarded searching look.

"It's nothing. Just... trust me?" he implored, tipping her chin up with the tip of his finger.

She hesitated, but not for as long as he'd anticipated. Her smile was wary, but she nodded. Still, the tension didn't leave her shoulders.

He knocked violently on his soldiers' minds, and blasted emotion at them—anger, a touch of violence, a vehement need for privacy. Giant clues that came together to scream: *Go away.*

Long minutes passed as he and Dani made their way to the exit of the rink, then went to return their skates. All the while, he kept his senses open. He could still feel them close by. He couldn't see them, and they didn't come any closer, but they hadn't left.

Waiting. They were *waiting* for him. *Fuck.*

He and Dani switched out their skates for sneakers and boots, then returned their skates. Once they'd ordered hot chocolate—with heaps of whipped cream—he handed both of them to her.

"Hold this for a sec," he said. "I'll be right back."

She gave a tight nod, concern and caution etched in the lines of stress around her eyes.

"I'll be right back," he said, backing away from her. "Don't... don't leave yet. Please."

Her shoulders loosened a bit, and her chin rose a fraction. "I won't."

"I'll be right back, I *promise.* Just... a few minutes." And he turned and took off, jogging around the rink, until he was out of sight from the hot chocolate tent. He followed his senses and found two of his soldiers lurking behind some trees on the edge of the park. They were two of his favorites, but his patience was less than thin right this moment. The male was Basyl—as usual—and the female was named Sky, and while Slate knew her well enough from training, she was new to his *protective detail*. The moment they spotted him, they both pressed a palm to their chest and inclined their heads at him the moment he neared.

"What are you doing?" he hissed, temper soaring.

Basyl was even-keeled, but Sky, not as much. She frowned, narrowing her deep brown eyes. "What do you mean, what are we doing? We sensed you outside of the ward, my lord—"

"You can't be here," Slate blazed over her. "You have to leave. Now."

"Our job is to protect you—"

"I know what your job is," he growled. "But I'm busy right now and you need to leave."

Confusion knit Sky's brows together, but Basyl's eyes widened a little. "That female, yes? With the red hair?" The ghost of a devilish smirk twitched at the edges of his mouth.

Sky whipped her face toward Basyl, then back to Slate, her mouth forming a little 'o' of surprise. "So it's true, then? There's a rumor at the base that you are courting someone..."

Slate pressed his palms together and begged all the kami and the Goddess herself to not lose his shit right then and there. Just what he needed—more rumors about him around the soldiers' base in Titan's Fen. But addressing the rumors was neither here nor there. "Please leave," he growled. "I'm begging you. Do *not* fuck this up for me."

"Absolutely not. Your safety is our highest priority—"

Slate didn't have the patience or the necessary brain capacity at that moment to parse his words neatly. "She's afraid of fae, and she can sense you here," he blurted in a fast string. "She's... she's aura-sensitive? I dunno, but she knows you're here, and you're going to mess this up for me."

"Is she a lorebeing? Why is she afraid of the fae?" Sky pressed insistently, Slate's magic picking up the curiosity lighting through her.

"Sky..." Basyl drawled.

"What? Do we not have a right to know about her, if she's going to be with the prince?"

Slate shifted his attention to the fae male, choosing not to get into Dani's aversion to the fae. He didn't know enough about it and frankly, it wasn't his place to spill her secrets. "Basyl," he said, knowing he had a better shot of convincing him than Sky. "Do this *one* thing for me. *Please.*" Slate dropped his hands on Basyl's shoulders. "Dani's uncomfortable. I won't have it. Leave, or I will find my own way to leave."

Basyl regarded him for several agonizing heartbeats, pinging his silver eyes back and forth between Slate's. Basyl was one of the few Slate counted among his inner circle at Titan's Fen. Many in Titan's Fen were friendly with him, but few were *friends.* Not many saw him as *Slate,* as a half-fae man dumped into a situation he didn't ask for and was trying to make the best of it with what he had.

Basyl was one of those. He was one of the first who respected Slate as a fighter, as his prince, as his future king, and as just... an equal. It was refreshing, and because of his connection with the male, Basyl ended up on his protection detail more often than others.

"We will leave, my lord," Basyl said with a nod. "However. We will be back every quarter hour until you are safe behind the ward of either Titan's Fen or the Eastern District."

Slate's entire body melted in relief, even as Sky bristled with indignation.

"Basyl!" she hissed.

But Basyl shook his head. "Our prince has given us a direct order. It is not our place to question it."

"*I'm* questioning it!" Sky hissed. "Our duty is to protect him. *Especially* if he's courting a female who could become—"

"We will leave," Basyl said curtly.

Sky opened her mouth again, then snapped it shut and nodded. Once. "Fine. When the lieutenant asks why we skirted our duties, *you* get to explain, Basyl."

"Kallen can take it up with me," Slate said with more confidence than he felt. He turned to Basyl. "I owe you, Basyl," Slate said gratefully, backing away. "Seriously."

He waited until Basyl and Sky disappeared through a portal before he hurried back to the heated tent where he'd left Dani.

She was blessedly where he'd left her, his cup on the bench beside her while she held hers in her lap. She was a little pale, eyes trained on the floor before her as she ran a nervous thumb in a circle on her hot chocolate. She blinked rapidly when she spotted his approach, and a smile crinkled her freckles as relief flashed through her grid.

"That was quick," she said with a smile. She'd taken off her jacket and had it draped over her knees, revealing a simple white long-sleeved shirt. "Everything okay?"

He pulled up a smile. "Yeah, everything's fine." He picked up his cup and sat beside her.

That's when he noticed it. Barely visible against the naturally pale cream of her flesh—exposed now without the collar of her jacket in the way—was the edge of two crescent-shaped white scars peeking out from under her shirt, at the juncture of her left shoulder and neck.

His entire being locked on the sight of that mark, time coming to a standstill. It was still *there*. The *mayt*-mark. *His mayt*-mark, right there. It was physical evidence of his claim to her, the nascent beginnings and the undeniable endings to them. The fae believed that the shape of the two crescents represented two halves coming together to form a single, perfect whole. Two beings meant to be together.

Dani was speaking. Slate shook his head minutely, slamming back into the present. "What?"

She furrowed her brow at him, a little smile playing across her face. "I asked if you'd been to that new sushi restaurant Kari keeps raving about..."

"Oh... oh, yeah..."

And the conversation and banter continued, even as a part of Slate's mind dialed into that mark on her neck... and hope burned brighter inside him, igniting a warmth in his chest.

"This was a lot of fun," Dani said later.

They were holding hands—holding *hands*—and walking back to her bike. Slate didn't think he'd been breathing properly since the moment she'd scooped up his hand and threaded her fingers through his. Skin to skin this time. So simple, so innocent, and yet... The contact was nearly painful in how good it felt.

"Worthy of a second date?" He flashed her a wicked grin. They stopped beside her bike, parked a little bit away from the main crowd of vehicles in her own made-up spot.

She made a good show of thinking about it, and he pouted at her. She laughed. "Maybe. What does your Monday look like?"

"Looks like anything you want it to look like."

"You make it too easy."

"You know I don't do subtlety well, love."

Another light chuckle from her. His heart crawled into his lungs. With her free hand, she tucked a stray piece of fiery hair behind her ear. "Monday, then. You text me."

"Alright."

A beat of silence. The easy smile on her face faltered a little. He was racking his brain for something to say—*anything*, to keep her for one more moment—when suddenly she was moving. His scattered brain registered her fingers against his sternum as she rose on her toes, but didn't connect the dots until her lips were already on his.

She was kissing *him*.

For the second time in less than two days, Slate's entire body short-cir-cuited. The kiss was hardly longer than the space between heartbeats, but it rocked him to his very core. A kiss should have just been a kiss—it wasn't like he hadn't kissed her plenty of times before—but it didn't feel like *just* a kiss. It signified a level of trust and comfort from her that he'd been missing. Craving. A space he'd desperately wanted them to get back to.

A space where she trusted him. At least, enough to kiss him.

She rocked back onto her heels and smiled, a flush flirting with her freckles. She opened her mouth, drawing in a breath like she intended to say something...

He moved before he could overthink it, closing the gap to find her lips again.

He tasted her small, sharp intake of breath. Her fingers on his chest flexed into his jacket. Heard her small sigh before some of the surprised tension bled from her shoulders, leaving her pliant against him. It sent a shot through him, making him ache for bedrooms and dark nights and privacy.

He slipped a hand along her jaw, tipping her face to kiss her a little more thoroughly. He had to resist the urge to really *go* for it, resist the urge to open her mouth and taste her properly, a little afraid his self-control would cave and this would go further than either of them were ready for.

Especially considering they were in a parking lot.

So he eased off, using every ounce of discipline he possessed to put a little breathing space between them. She leaned into him, as if chasing his lips, and it almost undid him. The heady, insane urge to toss her into a portal and disappear somewhere nearly drowned him, but by the grace of the gods themselves, he held firm. Both of them were breathing a little irregularly as he stared at her, and noticed her irises were once more, ever so faintly, limned in an iridescent green.

It faded between one blink and the next. She swallowed visibly, reluctantly pulling her focus from his lips as she gave herself a little shake, and took a step back, absently reaching behind her toward her Vespa. He noticed her fingers were shaking when she slipped the helmet from the handlebar. "Can you... are you okay getting home by yourself?" she asked, and her voice sounded hoarse.

He nodded, flashing a grin to cover his racing pulse. "I'll survive, don't worry."

She mirrored his nod and tugged the helmet over her head. She threw a leg over her bike and started it with a quiet rumble. Once more, her eyes locked on his. She hesitated a moment, then flipped up the visor, a hint of a smile pulling at the corners of her eyes. "Text me?"

"I will."

With a rev of that little engine, she eased away from the curb and out of the car park. At the stop sign before the road, she turned and looked back at him.

He gave her a little wave... and vanished through a portal.

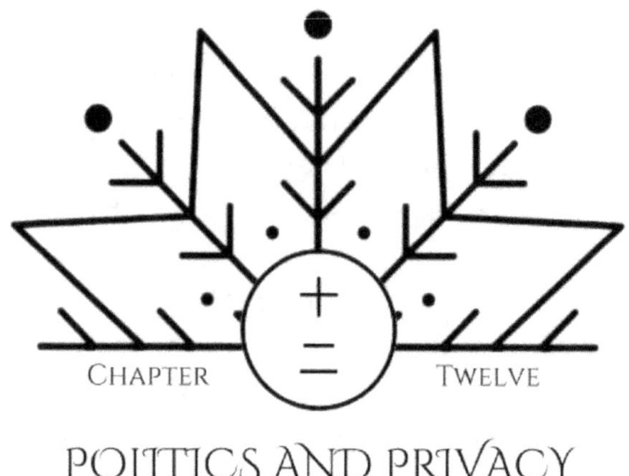

POLITICS AND PRIVACY

... her death was discovered, reported as 'unknown cause' by the Acolytes of the Silver Valley, but whispers suggest Zeyphar Titania's involvement in his sister's...

- Gherald Schmidt, Faerloch Historical Archives

Slate stormed into the council room in his manor at Titan's Fen.

"Alright. I've had enough," he growled, slamming his palms into the heavy, ornate wooden table in the center of the room. "Call off the guard dogs. I'm *done*."

Seated to the right of the head of the table was a fae of refined taste and stature; tall and lean, with silver hair combed back from his brow. He put down the document he was reading and leveled an inscrutable look at Slate. Slate didn't miss the way his gray eyes flitted over him, from his palms pressed hard into the table, to his pulsing tattoos—currently a mild shade of henna—all the way up to Slate's blazing expression.

Galyn Alva sighed through his nose. "We've had this discussion before, *mai tatya...*"

"And we're gonna have it again. I do not *want* or *need* a full-time babysitting service." He turned his attention to the other fae seated at the table across from Galyn, none other than Slate's current full-time nanny, Kallen. "I want some fucking privacy." The presence of his soldiers had nearly ruined his date with Dani. He would *not* risk spooking her again.

"The escorts are wise and discreet—" Galyn started, even as Kallen's unreadable heather eyes studied Slate.

Slate whipped his attention back to his only remaining council-fae. "I *get* that," he said to Galyn through gritted teeth, "but it's not the same."

"I'm afraid I cannot be swayed, young lord."

Ah. Slate knew a conversation with Galyn was over when he was demoted from 'my lord' or '*mai tatya*' to '*young lord*'.

Forever reminding Slate that he was nothing more than a *faeling* prince.

It didn't matter that he was almost 31 years old and a functioning, responsible adult. To the fae, he was young. The equivalent of a wily, rebellious teenager.

He hated it.

"Galyn," Slate tried again. "You *gotta* give me this one—"

"A guard is traditional—"

"I don't give two flying fucks about *tradition*." His mother before him had been raised in a quintessential royal house; complete with a personal guard following her around constantly, nobles she rubbed shoulders with, and ladies-in-wait to attend to her every need.

Slate had zero desire for any of that. He could take care of himself. He didn't care about the subtleties of politics, had no interest whatsoever in holding court or attending boring political meetings with stuffy nobles who had ulterior motives. No desire to be a prince, really, but here he was.

All he wanted was to date Dani with some goddamned privacy.

"Non-negotiable, young lord. Until you have complete mastery over your mind and your magic, the escort *must* remain."

Slate could practically taste Galyn's fearful hesitancy about letting the rightful heir to the *fae* throne galavant willy-nilly around an iron-clad city while they were in the middle of the civil war, one that seemed to grind far too slowly for his mortal mind. Fae didn't act quickly, since they lived so long. Thinking and diplomacy were slow, a practice natural to a society that had all the time in the world to consider every element. It was both irritating and somewhat intimidating to Slate.

It was like Zeyphar wasn't even worried about him. Like he didn't even pose a threat.

Like he didn't have a chance.

He stared at Galyn. Galyn stared calmly back, but the emotions leaking from his door said differently. His sole political advisor was still bleeding from the death of his mother, as were the rest of the faerfolk in this town, their grief deep.

She'd even had her personal guard with her when she'd died, a fact that no doubt exacerbated their anxiety.

Kallen was all that remained of his late mother's personal guard. He hadn't been present at the time, something Slate knew he regretted heavily.

"Galyn." Slate eased off the table and walked around it until he could drop into his seat at the head of the table, bringing himself eye to eye with the council-fae. "The escorts nearly ruined my date with Dani." Slate's eyes flickered to Galyn's collar, where he could see the barest peek of a *mayt*-mark on the council-fae's right shoulder. "You know better than anyone... you have to do this for me."

The fae male mustered a deep, even breath. "I understand, young lord, but you are the *crown prince*—"

"—who is a fighter first and foremost—"

"—and as such, protections are put in place—"

"I'm going on dates with *Daniella*. I *need* this."

"—to keep you safe."

"Galyn, Galyn, *Galyn*." Slate leaned over to drop his hands on the older male's shoulders. "Listen to me very plainly. I. Am. Not. Aredhel."

That got the reaction he was looking for. Stillness spread through the council-fae, seeping through the room. Hands still on Galyn's shoulders, the male's emotions curled against Slate's magic like wisps of smoke. Strong emotions seeped past the male's shields as sadness, anxiety, and a touch of guilt vibrated inside him.

"I'm aware, young lord," the council-fae started softly, "but—"

"No buts," Slate interrupted. "No buts, ifs, ands, whatever. I'm not a cultured fae noble. I am a fighter, a martial artist. I am not a politician. Never will be." He tapped a hand on Galyn's shoulder. "That's why I have you."

Slate wasn't his mother. Aredhel had been smart and cunning, but not a fighter. She fought her wars with wit and a sharp tongue, not fists and blood

Galyn regarded Slate for a long beat of silence. Slate met his focus steadily, not yielding an inch.

"I see so much of your mother in you sometimes," Galyn finally said. "And I forget you have your father's fighting heart."

Slate's soul soared. "So... no escort?"

Galyn turned his attention to Kallen with a questioning tilt of his brow. Kallen huffed a short breath. "You would like my professional opinion?"

"Of course, lieutenant."

Kallen's eyes tracked over Slate in deliberate assessment. "The Goddess has gifted us a warrior prince. It is as he said—he will not be satisfied within the confines of a court, with his words and his tongue as his weapons."

"He must be *protected*—"

"He will be. I assume he will not venture into the city for long stretches of time, yes?" A cut of those heather-violet eyes. Slate gave a curt nod, trying not to choke on his own excitement. "And since he will be with Tanyiel-*tana*, it's also my assumption he will not be engaging in large displays of magic, and he will take care to glamour himself if he leaves the Eastern District."

"Yes, all of the above." Slate nodded.

"And we currently have no intel that Zeyphar has made any appearances in the city in months. We have no proof, but it is Karisi's understanding that the vampire Roger Addington and the werebear Loraine have added extra protections to Tanyiel that are dissuading full-on confrontation with Zeyphar as of yet," Kallen said with calm professionalism.

"Should that intel change…" Galyn said with a pointed look.

Slate nodded in understanding. Should Zeyphar decide to make a move to approach Slate, either the escort returned, or Slate was confined to Titan's Fen. Which had happened before, once in the late summer. His uncle had sent some faerfolk after him again—a thinly veiled kidnapping attempt under the guise of 'negotiations'—and Slate had been more or less grounded to Titan's Fen for a couple of weeks.

"I'll do my best to stay within the Eastern District," Slate assured them both, particularly Galyn. The ward around the Eastern District protected him, and his escort had long since been removed while he spent time at home.

Galyn regarded Slate once more. He nodded. "A trial run, then, young lord." He turned back to whatever dry, though undoubtedly important, political document he was reading. "Perhaps with any luck, we will have a future queen consort." It was a lazy comment, but Slate heard it crystal clear.

An annoyed flush heated his cheekbones and he shoved himself to his feet. "We aren't discussing that." He didn't want to say it was a *frequent* conversation with Galyn, but it was a topic the council-fae had brought to Slate's attention more than a few times.

"It's a wise political move—" Galyn called after him.

"I don't care," Slate replied, and he stormed out of the room.

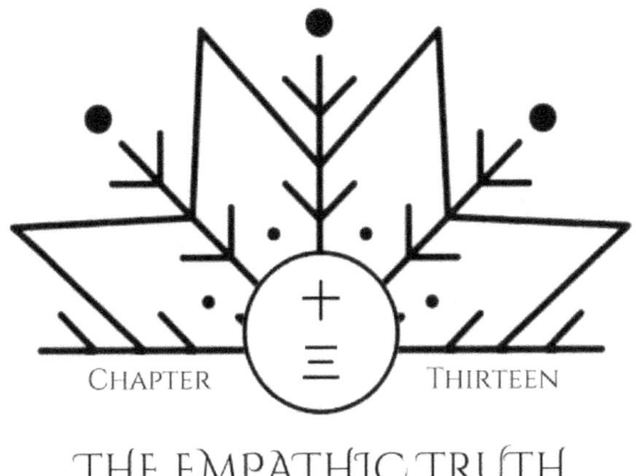

THE EMPATHIC TRUTH

Following the trials of Salaì, da Vinci's lover, the abduction of mortals for fae amusement or curiosity rose in number, until Titania Rywin began curbing the practice after her daughter advised her that...

– Gherald Schmidt, Faerloch Historical Archives

The next few days flew by in a chaotic blur. Slate found his attention scattered in several different directions—dating Dani, ramping up for the Winter Solstice festival in Titan's Fen, along with his regular activities of training, teaching, more training...

Not to mention a slow but rising tension with Zeyphar and his troops from the Silver Valley. It was frustrating, waiting for the fae to take action. Slate *needed* action, liked getting shit done. He wasn't so good at the waiting game.

Galyn and Kallen were true to their word in easing up on Slate's escort. And Slate was good on his. The couple times he and Dani saw each other, they remained in the Eastern District. The one time they'd ventured out, Slate made good on checking in with Kallen via a quick text. The lieutenant wasn't so savvy with the tech yet—it was only in the last handful of months that Slate and the twins managed to jerry-rig stable wifi for the town using a network of satellite phones, magic, and a lot of swearing—so the text he got in return was a little sloppy, but the point was conveyed.

Dating Dani was... steady. Slow, but steady. The tension that coursed through her every time she sensed him using magic had ebbed to little more than an active awareness. Sometimes a shot of fright still zipped through her, but he noticed that she recovered faster.

He found himself picking his words a lot. Pausing more. Stretching silences.

He didn't know what to think about it. Cautiously optimistic, he supposed. But... he wasn't entirely sure what he was optimistic *for*. For them to date seriously? For commitment? For a *mayting*? Where were they headed? What were they going to do? The fact that he didn't have some sort of target to shoot for bothered him. And the fact that they were more-or-less using the dates as 'exposure therapy' to almost cure her of her fear of the fae left a foul taste in his mouth.

It didn't feel right, and he still waffled over whether or not he was good for her mental health.

He tried not to get too far ahead of himself. Tried to just focus on one date at a time. Tried not to think about what would happen if she chose to be with him... if she chose to *mayt* him—

Or anything after that. Because despite what Galyn thought, Slate couldn't imagine Dani wanting anything to do with his life. *He* didn't want anything to do with it. He couldn't imagine *himself* being a king, let alone imagining her as a queen consort. And it annoyed him to talk about it. To speculate about what she would want without her in the room to have a say in it herself. It *more* than annoyed him that *mayting* Dani was seen as a political maneuver because it was politically advantageous. As if Dani's only value was as his queen consort, and not as a person with her own agency.

A smaller part of him wondered if he should be offended, if his value as a leader was dependent on a female at his side. Fae were, traditionally, a matriarchal society—there was a reason why only males remained from Aredhel's court. All of the high-ranking females had been eliminated.

It was a thorn in his side, that his personal life had been reduced to whether something was a good political move or not. Who he was friends with, where he went, who he dated… all because of his status, his *title*—shit he didn't even *choose* for himself.

He'd gone from making his own path in the Eastern District to having all the pieces laid out *for him* in a monstrous game of thrones and politics. From the relative privacy of anonymity to one gigantic public display. Nothing was sacred when you were *royalty*.

The icing on the cake? He, a fae prince, was dating a woman who was afraid of the fae. What a wonderful combination *that* made. Like gunpowder and fire—part of him was waiting for all this to blow up in his face.

All these thoughts chased through his head, night and day. They only ceased during the few times he'd actually *seen* Dani, her very presence the ultimate distraction. It'd been nearly a week since that first official date, that first kiss. A week that had felt a lot longer, as he desperately tried to keep his cool around her, tried not to think about *mayting* at all even though his eyes were constantly drawn to the scar on her neck.

Fae and magic aside, nothing freaked her out more than *commitment.* Even if she said she wanted to try.

"So," Dani hedged from her place on a stool in his kitchen in the Eastern District. The reluctant edge to her voice instantly had Slate on guard. "I have… I have a question for you."

Slate paused from where he was preparing the vegetarian sushi he was showing her how to roll. "What's that?" Dani had taken the night off, and they were having a low-key date night—dinner, and then they were going to see a Kabuki play.

She went silent again. Slate peered at her, then pressed his ear to the proverbial 'door' of her emotions, picking up on them with an uncanny ease he experienced with no one else. She was nervous and jittery, a tightness of fright wrapping around her, but it was tempered by a reluctant determination, or maybe a wild desperation.

Slate wasn't telepathic, but with Dani, and with so little effort, her emotions were so clear to him he could *almost* translate her emotions into thoughts; she wanted to know something, and she was hoping it would help whatever demons she grappled with.

Maybe.

"I wanted to ask you…" Her eyes fell from his face, down to the tell-tale nervous gesture of her own fingers tangling together. "How does… how does your empathy magic work, exactly?"

Slate paused, heart skipping a beat as his throat closed up. He'd avoided talking about his empathy magic around her. They'd eventually discussed other aspects of his newfound magic, like teleporting, mental wards, and telekinesis. She'd even asked for more demonstrations one night, and he'd taken her to the studio to show her some of the practical applications of his telekinetic magic.

He'd been dreading this moment, though, when his empathy magic took center stage. And he realized with a kickstart to his heart that he was dreading it because *she* was. Her anxiety was feeding his own.

"Umm, well…" he hedged, focusing on julienning some cucumbers for their sushi as he carefully picked his words. "It's a pretty nuanced piece of magic. And uncommon, apparently, especially in males. Most empaths are female. And those who do have it, they generally have… less… than what I have."

He felt like he was walking on glass; he was acutely aware of the spike of anxiety his words caused, but he couldn't lie to her.

It took her a long time to speak, and Slate kept his attention on his task, even as most of him was focused on her. Finally, she drew in a slow breath. Her voice was hesitant, but there was a steel spine of determination coming off her. "Will you tell me more about what you do with it?"

Again, he didn't answer right away, opting instead to peek through that crack in the door to her emotional grid. He pulled back when a potent shot of panic raced through her. He abandoned his cucumber-cutting and turned to find her watching him, eyes a little too wide in a face that was a little too pale.

"I can… I can tell you're using it now. Well, I can tell you're using magic of some kind, and since nothing is flying around, I assume it's your empathy magic." Her words were a little too fast, another sign of her nerves. She wavered a moment, then straightened her shoulders in a decidedly stubborn gesture. Her voice came stronger now, her brows flicking together. "What are you doing with it?"

"Nothing," he said hurriedly, flushing at being caught. "I just... I was just studying your emotions, wondering what you're feeling and what you're expecting me to say."

She was silent for a long time. Long enough that he was ready to say just about anything to break the silence, but her voice came first. "It shouldn't matter what I expect you to say... I want to know the truth. You're studying my emotions?" She cast him a look that was impossible to decipher, and he didn't dare peer at her emotional grid now, not after she'd just called him out for it. "You do it a lot, you know." She watched him closely.

"It's..." Honesty. He would have to be completely honest with her. Jian's words echoed along with her own. She deserved the whole truth. "It's automatic for me now," he admitted. It was tempting to look away, but he held her gaze, hoping she could see he was being completely truthful with her. "I do it to everyone. Only... no one else notices like you do."

"I can see it in your heartfire," she told him slowly. "Your fire flares when you flex your magic."

So he'd been right, it did have something to do with that magical fire she could see in people. He watched her, still as stone. "You can tell each time I use magic?" He sucked everything back, magic, aura, everything. Tucked it in as close to his own self as he could, a skill he was still perfecting.

She nodded. "Every time, I think. Like... right now, your heartfire just cooled right down."

"I just pulled it all back," he explained instantly.

"I see."

Even without using magic, he knew her fright spiked—it was written all over her face. "I didn't... I don't mean to make you... uncomfortable, but that's the truth. Even if it isn't what you want to hear."

More tense silence. Finally, she sucked in a deep breath. "That's scary, you know. You can read anyone's emotions all the time. No one has any privacy around you."

It was like she'd vibed the direction of his recent thoughts—wasn't he just thinking about privacy? "It's not... it's not *quite* like that..." he trailed off, studying her face, the cautious suspicion that darkened her eyes to midnight pine. "How do *you* know how I feel about something, without me telling you?"

Dani blinked, clearly not expecting the question. He waited, and after a moment, her eyes slid away and he could tell she was seriously considering the question. Finally, she cast him a sidelong glance and her lips quirked into a wry half-smile. "You're pretty expressive, I guess. It's usually written all over your face."

He grinned wide, cocking a brow. "So how do I feel right now?"

She studied him a moment, her smile fading. "You're nervous."

"How do you know?" His smile dropped.

She shrugged. "I mean... you're smiling, but your shoulders are tense, and the smile isn't reaching your eyes."

Swallowing his heart, he nodded. "How do you know when Maddie is happy?"

As if the mere thought of a happy Maddie made her smile, Dani's lips twitched, a little bit of light coming back into her eyes. "She smiles, she laughs, and she uses more French. I don't know, it's in her face, I guess. She gets... bubbly."

"And how do you know when Roger's upset?"

She paused, and her gaze flickered back to him, suspicion beginning to eclipse the wariness in her eyes. "He has his signs."

"I'm sure he does, and I'm also sure you are one of the few people who can read them." Dani gave a reluctant nod. "What I can do? With my magic?" He gentled his voice, knowing this was a difficult subject for her, for whatever reason. He had his suspicions, but no proof yet. "Where I read people's emotions? It's not much different from what you do with your friends, or with your animals. It's just a little easier for me, but it's not that much different. I can't read Roger with my magic any more than most people can read his expressions, but for others? It's much easier."

She didn't say anything, clearly processing his words, and he found he couldn't stop himself now that he'd started. The fact that she wasn't running for the door was giving him an unreasonable amount of hope.

"Reading emotional grids is like... being surrounded by doors," he continued. "I can listen from the outside and usually pick up faint hints of emotion. There's a risk of picking up too much, so I have to be careful with myself. If I wanna know more about someone, I have to go through their door. Really, the door is just a mental shield. Even some of the stronger ones—like Jian, for example, he's got a pretty sturdy door—I can still hear emotions, but I can't open the door without using some powerful magic."

"Do I have a mental door?"

He nodded. "Yeah. It's not as strong as others, but you could fix that with practice."

Dani was watching him, expression shuttered, but he didn't dare reach for her with his magic, not when this was all about trust. "So you can hear my emotions through my door?"

Again, Slate nodded. "I can't turn off the voices behind the doors," he continued. "I hear it even if I don't want to."

"Then why do I sense you using your magic actively sometimes?" Dani asked, brows twisting together.

He studied her for a moment, thinking. "You might be sensing moments when I press my ear to the door to hear more clearly."

"And if you want to hear even more?" she asked slowly. "That's when you open the door, right?"

"Yes, if the mental ward—door—isn't too strong for me," Slate said honestly. "I don't like to do that, though. People tend to hide their deeper emotions behind their mental shields. It's a little too private for me."

Wariness returned to her face. "You do that without permission? Can you... do stuff inside someone's emotional grid?"

Some instinct told him that lying to her would do irreparable damage, even if the truth frightened her. "Yes... I can." The words were like rocks in a still pond, clunking through the tension between them and creating ripples.

Ever-so-slightly, the edges of her irises limned with fluorescent green, like the way a cat's eyes catch the light in the dark. She sat silently, staring at him, and he held his breath, fighting the need to explain himself, to give excuses as to why she shouldn't be afraid of him.

But he had to be honest, because he wouldn't be able to live with himself if he talked his way out of this, charmed her and convinced her not to be afraid of him. It would be a manipulation, even if it wasn't magical.

"Tell me." She lifted her chin, watching him with less caution now, and he thought he saw a spark of curiosity, feeding his hope.

Slate leaned over until he could snag one of the stools, positioning it across from her. He rested his elbows on the counter, holding her gaze as he continued. "I can make people feel things, feed them emotion, if I can get into their emotional grid. Good, bad, anything. It's a sandbox in there. I can do whatever I want."

Dani paled a little, but the way she tipped forward slightly, she seemed to be hanging onto his every word with desperation, a shade of determination tightening her brow. Like she had to know everything.

And frankly, he'd deny her nothing.

She was as still as a statue, frozen in a way that scared him, and his smile slipped. He wanted to reach for her, to reassure her, but he forced himself to stay where he was.

"How... how do I know when you are manipulating my emotions instead of just peeking at them? Your heartfire only tells me when you're using your magic, not what you're doing with it." She was chewing her lip, staring at him, but he had a feeling she was staring at that fire inside him she could apparently see.

"You'd know," he hurried to tell her. "It might feel like real emotions, but deep inside, you'd know they aren't yours, not really. Sometimes it's hard to tell if you aren't focusing, but if you concentrate on how you're feeling, you'd be able to tell the difference between real and manipulated emotions. Jian says it's like when your hand goes numb, and you touch it with your other hand. It doesn't feel like your hand, but you just *know* it's your hand, even if your senses say it's not. You just know." He shook his head, unable to describe it better. No one had played with his emotions—not yet. His uncle was the only one strong enough to go against him in terms of empathy magic, and so far, he'd been spared that manipulation.

Dani's eyes unfocused, her breath catching a little, and Slate had the impression she wasn't seeing his kitchen anymore.

"I don't like doing it, to be honest," he told her quietly, not sure if she was even listening at this point. "It feels... slimy. The only time it doesn't is when I'm sharing how I feel with Jian or Kari. Maybe it's because all parties know what's happening, so it doesn't feel like an invasion of privacy or a manipulation." He shrugged, anxiously watching her face.

She nodded slowly, and he could see her processing all this information. She'd regained some color in her face, and her shoulders weren't so tense anymore.

Pride filtered in through his anxiety and concern for her. He didn't know the reason for her fear, but he'd felt the strength of it, knew it took a great amount of courage to face it, to try to tame it and overcome it. But she looked so small, so vulnerable right then, that he wasn't sure his heart could take it.

He reached across the kitchen island, and gently tipped her chin up. "Look at me," he murmured, and sluggishly, her eyes drifted up to lock with his. He offered her a small smile. "Go home, love. We can reschedule our date for another night, *ne*?"

Russet brows drew together, a spark of determination bringing some life back into her expression, and he knew she was about to argue. To insist that she was *fine*, even though she wasn't. "If you need time, that's fine," he continued. "Don't rush yourself. I'll still be here when you're ready."

She hesitated, then gave a tight nod. He dropped his fingers from her chin, and she slid off the stool. Slate walked with her down through the studio and out to her Vespa. She paused before getting on her bike and turned to look back at him, a starkness to her face.

"I'm sorry," she whispered.

A touch of panic threaded through him, her words bringing to life the memory of her driving away from the Den. Of zero communication for almost two weeks.

He swallowed his heartbeat. "Don't be. It's okay."

He didn't dare try to probe her emotions, not yet, but he couldn't stop himself from closing the gap. He brushed his lips over her brow, savoring the short moment of contact, her warm scent washing over him.

She let out a soft breath, and he wanted to believe she found comfort in the touch as much as he did. When he stepped back, he found her searching his face. He cracked a wicked grin for her and was rewarded with a ghost of a smile. "Text me when you get home."

She nodded. "I will. Promise."

"Goodnight, Daniella."

"Goodnight, Slate."

The Vespa rumbled softly out of the alley. Slate stood there until he could no longer hear the sound of it before he headed back upstairs to his now-empty apartment. The remnants of the sushi date night stared at him from their vigil on his counters.

A thrum of anxiety shot through him, a breath of insecurity. Had he fucked this up, being so brutally honest about his magic?

No. It was the thinnest whisper inside him, the smallest assurance that he'd played this exactly as he should have. Because there could be no more illusions and lies and charades between them anymore. The foundation on which they were building—whatever it was they were building—had to be crafted out of *trust.* Or the whole thing would crumble underneath them.

Trust... and patience. A fuckton of patience.

He still let out a long breath of relief when his phone vibrated some fifteen minutes later, the screen glowing with a text notification.

Dani

I'm home. Thank you.

MIND MAGIC

Because the Goddess created the Wild Fae first,
she created them in her image, therefore they...

- Gherald Schmidt, Faerloch Historical Archives

"Are you sure about this?" Slate's voice held a wealth of reluctance, and that soothed Dani's nerves like nothing else could right now.

She held back a sigh. "Yes, I'm sure. For the third time."

The afternoon was mild; most of the snow had melted in an uncharacteristically warm stretch of days leading up to the Solstice. Since their sushi date last night had been a colossal failure, Dani had asked Slate to come over before his own Solstice celebrations with the fae and to bring take-out with him. They'd set up a picnic in her backyard on a large waterproof blanket. A portable fire pit burned next to them, banishing the lingering chill in the air.

"And when you come over," she'd said on the phone that morning, *"we're going to talk more about your empathy magic..."*

He'd agreed, but apprehension was still a visible weight on his tense shoulders.

"I just... it doesn't have to be now," Slate murmured. "If you wanna sit on it for a few days..."

He clearly didn't want to do this, and that was completely in line with all of her instincts. It was against Slate's nature to cause her discomfort. She needed to start listening to her instincts more.

"I want to do it right now. Just... go slow, okay? And... talk me through it all. I want to understand." Dani squared her shoulders and lifted her chin. Understanding was key, and she already felt better about this empathy thing since his explanation.

It had certainly helped when she'd realized she didn't need magic to read Slate's emotions; he wore them on his sleeve. That realization leveled the playing field between them a bit, made her feel bold enough to handle this.

At her back, Sellie clinked her beak with a rumble of a growl. The griffin wouldn't stop staring at Slate like she was considering the best way to eat him. The unblinking stare of a snowy owl was unnerving at the best of times, and positively sweat-inducing when that owl face was attached to a griffin the size of a small car.

Slate was bearing it gracefully. She would bet Sellie was impressed too, even if she refused to acknowledge it—most people, even lorebeings, would wet their pants from that glower.

Slate let out a breath, rubbing at the back of his neck, and his eyes flickered away from Dani's face and up to Sellie's. The griffin let out a croon that should have sounded soothing, but it came off more like a quiet threat. Slate's brows lifted, and his grin was a little tight, but he spread out his hands in a distinctly non-threatening way. "Don't worry, Lady Selene, I swear I won't hurt her."

"Sellie," Dani scolded in a low voice, reaching up to soothe her friend with a stroke through the feathers under her chin. The griffin didn't so much as blink, keeping her laser focus locked on Slate. Dani sighed, casting an apologetic glance back at Slate.

He looked inclined to back out, so Dani scowled and tapped Sellie on the beak, before pinning Slate with a look. "Both of you... stop treating me like I'm made of glass. Dash is the only one here who is absolutely okay with my decision."

That's because he is vermin, Sellie responded tartly.

Dash lifted his head from where he was curled against Dani's hip, and the fox let out a little rolling yip, oblivious to Sellie's mild insult.

Please... I need to do this, she entreated the griffin, and Sellie finally broke her death stare, blinking her big silvery-blue eyes down at Dani. She didn't answer, but she let out a short rumble of irritation. She turned her head to study something else in the backyard, promptly ignoring Slate with all of her significant dignity.

"It's... it's not that..." he trailed off.

"You don't like making me uncomfortable," Dani finished for him, and she knew she was right when his vibrant eyes flickered. The tattoos she could just barely glimpse from the collar of his shirt had darkened to a rich mahogany, darker than the soft henna they were when he was relaxed. "Well, too bad. This has to be done, so let's... let's do this." She sucked in a breath, rolling her shoulders.

"Shit, Dani, you look like I'm about to hit you," Slate said tightly, shifting onto his knees. He looked ready to jump to his feet and pace. Or bolt.

She made an effort to release the tension in her body. "Stop worrying. I can do this," she told him firmly. "You said it yourself, it's *not* going to hurt. So... start by letting me feel *your* emotions."

Slate opened his mouth, looking like he was about to ask her, for the millionth time, if she was *sure*, so she let her eyes narrow in warning.

"Right... okay," he muttered, blowing out a breath. She saw the heart-fire inside him flare... and then she was feeling distinctly... *nervous*. But it wasn't her own nervousness, which was tinged with apprehension. This nervousness tasted like caution, a tentative hope, and a...

She didn't have words for it, but she got the distinct impression of trying to overcome a protective urge, like when she had to force a shy dog into contact with other dogs, even if it made that dog uncomfortable.

She didn't like the way she felt when she did it, but exposure therapy was important for many rescue dogs. This seemed similar and yet different. His protective urge felt *stronger* than the kind she felt about her animal friends, and it was taking a big chunk of his self-control to trample that feeling.

The emotions were tinged with self-loathing, and it spurred words from her lips before she even knew what she was saying. "I'm okay," she said, her anxiety being swept away by her own need to protect him—from himself. "I'm okay," she repeated, tasting the absolute truth of her own words.

She really *was* okay, and her confidence in this decision grew stronger. A smile tugged at her lips, and pride—this feeling distinctly *hers*, though she didn't know how she knew that—bubbled up. "Really, I am. It feels... strange. But not bad. You feel... Please stop being so nervous. I can handle this."

His emotions shifted, and she *felt* it. Felt his overwhelming relief as an answering smile spread across his face. It was one thing to logically understand his explanation, but quite another to feel it, and he was absolutely *right*. With Slate, at the very least, she could have already guessed all of these emotions he fed her if she was paying enough attention to his features.

Her smile widened, a sense of victory making her light-headed from her own relief, and slowly, the emotions that weren't her own faded from her awareness. "Does it cost you to share like that? Is it a lot of effort?"

Her ability to sense heartfires was a terrible gauge for exactly how much magic was being used. The flare in a heartfire was effort-based—how much of a being's life energy went into the magic. Roger's heartfire might barely flicker for a feat of magic that might make someone else's fire near-explode, because Roger was incredibly strong and so the effort cost for him was so much smaller than for someone weaker than him.

Slate's brow furrowed in thought, though he was visibly more relaxed by her reaction. "More than when I want to hear someone else's emotions, but not by much."

"What about when you manipulate them?" Dani bit her lip, memories of Kat hovering at the edge of her mind. "It sorta seems... the same. I mean, you made me feel a certain way right now. When you manipulate someone's emotions, can you... can you make them feel *more* than what you feel?"

Slate studied her face, and his heartfire flared. Since she wasn't feeling unusual emotions, she assumed he was just checking on her. Listening, as he said. She waited for any fear to curl through her... but it never came. With Slate so close, with the sensation of his own apprehension still fresh in her mind, it was tough to be scared when a part of her was so focused on reassuring him.

"It's kinda the same..." Slate started slowly. "It's the same method, at least. Instead of funneling my own emotions, I find the emotion inside them and amplify it. Or I feed it to them myself. Even a wisp of a feeling can be nurtured into a tornado. Like, I can make someone happier than I have ever felt, just by amplifying it with magic. The innate feelings inside their own mind attach to the emotion, amplifying it more, like a constant feedback loop—" His brow furrowed. "It's sorta hard to explain. And it's situational, if that makes sense. The strongest empaths manipulate emotions based on the situation..." His expression darkened slightly. "It's how Zeyphar got the entire fae council in his pocket so swiftly. Subtle emotional manipulation. Made them feel a different way about something to get what he wanted, in such small increments that they didn't notice."

Dani's lungs stuck to her ribs as his words resonated with her memory. Of manipulating someone into an action, like... making a young girl feel like she *wanted* to leave...

This is the part she'd been dreading, but her success so far buoyed her above her childhood fears. So she reached across the distance that separated them, and slowly threaded her fingers through his. The slide of his skin lit up her senses, melting away the residual nerves. His eyes flicked to their joined hands, and she didn't need magic to see he was startled by the contact, but desperate for it. His fingers clenched convulsively around her own, curling against her skin like they had been waiting to do that since the moment he'd arrived.

"It's not a great offensive magic," Slate hurried to say. "Though I did practice on Jian once and that was pretty horrifying—"

"What happened?"

"I uh... I escalated his fear. We were both curious about what would happen and you know how Jian gets. Obsessive and hyper-fixated on results. And... well, we all slept in my room for a week because we were all too afraid to be alone after that. Kari felt it through their twin bond, so yeah... it was a bit of a disaster."

The image of the three of them having a sleep-over like children made her lips twitch with amusement, easing her anxiety. She sucked in a breath and squeezed his fingers. "Do it to me. But not fear. Something happier. And before you ask, *yes, I'm sure.*"

That got her a flicker of a smile, and she braced herself. She couldn't get Kat's horror-filled eyes out of her head, a twisted contrast against the pleasant smile on her full lips. Dani hesitated. Wait. What if—

And then she was laughing.

The image of Kat was chased away by an overwhelming mirth that had her snorting out a laugh before she could stop herself. Sellie's head whipped back toward them, wide eyes watching as Dani covered her mouth with her free hand, startled by the sound. Dash wiggled into her lap until he could lick at her face, plainly delighted in her amusement. Planting his small paws on her chest, he licked at her face, happy yips punctuating each washing.

It was strange, because the mirth felt like it belonged to her, until she truly focused on why she was happy and came up with something... fuzzy. As if analyzing the emotion forced the vision of it to become blurry, and somewhat awkward. Like clothing that almost fit, but still left you fidgeting.

It was the answer to a question that resounded inside her over and over ever since she'd learned about Slate's magic.

Had Kat known she was being manipulated?

Or... had Kat left that night fully believing that she was happy to leave Dani? Her parents? Her life? Had she not realized she was being abducted?

The adult in Dani reasoned that the emotions of an adolescent were complex to begin with, so perhaps Kat hadn't fully understood her own feelings. But the child in Dani harbored a deep fear that had clawed its way into her heart over the years, and it was only after Slate had explained how the magic worked that Dani was able to unearth it.

Had she imagined everything?

Perhaps Kat had left willingly. Perhaps it hadn't been magic at all, and Kat had left with the beautiful and mysterious fae because Dani wasn't a good enough friend.

Now though... now she had concrete proof that she *hadn't* imagined that. That Kat hadn't *wanted* to leave her, not really. The terror in Kat's eyes had been *real*.

It hadn't been *Dani's* fault Kat had left.

The hilarity bled from her mind, leaving her hollow inside. She pushed Dash down gently and squeezed her eyes shut. Tears pricked behind her lids as two kinds of relief clashed with a different kind of guilt. Relief that she knew she couldn't be manipulated by Slate without her knowledge... and relief that Kat *had* actually been manipulated. Which left a twisted, sick feeling inside her.

How could she be happy about that?

"Dani..." Distress colored Slate's voice, and there was a tentative touch on her shoulder. Behind her, Sellie crooned softly, and a wing brushed against her hair in a caress as the griffin pushed impressions of comfort on her. "I'm sorry, love, I didn't mean to—"

"It's not that," Dani said, opening her eyes to find he'd shifted closer, watching her closely, his brows twisted in alarm. She offered him a watery smile. "It's... something else. Your magic... I could feel that the emotion wasn't mine. It felt real, but you're right, it wasn't quite the same."

His eyes pinged back and forth between hers. "So wait... then why?" Uncertainty laced his voice.

"It's... complicated," she started, reaching up to slide her fingers down the line of his jaw. All of the tethers and restraints she'd forced on herself had dissipated, and she no longer moved through molasses around him. With Slate, with this male who had gone to great lengths to help her face her fears, she suddenly felt as light as air, the movement easy and natural as she soothed him with a touch. "But... you've given me a gift today. You respected me enough to let me face my nightmares on my own. Thank you."

His hand moved to cover hers, holding her fingers to his face as if he wanted to absorb all the contact he could, but he still watched her with a certain amount of cautious vigilance. His movements, his expression, all of it spoke of a restraint he'd been showing around her ever since he'd come back into her life. Like he was walking on eggshells whenever she was around, and it was so very un-Slate-like, so very *wrong* to see him holding himself back around her, it struck a sour chord in her soul.

She was done with it. Done with being restrained by her own weaknesses, done with letting their situation get in the way of what had always felt so *easy*—being with Slate.

"I'm not afraid of you," Dani murmured, rocking forward onto her knees. She raised her other hand until she was cupping his face between her palms, looking him right in the eye. "I never have been, and I refuse to be afraid of your magic. It's a part of you, and I have never been afraid of *you*."

"That's not true," he whispered.

"Your magic scared me, but *you* have never scared me. Deep down, I know you would never use your magic to hurt me. I just... *know*." She gave a little shrug and offered him a small smile. "You would know if I was lying to you."

The look in his eyes was heartbreaking, a desperate hope, a yearning that was twin to her own. She followed her instincts, slipping her fingers past his face to twine at the base of his neck, bringing her closer until she could brush her lips against his in a gentle caress.

She coaxed him with another little kiss, trying to prove to him that she was *fine*, that *they* were alright. He lasted all of a breath before his arms snapped around her, tugging her tight against the hard planes of his chest as he angled his head to deepen the kiss.

He stole her breath, then gave her his, until the world around them faded but for the taste of him, the heat of his body searing into hers. He clutched at her like he was afraid she'd vanish, afraid she'd bolt, and she clutched his shoulders and teased her tongue along the seam of his lips in an effort to assure him she wasn't going *anywhere*.

Not when he so effortlessly caused an inferno to erupt inside her.

His mouth opened for her, and he was devouring her, rising onto his knees and bending her back. One hand slid up her spine to grip her nape while his other splayed wide across the small of her back, pressing her tighter to him until she could feel his galloping heartbeat echoing against her own.

Faster, faster, they spiraled out of control, kissing each other like they were starved for it—which they were. Fire raged in her bloodstream, setting off tiny explosions of sensation as the muscles of his stomach contracted against her own. The tips of his fingers dug into the flesh of her back, and he gently squeezed her neck as he angled her head just the way he wanted.

She plunged her hands down the back of his shirt, splaying her fingers wide to touch as much of his hot skin as she could reach, fingernails digging in as his hand shifted lower, lower, until he could palm her ass and tug her hips against his own.

She moaned into his mouth, his erection a statement through his pants, a hard ridge pressed tight against her stomach. Heat tightened in her belly. It had been so long and she was suddenly starving for him—

"*Ahem.*" A voice filtered in through the haze in her mind, edged with a *loud* clearing of someone's throat. It was followed by a low hiss and the distinct susurration of giant wings at Dani's back.

Slate stiffened, a distinctly inhuman snarl vibrating through him as he tugged his lips away from hers and clutched her to his chest, shoulders curving in an attempt to shield her from view as he twisted his head around.

"Kallen. *Go. Away.*" If looks could kill, the male standing just on the edge of the ward perimeter behind him would have expired right then and there.

Dani struggled to catch her breath, pulling her scattered thoughts together as she peered over Slate's shoulder. The male was lean and tall, with fair skin contrasting against rich brown hair long enough to brush the tops of his shoulders. It was pulled back into a neat half-ponytail, exposing the tips of slanted ears; a fae male.

Her heart skipped a beat, but her body was too full of fire to feel the cold tingle of fear. The fae's face was calm, but with a hint of pink on his cheeks, and he studiously observed his own feet, avoiding eye contact with both them and the large griffin at Dani's back. Sellie was making her displeasure at the sudden interruption known through a series of low rumbles and sharp clicks of her beak.

"I'm afraid I cannot, my lord, considering what time it is. You are already late." The male spoke with a slight lilting accent, his tone soft and yet perfectly clear to the ears, and heavy with an unvoiced apology.

Dani pushed at Slate's shoulders, studying the fae as her breathing leveled out, and Slate reluctantly relinquished his hold. He got to his feet with a surge of fae grace and speed, moving so fast that Dani blinked and nearly missed it. She was still on her knees while Slate stood facing the fae, shielding her with his body.

She drew in a steadying breath as she slowly pushed herself to her feet, reaching out to press a hand to Slate's back. Heat bloomed across her cheeks as she willed her racing heart to calm. She'd been utterly oblivious of everyone and everything while Slate had been kissing her, and she wasn't ignorant to what might have happened without the interruption.

She suddenly wanted to throw a rock at the male. Her body was primed for sex, starved of it for so long, and that frustration—not to mention embarrassment—overwhelmed any sense of nerves at being in the presence of a full fae male. She knew fae had acute senses and her face darkened to a ripe beet as she squeezed her thighs together in an attempt to disguise her physical reaction.

"I'll come find you *later*," Slate said, his voice still edged with a growl—a barely disguised threat.

The fae Slate had called Kallen finally looked up, and Dani saw his eyes weren't quite blue. They were a soft purple, and while the male looked to be in his mid-thirties, the age of his eyes spoke of someone older and wiser. A hint of amusement made them wrinkle in the corners, and the urge to pelt him with small rocks intensified.

The fae male's gaze shifted from Slate's to Dani's, then over Dani's shoulder to Sellie behind her. "Forgive me for the intrusion into your domain," the male said smoothly and offered a half bow toward Sellie. His purple eyes slid back to Dani. "I do apologize, my lady, but I have delayed for as long as I could. Tradition requires him to be in attendance before sunset." Kallen looked right past Slate, addressing her with a courteous tipping of his chin, before he gestured toward the setting sun.

Dani blinked and glanced down to where her phone lay forgotten on the corner of the big blanket she'd laid out over the frosty ground for them. With a nudge of her foot, she saw that she still had 30 minutes or so before she needed to leave for work, but the sun was already edging close to the horizon, casting long shadows across her backyard. It was the longest night of the year tonight, the Winter Solstice... a big holiday for the fae. Maddie, too, was hosting an event at her house that Dani would be headed to after work.

Time had had no meaning when she was with Slate, and it had gotten away from both of them.

Slate stiffened, staring at Kallen with a hint of mutiny on his face as his hands flexed at his sides. His posture hinted at his thoughts: *To hell with tradition.*

It warmed her, to see him so ready to toss aside everything and anything for her sake, but that wasn't who Slate was. He might be a hothead at times, but he was the lead instructor in a respected martial arts school that taught discipline to the young and old alike. As much as he might not like it, he was, in truth, a responsible leader, and although she'd like nothing more for this fae male to disappear and for Slate's hands to resume their wanderings, she knew it wouldn't be right.

"You have responsibilities, right, Sailor Scout Slate?" she teased him, needing some humor to find her feet again. She'd gotten past her nerves with Slate being fae, but being in front of a full fae was another matter as she came down from her sexual high. Still, the courtesy and distance the male maintained did a lot to ease her discomfort, and she was startled to find that she was grateful he'd addressed her directly, rather than dance around her like she wasn't there.

His demeanor, too, was so calm, so different from the buzzing power that surrounded the fae warriors she'd encountered in the past. It was a stark reminder to herself that her experiences with the fae were extremely limited, and she would only be doing herself—and the fae before her—a disservice by continuing to assume all fae were alike.

Slate broke his stare with Kallen to cast her an incredulous look, and she couldn't tell if it was because she was suggesting he leave her to go with the fae, or because of her Sailor Moon reference.

"It's okay. You should go," she said quietly, offering him a small smile, letting him see that she was being sincere. She reached out a hand to thread her fingers through his, and the tension visibly lessened in his broad shoulders. "Not that I want you to leave, but I don't want you to miss your big event."

He studied her face for a moment, and she squeezed his fingers in assurance, a silent message: *I'm okay with this, I'm* okay, *I promise.*

Slate finally let out a breath, casting Kallen another glare, before he shifted to face Dani, once more shielding her from view with his wide frame. He reached up with his free hand, slipping his fingers along her nape in that familiar possessive hold.

"Do you... you can come with me, if you want," he offered softly. He must have read the hesitation on her face—or with his magic—because he quickly added, "It's okay to say no. No pressure at all, love."

Go to Titan's Fen, a city *full* of fae?

"I think I've used up all of my courage for today," Dani confessed in a small voice, biting her lip. She had every intention of pursuing a relationship with Slate, and that meant she'd have to find the courage to go there one day, but venturing into a fae settlement for the first time during a massive festival might not be the best choice for her. Still, it stuck in her throat like the taste of cowardice. "Maybe another day—"

"Hey." Slate released her nape to tip her chin up, squeezing her fingers with his other hand as he offered her a smile. There was absolutely no judgment, no disappointment, on his face. "Don't worry about it, love, I understand. If I had any say in the matter, I'd avoid Titan's Fen today, too." His smile turned into a lopsided grin, calling up a responding smile from her. "I'll see you this weekend? Maybe tomorrow afternoon?" More of that painful hope colored his voice, and Dani wanted to banish that hope and turn it into confidence.

She liked confident Slate much better than uncertain Slate, and it was *her* fault that he defaulted to that unsure state around her. "Yeah, I... I would like that." She nodded and was rewarded with a flicker of intense happiness in his expressive eyes. "Hopefully we won't be... *interrupted,*" she murmured in a low voice, heat still simmering beneath her skin.

His eyes darkened from sapphire to indigo, heat springing to life in them, and his hand at her chin shifted until his thumb could feather against the scar on the juncture of her neck and shoulder. It sent a bolt of liquid warmth to her core, and she squeezed her thighs together again.

"I'll make sure of it." His voice was a silken promise.

Dani needed to keep herself from catching fire again, even with the fae male standing mere feet from them, so she let a bit of mischief creep into her face. "I guess being a Sailor Scout Princeling isn't all it's cut out to be, huh?"

A wicked grin sharpened his face, sharpened his eyes, making that faint inner glow more prominent. A wicked grin that bespoke of bedsheets and skin. His hand shifted up, up, up her throat, caressing her skin until his palm rested along her jaw. He shook his head. "I will *never* hear the end of that, will I?"

"Never." She offered him a bright smile, and she leaned on tiptoes to feather a kiss against his jaw.

Kallen cleared his voice again, and Slate's face soured. Chuckling, Dani stepped back from him and peered around Slate's broad form to offer the fae a timid smile. "Take care of him, okay?"

Surprise made his violet eyes flare a moment before the fae offered her a smile with an incline of his head. "A tall order, my lady. He is certainly spirited," the fae said dryly. "It has been a pleasure to meet you." Kallen's eyes shifted over her head to Sellie, and he inclined his head once more. "And you."

Dani glanced back to see Sellie's feathers puff out with self-importance.

"I'll call you, *ne*?" Slate murmured. He hesitated, then leaned down to feather his lips over hers. Before he could pull back, she caught at his shirt and pressed her lips more firmly to his for a proper goodbye kiss. Releasing his shirt, she stepped back to place her hand on Sellie's back as Dash wound around her ankles. Slate looked a little dazed from the kiss, and warmth spread through her chest.

Slate was still staring at her when Kallen threw down a fae portal right over the boundary of the ward around her property. Slate was still watching her with longing written plain on his face when he stepped into the ring... and vanished.

CHAPTER · FIFTEEN

MIDWINTER MISSIVES

... returning to the more rigid social hierarchy of ages past. Zeyphar Titania cited the relaxation of the unofficial caste system during the later years of his mother's reign as the cause of the unrest and diminishing power of the fae people. The prince stressed that maintaining social hierarchy was key to...

– Gherald Schmidt, Faerloch Historical Archives

The large, heavy door hinged open on a mere whisper of sound.

"You requested to see me, my lord?"

"Yes," came the soft reply from the male standing at the other end of the expansive hall. The luxury of the room was subtle—it didn't scream royalty but rather whispered it like a lover might. Wood and stone married gracefully, the floor inlaid with blue lapis stone in a wash of color, vaulted ceilings supported by column-like tree trunks. Floor-to-ceiling windows adorned the end of the hall, overlooking one of the handful of town squares scattered around the city.

Zeyphar, king of the fae, turned to see a tall fae male standing to attention just inside the doors. The male stood with military readiness, expression hard yet stoic, a hint of cruel arrogance along the line of his jaw. He was one of Zeyphar's highest-ranking confidants, a noble who'd made a life in the military while maintaining a seat in the fae court. But he was not a Second to Zeyphar, no, because he had no need of such relationships.

"What is your will, *Titania*?" Gelayeth asked, a hard glint in his gray eyes.

Zeyphar wandered over to the wide windows that overlooked his city. "Zlaet will be in Titan's Fen for the Solstice Festival this eve. His... constituents will assure he is there to uphold traditions."

Gelayeth nodded.

"I want Zlaet's eyes on Titan's Fen in the morning. His eyes, the lieutenant's eyes, that Mystic witch-doctor and his sibling... draw their gazes to the town. Keep them busy. Keep them *out* of the mortal city."

"Yes, my lord." But there was hesitation in his voice, uncertainty drifting off Gelayeth's emotional grid.

"What is it, commander?"

"May I speak freely, my lord?"

A wave of a hand in permission, though Zeyphar's gaze remained on the small forms of his people below.

"It is your belief that Zlaet's mind is... truly corrupted?"

Zeyphar flipped hard sapphire eyes to the commander, understanding precisely what was being hedged. "Zlaet is young, hardly out of faeling-hood. His rearing in the mortal city makes him vulnerable to the frivolous ideas of the desperate. He does not know the narrative he hears is naught but lies, because he has nothing to compare it to. He belongs here, with me, in the Silver Valley. He does not know he's little more than a prisoner. The denizens of Titan's Fen will use him as a martyr for their perceived need for rebellion."

"You are certain of this, my lord?"

"You fear he is making his own choices?" The question was a silken response. "That he is sound of mind? He is a faeling, commander. He does not know what he does not know. He is your prince, and he is unsafe there. I will see him and Tanyiel in this court by whatever means necessary."

A beat of pause. Then Gelayeth nodded. "Yes, my lord. I trust your judgment."

Zeyphar tilted his head, watching the commander. There was something calculating about him, though his emotions gave nothing away but unwavering loyalty. "Schedule a meeting with Zlaet. Send a message at dawn. Perhaps we can sway him yet to abandon the riff-raff."

"Will you be attending this meeting, my lord?"

"No. But do not tell Zlaet as such. I will be in my own meeting, but I need Zlaet busy for this meeting to be... successful." He trusted Zlaet's instincts would certainly interfere, should the young male not be otherwise engaged. It would be challenging enough, working around the protections the vampire and the she-bear had put in place. A risk, certainly, but he understood the boundaries of such protections, and so long as he played by their rules, it was a risk he was willing to entertain now. "Am I clear?"

"Yes, *Titania*."

Zeyphar waved his hand dismissively. Gelayeth pressed his palm to his sternum and inclined his head.

Zeyphar turned back to the sprawling windows once more, glancing over his city. The Solstice celebration was soon to begin, the citizens performing the last of the decorating and preparation. And he would enjoy the evening as he always did.

Come dawn, he would make another careful move toward securing Zlaet at his side. Another careful play on the proverbial chessboard.

It was time to speak with the power behind Zlaet's throne.

Power in the shape of a female.

CHAPTER SIXTEEN

LETTERS, LEGACIES, AND LIES

... was led by both the Sanguine Scholars and the Acolytes of the Goddess. The Vampire-Fae Accords are considered to be one of the only...

- Gherald Schmidt, Faerloch Historical Archives

Slate stormed into the training facility, already annoyed.

Eager to see Dani despite the late-night partying, Slate had been awake at dawn. He immediately set a course to hunt down Kallen to let him know he was leaving town—otherwise, he couldn't be sure he'd get any fucking *privacy.*

Before he made it halfway down the stairs, Autymn caught him and handed him a note from Saida, telling him to report to the training facility straight away.

And Slate knew better than to just leave without seeing what the captain wanted.

The few soldiers haunting the facility this early glanced his way, but none paid any additional attention to him as Slate headed for the stairs that would take him up to Saida's office. The facility was large but simple, with the first floor consisting of a few training rings, benches, tables, and racks with practice weapons. The upstairs featured a mezzanine overlooking the floor below, with the back wall housing a few offices and a small healer's ward.

Slate rapped his knuckles against Saida's office door, and when her voice beckoned him, he entered, mustering a deep, even breath to quell his annoyance. "You needed me?"

"Yes. Close that." Saida pushed herself up from her seat behind her desk. She was a small female, but there was an authoritative edge to her that instantly triggered Slate's student mentality. Her predator-sharp gaze missed nothing, and her mind was as honed a weapon as her fists. She was brutal, efficient, and no-bullshit.

Slate liked her immensely.

She leveled him a hard look. "I want to talk about your attitude lately, before you disappear into the depths of the mortal city for the day."

"What's wrong with my attitude?" The words were out, and Slate pressed his lips together when he heard said attitude articulated clearly in each syllable.

Saida raised a brow, lips thinning. "That attitude." She studied him, strong arms crossed over her chest. "You've been on edge. Hyper aggressive in sparring matches, brutal, merciless."

"I like to fight," Slate replied, a jittery, icy tension jacking through him. There was nothing to say beyond that—what Saida said was true. He was on edge lately, as if he had a tight, icy ball inside his chest all the time, and one small upset could turn it nuclear. He idly wondered if it was stress-related, particularly where Dani was concerned. Because it seemed the tightness inside him lessened significantly when he was around her.

"Normally I wouldn't complain." She unfolded her arms to brace her palms against the desk before her. "But it's getting more pronounced, and I can't have you here if you are out of control. It's not my business what you do with your personal life, but I will say something I'm certain you are already acutely aware of." She leveled him a look, and Slate held the gaze, hackles bristling. "Fae are closer to beasts than they are to humans, and we become agitated if we go long periods without touch or sex. You need to understand that about yourself—you are not *human* anymore."

"I'm aware of that, thanks," he snapped, instantly agitated.

"Touch-starvation can cause fae to become irrational and—"

"Are we done here?" Standing here, having a discussion with his guard captain on whether or not he fucked Dani was *not* what he wanted to be doing whatso-fucking-ever.

She raised both brows this time, giving him a knowing, pointed look. "We're done when I say we're done, soldier."

Slate had the grace to flush and zipped his focus to a spot on the wall. It bothered him more than he cared to admit that he wasn't at the *top* of this particular martial community. It'd been a long time since he had to take orders from anyone.

"I understand courting Tanyiel is high-stakes for you," Saida continued, "and that you are under an unprecedented amount of stress. However... you are not above reproach, not in my military. Get your head screwed on correctly before you hurt someone. Do you understand me?"

He nodded once. "Yes, ma'am."

She tipped her chin toward the door. "You're dismissed—"

The door to the office burst open, revealing Kallen in the doorway, his normally neat hair coming loose from the tie at his nape. "Captain!"

"I'm *busy*," Saida growled.

"It's urgent." Kallen's eyes shifted to Slate quickly, before returning his attention to Saida. "We haven't heard from Basyl's team in hours... and we just received this."

He stepped forward and handed a scroll to Saida, but before he released it, he turned to Slate. "It's addressed to you as well."

The captain uncurled the scroll, and Slate watched as she scanned it, as her hard features grew paler and paler. The echo of her emotions was difficult to ignore— urgency, anger, a touch of fear.

Wordlessly, Saida held the scroll out to Slate. Snatching it, he tugged it open.

Addressed to Captain Saida Bhryt, and my dearest nephew Zlaet Titania,

I have within my possession three young, sprightly soldiers who live within the hamlet of Titan's Fen. My own soldiers encountered them close to our borders early this morning, and thus secured them into our custody. While they are always welcomed within the fold of the Silver Valley, I thought it to be a gesture of good faith to return them to you in excellent health. In exchange, I would ask for a brief meeting with my nephew.

Zlaet, on behalf of our people, I would implore you to reconsider my proposition from the summer. The well-being of our people remains uncertain unless you and I seek to be a unified front. I would deeply encourage you to consider the future of our people, and the impact a civil war would have on the fae. Many lives have been and will continue to be lost should this petty family feud continue.

I shall prepare another proposal for you to consider. We will await your arrival at Faerie Glen at midday today.

Charmingly yours,

Zeyphar Titania.

Slate was silent for several long, thumping heartbeats. A *family feud*? This civil war was so far beyond feud status and it certainly wasn't exclusive to his family anymore. A shaking roared through him as he turned the words over in his mind, processing the subtle meaning, the nuances hidden between the lines. He thrust the scroll toward Kallen so he could read it before Slate ended up shredding the fucking thing in his hands.

The lieutenant read it over, his face carefully neutral. Then, with the same careful neutrality, he rolled the scroll back up and placed it on the table next to Saida. "We have intel of a significant increase overnight of Silver Valley fae around Faerie Glen," Kallen said into the quiet.

"The *gall* of that male..." Saida growled, voice hardening. "As if he's not the reason Ari is—" Saida cut herself off, shaking her head.

"You're certain it's Basyl's team?" Slate asked Kallen.

Kallen jerked his head in a nod. "We are certain."

He felt like all the air was being sucked out of the room. Basyl? *His* Basyl?

"He cannot know precisely where Titan's Fen is," Slate heard Kallen's voice through the rising pulse in his ears, "or else he'd be on top of us... my assumption is he only has a best guess—"

"What would it take to convince you to go to Tanyiel's and stay there?" Saida cut Kallen off, turning a hard gaze to Slate.

The question threw Slate out of his own headspace for a second, so focused on thinking ahead, playing out the moves in his head, on what it would take to get Basyl back. "What?"

"Let us handle this."

His mind froze for a second, as selfishness warred against his ingrained sense of duty and responsibility. How easy it would be... just say *sayonara* and peace out and go to Dani's house, have uninterrupted time with her.

He'd never forgive himself though. As much as a giant part of him wanted to walk away, he couldn't. He wouldn't be able to live with it if he did nothing and something happened to Basyl and his team.

"This is where your life is now, Slate. This is where you were always meant to go. It is not a choice. It is fate."

Words said many moons ago by his father, an iota of wisdom he'd needed at the time. Nothing was ever going to feel *right* unless he made it right. If this was where his future was... then, it was as Zeyphar said in his letter: Slate needed to think about the future of his people.

Damn his ingrained sense of responsibility.

"No." Slate shook his head. "My presence was requested, so I'll go."

"He has no authority to request anything from you," Saida said curtly. "He is a false king and you are the crown prince."

"I'm *uncomfortably* aware of that," Slate replied, a cool edge to his voice.

"This is a thinly veiled kidnapping attempt..." Saida continued, no part of her phased by Slate's icy attitude.

"They usually are," Slate nearly growled.

She picked up the letter again, eyes flitting over it. "He... seems to be under some delusion that you are a prisoner here."

Slate frowned a little. "I mean, sometimes it feels that way."

Two pairs of eyes snapped to his face, and after a heartbeat of silence, Saida quietly murmured, "Do you truly feel as such?"

"Well, I didn't exactly *volunteer* to be a fucking prince. Wasn't like I had much choice in the matter, so yeah, sometimes it can be a bit... suffocating. Though I'll take this place over being under Zeyphar's thumb, that's for sure."

Slate understood something about his uncle now that he hadn't before, back in the arena—his uncle suffered some kind of magical psychosis. The 'Malady,' the healers called it, a condition strong male empaths were especially prone to. Slate had seen glimpses of it in the summer; a rapid shift of emotions when things didn't play out to Zeyphar's plan. The icy, cruel aura of magic around him, sucking the life and air and warmth out of a room. It had made the hairs on Slate's neck rise then, and now that he had a word for it, it simply reaffirmed his notion that nothing good awaited him in the Silver Valley.

Whatever challenges he had in Titan's Fen were child's play compared to whatever his life would be in the Silver Valley.

"Such are the trappings of politics. Perhaps we are all prisoners to it," Kallen stated evenly.

"If uncle dearest thinks I'm a prisoner here..." Slate wondered, mind shifting rapidly through thoughts, "then it stands to reason the *rest* of the faerfolk from the Silver Valley think I'm a prisoner too."

Saida studied him. "That would certainly feed Zeyphar's narrative. To admit you are anything *but* a prisoner would be akin to admitting you are a threat to him, and thus, a threat to his stolen power."

"And if he paints this pretty picture of me as a prisoner, and he's rescuing me, he covers his ass in both ways; if he somehow convinces me to join him, I'm lauded as a prince returning home, and if he forcibly kidnaps me, then he's simply rescuing me for my own good." Slate linked his hands behind his back, twisting his fingers together to stifle the urge to pace.

"Either way, he'll want to remain in your good graces," Kallen supplied with an incline of his head, expression grim.

"I'd think so. Or else it fucks with his idea of getting me to trust him. At least, that's how I'd play it... but I'm not crazy, so..." At least, not yet. Hopefully, not ever. His uncle was a visceral reminder of what he could become if he wasn't careful. There was a reason male empaths were scarce.

"Also true." Kallen nodded. "The Malady poisons his mind. He might have truly convinced himself you are a prisoner here, and you are being groomed and corrupted... and yet, within a breath, he could choose to kill you. Zeyphar is very much the kind of male who believes if he cannot have someone, no one can."

Zeyphar wanted Slate because he wanted a puppet to control. Controlling the fae population would be infinitely easier with the true heir under his control. He hadn't been able to control Slate's mother, Aredhel, so he'd killed her.

Slate wondered if the same fate awaited him when Zeyphar realized there was nothing he could do to sway Slate to his side.

The captain leveled Slate a look. "He could be seeking this meeting in an attempt to get close enough to manipulate you by magic. That would be well within his power. You might be a strong empath, but Zeyphar is at least as strong and has had centuries to practice."

"But as an empath, I'd know the difference pretty quickly. And that would kill my trust in him."

"If he kept you enchanted for long enough, you would not know anything different. You'd not ever trust your own emotions again."

... Valid. And not something Slate had considered. Magical gaslighting.

Saida leveled him a look. "I do not like this. Using our scouts as an excuse to get close to you. I would prefer you stay—"

"No way." Slate's tone shifted, instantly icy and acerbic.

"My job is to protect the interests of the people, and *you* are part of that interest—"

"If you're suggesting I hole up in the manor and hide, you're fucking mad. Not that kinda guy. I will *never* be that kinda guy. That kinda... *king*." The word felt foreign on his tongue still.

Another withering look from Saida that would've made a better male than Slate quiver at the knees. "To be king, you must *live* long enough to be crowned."

Slate smiled grimly. "Where's the fun in that?"

Saida's eyes narrowed. "It is part of our duty as soldiers, and our allegiance—"

"Hold up. Allegiance? *What* allegiance?" His temper instantly snapped, bursting forth like an avalanche. "No one here is loyal to me yet." He gestured pointedly to both Saida and Kallen. "Not even the two of you are loyal to me. You're loyal to the memory of Ari."

It was a low blow, and the impact rippled through the room, but Slate tasted the truth of his own words.

It tasted sour.

And for a moment, he faltered. Why? Why did he have to care so much for these people? If he were to jump ship and switch sides in this war, who would mourn him? Who would mourn Slate as his own person, and not as Slate, son of Aredhel?

The list felt alarmingly short.

He'd been trying to make it right here for *months*... working his ass off, flipping his entire sense of self upside down... and for what? The faerfolk had loved Aredhel... and now they were settling for Slate.

He knew all this, and it stung him to his core, and yet... the part of him that even considered the idea of running away wanted to vomit right there in the middle of the floor. Slate didn't consider himself a coward; he ran away from nothing.

Especially not the people his own mother had cared about, even if they didn't care for him.

"That's not entirely true."

Slate flipped his eyes to Kallen. The lieutenant studied him carefully. Slate's magic might not have detected even a whisper of emotion from him, but his heather eyes certainly gave some of them away. A troubled sadness, a pinch of guilt, a shot of acute memory. "It's true that much of you takes after Ari," Kallen continued, "but I will speak only for myself when I say that *my* loyalty to you does not start and stop with those similarities. Though I won't deny that many of us possibly hold you too close to the chest *because* of Ari. But that is our error, and not yours."

Somehow, the sting inside his chest intensified and shifted, perhaps a piece of him influenced a little by whatever echoes of emotions were bouncing around the room.

"I do not think either one of us would disagree with you, however," Kallen continued steadily, "in that loyalty is not built within the confines of a throne room. The people are the spine of a kingdom, and a king is nothing without his people." The lieutenant nodded once, as though convinced of his words.

The silence that shifted through the room was tense.

"So... we bargain, then," Slate broke the silence first, needing to move on and shelf this conversation for another day and focus on the task at hand. "Get the kids back and what? Promise uncle dearest that we'll behave and not egg on a war yet?"

Saida frowned. "Kids?"

"Yeah. Basyl and his team."

"Basyl is *triple* your age."

Slate shrugged. "Still a kid."

Saida shook her head.

"The last time we parlayed with Zeyphar, it did not go well," Kallen hedged, glancing at Saida. "Though Ari did agree at that time to go to the Silver Valley for her negotiations."

Slate could hear the echo of grief in every word. "It'll be different this time," he said slowly, unsure of what to say. He didn't share the same heartbreak over his mother as the rest of the people in Titan's Fen did; his memories of her were nonexistent at best. "You've gotta stop comparing me to her... we're different people."

"I know. Again, some of us find that difficult at the best of times. But you are correct—you share the same... willful disposition as Ari, but she wasn't a fighter," Kallen said with a slow shake of his head.

"At all," Saida echoed with a firm nod. "She disliked physical confrontation." She pinched her brow. "Goddess help us, a warrior prince." She lifted her gaze to Slate's. "We will bargain—bargain *only*, if at all possible. We are in and out. No bloodshed."

"That's fair." Just because Slate *liked* to fight didn't mean he always wanted to.

Besides, a fight with fae was tenfold any fight he'd ever been in. He wasn't an idiot—the ending of a fight nowadays would not be when the ref stepped in and separated them.

It was a kill-or-be-killed. 'Til death do us part.

And Slate knew he wouldn't be spared from the other end of that either. At some point, someone would die by *his* hand. He was not looking forward to that.

Saida nodded. "You will not be alone. Myself, Kallen, Galyn of course, and several others will be with you."

"And Jian," Slate added.

Saida considered it. "I agree. The witch-doctor will be a valuable asset. He can see through enchantments, and he knows your behaviors and mannerisms intimately." She waved a hand at Slate. "Go. Fetch the witch-doctor and whatever else it is you need. With haste, or we will be late."

Chapter · Seventeen

EXCHANGE AT FAERIE GLEN

... is believed that treading on hallowed ground puts one in the eye of the Goddess herself. To break one of her Sacred Laws on such ground has historically been met with deep consequences for incurring the wrath of the Goddess....

- Gherald Schmidt, Faerloch Historical Archives

"This was not *at all* how I pictured this day going..." Slate muttered darkly as he, Kallen, and Jian materialized out of a portal. They stood on the edge of a small meadow. The midday sun sparkled off errant snowflakes, a fine layer of white powder brightening the otherwise dull winter grass. Conveniently, or perhaps unnervingly, Titan's Fen's current location wasn't far from the meeting place. Unlike Titan's Fen, Faerie Glen was static within the Forest, close to the heart of it, near the griffin breeding grounds.

"Big plans with Dani?" Jian chuckled. Around them and behind, several more portals glowed to life, and about a dozen soldiers materialized out of them. Slate recognized all of them; he noted that Saida had been extremely selective in her choices.

All of these soldiers were unquestionably loyal to Ari and thus, to Slate.

"Maybe..." Slate ground out, shoulders tense for what was to come.

Jian made a musing sound in the back of his throat. "Technically, it *was* your birthday yesterday..."

Slate decided not to feed into that comment. He hadn't made a huge deal of his birthday this year—it had seemed... like not great timing. There was so much other shit going on that it just seemed so inappropriate to shift all the attention onto him. He was under enough scrutiny these days as it was. The Solstice Festival was enough for him.

"When are you two just gonna fuck and get it out of your system? Watching you touch-starve is brutal, man," Jian continued lightly, gray eyes casually observing the edges of the meadow.

Kallen cleared his throat, and just as Jian's eyes snapped to the lieutenant in obvious, painful curiosity, Slate growled, "Shut the fuck up, both of you."

"I said nothing, my prince," Kallen replied smoothly.

"What did I *miss*?" Jian hissed gleefully.

"I could've *literally* peeled your skin from your bones yesterday," Slate growled at Kallen, eyes studiously on the far edge of the meadow. Fifteen minutes... if Kallen had just given him *fifteen more fucking minutes* yesterday, that's all he'd have needed.

Damn it, he *was* touch-starved, wasn't he?

"I'm aware." Graceful, smooth humor in every syllable, even as Kallen's face remained carefully neutral.

Jian chuckled darkly. "Kallen interrupted *birthday sex*?"

"Shut *up*, asshole."

Saida and Galyn appeared at Slate's elbow, killing all cackling and conversation. "We've swept the area and I've placed reinforcements in the Forest," Saida said by way of greeting. "No sign of Zeyphar's ilk."

"This is the spot, though, right?" Slate asked.

She gave a sharp nod before slipping away. Galyn remained, poised and distinguished as usual with his silver hair neatly combed back and his Titania-blue doublet and gray breeches spotless.

Long seconds ticked by. Slate resisted the urge to check his watch, nerves beating in his throat. He swallowed them, actively breathing evenly, trying to slip into fight-mode—the mindset he flourished in whenever he stepped into the ring.

He'd not seen his uncle since the day he'd blown up the arena. Back then, he'd been powerless, his friends at the mercy of his decision, lives hanging in the balance—

Jian was watching him. "What?" Slate asked. He noticed that Kallen and Galyn were eyeing him too.

Jian's sharp eyes swept his form. "Your *chi* is doing that weird shit again. Where it's... thrumming. Swelling, almost... I thought it'd go away after the glamour." Jian shook his head. "It's cold. Icy, almost. And..."

"Unstable," Kallen said softly. A little furrow rested between his brows. "Do you feel alright?"

"I'm fine," Slate shifted his attention back across the meadow. "Nervous, I guess. Trying not to think about what happened the last time I saw this guy."

Jian hummed. "Definitely one of the worst nights of my life. Right up there with the first time Kari died."

It was still baffling, how casually Jian talked about Kari's death. But death for a three-tailed *kitsune* was not always permanent, he'd learned.

Jian frowned suddenly. "Someone's coming."

Portals appeared on the other side of the meadow, two, then four, then eight...

The drumming of nerves in his throat amped up tenfold. Every time he encountered Zeyphar's fae, shit went south.

Several figures started walking toward them with the smooth grace becoming of fae.

Slate twitched, muscles primed for some kind of action, but a hand settled on his shoulder.

"Stay here," Galyn's voice whispered near his ear. "Make them come to you. You owe them *nothing*. Chin up, stand straight."

Slate sucked in a slow, deep breath. He might not *feel* like a prince or a king or *Titania* or whatever, but that didn't change how others perceived him. Perception was reality, and in the case of the fae, their perception, their reality, was that he wasn't Slate Melisande, master martial artist. He was Zlaet Titania, crown prince of the fae.

It was a part he had to play and little more. As much as he hated the pomp and circumstance of it.

The approaching fae stopped a dozen paces away. Slate's eyes swept them, frowning, senses flaring as he deliberately fed tendrils of his empathy magic to listen at the threshold of each and every mind. It was information overload, but he bore it with stoic silence, needing every advantage he could get.

He didn't like infiltrating minds, but it was a necessity.

"*Tatya.*" They laid their palms against their sternums in a fae greeting.

A kernel of annoyance stabbed him in the center of his chest at the title. "Where's Zeyphar?" Slate demanded without greeting or preamble.

A beat of pause. "The *Titania* is otherwise engaged," one of the fae stated, a male with hard gray eyes, like iron in winter—unforgiving and unyielding. Slate had met this male on several other unpleasant occasions.

Gelayeth.

Slate's expression narrowed, and he tuned his magic to listen more closely to the commander's emotional grid just as Galyn spoke. "We were informed that he'd be present."

"All due respect, councilor, but our king is a very busy male. He will see you at his leisure and not a moment before."

"All due respect, commander, but Zeyphar is not my king," Galyn replied smoothly. "This meeting was organized on the condition that Prince Zlaet would indulge in a proposal from Zeyphar."

Gelayeth hummed in the back of his throat but said nothing further. Red alarms blared through Slate's mind as he rapidly began to pick apart every word of the letter. The fae were masterful with words and loopholes and cleverly disguised lies. While he didn't get the sense that Gelayeth was *lying,* per se, something definitely wasn't right.

"Where are my scouts?" Slate growled, his voice cool and icy and more than a touch angry.

There was a ripple of stillness among Zeyphar's fae. Slate heard echoes of caution coming from Jian, and a tickle of wary anger from Galyn.

Gelayeth's expression was unwavering. "I see you would prefer to get right to business."

"You're fucking right I would."

Gelayeth nodded once and turned to snap a few commands in Faerish to his own soldiers. Slate surveyed them. Two dozen fae soldiers in blue Silver Valley armor—double what Slate had brought. Many of them held a nugget of reverence and concern toward Slate. The reverence was understandable, but the concern...

They were concerned for Slate. He threaded magic toward those with weaker minds, tuning into them. What bounced back was a mixed bag of concern and conviction. Emboldened with a sense of good purpose and faith...

Interesting. Were their emotions a reaffirmation of Slate's suspicions that his uncle was painting this narrative that Slate was somehow a *prisoner* in Titan's Fen?

"I do not like this..." Kallen whispered, his voice a low current meant only for Slate, Jian, and Galyn. "Something is wrong."

"Indeed," Galyn added softly. "The correspondence was vague; Zeyphar might not show himself. Be on your guard, my prince."

"I know," Slate replied, straightening as Gelayeth returned, and gestured for three soldiers to come forward.

Each soldier had a scout, secured in iron wires. Slate's anger soared immediately, seeing each scout wobbling on the spot, half-conscious, held on their feet by the strength of the hands holding them up. Basyl was in terrible shape, bruised, beaten, fresh blood still drying on his cheek.

As if he'd put up a hell of a fight.

"*What did you do to them?*" Slate snarled as each scout was shoved to their knees in front of him. Jian dropped instantly, a soft orange glow limning his hands as he reached for the first scout.

"An enchantment, nothing more, to erase their memory of the Silver Valley's current location," Gelayeth said, watching Jian assess each scout. "Are they to your liking, witch-doctor?"

The look Jian gave the commander would've withered a lesser male.

He turned to Slate. "The enchantment is complex. They will need fae healers and time."

Slate tipped his head, permitting Jian to take the scouts. The witch-doctor wasted no time; a handful of Titan's Fen soldiers edged forward and gently pulled the scouts to their feet and whisked them away.

"Are you satisfied then, Prince Zlaet?" Gelayeth inquired the moment Jian and the scouts disappeared.

There was a subtle shift in Gelayeth's emotions then. Subtle, but it sent more warnings blaring through Slate's mind. The commander's emotions didn't quite jive with the rest of the Silver Valley soldiers.

Gelayeth watched Slate like an opponent in a ring match. He was sizing Slate up, looking for tells, for hints about what he was going to do next. The commander's shields were much better than his soldiers', but even despite that, Slate could sense a hint of... amusement. Something was definitely off, but Slate couldn't put his thumb on the pulse of *what* was wrong.

They needed to leave. Now. While the going was still good.

"We're done here," Slate announced.

Gelayeth's eyes narrowed, glinting like cold iron. "I do believe you must uphold your end of the bargain, Prince Zlaet."

Slate's gaze flickered around the meadow, to each soldier before settling on Gelayeth once more. "Zeyphar's not here. He failed to uphold it himself."

"Did he?" Gelayeth said, his expression edged with airy hostility. "I do believe the terms were 'an exchange for brief meeting' were they not? My *Titania* is quite busy—"

"Too busy or too afraid to talk to me?" Slate growled. "Easier to manipulate a mortal than a fae prince, I'd think. Is his ass still chapped from losing to me in the arena?"

The fae commander's lips thinned; a subtle change in expression even as his emotions shifted from amused to annoyed. He waved his hand and a portal appeared at the toes of Slate's sneakers.

Kallen reacted faster than Slate, fisting a handful of Slate's jacket and jerking him back a step, putting distance between Slate's feet and the glowing ring.

"If you wish to hear the proposal directly with my *Titania*, Prince Zlaet, we will gladly escort you to the castle in the Silver Valley."

There was a rustling behind Slate as his Titan's Fen soldiers closed in. Kallen tightened his grip on Slate's jacket, strangling the fabric and pulling it taut, as if the lieutenant did not plan to let him go without violence, regardless of Slate's decision.

Another hand came to rest heavily on Slate's shoulder. "We will hear the proposal here and now, commander," Galyn interjected smoothly, "with the Goddess as witness in the hallowed ground of the glen."

A tense silence stretched, swelling through the entire glen like a collective breath.

Finally, Slate nodded. Once.

The portal disappeared from his feet and the soldiers backed up two steps.

Gelayeth gestured and from the line of Silver Valley soldiers, a wiry female edged her way through. She wore a long robe of silver with white embroidery around the cuffs, hem, and collar, following a straight line down the meridian of the garment.

Slate frowned, and as if he'd read Slate's confusion, Galyn whispered, "An Acolyte of the Goddess."

Slate nodded as the Acolyte came forward, a scroll clutched in her hand. She inclined her head at Slate and pressed her free hand to her sternum in greeting. "I have the proposal here, my prince. I've been instructed to present it to you."

Slate nodded.

She broke the seal on the scroll and unwound it carefully.

And unwound it.

And unwound it.

Until the bottom of the scroll touched the frosted grass under their feet.

"Are you *fucking* kidding me?" Slate snarled. "What the fuck is *that*?"

The Acolyte flushed scarlet at his tone and glanced at Gelayeth. The commander offered her a gracious wave. "Continue, Ellyea."

Slate's vision tinged red at the edges, an icy frost creeping through his blood. "Absolutely not—"

Galyn's finger gripped Slate's shoulder harder, an interruption, a warning. "Proceed," the council-fae said.

"Are you out of your mind?" Slate hissed over his shoulder as the Acolyte began to read what promised to be a lengthy and boring as fuck introduction. "It'll take her hours to read that."

"If we do not hear every word, we cannot know if we are being deceived somewhere," Galyn said evenly. "This is quite normal, my prince. Remember, fae understand time differently."

Un-*fucking*-believable.

"I quit this job," Slate muttered darkly under his breath.

Amusement trickled out from behind the council-fae's mental shield, just a thin thread compared to the unwavering focus and attention Galyn was giving the Acolyte.

Slate's eyes slid to Gelayeth. Whereas the other fae around them were dutifully focused on the Acolyte, the commander was watching Slate instead. A ghost of a smug smirk danced around the commander's mouth, igniting Slate's rage and frustration.

"Are we keeping you from other pressing matters, Prince Zlaet?"

Slate smothered his emotions, locking them behind a barrier of ice and nothing. "No," he ground out. "Carry on."

A FALSE KING'S PROPOSITION

... formal request from the Silver Grace Coven to dismantle Dagby's Creature Emporium was denied. The only proof regarding the heinous nature of Dagby's capture methods came from the testimony of a lorekissed female, who claimed to be able to speak to the creatures. This proof was not sufficient for...

- Gherald Schmidt, Faerloch Historical Archives

Dani slept until noon after her late night at Maddie's house for the Winter Solstice and found a sweet message from Slate on her phone that he'd sent much earlier in the morning. She sent a reply, eager to arrange their date, but when he didn't respond over an hour later, Dani left her house on her Vespa.

Needing to keep herself busy, Dani headed downtown to the magically hidden Dark Arts Market, the same place she'd rescued Sellie from years earlier. She came here at least once a month and strolled the narrow street with the hope of rescuing others from the fate Sellie might have faced if Dani hadn't intervened. In Sellie's case, she likely would have been imprisoned and used for her valuable feathers, blood, and ability to see through glamours of any magical nature.

Sellie had managed to escape all on her own, and Dani had found her in an alley branching off the Dark Arts Market, cornered by hellhounds. Dani didn't know if they'd been employed to bring Sellie back to her seller, or if they'd had more predatory interests in the hatchling, but Dani had managed to rescue the small but defiant griffin.

As she strolled, she kept her senses open for signs of creatures in distress. She was surrounded by magical beings, but their magical 'flames' felt different to her than those of wild creatures. Animals—both the mundane and magical—had much smaller fires, and much wilder. Disorganized, like a snarled mass of fire as opposed to the bigger, groomed fires of lorefolk.

A vibration in her pocket startled her, and she nearly tripped as she fished her phone out, all attention immediately zoning into the illuminated screen. Excitement was a balloon in her chest, one that popped and deflated when she saw it was a Snapchat from Caroline.

Nothing from Slate.

It was late afternoon. She'd expected him to text her by now...

"Daniella O'Callaghan."

The lilting, masculine voice came from her left, and Dani's right hand was already slipping into the pocket of her green jacket as she turned, fingers curling around her handgun concealed within.

Brilliant cobalt eyes that seemed to glow ever-so-slightly from within speared through her, pinning her into frozen shock as she found herself a few paces away from Zeyphar Titania.

She never would've noticed him—he was dressed simply in almost modern clothing. His simple black cotton breeches and double-breasted jacket could have passed at first glance as a sharp suit, and his long platinum hair was pulled back into a ponytail.

Beautiful yet dangerous.

Thin lips curled into an amused smile, and Zeyphar held both hands out before him in the universal gesture for peace. "Might I borrow a moment of your time?"

It was a moment before Dani was able to suck in enough oxygen to kick her brain into gear. Sellie reacted faster, letting loose a piercing shriek that had Zeyphar's eyes flicking upward, but there was no space for the griffin to land without doing so on top of other beings, so she circled above their heads, flying in a tight circle as her luminous owl eyes locked predatorily on Zeyphar's lone form in a clear message that Dani was able to translate from the images and clips of words Sellie was screaming at the fae: *Make a wrong move, and I don't care how many innocent bystanders get injured in my attempt to rip your head from your shoulders.*

"I am alone, I assure you both," Zeyphar said calmly, with no indication of fear for the griffin who'd set her sights on him, even as other individuals ducked and glanced upward in alarm. He continued to hold his hands out and speak in an even tone, looking between her and the griffin with a pleasant smile on his face. "And we are in a public place, one where I hold no authority." Zeyphar lowered his hands slowly, then crossed them with all the confidence of someone who *wasn't* being considered as a snack by a griffin. He propped a shoulder casually against the frame of one of the market stalls. "I vow to the Goddess that you are safe from me, that you—and your griffin—will leave this market unharmed and of your own free will."

A vow to the Goddess was taken seriously by lorebeings—misfortune followed those who broke their vow. Dani hesitated from pulling the small handgun from the pocket of her jacket.

This was the Dark Arts Market. She was safer here facing the king of the fae than she would be even at her own home with all her wards. This place operated smoothly on an unofficial set of rules enforced by all beings who enjoy its services. Mainly, that starting violence in the middle of a market was bad for business, and anyone bad for business was *not* welcome in the Dark Arts Market.

Not even Roger messed around here.

Zeyphar was not wrong—he had no authority and power here, and that knowledge more than his vow was what kept her from turning tail.

And a thread of curiosity tickled her underneath the terror. What reason did he have to *talk* to her? She had little to do with this war aside from her relationship with Slate. It would make more sense for him to simply manipulate her and kidnap her, but he'd just sworn to the Goddess not to do that.

Sellie was gathering too much attention now, and not all of it was tinged with fear. She was a highly valuable creature who was under strict orders from Dani to keep a low profile any time they came to the market.

Sellie, pull back. I'll let you know the moment I need you, okay? Dani's skin felt too tight over her bones as her heart hammered out a staccato beat against her ribcage. She kept her fingers wrapped securely around her weapon, doing her best not to look like a frightened rabbit cornered by a wolf.

Sellie protested instantly, but Dani injected her will into her words as she urged the griffin to stay close, but lose the visibility. Snapping her beak in warning, Sellie pumped her wings, catching a warm updraft from the narrow street. The griffin landed silently on the lip of a neighboring building, and settled so she could peer over the edge and down at them, eyes zeroed in on Zeyphar.

The fae male paid the griffin absolutely no heed, and instead, he watched Dani with a pleasant smile on his face.

Dani tipped her chin up, reminding herself to stand straight and strong despite the terror wrapping long, icy fingers around her lungs. "What do you want?" she asked, finally finding her voice.

Zeyphar uncrossed his arms and straightened from the market stall, sweeping out a hand to gesture toward a small cafe run by one of the smaller witch covens in Faerloch. He inclined his head with a polite smile and took a step closer to her—and smoothly stopped his advance when Dani instinctively fell back a step and Sellie let out a hiss audible even from up on her perch.

"Apologies. I assumed you'd prefer to sit?" His polite tone matched his polite smile, but it made the tiny hairs on the back of her neck stand straight from instincts that whispered she wasn't looking at a man, but a predator who would love to eat her for dinner.

It took considerable effort to unglue her feet from the pavement and force her legs to fold into the chair opposite the one Zeyphar slid into. She kept her hand in her pocket, sitting stiffly on the edge of her seat. He leaned back in his chair and regarded her with an expression that was a mixture of delight, fascination, and a hint of excitement that had her spine locking against the instinct to *flee* this dangerous being.

She really should just leave. She had no business speaking to him, and frankly, there was nothing he could say or do to curry her favor.

"As you know, my dear, there is some... tension amongst the fae," Zeyphar began, speaking airily as if such a statement was a mild, inconsequential one. "And I do not relish this *contention*."

Dani studied his face but didn't reply.

"I believe *you* might be able to help me solve this problem, you see," Zeyphar said, smile widening as he spoke. "I believe you might be the key, in fact, to bringing peace to the fae, and to Zlaet."

"Me?" Dani scowled at him.

"Indeed, my dear." His smile was pure feline, and despite the answering chill that smile caused, Dani had the distinct impression he deeply believed what he was telling her. "I believe that you hold the power to sway my nephew, to encourage him to make the right choices, for the benefit of all fae."

"And why do you think that?" Dani raised a brow.

Zeyphar's eyes dropped to her neck, lingering there as his nostrils flared slightly. When his gaze returned to hers, she resisted the urge to touch her neck as his pleasant smile widened. "Trust me, you hold *considerable* sway on my nephew. Moreover, I believe that should you convince my nephew to see reason and join with me, you would make a stunning queen-consort to the fae. You and my nephew, under my guidance, would learn how to truly guide our people toward greatness. You would be royalty, with the ability to make a difference."

Dani stared at him, not quite sure she had heard correctly. Queen... consort?

The word, in relation to herself, felt like fitting a round peg into a square hole. A queen? Her? That was the logical conclusion to dating the prince of the fae, she supposed, but it didn't feel like an accurate description for her and Slate. They were just... Slate and Dani.

It was several seconds before she found her voice. "You can't mean this. Where's the catch?" She struggled to keep her tone neutral as she studied Zeyphar's face warily.

"No catch, I assure you. I speak in complete earnest, for the good of my people. I want my nephew by my side, to *learn* from me, to become the leader the fae deserve. Under my tutelage, he would learn to be a *true* king. For the good of all fae."

His words seemed reasonable... and yet the tiny hairs at the back of Dani's neck stood straight up. She had the distinct impression that when Zeyphar said *true* king, he meant *his* kind of king.

Dani didn't answer him, studying him carefully, when she sensed Zeyphar's heartfire flare. Exactly like when Slate was feeling her out. Swiftly, she shut all of her emotions down, sick to the stomach at the idea of allowing this fae access to her private feelings.

She might trust Slate not to abuse his power, but she had no such faith in Zeyphar.

She had no idea what Zeyphar gleaned from her emotions, but his eyes narrowed, even as his smile widened. "Take time to consider this offer, my dear. It would be unfortunate to rush yourself on such an important matter; mistakes in matters of war and royalty can be... disastrous."

"Is that a threat?" The words were out before she could stop them, a bit of spine despite her fear, and she suspected that spurt of courage came from the threat to Slate more than for herself.

"No, my dear, *that* is politics." His gaze flickered over her stiff form, perched on the edge of her seat like she was ready to flee at any moment, and lingered where her hand remained in her pocket. "I shall leave you then, to consider my generous offer. Remember, not only would Zlaet, and yourself, benefit from my proposition, but *all* fae would be richer for our alliance."

Dani said nothing. He considered her another moment before his lips thinned and his pleasant demeanor threatened to slip. He got to his feet with eerie grace, looming over her for a moment and causing her heart to stutter in her chest. Her fingers spasmed around the small handgun in her pocket. "Choose wisely, Tanyiel."

Unlike his other words, veiled in civility and dressed in a pleasant smile, these sounded very much like a threat. His brilliant eyes flashed with brief, arctic menace before he disappeared into a portal.

By the time Dani pulled into the alleyway next to Melisande Martial Arts, her hands were shaking.

Breathe... breathe...

"You would make a stunning queen-consort..."

She couldn't rinse off the feeling Zeyphar had left her with, that impression of an ice so cold, her bones felt brittle from it. During the long months that Slate had been gone, her mind and her dreams had blended and blurred the lines between Zeyphar's aura and Slate's, but having faced Zeyphar's anew, she'd never mistake them again. Slate's power tasted like the first breath of winter, like fresh snow; crisp and clean.

Zeyphar was little more than a desert of frigid ice. Arctic. Empty.

The streets of the Eastern District were saturated with sunset reds and oranges, but the studio windows were lit, and people were inside. Dani pushed open the front door, her breathing becoming harder and harder. *Slate, Slate, Slate.... Where was Slate?*

The sound of the martial arts classes was weirdly comforting—the sheer normalcy of it was a stark contrast to facing a fae king with deadly intentions. A tall figure clad in a black uniform stepped into the waiting room as the door snicked shut behind her, and Dani's heart stuck in her throat for a moment before she realized it wasn't Slate.

The man was too narrow to be Slate, and far too young—barely beyond a teenager. His uptilted dark eyes studied her curiously as he offered her a polite smile. "Hello, can I help you?"

It took a moment for her disappointed brain to switch gears, and she sucked in a steadying breath, forcing a small smile on her face. "I'm looking for Slate."

The young man's brows furrowed, and one slender hand rubbed at his sharp jawline somewhat shyly. "Oh, sorry, ma'am, but Master Melisande isn't here today. Is there something I can help you with? My name's

Ronin—"

"No." Dani shook her head, eyes tracking over the space, as if Slate might materialize out of the shadowy corners. Which, a part of her reckoned, he could. "I just... thank you."

She stepped around him and walked through the waiting room toward the back hallway that led to the stairs to his apartment.

"*Onee-san!*" the young man called after her. "Lady, you can't..."

Dani ignored him, hurrying down the hallway and pulling open the door leading upstairs with a sharp yank. The young man's voice echoed in the narrow stairway as she pounded up the stairs in time with her pounding heart.

She exploded into Slate and Ebisu's home to an answering, deafening... silence.

Empty.

Empty. And it tasted empty too. Like no one had spent a significant amount of time here for a while.

Empty. Empty.

Down the hall, she slid open Slate's bedroom door.

Empty.

Breathe, breathe.

She stood in the doorway, counting her breathing, searching the small room. A part of her recognized that she was acting irrationally, but the adrenaline in her system had her on overdrive.

She scanned the space. Dresser. Television on top. A narrow shelf of martial arts movies next to the dresser. Futon on a simple wooden frame. Functional. Neat. Clean.

And still empty, despite the three scans she made of the small space.

The last time she'd been in this apartment, he'd explained his empathy magic to her. Over a failed sushi dinner. Had that only been a couple of days ago?

And the last time she'd been in *this* room... well. Very different circumstances.

Dani pulled her phone out of her jacket pocket and dialed Slate's number again. It rang... and rang... and fucking *rang*—

"*Yo, It's Slate. You know what to do...*"

His voicemail. She hung up. She didn't need to leave him another message. Her heart jacked into her throat again.

Where was he? Had something happened in that little village? Titan's Fen? Is that why Zephar had come to her?

No, no, Slate could take care of himself. He was strong—

Screaming, screaming like someone was killing him, blood pouring out of his face, his eyes, his nose, as if his brain had turned into a bloody pulp inside his skull and was leaking out—

"Stop it! You're killing him!"

No.

No. He was fine. He wasn't the same person as he'd been in that arena, not anymore. Well, he was. But he wasn't.

He was fine.

Blue-gray eyes locked on hers for several frightened heartbeats. A beautiful, wrong *smile, as Kat was led away.*

The police at her door. "Your parents...There's been an accident—"

Dani slapped her own cheeks. "I'm safe here," she reminded herself. "Slate is fine. Slate is fine. Slate is *fine*."

She turned and walked out of the room and back down the hall. And paused in the living room.

She could stay here. She was safe here. And if Slate came home or finally answered his phone, he'd find her here.

But she was alone here.

Not alone, Sellie's voice echoed through her mind. *Have friends. Me. Pretty faeries.*

Friends. Right. Dani had friends.

You are not alone.

Roger.

Dani whirled around and stormed up the stairs and burst out onto the roof. Ebisu's beautiful garden greeted her, the sunset draping the plants in reds and golds and deep navy shadows. Sellie roosted in the corner in her nest, but the griffin ruffled her feathers and clicked her beak at Dani, following Dani's train of thought.

"Sellie, will you take me to the Den?" Dani asked, crossing the lovely garden—blooming still in the middle of winter—to where the griffin roosted. At Sellie's mental query, she pushed impressions of Roger, of Maddie and Loraine, and a sense of urgency.

Sellie didn't hesitate, soft white and gray feather ruffling as she lowered her haunches, and Dani slid on.

A PLEA TO SHADOWS

... resulting in the decimation of vampire numbers as well as a number of high ranking fae nobility. The fae's agreement to the Vampire Accords was predominantly attributed to Rowan Fafnir's senseless death after striving to resolve the conflict nonviolently...

– Gherald Schmidt, Faerloch Historical Archives

Roger swirled the glass in his hand and indulged in another sip. "This is delightful, Madeline," he said, a rare smile ghosting over his features. "Best batch yet."

"Tony will be thrilled, *cher*. He was trying to bring the sweetness back into this batch." With practiced efficiency, Madeline swept away the other empty flight glasses from the table.

"He has succeeded. My compliments."

The Den was quiet for the evening—most of the patrons were still celebrating the Solstice from the night before. Though, in fairness, it was still quite early. Loraine was taking care of some business in her office, leaving Madeline to tend the bar and one waitress flitting between the three sparse tables that held patrons.

Roger drained his flight and handed the glass over to the witch's waiting hand. "How was your Solstice?" he asked.

"Lewd and lascivious, as usual," she replied with a laugh. "Carrow managed to coerce a handful of the women to jump naked into the pond—"

He sensed her before he saw her, and his eyes flipped to the entrance as the door burst open, spilling Daniella into the bar.

Something was wrong.

He was moving before he had a conscious thought, sliding from the booth to stand as Madeline turned to follow his gaze. Daniella was practically running as she hurried toward them, not even sparing Madeline a glance before she near-collided with Roger, small fingers curling into the silk at his biceps.

"I need help, Roge," Daniella whispered urgently, verdant eyes too big in a face that was too pale.

Roger shifted minutely until his shoulders blocked her from the view of the occupied tables, gently untangling her grip from his arms as he took her hands.

"Breathe, Daniella," he murmured, turning her toward the privacy of the back kitchen door as Madeline flanked her other side. "What is wrong?"

"I need you to find Slate," Daniella explained, and the pitch of her voice was bordering on frantic. As Roger pushed the door open and ushered her inside, Madeline whistled, gesturing to the other waitress to keep an eye on the front as she slipped into the kitchen after Roger.

"I can't get ahold of him," the words burst out of Daniella, a hint of panic in her tone that had Roger's darkness bucking inside him, the sinister beast straining under Roger's relentless control. He forced himself to release Daniella's hands, but he couldn't make himself step back from her as she sucked in a shaky breath and continued, "Something is wrong, he's not answering his phone and Zeyphar said—"

"Take a breath, *cherie*," Madeline said, laying a hand between Daniella's shoulder blades.

"Zeyphar?" Roger said sharply, his darkness snarling to life inside him. "You spoke to him?"

"Yes." Daniella jerked her head in a nod. "I... I was in the Dark Arts Market, just... checking things out, you know, like I normally do, and he was just... *there*. All by himself, and he came right up to me."

She was babbling, and the darkness hissed at the idea of Zeyphar so close to her, coiling ever tighter against the grip he maintained on it.

Of course she'd been in the Dark Arts Market, the one location so saturated in protective magicks from all factions of the Lore that his own shadows were useless. There were countless anti-theft and anti-detection charms covering every inch of that block. It explained why he hadn't been alerted of a fae presence near her.

It also explained why Zeyphar had been emboldened to approach her.

The urge to ban her from going there again was strong, but he knew better than to limit her freedom for her own protection; he refused to cage her. He also knew it was fruitless to expect her to abandon any potential creature she could save from being trafficked.

Roger's nostrils flared, but he scented no blood. All the same, his gaze tracked over her, fighting back his bloodlust. "Are you alright? Did he touch you?"

"No, he didn't, I'm fine." She gave a sharp shake of her head, voice pitching. "This is not about me, Roge, it's Slate! Please, I can't get ahold of him and I don't know where to even begin to find him. I need you to go get him. Something is wrong, I can feel it—"

His mind was rapidly putting together information, trying to fill in the gaps in her story while also respecting the urgency with which she arrived, clearly distressed. "What did Zeyphar want?"

"He... he wants Slate and he wants me to bring Slate to him—it doesn't matter!" She latched onto his arms again. "You have to find Slate. I know it doesn't make sense for Zeyphar to ask me to bring him Slate if he already has him, but... Slate should have called or messaged me by now. What if something went wrong, or..."

There was panic written plain on her face as she stared at him, and his heart clenched in his chest. He slid his hands into the pockets of his slacks to keep from reaching out to her, the need to soothe her a thrum in his blood. He gave a sharp nod. "I will do my best, Daniella."

"Don't worry, *cherie*," Madeline urged as she slid an arm around Daniella's shoulders and squeezed her gently. "We can scry while we wait for Roger."

Daniella bit her lip as she nodded. "Please, Roger. I... I can't lose him again..."

Roger leaned down until she met his eyes, and offered her a smile because it was what she needed right then. She needed to see his confidence, and he would deny her nothing. "Trust in me. I will find your princeling. You can stay here or go home with Madeline."

He didn't wait for a response, knew the witch would look after her, before he stepped back into the waiting shadows.

Roger had never been to Titan's Fen before, had considered it a rather rustic little hamlet that floated the drifting currents of L'el like a small raft in an ocean of trees, but he was impressed with the ward he encountered when his shadows finally located it. It gave him pause, and made him reassess his estimation of the might of such a small settlement.

He decided shattering such a ward and fending off a battalion of fae soldiers would not expedite his mission, and besides, killing Slate's people seemed like the kind of thing that might upset Daniella further, and she was already distressed enough.

So he materialized on an ancient stone bridge in full view of an unassuming part of the Forest—nothing but trees all around him. He knew the scene was not what it appeared as he deliberately held his hands out to his sides. "I come seeking Slate Melisande," Roger announced in Faerish.

Silence was his reply, but Roger held himself perfectly still. Beyond the bridge, the trees shimmered and rippled until a narrow mountain pass materialized. Between the unsurmountable sheer cliffs was a fortified and crenelated stone wall spanning the pass. In the center of the wall, a large wooden gate slowly opened.

It was a formidable defense for such a small village. It would do nothing to stop him if he was of a mind to get past, but it would certainly deter a platoon of Silver Valley soldiers.

A wandering thought crossed his mind that he could assist Slate's fae in strengthening their defenses. He'd learned much over his lifetime in the ways of war and strategy, and it was becoming increasingly clear that he would have to keep Slate alive to keep Daniella happy.

As bows creaked along the top of the wall, a single figure appeared in the partially opened gate. "Who is asking, vampire?" the fae figure asked, one hand on the hilt of a sword.

"I am not currently a threat to you. I wish to speak with him. He will know who I am," Roger said, a hint of dry amusement lacing his tone.

The fae didn't take his eyes from Roger as he turned his head and shouted behind him. They waited, Roger sliding his hands into his pockets as he held the fae's gaze. It wasn't long before a familiar voice reached Roger's sharp hearing, one that brought a begrudging sense of relief. If Slate had indeed been taken by Zeyphar, Roger wouldn't have been able to retrieve him, especially if he'd been taken within the ward that surrounded the Silver Valley.

"Don't fucking shoot him," the voice grumbled from the other side of the wall, before a second figure stepped through the gap in the heavy wooden door.

The dark hair and unusual eyes were familiar, but the icy, near-arctic aura that radiated off the male had Roger's muscles tightening as Slate approached him. As Slate closed the distance, the chill of Slate's aura burned Roger's nose, and he curled his lip the darkness inside him strained.

Little in this world gave Roger pause anymore. But a young half-fae prince in his third decade of life with such a frozen, burning aura certainly made him pause. Even for the briefest of moments.

Inside him, almost gleefully, his darkness whispered, *Dangerous...*

To whom, Roger wasn't yet certain. Not to him, not yet, but to Daniella? To Slate himself? It made Roger uneasy, but he wasn't in much of a position to do anything about it, not without betraying Daniella's trust.

"Why are you here?" Slate demanded, storming toward him. "Is Dani alright?"

"She is fine. She is safe, but she is frantic," Roger supplied, watching Slate closely as he withdrew his hands from his pockets to hang loosely at his sides. Slate wouldn't know him well enough, but it was quite the compliment—it meant Slate's aura had Roger on his guard, and not much did that these days. "She has been trying to contact you." He allowed a little reprimand into his voice, brows lowering as he stared at the once-mortal.

Slate's hand absently patted at the pocket of his pants, scowling. "Phone service is spotty out here, depending on where we are in the Forest."

"Your uncle approached her this afternoon."

The arctic chill around Slate exploded outward until the air noticeably cooled around them, the color of Slate's eyes frosting over as he took a step closer to Roger.

"What?" he demanded, voice harsh.

"It appears he merely wished to talk and did not harm her." Roger held his ground to the storm of Slate's power, studying the hint of frost dusting the stone beneath Slate's feet with wary curiosity. "Over the summer, Loraine and I fed information to the Silver Valley that we would not tolerate anyone harming her." Roger's tone was grim, his temper simmering. "Zeyphar did not technically break our decree, he will argue, by speaking to her."

"That fucking *bastard*," Slate seethed, and Roger noticed the tattoos visible at the collar of his shirt darken in color. Slate ran an agitated hand over the shaved side of his head. "You're sure he didn't hurt her? What did he fucking say to her? *That's* why he didn't fucking show..." Slate growled, dropping his arm and fisting his hand. "Where is she?"

Roger paused and mentally reached for his shadows. Slate's eyes dipped, widening minutely, and the arctic cloak around him faltered. Roger almost smiled, knowing the sight of his personal shadows, much like snakes writhing around his body, could be rather disconcerting. It didn't take them long to whisper in his ear.

It went against his every instinct to let Slate near her in such a state. Slate's frost continued to coat the back of Roger's tongue, a stinging reminder of the madness that plagued male empaths.

But he couldn't deny Daniella her princeling, and he had to trust that this male would sooner kill himself than hurt his *mayt*. With only a brief hesitation, Roger inclined his head as his shadows retreated. "It appears Daniella has returned to her home with Madeline."

"Shit," Slate growled. "Shit, fuck, shit." He stormed across the bridge, and Roger turned to watch him. Without another word, Slate waved a hand and tossed a portal down by his feet.

"Tame that aura before you speak to her, or you will frighten her," Roger spoke, voice like a whip as the darkness inside him writhed with a protective fury, even as he held himself perfectly still.

Slate froze, one foot in mid-air, but the glare he shot Roger held enough heat that Roger hoped it would help thaw his icy aura. He offered the male a taunting smile, to stoke those flames, and Slate muttered a curse before he disappeared through the faerie ring.

Roger's cruel smile faded as he cast one more glance at the crenelated wall in the narrow mountain pass of Titan's Fen, noting the fae who continued to watch him suspiciously, bows at the ready. He inclined his head, then stepped into the abundant shadows cast by L'el's giant trees, vanishing.

CHAPTER · TWENTY

FORGIVENESS

… tying magic to the modern sciences of mortals, and as such, the ability to manipulate water has been recently used to investigate the molecular structure of a person and determine future magical strengths. This has been compared to the human study of DNA, though its uses…

– Gherald Schmidt, Faerloch Historical Archives

"He's fine, you know," Maddie chided gently, then patted the cushion next to her on the sofa. "Sit and drink your tea."

Dani moved on autopilot, plopping down on the couch and reaching for the tea without a thought. The hot cup warmed her fingers, and tugged her mind away from Zeyphar's cruel, calculating attention.

She couldn't stop replaying her encounter with Zeyphar over and over in her mind, processing the subtle nuances of his words. One seemingly insignificant detail kept nagging at her. He had called her *Tanyiel*, and something about that name sounded so *familiar*. She was certain she'd heard it before, or something like it, and yet she couldn't place where.

Dani turned her head toward Maddie, tea forgotten in her hands. "Hey, have you ever heard—"

An insistent knocking cut off her words, echoing from the hallway leading to the front door.

The knocks were forceful and sharp, and her heart knew who it was even before she heard the muffled voice calling her name. For a moment, she froze, relief crashing through her and leaving her head spinning in its wake.

Beside her, Maddie leaned over to gently bump Dani's shoulder with her own, chuckling. "*Bon*, I'll be on my way." She got to her feet, then offered Dani a coy smile. "Text me, *oui*?" she whispered with a wink, then whisked out the back sliding glass doors before Dani could say a word.

Dani was already moving, Maddie forgotten and the tea left haphazardly on the coffee table. Dash nearly tripped her as the little fox skidded to a stop in front of the door a breath before Dani reached it, and she had to shoo him to the side with a foot as she fumbled with the lock, heart pounding against her ribs.

The door hadn't even swung all the way open before Slate was inside the doorway with a burst of inhuman speed, large hands coming up to frame her face. "*Are you alright?*"

"Yes. I—" Her throat stuck, an overwhelming *relief* at the sight of him stealing her voice. He was alright. He was here. He hadn't left her.

Nothing had happened to him.

Slate's scent, like a brisk winter storm, slammed into her, calming her as the tension she'd been holding in her muscles eased.

His hands left her face, only to whisper down the sides of her neck, over her shoulders, and down her arms, his gaze sweeping over her, assessing her well-being both visually and physically. "I got here as fast as I could. I..." His nostrils flared and his eyes shot up over her head to scan the space behind her, his hands settling on her shoulders.

Dani glanced over her shoulder, then realized he must be scenting Maddie, but probably didn't know her scent yet. Looking back toward him, she gave into her needs and splayed a hand over his chest, soaking up the warmth of him. "It's just Maddie," she assured him. "She left when she heard you knocking." Which reminded her, so she mirrored him as she leaned to the side to look behind Slate. "Roger—"

"—is fine. Everyone's fine, nothing major." A warm hand pinned hers to his chest as Slate leaned down, and Dani moved on instinct, angling her head back. Slate hesitated for a breath right before his lips met hers, then he was kissing her in a way that sent fire to chase away the lingering ice of nerves from her blood.

It was over far too quickly, and Slate was ushering her inside, swinging the door shut behind him. His attention snagged downward, and Dani saw Dash winding through his legs. The little fox expressed his vexation at upsetting Dani in a series of annoyed chitters and yips.

"Hey, little guy." Slate reached down and stroked his palm over Dash's back and along his bushy tail. "Sorry, I didn't mean to freak you out."

Dash huffed out a breath, but he turned his head to lick at Slate's fingers before he scampered away from them and down the hall.

"Dash doesn't hold grudges," Dani said with a smile.

"He's a good boy," Slate agreed, but he glanced toward the door leading to the garage, and winced. "Sellie, however..." he whispered, a flush appearing over the top of his cheekbones and the tips of his ears. He glanced sheepishly at Dani. "Apologies, Selene," he called toward the garage door, hardly raising his voice.

Silence was the response, though Dani knew Sellie had heard, could hear the mental grumblings from the griffin and chose not to repeat them. "She heard you, she's just... stubborn," Dani explained, glancing toward the garage.

"I don't think Sellie's *ever* going to forgive me." Slate sighed, shaking his head. "Not that I blame her," he added hurriedly, rubbing at the back of his neck as his gaze swung from the garage back to her.

"She'll come around," Dani said with a little nod.

Slate's fingers whispered over her cheeks as he cupped her face once more, shoulders curving in as he leaned over her, gently tipping her face back to look up at him. "Are you *sure* you're alright? Roger said Zeyphar—"

"I'm fine," Dani assured him. The mere memory of the encounter was enough to make her break out in a cold sweat, but she refused to give in to the fear. She was done with it taking over her life. "I was more worried about you, because I couldn't get a hold of you. I thought maybe he had done something to you." Needing to touch him again, she flattened both palms against his chest as she stared up at him. "Where *were* you?"

"Some... political shit. Zeyphar got his hands on some of my scouts this morning, wanted to meet to exchange them. But he didn't show, sent one of his commanders in his place..." His expression suddenly tightened, a blaze of fury snapping across his face, so sharp and so sudden that her heart froze for a breath. "He planned that... to make sure he could see you without interruption." Dani could have sworn the temperature in the very *room* dipped.

She slid her fingers up from his chest to curve around his jaw, cupping his face as she held his gaze, wanting to soothe his agitation. "I'm fine, I promise. Sound of mind. Sellie had my back, Slate. I was fine. Besides, not even Zeyphar would have been able to cause trouble in the Dark Arts Market."

At her touch, he seemed to visibly calm, his eyes sliding shut for a moment as the air around them warmed in time with the deep breath he took. When his eyes opened, she smiled at him, and small butterflies took flight in her belly when he smiled back.

She stepped back from him and gestured vaguely behind her. "Do you... why don't you stay here for a bit?" She needed to be around him, needed to soothe her nerves with his presence.

He watched her, a heavy pause settling between them, and his heart-fire flared as he felt her out. She stared back, leaving herself as open as she'd closed herself for Zeyphar. His lips curved upward at whatever he must've found. "I'd like that, if you don't mind."

"I don't mind," she assured him, smile widening as she slipped her hand into his and led him toward the living room. She savored the way his fingers curled around hers, and chose not to relinquish the touch as they sat on the couch together. "So you're really okay?"

"Totally fine," he said. "There was a little miscommunication, but Kallen and I figured it out. They tried to get us to go to the Silver Valley, but... we didn't, obviously. We worked it out." He paused, assessing her once more as she gently squeezed the hand he held in his lap. "What did he say to you?" he asked softly.

Dani shrugged, pulling one knee to her chest and wrapping her free arm around her leg. "He... offered me something. A proposition."

His eyes narrowed. "What proposition?"

"He said... he said I should convince you to join him. So he can take you under his wing. Said it was for the benefit of all fae. He said... I would be a fine queen-consort." She glanced away, heat rising to her cheeks at the implications involved.

Slate froze stiller than stone, a silence stretching between them. He let out a slow breath and turned to look at her. "I... didn't want this," he finally admitted quietly. "I didn't want to bring... this... shit into your life."

Dani's heart skipped a beat at the anguish in his face, a reflection of his truth, a shot of vulnerability. She offered him a small smile. "You are definitely more trouble than I originally signed up for."

A little grin crossed his face, a touch wicked. "I'm more trouble than *I* signed up for, love."

She realized with a start that she'd missed that the most; his wicked charm. This new Slate was far more guarded around her than the old Slate had been.

She hated that, suddenly and fiercely.

"I've decided you're worth it, though," she said, eyes drifting away from his to where he still held her hand in his lap. "I don't think I'd ever be the same without you in my life. I..." she faltered, face heating.

She'd accepted his apology for leaving for six months, but she hadn't told him that she'd forgiven him. She hadn't really known for sure herself if she *had* forgiven him until she'd been faced with the possibility of losing him again. None of her anger or loneliness had mattered in the face of the possibility that Zeyphar had done something to him, that she might never see him again.

Putting those sentiments into words, however...

"Daniella," Slate murmured, reaching out to slide fingers over her skin until his palm gently circled her throat in that familiar, possessive touch. "It's okay... I can hear your feelings," his voice was a little raw around the edges.

For the first time, she was relieved by his use of magic, relieved that he could know how she felt without the messy miscommunication words often brought. Wrapping her free hand around his wrist, she untangled her other hand from his to slide her fingers over his jaw as she leaned up to feather her lips over his.

"I just... I want you to know that I forgive you, for leaving. That—"

"I know," Slate murmured against her lips. "I said I could hear your feelings, *ne*?"

Lips quirking, Dani savored the warmth of him, his comfort, his scent. His hand tightened gently on her throat, but he made no other move to deepen the kiss, displaying more of that restraint she was coming to hate. Needing more of him, needing to feel the vitality of him in her very being, she leaned into the kiss.

He released a breath against her lips like a sigh of relief, of yearning. Her eyes closed as her fingers slipped over his jaw, past the shorn hair above his ears and into the long strands tied up from his neck. She gently plucked the hair tie loose, dark silken strands cascading to his shoulders and tickling the backs of her hands.

"Daniella..." he whispered, and the ache in his voice sparked an answering heat inside her. She deepened the kiss as she teased his lips with her tongue, earning herself entry with a deep moan from him. His fingers at her throat tightened gently as he angled her head to slide his tongue along hers, claiming her mouth so thoroughly, her head spun.

Dani shifted, sliding a leg over his to straddle his lap. His hands landed at her waist, nudging the material of her shirt up until he splayed his strong fingers against the bare flesh of her waist.

He shifted a palm to her ribs, his thumb feathering against the flesh below her breast, and her back arched instinctively. A fierce, pulsing need thrummed through her. "Slate," she whimpered, breaking the kiss.

His mouth shifted down her neck, and something uncorked between them. His fingers tightened at her waist, clutching at her as his lips left a trail of heat over her collarbone, and her head fell back. An inferno was building inside her with every brush of his lips, and she found herself rocking her hips against his as she clutched at his hair.

"Can I spend the night?" His voice was raw and ragged, kissing her throat as his fingers delved under her bra, fingertips teasing her nipple.

She might combust then and there. "What's in it for me?" she teased breathlessly.

His answer was a searing kiss, a tangle of lips, teeth, and tongues that had her stomach clenching and heat spearing through her veins like hot lightning. He didn't need words to express his intentions with a kiss like that...

Her world tilted suddenly, strong arms sliding down to cup her bottom as Slate hefted her up and straightened in one smooth move. He held her flush to his body, and another whimper escaped her as the hard evidence of his arousal pressed tight to the juncture between her legs. He hissed out a curse as she writhed helplessly against his length, and his legs ate up the distance to the stairs.

He took them two at a time, moving with fae speed until her back was hitting her mattress. She didn't have time to bounce even once before his body was blanketing hers, his hips settling firmly between her legs as he ground down mercilessly, lips finding her throat. She gasped, breathing fast, fingers digging into his shoulders.

His teeth found the little half-moon scars where her neck met her left shoulder, and he bit down at the same time as he thrust against her.

Dani's back arched as a cry escaped her, her orgasm catching her off guard and exploding through her. Pleasure stole her breath, and all she could do was cling to him and writhe as he continued to thrust against her, drawing it out until she was gasping and pushing at his shoulders.

She still had her pajama pants on, for goodness sake.

His teeth released her neck, his tongue stroking her skin. A shiver raced through her bones.

Then he was kissing her again, tongue sliding along hers, devouring her. She was drowning. Drowning in his mouth, in his hands, the aching need along her skin, the same ache between her thighs. She could practically taste the twisting swirl of sexual energy in the room. She couldn't get enough. Enough of him. Enough of his touch. Enough breath.

They came up for air only to shed pieces of clothing. Shirts slipped to the floor. Her bra followed. His hands shaped over every inch of her, as if he were a starving man and she a feast.

She let out a whimper of protest when he sat back, but it died in her throat when he started tugging her pajama pants off. Her eyes landed on the breadth of his exposed shoulders, his muscled chest, and a gasp slipped free.

His hands stilled for a second, eyes lifting to catch hers.

She swallowed her dry throat. "Your tattoos..." She hadn't realized the *extent* of them—from his wrists to his collarbone, right down to his hips. They covered his entire torso and arms in a stunning display of characters and sharp strokes, scrolling over his skin. They were tinted a different color than the pale color she'd spied on his arms before, now they were a deep, mahogany brown... almost *alive* with color.

She suddenly wanted to lick every single one of them.

She saw his breathing hitch, his chest heaving as he noted her stare, the heat in her eyes. He swallowed hard. "You like them?"

"Yes," she breathed, voice husky with the heat swirling through her blood.

"Holy *fuck*, Dani. Keep looking at me like that, and I'm gonna come right now."

Her stomach clenched at the raw, unbridled arousal on his face. She shimmied out of her pajama pants, leaving herself clad only in her panties, before she reached forward for his pants. She hooked her fingertips into the waistband and tugged him closer to her. His own hands joined hers, to help, to stop, she didn't know, but she batted his hands away as she shot him a look. He fisted his hands at his sides as he indulged her, watching with rapt attention as she tugged them over his hips.

His cock sprang free, and molten heat pooled between her legs as she reached out to wrap her fingers around him.

Stroked once.

"*Fuck*," Slate hissed, and his hips jerked as his eyes rolled back, face tipping toward the ceiling. She stroked again, from the base of his cock right up to the tip in a long, single pass. He groaned loudly, and his tattoos shifted from deep brown to something a shade darker, a rusty ebony.

Unspoken was the fact that he was teetering on the edge of his control, his entire body practically vibrating with anticipation.

What would it be like, for Slate to snap that tether of control? Her throat dried up at the knowledge that her nerves around his fae strength stood no chance against the arousal that rose at the idea of him dominating her with all of that unleashed fury. Her face in the pillows... his cock buried to the hilt, seed spilling down the inside of her leg as he pounded into hers... teeth at her neck...

Goddess help her.

Part of her wanted to have it his way.

Slate's nostrils flared, and she was on her back, his heavy body pinning hers to the bed as he slashed his mouth over hers. Consuming her. His free hand curved around her throat and slid up her jaw, tilting her face to kiss her harder. Deeper. She moaned, digging her fingers into his shoulders.

He pulled back, both of them gasping for air. "I need to be inside you."

"Yes," she breathed, hips rolling.

He braced one elbow by her head and reached between them to grasp himself. He dragged the head of his erection along her soaked panties, swearing at the wetness he found.

Releasing himself, he pushed back onto his knees and hooked a finger in the hem of the panties. He dragged the material down her legs, over her ankles and toes, then tossed them over his shoulder. He ran that same finger down the very center of her, gaze locked on what he was doing.

The utter focus, the raw hunger there, had her pulse jacking higher as she rolled her hips, pleasure melting through her at his touch. She gasped his name as he slipped two fingers into her, the pressure intense and sharp. More. Goddess above, she needed *more.*

"More," she moaned, thrusting her hips into his hand. "*Please.*"

"Easy, love. You're so tight."

He worked her with his hand, harder, deeper, his other hand wandering over her skin, teasing her breasts, palming her throat, his thumb stroking the scar on her neck. Just before she was ready to fall over the edge into another orgasm, he pulled his hand back. She watched, breathing hard, as he sucked his fingers into his mouth.

A whimper escaped her.

Simply watching him was pleasure itself. She wanted his hands on her body, ached for his mouth on hers, ached for every inch of him to fill her...

There was a near feverish light in Slate's eyes as he shifted to angle his cock against her entrance, his own breathing accelerating as a fine sheen of sweat coated his skin.

He pressed his cock into her, and she swallowed another moan at the fullness of him. Her fingers clenched into the sheets in sheer ecstasy as Slate worked himself inside her in a series of short, powerful thrusts, his hands sliding under her thighs to push her legs wider apart. It was intimate, wild, and satisfied some deep, primal need inside her.

"Fuck yes," he growled, fucking her in deep, hard thrusts that would have moved her across the bed if he wasn't holding her in place. Again, and again, and *again*...

She needed this. Needed him. Needed his body inside her. Needed this like she needed oxygen.

Slate's gaze locked with hers, and he dropped his elbows on either side of her head. The glow behind his eyes blazed with an emotion that had her breath catching, but his mouth claimed hers again, rendering her mindless as he pumped his hips powerfully, deep, hard, fast.

Slate slipped a hand under her ass, hauling her up and angling her as he picked up the pace, his warm breath finding her neck. Dani's fingers curled into his hair, holding him tight as she writhed beneath him, breath sawing from her lungs as her pleasure mounted with each thrust.

"Goddess... Slate..." she gasped.

His grip on her ass tightened as he growled and nipped at her neck. His thrusts reached a frenzied pace, and she knew it was coming before he did it.

And Goddess above, maybe she was crazy, but she wanted him to do it.

He bit her neck. *Hard.* Pleasure burst in a kaleidoscope behind her eyelids as her orgasm raged through her. She screamed his name, arching back, her fingers digging into his back, gripping hard.

He released her neck and shoved himself up onto his free hand, fucking her wildly. "Fuck, Daniella, I'm gonna come—" and his pace staggered as he shouted her name as his own climax ripped through him, sending another bolt of pleasure rioting through her.

The pleasure ebbed like a wave receding from the beach, leaving Dani limp and breathless. Slate's chest heaved above her, and his eyes were wild as he stared down at her. Neither one of them spoke for several racing heartbeats. Until finally, Slate eased down onto his elbows again and tucked his face into her neck.

"Daniella, listen..." he said quietly, his voice gravelly. She felt his mouth trace the scars on her neck in a tender kiss. "I have to tell you something."

"Hmm?" She traced her fingertips over his shoulders, feeling boneless and utterly content for the first time in months.

He was quiet again for a moment. "Just. Listen. We... I—"

The backyard windows exploded inward, showering them with glass.

Time seemed to slow. Dani's world flipped once again, and she found herself pressed face-down into the carpet on the far side of the bed, away from the window, Slate's body covering hers.

Several rapid heartbeats ticked by as her pleasure-soaked mind desperately tried to catch up to what was happening. "Slate... what—"

"Someone's here..." his voice was rough around the edges, decidedly not human.

SMOKED OUT

... like their counterparts in other magical cultures, the Xtabay (esh-ta-bye) are an exclusively female race who are thought to lure male travelers to their deaths. However, Lore researcher Elke von Turig spent time among the Xtabay on the Yucatan Peninsula and discovered...

— Gherald Schmidt, Faerloch Historical Archives

Someone was here.

On Dani's property.

Slate spread his senses out, casting his net wide as he swept the vicinity for emotional grids. It was an effort when the scent of Dani's fresh blood made his head roar. Her cuts were minor, grazing, but instinct had rage exploding behind his eyeballs.

That tight, icy ball of energy that lived inside him cracked, spearing through his veins, through his head, sharpening and narrowing his focus to two simple facts—Dani was trembling beneath him, and the cause of her acrid fear was an unseen threat outside the house.

"Stay," he said to her, and slowly, he shifted off her, reaching for his pants and hurriedly tugging them on. Dani sat up and snatched her t-shirt and pajama bottoms from the floor, tugging them on with shaking hands as she remained crouched next to the bed. Her terror was a tangible taste in his mouth, his fae sense of smell and his empathic magic blaring alarms at him to *fix this*.

To have his *mayt*—to have *Dani* be afraid... no. Not on his watch. Those responsible would *die*. His bare feet avoided the broken glass as he silently crossed the room to peer out the window into the backyard.

Darkness greeted him at first. Then... he saw them. Three tall, lithe figures stalked along the border of her ward beyond her backyard, surveying the house.

He swore violently under his breath.

"What?" she whispered, peering over the edge of the bed.

He slid his gaze to her, and from the way her eyes widened, he could tell his own must be doing that almost-glowing thing they did when his magic was close to his skin. "Looks like Zeyphar sent some friends."

Her panic spiked hard, nearly smothering him. "*Fae* friends? But I have a ward for the house."

"Looks like they threw some Molotov cocktails," Slate growled, rage building in his blood. "I imagine your ward isn't spelled against ordinary objects, or you'd never get mail." Would a ward be enough to keep out three determined fae soldiers?

He wished he knew more about wards. He peered out the window again. Had he been followed here? Impossible. He'd taken every precaution. He'd covered his tracks and his magic before coming here.

"Sellie's aware. She's... upset," Dani murmured, eyes wide as saucers, and her tone implied the griffin was more than *upset*. A hint of a viridescent glow flickered at the edges of Dani's irises, stark against her too-pale face.

"I fucking bet she is..." he muttered, turning his attention back to the fae prowling outside. Two of the fae had unfamiliar emotional grids, but the third?

Gelayeth. He'd recognize that cold, rotting mind anywhere.

Voices drifted up to him from out the window. He tuned his hearing, angling his head to catch the words more clearly.

"This is the correct location?" one of them said. *"I cannot sense her presence here."*

"It's a witch ward... Do you not scent her? This is her property."

"She must be here. Drive her out. We cannot portal from her property, and we cannot get in the house without permission of the host."

Her?

Slate's ire heightened, swelling under his skin in a frigid ball of violent anger.

These High Fae weren't here for *him*... they were here for *Dani*.

His eyes shot to her, and too late, he realized his expression had given it away. Color drained from her face, the freckles across her cheeks standing out like blood splatter.

"They're not here for you, are they?" she asked, her voice barely a thread of sound. Her tone pitched higher, even as she struggled to keep it even. "They didn't follow *you* here... they followed *me*." Her eyes widened in horror at the realization.

"I won't let anything happen to you," he said firmly. He leaped over the broken glass and back to the bedside next to her. He curled his palm around her throat, protectiveness surging through him, heady and sharp. "Dani... look at me." Her gaze snapped to his, her breathing growing erratic, panic and terror steadily spiraling together. "Nothing is gonna happen to you."

"Why are they here? Why me...?" Her eyes slipped from his face, becoming unfocused, before they widened and snapped back to his face. "I'm bait."

The fingers around her throat spasmed as fury pitched through his head. They'd both refused his uncle. And now... Zeyphar was coming for what he knew would break Slate the fastest.

The problem was that it was a flawless plan. If his uncle had been successful in luring Dani—or nabbing her if she refused— to the Silver Valley, Slate would follow. Without question or consequence. "We need to leave. Now."

"Leave?"

"Yes. Leave." Her property was warded against portalling, and the house itself was warded against physical entry from any who didn't have permission to do so. They couldn't come into the house, but he couldn't portal them out, either. They were, effectively, trapped. He pulled her to her feet, but she resisted when he tried to tug her toward the door.

"No, we're safe here," she told him with a sharp shake of her head, some of the panic ebbing from her wide eyes. "The ward will keep us safe. So long as I don't invite them inside the house, they can't get in. We should stay and—"

There was a loud *boom*, and Dani let out a startled scream as the house shook abruptly. The sound of breaking glass filtered in through the open bedroom door as the rest of the windows in her house shattered.

There was a heartbeat of eerie silence as they held their breath... and the darkness of her bedroom was chased away by an orange light. In the dark of the night through the broken windows, flames leaped up the siding to flirt with the edge of the windows.

Dani's hand flew to her mouth as horror bloomed across her face and her emotions, so suddenly and jaggedly that she swayed where she stood. "My house..."

Driving her out. They couldn't sense her, couldn't get in through her ward, but they were acting under the assumption she was here... and if they couldn't get in, they were going to try to smoke her out.

Another rumbling shake, and a picture frame next to her bed tumbled to the ground, glass cracking, books jumping free of the bookcase. Trinkets danced across her dresser and a lamp crashed to the floor. Dash flew into the room, gekkering in panic, and Dani scooped him up, holding him to her chest.

"Time to go," Slate said, tone leaving no room for argument. He scooped Dani and the fox up into his arms. He made it one step over the broken glass before Dani's cry stopped him. She was reaching for the fallen picture frame.

He flexed his telekinesis, and the picture frame shot toward them. He was already moving as she snatched it out of the air. He flew down the stairs two at a time. "What about your other animals?"

"I ordered them to run," Dani told him, and it was all he needed to hear before he was shouldering his way into the garage, the door banging against the wall from the force of their entry.

Half-crouched between her nest and the closed garage door, Sellie hissed her displeasure when she saw them. Slate wasted no time, rushing forward to dump Dani and Dash onto the griffin's back. For once, he and Sellie seemed to agree, because she lowered her haunches to make it easier on him, beak clicking anxiously.

When he was certain Dani wouldn't slide from Sellie's back, he moved to grab a shovel from the corner of her garage, and with a hard snap, he broke off the metal head and twirled the handle like a staff.

"Slate..." Dani's voice was uncertain.

Sellie moved to flank him as Slate hurried to the garage door, reached overhead, and yanked the red cord hanging down, disengaging the door from the power supply.

"Ready, Sellie?" he growled, and the griffin snapped her break sharply. He latched onto the door with his magic and yanked it open hard and fast.

And stopped short

Gelayeth stood in the driveway, a mere handful of feet from them, and in his peripheral vision, he spied the other two coming around from the sides of the house.

An effective barricade between them and the edge of the ward, and not enough space for Sellie to get out and airborne.

"Ah, Prince Zlaet," Gelayeth greeted with a cold smile, hard gray eyes sliding between them. Slate caught an echo of surprise from the other two fae as they closed the distance, flanking their commander on either side. "We meet again this day."

"Surprise, mother-fuckers." He pointed his makeshift staff at the trio of High Fae. "Leave. Now."

Gelayeth made a musing noise, gaze bouncing around, taking in the house—and the flames that hungrily ate up the siding—eyeing the trees and the neighboring homes. A slight pressure to his senses told Slate that the reason none of the neighbors had noticed that Dani's house was on fire was due to a glamour, one held in place by all three of the fae, but anchored by the male to Gelayeth's left. The fae commander's smile slowly widened. "Where is your entourage? Did you leave the guard dogs at home this evening, Zlaet?"

Sellie's wings ruffled as she took a threatening step forward, fur and feathers alike puffing up until she appeared much larger than she was. Lowering her head, she opened her beak and let out an enraged hiss that ended in a dangerous feline rumble, as though to say: *Who need a guard dog when you have a guard* griffin.

If he wasn't so pissed off, Slate might have smiled at the way the two fae accompanying Gelayeth paled. "I said *leave*," he snarled at the trio. "We won't ask a third time."

"I'm afraid we cannot leave. You see, we have business with Tanyiel. And since you are here as well, and alone, we will take our business up with you." Gelayeth's smirk was feline in its delight, like a cat who'd cornered not one, but *two* mice, and didn't know which to devour first.

"Touch her, and your death will be swift." Despite the flames mere feet away, the temperature around them dropped. In his periphery, he saw Dani's breath fog the air as frost crept out along the cement beneath their feet.

Gelayeth tipped his head. "Interesting. The Malady's ice is beginning to sink its claws into you—"

Something popped inside the house. A hiss of air as fire devoured her home. Dani let out a pained whimper, head jerking as she looked up as if she could see through the ceiling of the garage and into her house. Slate didn't take his eyes off the trio in front of him, even as Dani's unbearable emotional distress beat against his senses. He knew how much her home meant to her—it was all she had left of her parents.

He forced himself to focus, to close off Dani's emotions. The end of her driveway marked the end of the ward. Beyond it—safety. He knew as well, that behind her house, the edge of the treeline was the demarcation of the ward on that side.

If he could get there, he could portal her out.

Gelayeth beckoned them with his hand. "I tire of playing games with you, princeling. You and Tanyiel will come with us. You will be perfectly safe, I assure you."

The shift was subtle, nuanced, and if he hadn't been an empath himself, he might not have realized it. The cold rage swirling in his chest... calmed. Hints of joy, relaxation, and assurance slid in through cracks along that ball of fury inside him.

Behind him, Dani let out a relieved sigh, and he glanced over to see she'd loosened her death grip on Sellie's ruff, a hint of a smile tugging at her lips. Dash, held to her chest by one arm, wriggled and let out a yip, clearly disturbed by Dani's sudden change in behavior.

Renewed fury obliterated those foreign emotions from his grid, and he bared his teeth at the fae as he used his magic to snatch those emotional threads. With a flex of his magic, he snapped the threads free from Dani and himself, and on instinct, he did something he'd never done before. He yanked at those mental threads. Hard.

The female fae to Gelayeth's right gasped. He honed in on that sound, blasting a cacophony of anguish, sadness, horror, and blinding fury back up the threads with enough force to blast her mental door right off its hinges. Going deathly pale, the female fae staggered a step, long fingers flying up to either side of her head.

Next to him, Dani sucked in a wobbly breath as Sellie let loose another vicious hiss. Slate caught a whisper of hysterical panic and confusion twisting from her, emotions that tasted solely of Dani's own true feelings.

"*You*," Slate snarled, pointing his staff at the female, "are so far out of your league, we aren't even playing the same fucking *game*."

He amped up those negative emotions that he shoved at the female, and added to them a replica of Dani's feeling of pure panic, confusion, and that helplessness of violation. Fed them back multiplied to an untold degree.

The fae female dropped like a stone, right to her knees, a scream ripping from her throat. He shifted his attention to the other two fae, but came up against hastily reinforced, iron-clad mental defenses, even as they fell back a step.

"Fascinating," Gelayeth murmured, eyeing the female fae but offering no assistance to his comrade. "You've inherited your mother's gifts."

But Slate's focus was already back on the female fae. He kept funneling horror, relishing her scrabbling mental claws as she desperately tried to dislodge him. This fae *garbage* had threatened his *mayt*, violated her, and tried to manipulate her. Had tried to do the same to himself. He took an unconscious step closer, all personal emotion eddying out of his head. A wall of ice closed in around his mind as he watched the person who threatened his *mayt* writhe, pumping more fear down the thread between them—

"Slate." Dani's voice cut through the rush of icy fury. Still clutching Dash to her chest with one arm, she reached out to brush her fingers over his shoulder with the other. "Slate, stop."

Like sunshine cutting through the wild winter storm that brewed inside him, her touch and her words grounded him, shooting clarity through the cloud of anger. Slate blinked, then dropped that thread of magic connecting him to the female fae. With a snarl, he sent out a blast of telekinetic magic. All three High Fae staggered backward at the same time as he whirled around and snatched Dani from Sellie's back.

Dash yipped uncomfortably from Dani's arms, but Slate was already moving, hauling both of them toward the garage door to the house.

"But Sellie!" Dani cried, trying to turn back. She shifted Dash to one arm, supporting the fox under his bottom with his face peering over her shoulder.

"She'll be fine, she can take care of herself. They're after us, not her," Slate urged, pushing her through the door and into the house. Smoke suffocated them as he hurried Dani down the hall toward the back slider door. She stumbled, coughing, but Slate grabbed her free arm and hauled her after him and through the broken slider doors.

They shot into the backyard. Slate clasped her wrist in a bruising grip as they sprinted across the grass. A shriek pierced the air behind them, and Slate angled his head to spy the High Fae rounding the corner of the house with Sellie hot on their heels.

A shimmer rippled along the grass, and he pulled up short as binding circles peppered the ground around them. He yanked Dani and Dash close to him and reached deep inside him into the well of magic thrumming under his skin. It spiraled up the shovel handle, swelling and fracturing the wood before he slammed it into the ground, creating a shockwave that surged toward the High Fae.

The binding circles died in a shimmer of sparkling gold, clearing their path.

He yanked Dani to a halt just beyond the ward boundary. "Go to Kari's," he said. His voice shook with rage, the ice storm in his chest growing, his tattoos pulsing closer and closer to a bright crimson. The High Fae were closing in on them. "I'll take care of the fae."

"Wait—what? Slate... Slate, no," Dani started, her grid lighting up with a greater panic than when she realized her house was on fire. She shifted Dash and the picture frame to one arm and reached for him with her other, her eyes impossibly large in her faerie face. "Don't leave me alone—"

He grabbed her face and pressed a hard, fast kiss to her mouth. "You won't be alone, you'll be with Kari. I need you to be safe." He made a portal at her feet. He locked eyes with her, sapphire clashing against stark emerald. "I love you," he told her.

And he pushed her into the portal.

CHAPTER   TWENTY-TWO

PROTECTIVE PANIC

... for they believe chi is inhabited by all living things, and not exclusive to magical folk. This has been the standard philosophy of the manyeo, whose magic is rooted in the manipulation of chi...

– Gherald Schmidt, *Faerloch Historical Archives*

The absolute stillness of the night was near-suffocating as Dani emerged from the portal at the edge of the ward around the Eastern District. She stared across the bridge as panic rioted through her. For several erratic heartbeats, she stood in place, disoriented, wrestling with her own out-of-control emotions. Dash let out a yip of protest, and she instantly loosened her grip on him as her mind *raced*, trying to keep up with the adrenaline surging through her.

The High Fae had *followed* her home. Slate hadn't said as much, but she'd read it in his eyes, in his expression, in the fury and intense protectiveness on his face. They'd come to take her to the Silver Valley. To lure Slate.

Furious purpose flooded her, and suddenly she was sprinting down the bridge toward the Eastern District, heedless of her bare feet. Her pajama-clad legs ate up the distance as she rounded the corner at the end of the bridge and shot toward Kari and Jian's house. When Dash started wiggling, she released him, and he streaked alongside her.

Dani *reached* with her senses. Strained with everything she had to try and reach Sellie... but the griffin was too far away. She knew Sellie would be safe, but Slate's face from the arena last summer, bleeding after Zeyphar released the glamour on his magic, kept flashing in her mind. Dani bit back a sob and pushed herself to move faster, her breath sawing from her lungs.

Dani slammed through the small waist-high gate and into Kari and Jian's small front yard, bare feet catching on the stepping stones. The broken picture of her parents skittered from her hands as her knees hit the mossy ground hard. Dash let out a sharp yip of concern at her side, but she was already scrabbling to her feet.

Ahead of her, the door slid open. "Dani!" Kari was moving with all of her inhuman speed, the *kitsune's* deceptively delicate fingers steadying Dani before she even got to her feet. "What's wrong?" Kari demanded, her gray eyes missing nothing as she took in Dani's bare feet and pajamas.

"Slate's in trouble," Dani nearly sobbed, clutching at Kari with both hands. "The fae—Zeyphar's fae came. They followed me *home,* Kari. It's *my* fault. I need you to take me back. We have to help him!"

"Slate's in trouble?" Kari's eyes sharpened, her expression hardening in the blink of an eye. A shiver raced down Dani's spine as a hint of ghostly cyan flames danced within her pupils. "At your house?"

Dani nodded frantically. "Yes. I need you to take me back there. I know you can teleport or something. You can take me with you! We need to help him, Kari. I can't—he can't *leave* me like this!" Dani knew she sounded hysterical, knew her words didn't make much sense. Technically, *she* had left him, but it didn't feel like that in her heart.

What if he was taken? What if he *died*? Then *he* would be leaving *her,* and that caused a panic inside her that wiped all rational thought from her brain.

"Calm down," Kari urged her as she gently disengaged herself from Dani's grip, and when Dani opened her mouth to demand they start moving already, Kari's hand came up lightning fast.

She flicked Dani's nose. Stunned, Dani stared at the smaller woman, eyes watering from the sting, but panic no longer overrode her senses.

"Slate needs you to stay calm right now," Kari said in a quiet but sharp voice, and Dani sucked in a breath. "I'm talking to Jian. He's headed to your house with Kallen right now."

"Dani-*san*," a deep voice interrupted, and Dani whipped her head to the side to see Joon, Kari and Jian's father, stepping down from the porch with a steaming mug of tea held between both hands. "Drink this," Joon ordered in a pleasant, steady voice, his dark gaze holding hers as he smiled.

Dani blinked at the older man she'd only met a handful of times, at the calm smile he offered her, before her gaze dropped to the handleless mug in his hands. An ingrained sense of politeness had her taking the mug before she even realized it.

"Drink, please," Joon repeated calmly, gesturing to the tea, and Dani drank, the movement as automatic as taking the tea had been. Warmth slithered down her throat, and the jittery anxiety in her chest eased, shoulders relaxing a fraction as the scent of mixed herbs invaded her nose.

"Good. Now come inside. My son will find Slate-*kun*," Joon ordered once more, the gentle but firm inflection in his voice unwavering. As if he had full confidence in his son. He smiled and winked at Dani, cheerful despite the situation. "You will not help him out here."

Dani hesitated, a part of her still frantic to get to Slate herself, but the tea and Joon's voice grounded her enough to keep from making a spectacle of herself in plain view of the street. She turned toward the house, then stopped and whirled back.

Kari was right there, holding the cracked picture frame of her parents. Relieved, she took it from Kari and followed Joon inside, careful not to trip over Dash.

"Karisi, prepare the clean room for your father and brother, just in case," a stern female voice snapped out as the door slid shut behind the three of them. Kari's mother stood in the small sitting room, hands on her hips as she studied Dani. "Dani-*chan*, come here."

Anzu, as usual, had a no-nonsense expression on her face as she gestured to the low table situated in the center of the room, the same table Dani often sat at to have tea with Kari. Unlike Joon's gentle cajoling, Anzu's order left no room for argument. The older *kitsune* stared Dani down until she reluctantly drifted to stand next to the table. Dani was intimidated by the woman enough that she didn't resist when Anzu's surprisingly strong grip on her shoulder urged her down to the floor cushions at the table.

"Sit and drink your tea. No talking until that cup is empty, understood?" Anzu instructed.

Dani didn't respond, but she brought the tea back to her lips and sipped, which seemed to satisfy Anzu, because the older *kitsune* nodded firmly and sat across from her. The warmth from the tea continued to chip at the icy ball of anxiety in her chest, but her mind wouldn't stop *racing* with images of Slate, injured after the championship fight last summer.

What if that happened again? What if it was *worse?*

Just as her thoughts began to spiral with renewed panic, shadows pooled in the corner of the room. Anzu snarled in a low rumble, familiar ghostly blue flames flickering over her hazel eyes as her head whipped toward the corner. Before Anzu could do more than rise to her feet, Roger stepped out of the shadows, eyes zeroing in on Dani instantly.

"Daniella."

Dani lurched to her feet, nearly dropping the tea mug, as a renewed sense of desperation overcame her. If Kari wouldn't take her to Slate, maybe Roger would. Dani cut in front of Anzu and launched herself at the vampire, fisting her hands in his pressed white shirt for the second time that day. "Roger! Roger, the fae... Zeyphar's fae came. Slate is in trouble, you need to—"

"Breathe." Roger's gaze flitted back and forth between hers. "Breathe, Daniella. You are not alone here."

She tried. Goddess above, she tried to breathe, but the panic in her chest was a vise. "People leave and they don't come back, Roger, he's gonna leave me alone—you need to take me to him, *please.*"

"No one is leaving you, Daniella. You need to stay here. *I* will go—"

"No, take me with you. Don't you leave without me." She tightened her grip on his shirt, stepping closer to him.

"No, you must stay here where it is safe—"

"I have to go *back*," her tone shifted, the panic inside her becoming something... harder, swelling inside her, larger and larger, a beating, pounding need. *Go back, go back, go back to Slate.* An instinct that started as a whisper the moment she'd met him, but had grown to a howl in her blood.

Roger's long fingers encircled her wrists as he tried to gently dislodge her fingers. "Daniella—"

Kari's voice interrupted, rose-gold hair flashing in Dani's periphery as she appeared at their side. "Jian says Slate's safe. They're coming back, right now."

Dani whipped her head around to Kari, fingers loosening Roger's shirt. "Is he hurt?"

The *kitsune* motioned with her hand. "Come sit, he'll be here soon."

"*Is he hurt, Kari?*" Dani refused to move.

Steps sounded outside on the stone pathway. The sliding door slammed open and two figures rushed inside.

No, not two... three.

Jian, the fae male Kallen, and on Kallen's back, limp and unconscious... was Slate.

Dani's knees gave out under her, but Roger's arm was already around her, catching her before she hit the floor. Her hands flew to her mouth, as if she could shove the sob back into her throat and keep all of this from happening.

Slate's cheek rested against Kallen's shoulder, soaked to the bone, dark hair in disarray and plastered to his face, as if he'd gone swimming. His tattoos had faded to a light henna, and blood dripped in thin rivulets down his face and his right arm, dripping off his limp fingertips.

Kallen stopped dead in the foyer, heather eyes locking on Roger.

Dani got her feet underneath her and pushed herself off of her best friend and toward Slate.

Kallen's eyes shifted to her. "He's alright, *Tana*, he simply expended a great amount of magic."

She brushed her shaking fingers against Slate's face, pushing his hair off his forehead. His brows knit together at her touch, and she sucked in a hard breath when one bright eye slid open to focus on her, then fluttered shut again.

"Put him in there," Jian said to Kallen, gesturing toward a door to their right—the room Kari had been preparing. Joon's workroom.

Kallen gave Dani a slight bow of his chin, and his gaze flickered warily back to Roger once more before he headed toward the clean room. Dani made to follow him, to keep Slate in her line of sight, but Jian stopped her with a hand on her shoulder.

"I need you to stay out here," the witch-doctor said gently. "As soon as *to-san* and I patch him up thoroughly, he's all yours." Joon was already stepping into his workroom, gesturing for Kallen to follow.

Dani stared at Jian, then she glanced over his shoulder to where Kallen had disappeared into Joon's workroom. She knew if she protested hard enough, Jian would allow her in there. Panic had the words on her lips, her body leaning forward for the fight, but—

But Jian was a doctor. He knew what he was doing. Jian wouldn't let *anything* happen to his best friend.

She sucked in a breath, forcing herself to tear her eyes away from the doorway. She trusted Jian.

More importantly, she trusted him with Slate.

She nodded. "Alright."

CHAPTER · TWENTY-THREE

WAITING FOR WINTER'S TOUCH

... Éire, bringing many of their fae traditions, which were then deeply interwoven into the culture and lore of the human populace...

- Gherald Schmidt, Faerloch Historical Archives

"What happened to Zeyphar's fae?"

Kallen's focus shifted to hers from where he was standing vigil outside Joon's workroom. Dani sat on a floor cushion at the low table, a fresh mug of tea in front of her.

A long, tense hour had passed, but Jian and Joon were still working to heal Slate. Kari had disappeared a while ago to deal with the fallout of the fight. Roger too, had disappeared, but Dani had a suspicion he wasn't far away.

Leaving her alone in the living room with a full-fae male.

"Don't sugarcoat it, please," Dani added when the male regarded her carefully for several heartbeats.

"Zlaet did what needed to be done," he said simply.

Dani stayed silent, waiting for more. Kallen watched her, and he shifted slightly from one foot to the other, a movement so subtle she might not have noticed if she wasn't watching him intently. A nervous gesture?

Was she making him, a full-fae male, nervous?

"He killed two of them," Kallen finally admitted when the silence continued. "The third he managed to contain with his magic, and we took him prisoner. He's a high-ranking individual in Zeyphar's court."

Dani blinked, swallowing her horror at the idea of Slate killing people. She knew he was dangerous and powerful, even as a mortal, but to actually *kill* someone?

She didn't know how she felt about that.

Dash streaked into the sitting room and jumped onto her lap, gekkering softly as he planted both front paws on her chest and proceeded to wash her face. Dani smiled, sending a mental impression of appreciation for the distraction.

Slate protects us and house, Dash reminded her in a stilted verbal response, and Dani nodded, smoothing her fingers down his russet pelt. Sellie was nearby and had reluctantly agreed to stay in Ebisu's garden down the street, since Kari and Jian's home didn't have much space to accommodate a griffin.

"Zlaet tells me you can speak to animals."

Dani looked up from her fox friend to find Kallen still watching her, a curious spark in his eyes.

She nodded. "Yeah."

"A rare gift, even among full-blooded fae."

She frowned. "Is it?"

He nodded, and she noticed a delicate flush along the tips of his pointed ears and dusting the tops of his cheekbones. "My *tatkyr*—my father—was an Acolyte. A... you might have called him a religious scholar. He studied the stories told by our people. Legends say there was once a line of fae who could speak directly into the wild hearts of lorefolk, communing straight to the bestial heart that dwells in all of us, that piece of the Goddess of the Wild herself. We called them Wild Fae. Perhaps you have a drop of their blood…"

Dani's brows twitched together. "Like… a distant ancestor of mine?"

Kallen's brows creased too, but curiosity glimmered in his lavender eyes. He offered her a little shrug, and his expression smoothed back into a polite smile. "It's possible, I suppose." His tone said otherwise, though, and he cocked his head. Finally, he gestured toward the picture frame lying on the low tea table in front of her. A short but curvy woman with rich brown hair stood next to a tall red-haired man with bright green eyes, both of their arms wrapped around a small redheaded child, grinning with a missing tooth. "Can your parents speak to animals? Any other family members?"

She glanced at the picture frame, at the three figures smiling out at her from within, and her chest hurt as the smell of her burning house came alive again in her senses. She swallowed it, banishing the mental image of smoke and broken glass, and shook her head. She stroked Dash's fur, a soothing gesture meant for herself more than the fox. "No. My parents were unfortunately very mortal… and I have no other family that I know of."

A heartbeat of pause. "I see. I am sorry." He pressed a hand to his sternum. "May the Goddess hold them in the palm of her hand."

Dani blinked, the words snagging inside her. She peered up at the fae male. "What did you just say?"

Kallen offered her a smile. "It is a fae blessing."

"It sounds like… an old Irish blessing." One that her father would say often enough. She even had a woven tapestry of the blessing hanging in the foyer of her house, from Ireland. *May the Lord hold you in the palm of his hand.* She recalled the last time she'd seen her father, when she'd been 16 years old.

"Until we meet again, Tani." Her father kissed her cheek. Over his shoulder, the family car was packed with luggage and gear, for her parents to take a weekend trip up north.

A trip they never came back from, courtesy of a car accident.

But in that memory was that name again. *Tani…* which sounded eerily like Tanyiel. Her father had called her Tani as his personal nickname for her since before she could remember, and now she was struggling to connect it to Zeyphar calling her Tanyiel. Her father had been mortal...

The door next to Kallen opened, jarring Dani from her reverie. She surged to her feet, heart slamming against her ribs. Jian and Kari had both assured her—multiple times—that Slate was in no danger whatsoever, and yet...

Joon came out first, followed by Jian. The latter beckoned her with his hand.

Dani was already moving. Joon offered her a warm smile as she passed, and Kallen stepped back for her as her fingers curled around the door-frame. Steeling herself, she peered inside.

Slate lay on a twin-sized futon on the floor, covered up to his waist in a thin white sheet. The broad expanse of his tattoo-wrapped torso was bare except for bandages that wrapped their way down the entirety of his right arm, from shoulder to fingers. A line of butterfly stitches peeked out from under his loose dark hair, above his left brow.

More importantly, his chest rose and fell in the even rhythm of sleep. Relief nearly had her sagging against the door frame. She let out a breath, the tension in her muscles leaching away until her legs felt like jelly, but they carried her forward anyway. Gingerly, she knelt beside him.

She tracked her gaze over his face and down the bandages of his right arm. There was no hint of blood, but her gut twisted nonetheless at the sight of the injury, at whatever was beneath those pristine linens. She knew the kind of healing Jian and Joon were capable of, and to still need bandages after their magic?

Her heart squeezed painfully in her chest, and she reached for his left hand, threading her fingers through his, savoring the warmth of his skin.

Slate sucked in a deeper breath. Her throat tightened and her eyes flashed to his face to see his lashes fluttering open, revealing an azure like the richest depths of the sea.

"Slate..." she murmured, leaning over, and his lips curved in the sem-blance of a smile, lidded gaze locking with hers for a moment before they slid shut and his face relaxed back into sleep.

She could've sworn a soft, wintry hand caressed the edge of her mind, the barest breeze of fresh snow filling her senses before it vanished, and his breathing leveled out again, deep and even.

Dani stared at him a moment, part of her wanting to shake him, to wake him and see his smile again, but she forced that desire down. She settled on the floor next to the futon, gently bringing his left hand to her chest. She curled around it, tucking her free arm under her head, and her eyes drifted to his bare chest, tracing the lines of it as it rose... and fell...

Slate was here. He hadn't left her... he was breathing. Safe.

She kept her eyes on the rise and fall of his chest, letting each movement soothe her, until all that was left in her mind were his last words to her.

I love you.

Holding them close to her heart, Dani drifted off to sleep.

THE MADNESS WITHIN

... not chosen but rather born to suit the role of alpha and are believed to be blood-tied to the entire were pack. Characteristics are often displayed early, such as assertiveness, dominance, stubbornness, and...

- Gherald Schmidt, Faerloch Historical Archives

Roger touched the tip of his shoe to the blood-stained streak on Daniella's lawn, the scent of winter and crisp, fresh snow still permeating the air, having little to do with the current season and everything to do with the blood.

Inside him, the darkness swirled, sinking its claws into his throat. Storming against him to *kill the threat against Daniella—*

But Slate had taken care of it.

The shadows had warned him of the danger, too little too late. By the time the intel had reached him, she was already within the safety of the

Eastern District ward, far removed from the threat.

Interestingly, while his first thought had been to ascertain Daniella's well-being, his second thought had been: *Did Slate still breathe?*

He had actively chosen not to dwell too deeply into the thought. Into how pivotal Slate's well-being was now tied to Daniella's.

He glanced at her house, still smoking behind him. The sight had darkness roiling beneath his skin, sliding along sinew and bone, up vein and capillary, until it whispered in his ear: *This was Slate's fault.*

He'd sent Slate to Daniella, but he'd expected the male to take precautions against being tracked here.

A mistake he would not make again.

Slate had done this to her, had darkened her doorstep with these dangers and plights. From the moment that *faeling* had appeared in their lives, he'd done little more than shred the safety Roger had promised Daniella, all those years ago.

And yet...

Roger had known Daniella for over a decade—a blink to his long, immortal life but a decade nonetheless. He knew her, inside and out. And the woman he knew even as early as a year ago would not have nearly pushed him out of the doorway to return to a place of *fae battle.*

I have to go back!

The force of her words still echoed in his mind. He'd seen something in her this night, something fierce, had felt something stir in the very heart of him in response. It was a twist of nostalgia, a tangled thread to years and decades and centuries-long forgotten, little more than a feeling. As if he'd stood in the presence of such bright, flaring sunlight before...

His brow twitched; he had so *many* memories... to find a single one would be difficult, especially when his mind could only picture Daniella before him, and the more he pushed his memories, the less clear the feeling became.

He had, of course, seen hints of such a bright strength in Daniella before, but mostly when an animal was in danger. But tonight, she'd become sunlight given physical form, and he'd realized the light he'd basked in before today had been but the weak light of morning compared to the full force of the midday sun she'd become in that moment. She'd become powerful and compelling, and he'd never been so close to giving in when it went against everything inside him to put her anywhere near danger.

Was that a glimpse of who Daniella was, who she was supposed to be? Warm and bright as she's always been, but powerful and fearless, too?

And Slate...

Unbidden, the image of the small scar on Daniella's neck twisted inside him.

The darkness snarled, gleeful, and it caused a twist of that fear, a wild rage that someone would *dare* threaten to take that light from him.

Not when Roger so *desperately* needed that light. More than ever, the billowing shadow inside him was poised, eager to swallow him whole when there was no more *light* to keep it in check.

As Roger continued to inspect Daniella's property, he picked up that new note in Slate's wintry scent. He paused at the sub-zero sharpness invading the smell, and his nostrils flared as he inhaled deeply and felt it burn the inside of his nose. It was a *cold* burn... just a hint. A taint to Slate's scent.

Roger's eyes narrowed. It was the same taint he'd smelled earlier in the day, when he'd gone to fetch the princeling.

Slate Melisande... that male was crafted of winter snow and wild storms, but *this* kind of cold... Perhaps he was drawn to Daniella, to her summer sunshine in every smile, because of *that* cold, one to rival the shadows inside Roger. He'd heard whispers of the Malady among those empaths particularly blessed by the Goddess, and he had a suspicion Slate had not been spared.

Before tonight, he might have feared that such a frigid frost might snuff out Daniella's light. Yet now, he'd seen her shine so bright, it had resonated deep in his heart. The *faeling* prince seemed to be... *awakening* something slumbering in her. As if he were the wild storm and she the calm center, one that could be as strong as the storm.

Roger cast another look at the streak of blood on the frozen grass, banishing his thoughts. He crouched and touched the blood. It evaporated from the lawn into naught but shadows, leaving no drop behind.

The shadows had shared the details of the encounter with him, down to the minutia. Slate had portaled her away to safety, to the best place he could think. And he'd stayed behind, and not to simply deal with the threat.

To protect the *house*.

The house that Daniella loved so dearly, one of the few ties she had left to her parents.

As the shadows curled around Roger, it wasn't lost on him that he'd have done the exact same. Slate Melisande was not perfect by any stretch of the imagination, but... perhaps... there were worse males out there.

Slate stood in the middle of an ice cavern.

He knew, instinctively, that he was in his own mind. This is what his emotional grid looked like, or at least how his brain interpreted it. The circuitry of emotions resembled a stunning, echoing ice cave. Crystals streamed like shooting stars, ricocheting off the walls, spider-webbing out, disappearing and bringing back colors and emotions. A living flow of magical information.

And before him, in the center of the cavern, was a yawning chasm. Dark and deep. Icy, frigid air blew up from it. He shielded his face, bringing up a shield of telekinesis. The wind still seeped through, not because his shield was cracked, but because they were made the same—made of *his* magic.

The frigid air wrapped skeletal hands around him and yanked. Claws made of sharp ice dug into his arms and pulled, pulled...

Around him, the ice cavern shook. Stalactites loosed from the ceiling and crashed, shattering at his feet. The walls shook and shifted, closing in, herding him toward that icy ravine.

There was nowhere to go but down. Down, or be suffocated by his magic.

Down into the depths of icy numbness.

As the ice pressed against his back and those claws tugged, he took a deep breath and tipped forward—

A tendril of warmth, a ribbon of sunlight, and a single beam crashed through the cavern, bouncing and reverberating off the snow and frost in a sparkle of light and rainbows.

The claws loosened, disintegrating like ash, and the trembling, advancing walls ceased.

And he heard his name.

Slate...

Slate...

Slate.

Slate jarred awake, sitting up fast, breathing hard.

Where was he?

The ice. The numbness. The chasm of *nothing*—

His hearing came online first, and he could hear his name, sounding like it came from down a long tunnel. "Slate. *Slate.*"

Green meadows and sunlit trees—

He located the source and snapped his gaze around. It landed on Daniella, next to him. Worried eyes scanned his face, and tentatively, she placed her fingertips on his chest.

She was here. Safe.

Where was *here*?

He flipped his eyes around the room. He recognized it instantly as Joon's workroom. Things began to make sense as the flush of panic-fueled adrenaline faded from his mind, which made him realize that his body hurt.

A lot, and all over.

The pain shot straight to his head, and his vision spotted. He dropped back onto the mattress. A gentle hand splayed over his chest. Another on his face. He sucked in a deep breath, the scent of lush trees and fresh meadows filling him. He cracked open one eye. Dani was leaning over him.

He swallowed his dry throat. "Are you okay?" It sounded raw and raspy.

Her eyes widened. "You're asking me if I'm okay when you can't even sit up?"

He nodded, aware of his own lunacy.

She sighed, a little smile flirting with her mouth. "I'm fine. My feet were a little cut up, but Jian healed them." She slid her hand across his brow. "How are you feeling?"

Slate stuffed his left elbow underneath him and gingerly pushed himself into a sitting position. Waited a handful of heartbeats. Nothing spun.

He nodded and offered Dani a grin. "Whole and healthy." He felt like he'd been run over by a truck and then pushed over the edge of a cliff, but she didn't need to know that.

She looked doubtful, eyes flicking to his right arm. "What happened?"

He followed her gaze and found his right arm bandaged tight from shoulder to fingertips. He attempted to lift his arm, and pain spiraled down it. He hissed a little through his teeth.

A shot of intense—and loud—worry echoed into him. He flipped his eyes to her in time to see pain pinch her brow.

Pain for *him*. Concern for *him*. He wanted to touch her face and smooth away the lines of worry, but his left arm was the only thing holding him up. So instead, he thought back to the night. Windows exploding. Her house in flames. The trio of High Fae. That female fae who tried to get inside Dani's head and manipulate her into submission—

I love you.

He studied his bandaged arm, trying to ignore the heat across his cheekbones as he remembered the last words he'd said to her. Instead of repeating those words, however, he said, "I owe you a new shovel."

The handle had imploded under the force of his magic spiraling through it. Had sent him careening backward and shattering the bones in his arm. The pain had been excruciating before his mind compartmentalized it away. The precious seconds it'd taken him to get back on his feet had nearly cost him.

He'd been dragged across the ground, scrambling for purchase, iron wires tripping his feet, searing his skin, toward a portal just outside the ward line—

But he'd been so furious. Such mind-numbing fury that he hadn't felt any physical pain. The fae hadn't come for him, but had come for the beating heart of him. Had burned her house. Chased her out. Rifled around inside her head. Threatened to take away her safety and security.

Threatened to take *her*.

He'd heard their racing hearts, the swell of triumph as they'd snatched him. Gelayeth's voice, *"Tanyiel is next, princeling."*

There had been a screech of anger, of feathered fury, and blood had rent the air in an arc around him, turning those feathers red as the griffin tore into one of the fae. Slate had tuned into the sound of those beating fae hearts, had wrapped magical, kinetic hands around those organs—

The next thing he remembered was the arrival of backup. Jian and Kallen and a few fae soldiers. Water pelting from the sky from a blown fire hydrant, smothering the flames on Dani's house. Slate using every ounce of telekinetic magic he possessed to trap Gelayeth's living, fighting form to the ground. Sellie's low hiss and the drip-drip of blood from her beak as she crouched protectively over him—

A gentle hand on his chest pulled him from the memories. "Slate?"

Once more, he flipped his eyes to hers. Green and gold, like sunshine in summer, too big in her pale face.

The bedroom door slid open, and Jian's copper head peered in. "Wakey, wakey, eggs and bakey!" he sang, grinning devilishly. "There's my favorite Sailor Scout!"

Dani laughed out loud, and Slate had to actively fight to pull his focus around to his best friend. "Fuck you," he growled.

Jian was unbothered. "Damn, bro, you had a *night*, huh? How're you feeling?"

"Fine."

"Liar," Jian laughed. He came over to the side of the futon and touched Slate's forehead. "You blew your entire arm and hand to smithereens. Took Dad and I over an hour to set all the bones back into place." He slipped his hand over Slate's bandaged arm and an image appeared, projected above the arm. It was crafted of swirling white *chi*, unmistakably showing a diagram of Slate's arm, inside and out. Like a three-dimensional X-ray. "Everything is set though, healing nicely. Can you move your fingers?"

Slate did, touching each fingertip to his thumb as instructed. It was tight and difficult to move, and each one set a lick of fire up his arm, but he shelved the pain. Jian was too sharp, though, and reached out a hand to draw a character on Slate's forehead. Instantly, some of the ache disappeared.

"I've waterproofed the bandage, if you wanna take a shower. Dad's cooking breakfast." Jian turned his attention to Dani. "Kari said she sorted everything out with the insurance company. There's a team headed to your house right now, to assess the damage."

Dani nodded, an unreadable tightness to her face. "Thank her for me."

Jian smiled. "Of course, it's no problem. Kari's good at that kind of shit. Between you and me," Jian angled a hand by his mouth conspiratorially, and spoke in a hushed voice. "Kari's the reason the studio stays in business. We'd be lost without her management skills."

"I'd be offended but... it's true," Slate added dryly.

Dani smiled, and he quirked a little grin back at her.

Jian clapped him gently on his good shoulder, then flicked at a strand of hair by his face that was matted with dried blood. "Holler if you need help in the bath, *ne*?" He hopped to his feet, and with another smile toward Dani, Jian disappeared out the door.

Slate shifted to sit independently of his left arm supporting him, and he felt Dani's feather-light fingers as she moved to support him if necessary, hovering like some kind of worried mother-hen. "I'm okay, you know," he said gently, knowing Jian was going to mother-hen him enough as it was. He got his feet under him, determined to stand. "I don't go down easy."

On her feet now, she continued to hover anyway, hands ready to snatch him if he tumbled. She quirked her lips. "I know. You're big and strong."

"... you can still nurse me back to health, though. I don't mind."

He flashed a suggestive little grin at her, waggling his brow. "I like the attention."

She looked as though she were biting back a smile. Some of the anxiety leached out of her. "Of course you do." She stepped away from him, bare feet padding across the tatami floor to retrieve a *yukata* robe laid out over a chair. She held it out for him and helped him pull it over his shoulders. He hissed out a painful breath as they negotiated the robe over his shattered right arm, and she muttered out several fast apologies.

"Do you want help?"

He flipped his eyes to hers. "For what?"

"In the bath." She gestured to his arm. "Might be hard to... you know, wash your hair and stuff."

He followed her gesture with his eyes, watching his hand as he tried to flex his fingers. They moved. Slowly. "Maybe, yeah."

"I promise to behave myself," she teased.

Slate swallowed his suddenly raging heartbeat. "You can't know how badly I don't want you to behave."

She laughed.

"Which one do you want?" Dani turned, holding up two bottles of shampoo.

Slate hemmed for a second. "Kari's." He sat on a little stool in the center of the large bathroom, naked save his boxers. The *yukata* robe hung on a hook near the sealed and waterproofed door.

"Really? You want to smell like a—" she cut herself off, sniffing the bottle. "Oh. It doesn't smell like anything, actually."

"That's the point, love. It's not as... offensive to the senses. Kari's easily overwhelmed by a lot of the scented shit they sell to women. It might not smell like anything to you, but it does have a scent."

"Can you smell it? What does it smell like?" She put the bottle next to the stool and grabbed the shower head, turning it on and running her hand under the stream to test the temperature.

"A little. A faint smell of... like... flowers and grass."

"Did all your senses heighten dramatically after the glamour came off?" She touched his forehead, encouraging him to tip his head back a little, and when he did, she ran the water over his hair.

Slate closed his eyes, savoring the sensation, the heat of the water. "Yeah. I can hear and smell better than I could before, like... the scent of people, the scent of magic. I can hear voices better... my sight is the best, though. The shit I can see now is un*real*. I can see better in the dark, track even the smallest movements..."

"Like a predator," she offered. She squeezed the bottle of shampoo into her hand.

"Sorta, yeah. Fae are supposed to be closer to beasts than to humans, I guess. More animal. Sight is a critical sense to the fae. So is touch—" he cut off suddenly as her fingers speared through his hair, digging into his scalp.

The sensation was *heavenly*. The scratch of her nails against his scalp, the slight pull and tug of hair, the caress of fingertips along his temples and his nape where the hair was shaved short. A rumbling sound echoed in his chest, like the cross between a groan and a growl of pleasure.

"Your sense of touch?" Dani prompted, and he could've sworn there was a little teasing lilt to her voice. "More sensitive to it?"

"Yeah..." he said roughly. "Yeah... just... enjoy it more."

"Huh."

He fell silent, letting the scent of her and the warmth of her aura wash over him like her hands were. He actively tucked his own magic in close so as to not even listen and hear at the door of her mind. He didn't want to know what she was thinking. What she was feeling.

I love you.

He'd laid it all out there, hadn't he? Out loud.

The fact that she'd still been there when he'd woken up gave him an unprecedented amount of hope. That maybe, just maybe, she felt the same way.

Maybe she would choose him, too.

"I've decided you're worth it, though."

Maybe she already had.

He wanted to trust it. He wanted to trust that cautious flame of hope inside him, trust her words, trust her actions. She hadn't backed down from him *once* since he'd stormed back into her life. Not since the roof-top garden, where they'd laid everything out and showed both their hands.

But still... still he held back. Bit his tongue a little. Thought before he spoke. Kept his aura under wraps, and held everything close to the chest. Because he didn't want to chance scaring her away. Because he still remembered what it felt like when she ghosted him before the Championship Fight. He still remembered the months and months and *months* of aching, smothering loneliness without her, even though he'd done the leaving that time.

He didn't want to go back to that. A little bit of Dani was better than none at all.

"I killed those fae," he said suddenly into the quiet, his voice barely above a whisper. As much as he would stifle his feelings for her, he wouldn't straight up lie to her. That was a line he couldn't cross.

Her fingers stilled for a moment. "I know," she replied. He heard the rush of water as she turned on the shower head and rinsed the shampoo from his hair. "A part of me knew you had, even before... even before I asked Kallen about it."

"Part of me doesn't regret it at all. They came after you, tried to take you—" Ice crawled up his throat, and it wasn't lost on him that the temperature of the small Japanese-inspired bathing room dipped noticeably.

Dani's hands stilled again. "Breathe," she murmured, and her voice was calm and even, as though he were a wild creature in need of soothing. "Breathe through it."

He did, sucking in a deep breath through his nose. She ran her hands through his hair again, and breathing became easier. Her fingers scooped up his hair, gathering the long strands and pulling them up into a messy bun, away from his neck.

Her fingertips at his nape had the tension in his shoulders easing. "It was always a possibility," he continued. "You can't be... you can't be *me* without having to worry about it. But I just didn't..." He flexed his injured hand, flexed it hard, letting the pain and the tightness ricochet through him. Let it erase the surge of intense guilt raging up his throat. Let it erase the reality that he'd *stolen* lives from people. People who were supposed to be *his* people. "I don't regret it... but I don't think I like it."

A pause, and Dani said softly, "I'd be worried if you did."

"I could, though." The words felt tight and wrong, clipped and edged, as if they were forcing their way out of his mouth. "There's a part of me that could just be... I could let myself be numb to it." He'd tasted the ice. The numbness. He knew what lurked at the bottom of the frigid chasm inside him, and he'd seen a piece of it in him last night. "I don't wanna be *him*."

His uncle. Cold. Cruel. Unforgiving.

Still behind him, she pressed her fingers into his forehead to tip his head back to look at her again. "There's not a single person in this house right now that would let you be him. You really think Jian would hang you out to dry like that?"

"Jian would rather die first." The words came automatically.

She circled him, coming around to his front. She placed both hands on either side of his face, tipping his face back as she held his gaze. "You think *I* would let you be that?"

He thought about the warmth of her aura. Bright as sunshine, calm as a summer breeze, chasing away the cold and the ice and illuminating every part of him until he too, was bright and warm. Melting the arctic inside him until he defaulted back to crisp snow in midwinter. "I don't think I can be that. With you, I mean. Around... around you."

"Then stay. With me."

Slate stopped breathing for a moment, heart seizing in his chest with something that tasted a lot like cautious hope. He wanted to hate how much he pined after her, but it was impossible. He loved even the idea of her, even the process of *wanting*, he loved it all. He met her eyes, words failing him.

"Don't... I don't want you to leave me." She dropped her hands from his face and shifted her gaze away from his, studying the floor. "People tend to leave me and not come back. My best friend. My parents. That's why it's better to leave first, but... I won't—can't leave you." She was mumbling, speaking a little too fast. Finally, she bit her lip, sucking in a breath. "I don't... I don't want you to leave, either. I—I want to go where you go." A cut of those eyes and he felt that look down into his *soul*. "Then neither of us have to worry."

There was more to unpack about that statement than she seemed willing to share, so much weight in her words. Slate reached up and curled a hand around her throat, thumb stroking over the mark on her shoulder. His mark. "I'll always come back."

She tipped her head to the side slightly, giving him better access. A small, nearly subvocal growl of possessive pleasure zipped through his chest. *His*. He wanted to keep her so much, it physically hurt.

She let out a breath. "Just don't leave in the first place. Promise me."

He froze for a beat, mind and emotions short-circuiting a little. Promises were a big deal; even bigger among the fae. Nothing was ever promised lightly.

Then again, nothing between them had ever felt *light* to begin with.

"I promise."

MEMORIES IN ASH

... a summons of purple oleander will appear—known as lila kyochi—wrapped in a jade ribbon, which will transform into a scroll at the touch of the appropriate recipient...

– Gherald Schmidt, Faerloch Historical Archives

"*Yoo-hoo*, earth to Dani."

Dani ripped her gaze away from the window and turned to face Jian. He was washing dishes from breakfast, and she'd offered to help by drying the dishes and putting them away. "Sorry."

"You've been drying that pan for like, a *solid* minute." Jian's eyes followed her distraction, tracing out the window and onto the front yard. "Ah."

Dani returned her gaze to the window. Slate and Kallen were on the front lawn, having a heated discussion. Kallen was frowning and Slate was pacing a track in the winter grass, gesturing wildly, a chaotic grace about him. "What are they fighting about?"

Jian shrugged one shoulder. "Probably the usual. Kallen being suffocatingly overprotective and Slate clawing for independence."

There was just enough spite in Jian's voice that Dani shifted her attention from the lawn to the *manyeo*. "Why do you say it like that?"

Jian paused, then started deliberately and methodically washing chopsticks. Dani waited. She'd learned enough about Jian these last few months to know that if she waited long enough, he'd talk. And if he didn't want to talk, he'd deflect the subject with a devilish grin and snarky charm.

"Kallen was Slate's mother's best friend," Jian settled on, eyes focused on his hands. "He was the main person in charge of her safety for a long time. And, well, that didn't end well, so I think he projects a lot of his... survivor's guilt onto Slate."

"I see." Dani nodded slowly.

"Kallen knows Slate's different but..." Another half-shrug. "I dunno. I get where they're both coming from. Slate doesn't take orders well, and he's always been... aggressively strong-willed—"

Dani snorted, holding back a little smile. "That's a nice word for it."

That got a smile out of Jian. "And he's capable, *ne*? But Kallen... I mean. Aredhel was his best friend. And Kallen's not an offensive fighter. His magic is warding and portalling magic—defensive."

There was something in the way Jian said it, as if there was more to it, but Dani couldn't quite put her finger on the pulse of it. She sometimes still found Jian hard to read; he could be pretty reserved sometimes. A counterbalance to Kari's over-exuberance.

"Kallen couldn't keep Aredhel safe, so he's making up for it through Slate."

Dani placed some dried chopsticks into the drawer next to her. "You agree with Kallen more than you do with Slate."

"Well, yeah, I mean." A sideways glance. "I don't say this to freak you out, but if Slate ends up in the Silver Valley? The same kid that goes in will *not* be the same one we get back. His uncle will jumble the inside of his head so hard that Slate won't ever trust his own emotions ever again.

Magical brainwashing."

She swallowed hard. "I... I figured."

No one said as much, but she had a strong suspicion Slate had been closer to danger last night than people admitted. Not even Sellie would tell her what happened. But Dani had seen the grass stains on his knees last night, had seen the raw lacerations on his left palm, the dirt under his fingernails, as if he'd clawed for purchase against the frozen ground. She'd seen what looked like iron wire burns on his ankles and calves.

As if.... As if he'd been dragged across the ground.

Possibly toward a portal.

It made her want to vomit, the idea that he could get whisked away to the Silver Valley.

"I don't wanna be him..."

Her Slate—her wicked, devilishly charming, *good* boyfriend—manipulated into something ugly and cruel.

No. Not if she had something to say and do about it. What he'd said this morning: *"I don't think I can be that. With you, I mean. Around... around you."*

"Slate's not a politician or whatever," Jian continued, bringing Dani's mind back to the present moment. "He's a phenomenal fighter but still. I would prefer that he err on the side of caution, but that's not at all his modus operandi, so... we all just gotta get better around him, make sure we can keep up."

There it was. "You're worried you can't keep up with him," Dani murmured, watching Jian.

For a heartbeat, Jian tensed. Hands stilled. Only the sound of running water between them. "Always." He returned to rinsing off the bowl in his hands. "Never been able to. I don't *like* fighting. I'm a witch by birth, but a doctor by choice, and there's a reason for that."

"But you also chose to be a part of this... fae life with Slate."

Again, another beat of pause. Dani held her breath, certain this time he'd deflect her. "I did. Someone needed to be there to pick up the pieces of his life."

Dani nodded, understanding what Jian wasn't saying. Jian *wanted* to be there to pick up the pieces. Jian liked to be close to Slate.

Not that she blamed him. She liked to be close to Slate too.

"I don't know, Jian, maybe that's what it takes." She took the bowl from him to dry it. "Sometimes a perfect match isn't someone you can keep up with, but someone who balances you out. Maybe he doesn't need someone to fight at his side, but someone to pick him up after the battle," she offered with a quirk of her lips.

Jian turned and looked at her, really looked, head cocked slightly. "That was... incredibly insightful," he finally said. He reached out and flicked her nose. "Save some of those nuggets of wisdom for yourself, Dani-*chan*. You might need them." He grinned, with a pointed look toward Slate through the window.

She rubbed her nose with the palm of her hand, crinkling her face at him. He grinned, a low chuckle escaping him. "So. What's the plan for your house?"

She knew it was a deflection from the topic, and it was an effective one as her heart squeezed painfully in her chest at the thought of her parent's house being eaten by flames. "I... don't know." Jian's expression softened at the distress she must be giving away. She struggled to keep her grief from her face. "I haven't thought about it yet."

"Kari's already hired the contractors to repair the house, so there's that," Jian said with an encouraging smile. "She's good like that, organized and shit."

Dani jerked her head in a nod, grabbing another dish to give her hands something to do. She hadn't even let herself think about where she was going to stay while her house was repaired, either. Naturally, she could find a hotel or an Airbnb, but she knew Maddie and Roger wouldn't let her when she could easily crash with them. Hell, Roger's 'mortal' identity was a real estate broker, and he likely had many empty places to put her up in, if she asked.

And even if she didn't, knowing Roger, he probably already had a place in mind.

Yet the idea of bunking at one of Roger's places, or at Maddie's big house where she regularly put up covenmates, somehow felt... lacking. Probably because she'd allowed herself to consider another possibility.

Staying with Slate.

The idea caused such a riot of confusion in her, from excitement and anticipation to a cold sweat of old fear. Staying with someone was a big commitment. But the thought of being away from him was worse, making that old fear slip away until it was nothing but an echo.

"You can stay here, you know." A knowing look and a cocked brow. "Unless, of course, you have *other* ideas."

As if he'd read her mind. She'd blame his magic, but she was pretty sure he couldn't hear thoughts with his *chi*-reading ability. Which meant she was being transparent. Again.

She attempted to school her features into neutrality when the front door slid open with a loud bang, and Slate stormed in. Dani sucked in a breath at the swell of power that came off him, like the sudden heat of a roaring fire but icy cold. He caught her gaze, and his steps slowed. It felt like his entire being keyed right to her in that moment as the roaring cold fire banked until it was little more than a smoking ember.

"What's your deal, *Titania*?" Jian chimed in, grinning.

Slate wrenched his eyes away from Dani and flipped Jian off, which made Jian's grin widen. "As your best friend and physician," Jian mused, "I find it *deeply* reassuring that your favorite finger remains in working order."

Slate rolled his eyes and leaned his good shoulder against the doorframe. His other arm was in a sling now, which Dani knew Jian had insisted on, despite Slate's protest. Slate glanced back over his shoulder, but Kallen didn't make an appearance. "Just... Kallen being Kallen."

"Alright," Jian said with a shrug, but Dani had a feeling he knew *exactly* what the argument had been about, and that it was more than just Kallen being overprotective. Curiosity sparked in her, but from the expression on Slate's face, she didn't think pushing would get her far. Jian snagged the hand towel from her hands and dried off his own. "I'm out. Slate, brother, come see me later tonight when you have time. I wanna check your arm."

"Sure."

With a little wink at Dani, Jian disappeared toward the back of the kitchen, through a door that led downstairs into the subterranean greenhouse garden Jian and his father managed in the basement.

Leaving her alone in the kitchen with Slate.

All her senses dialed into him, her throat drying out a little. After the bath, they'd negotiated him into a black button-down shirt—the easiest shirt to get on over a broken arm—which Kari had insisted had to be paired with jeans instead of Slate's normal workout pants. It was a different look on him, and her eyes kept snagging to where the top button of his shirt was undone, letting some of his intricate tattoos peek out.

Warmth simmered under her skin, and she scowled at herself for the reaction. They'd had sex literally last night before the attack—how could she be this thirsty for him still?

Or maybe... maybe the thought of never touching him again had made her desperate to touch him all the more.

She tamped down her emotions, though, knowing that even without actively trying, he was probably getting a little taste of everything she was feeling. Probably meaning *likely* as she watched a subtle ripple of tension vibrate through him, eyes dilating even as he took in a deep, even breath through his nose. "So... you sure you're up for this?" he asked.

His question effectively poured icy water over that spark of heat. She dropped her eyes, busying her hands with the towel Jian abandoned. "Yeah." She looked back at him, squaring her shoulders. "Yes, I'm ready."

He nodded, and something like guilt chased across his face. "Kari said the damage is... extensive." He watched her like he was afraid his words would send her running.

Or to a meltdown.

Dani sucked in another breath but kept her shoulders straight. "I can handle it," she told him firmly, a little scowl between her brows.

Slate's expression softened, and he pushed off from the doorway to close the distance between them. He brushed the backs of two fingers against her jaw and smiled a little. "I know, you're stronger than you look."

Her lips twitched into a small smile, some of the dread inside her loosening. Somehow, with Slate at her side, she knew he was right.

Her strength took an immediate hit the moment she and Slate appeared out of a portal on the edge of her property. The sight of her charred house—the house her parents left her—was a punch to the chest, leaving her breathless as she blinked back tears, frozen in place. Slate stood close to her, a silent wall of support, as she digested the sight before her.

The whole backside of her house, from the corner of her small porch up to the bedroom window, was black and twisted from heat. Parts of the siding had completely burned away, revealing hints of the skeleton of the house. A tear escaped to trace a line down her cheek, but she sucked in a breath and scrubbed it from her face with the back of her hand.

She refused to wallow. She would not give Zeyphar the satisfaction.

Chest tight, she straightened her shoulders and glanced at Slate, who was watching her with a tight expression. Unspoken fury made the tattoos peeking out of his shirt pulse a darker color. Their eyes met, and he shifted until his shoulders blocked out the view of her burnt house. Gently, he cupped one cheek, thumb brushing at the wet trail there.

"I can soften your sadness... if you want... so you aren't so overwhelmed," he offered in a tight tone that told her how much her own distress was affecting him.

Dani bit her lip, then reached up to take his hand from her cheek, threading her fingers through his. The fact that he had offered, had made it *her* choice, meant everything. She shook her head. "Please don't. I... the ache means it's real, that *they* were real." She still remembered her mother's beaming face as they painted her bedroom walls, her father's calm instructions as he taught her how to use a hammer to build the porch.

They had loved this house, and after they were gone, the house was as close as she could get to feeling like she was in their arms again. Wiping away the pain would be another way to wipe them from her life... and she couldn't stand that.

"You're not alone, Daniella."

The same words Roger had used. The words resounded inside her like a mantra, and each echo of it had the air coming easier into her lungs. She offered Slate a watery smile. "I'm starting to believe that."

Slate blinked, then slowly, his lips spread in a smile. "Good. You should." He glanced over his shoulder. "Do you want to go in?"

"Yeah, I do. I can handle this."

"I know."

Dani wrinkled her nose at him, but didn't release his hand as they started for the house.

Dani noticed two figures standing outside her house, surveying the worst of the exterior fire damage. She didn't need her ability to sense their heartfires to know they were lorebeings—their mannerisms gave them away as werefolk. While were-creatures came off to her senses the same as anyone else in the lore, Dani spent too much time with animals not to recognize the wildness in their actions.

Glass crunched under her boots as she stepped inside. The stench of burned carpet and paint assaulted her as she came to a stop just inside her living room, throat tight. Three figures stood inside, conferring together. One of them offered her a smile, and she recognized the stocky woman as one of Maddie's witches.

Dani managed a weak smile in return, just as two dwarves sauntered past them and into the house, bickering about the qualities of good stone.

"Kari has a lot of friends," Dani observed, amazed not only by the number of workers but also by the variety. "I can't afford dwarf-work..." she added in a whisper to Slate. Dwarven-built goods came at a steep price, due to the high quality of their craftsmanship.

"Kari's already worked everything out, don't worry," Slate assured her.

"I'm not letting her pay for my house repairs," Dani argued in a low voice.

"Kari didn't spend any money. She called in favors that were owed to her. If you'd like to tell her not to do that, be my guest," Slate told her with a wry smile. Dani frowned, knowing that would be an impossible task.

And also because she knew she'd do the same for Kari. So she accepted the generosity, grateful to have such friends in her life, with a mental note to do something nice for Kari when she got the chance.

Once she had her emotions under control, Dani's first act was to consult with the general contractor to ensure they knew she didn't want any changes to the house, only repairs. Then she called her work, and after explaining that her house had caught fire, her boss insisted she take time off.

"You still have plenty of vacation days this year, Dani. If I see you before the end of two weeks, I'll be disappointed. Take some time for yourself, you've earned it. We can manage without you for a little while," her boss told her over the phone.

Somewhat relieved, Dani turned her attention to salvaging her possessions from the fire. Slate was a quiet wall of support next to her as he helped her go through her belongings, holding the garbage bag as she sorted between things that could be saved and things that couldn't.

They didn't speak much, and Dani was grateful for the silence, wondering perhaps if Slate's magic had warned him that she didn't have it in her to talk yet. Every charred item that went into the garbage bag made it harder and harder not to cry.

But she wouldn't let Zeyphar win, wouldn't let him force her back to being that weepy, cowardly person she'd been a year ago.

"It's okay to cry, you know," Slate murmured to her over an hour into the work, placing a warm hand on the small of her back.

Dani blinked, realizing she'd been staring at a charred tapestry she'd taken down from the wall for several minutes now. It had been her father's, an old Irish blessing. The edges of the tapestry were burned away, loose threads and slices from flying glass left patches of it in tatters.

It had hung in that spot on her living room wall all her life. After her parents had died, she'd wanted to keep everything the same, afraid that any changes would mean losing more of her parents, but her therapist had encouraged her to paint some walls, rearrange some furniture—make it *her* home, not just her parents'.

But the blessing? She'd kept it in that one spot. It was her morning's first greeting and her evening's last goodnight. She could still hear her father's voice echoing in her ears.

Until we meet again, Tani...

Tears burned in her eyes, but Dani shook her head and stubbornly dashed them away. She carefully folded the remnants of the tapestry, and set it in the box to her left, on top of the other items she'd managed to salvage.

She had to remind herself that this was just... stuff. Her house, her belongings, even the tapestry, it was just *stuff.* Last night, when she hadn't known if Slate was going to be alright or not...

Her sadness over her house was nothing compared to the panic and dread she'd felt last night. She'd rather this whole house burn down than lose Slate, and once that thought crossed her mind, she found it easier to go through her belongings.

The sun was flirting with the horizon when she was finally finished. The zipper was loud to her ears as she closed her duffle, and she was officially out of time.

Out of time to consider where she would be staying that night.

She stared at her fingers on the closed zipper, trying to find her voice and the courage to ask the question that had been dancing just out of reach in her mind all day.

A large hand covered her fingers, and she looked up to find Slate crouching across the duffle from her. He smiled gently at her. "Do you want me to take you to Maddie's place? Or Roger's?" That last offer came out reluctantly, but she knew he meant it.

Dani opened her mouth to accept... but stopped. For a beat, she hesitated.

She did not really want to stay with Maddie or Roger.

I want to go where you go.

Her mouth closed again, warmth flooding her cheeks as she looked away from him, down toward where his hand still covered hers.

"Or," he continued, his voice shifting to an almost painful casualness. "You could... stay with me... if you want."

Her gaze snapped up to lock with his as her heart skipped a beat in her chest. There it was, out in the open. She knew he meant temporarily, until her house was repaired, but staying with him would be a big step. It was a level of commitment she'd reached with no one else. Even though she'd already decided to keep Slate, even knowing that what they had together felt far more serious than just boyfriend-girlfriend… some part of her recognized that if she let herself live with him, she'd never want to go back.

It would be one more thing she would rely on him for, one more unbreakable link between them.

One more weight on the scale tipping precariously close to unrecoverable devastation if she were to lose him. She'd patched herself together after the loss of Katarina and her parents, but a little voice inside her heart whispered that maybe… there would be no coming back if she lost him.

… there hadn't been when he'd left for all those months. Who was she even kidding?

But then, if she stepped back now, she'd lose him all the same.

I want to go where you go.

"I'd like that," she said softly and smiled up at him.

His eyes flared slightly in surprise, and a tension she hadn't noticed eased from his shoulders as the corner of his mouth quirked up in a grin. "Me too."

THE L-WORD

... as permanent as the fae bite of the mayt-mark. Intense research has been conducted into why the fae instinct is driven to bite, and some peripheral studies have speculated that this instinct stems from the very core of the bestial fae heart...

- Gherald Schmidt, Faerloch Historical Archives

They stopped at Jian's on their way home, as per the *manyeo's* request. He spent some time working on Slate's arm, and Joon insisted they stay for dinner. By the time they walked out the door, more than two hours later, Slate's arm was no longer in the sling, but had black athletic tape wrapped strategically by Jian to support the arm while it continued to heal.

Dani wondered if it was just Jian and Joon's magic that was allowing Slate to heal so quickly, or if it was also Slate's fae blood. Not for the first time, she was overwhelmingly grateful for his fae heritage, the tight knot in her chest easing a bit at the sight of his recovery.

She could have lost him.

Slate led the way up the darkened stairs to the apartment above his martial arts studio, her duffle slung over his good shoulder. The smell was comfortingly familiar somehow as they emerged into the Japanese-inspired home. They left their shoes by the door and padded down the hall toward the bedrooms.

Slate hesitated by the door to his father's room and half turned toward her. He rubbed the back of his neck and gestured toward the door with his taped-up arm. "My father doesn't stay here much anymore, if you'd like your own room?" Again, he spoke with that painful casualness that sent a shiver of irritation down her spine.

This wasn't the first time it'd felt like he was walking on eggshells around her, and it made her heart sink a little in her chest.

She'd done that.

Never again. She slipped past him on quiet feet. She reached his room first and paused to find him still standing by his father's room. He watched her with a nervous expression she knew he was trying to keep neutral, but she'd always been able to read him like a book. Read him as well as he could read her with that new magic of his, perhaps.

Thinking of that balance between them felt... right.

She offered him a smile and pointed into his room. "I'd like to stay in here, with you, if you don't mind. The Eastern District gets chilly at night this time of year."

His responding grin, a mixture of wicked delight and blazing happiness, robbed the breath from her lungs. "Smart. We could... share body heat."

She laughed lightly, a slight blush heating along her cheeks. She stepped into the bedroom and flipped on the light. Moving into the center of the room, she turned in a circle, taking in the familiar sights of kung-fu movies and athletic gear contrasting against the minimalist Japanese decor and thick futon. Martial arts belts hung on one wall, and Slate's scent permeated everything, even though it was clear he hadn't slept here in some time.

When she'd been in here yesterday, she'd been in a state of panic.

She hadn't stopped to consider the room, the space, the things that had happened here...

She pivoted back to him. He was still in the doorway, good shoulder propped against the doorframe as he watched her with a small smile. She could practically feel his satisfaction at having her in his domain, but he didn't crowd her, made no move at all, in fact.

She was going to have to work on that... on teaching him not to be afraid of scaring her off again. Not like this. She'd made her choice, and she had chosen Slate. And she would have *all* of him, every ounce of his intensity. She would take him as he was, because that's what he deserved.

She closed the distance. She took his hand, and tugged him into the room. He gently dropped her duffle on the floor and held her gaze as he came willingly, closing the distance until they were practically sharing breath, but still, he did not reach for her.

"I won't fly away, you know," she whispered into the quiet. Her fingers found his chest, flattening against the hard muscle there as she pressed a kiss to where his tattoos peeked out over the unbuttoned collar. "I promise."

Slate let out an almost soundless breath, and warmth curled in her belly when his large hands came to rest on her hips... and drifted higher, until his fingertips brushed under her shirt to scorch the bare flesh of her waist.

She let out a sigh of pleasure at the touch. So simple, so small, but it was like an anchor, locking her to him. She wanted more, wanted to lose herself in his touch. Her fingers drifted up to slip around his neck and pull his head down toward her.

"Kiss me," she whispered.

He instantly obliged her. It was soft at first, the kiss. He eased his lips over hers as his hands slid possessively around to her back.

"Careful of your arm," she murmured against his mouth.

He chuckled darkly, angling his head to taste her better. He released the small of her back with his good arm and reached up to grip her jaw in a gentle hold as he tipped her head back. "The arm's not gonna be a problem, love," he promised, and his eyes were a deep cobalt now, heat blazing in them.

This time, the kiss was anything but soft. It was a claiming, and she melted against him as she opened for him. Drank him in as much as he devoured her, fingers curling into his shirt. Between them, something *powerful* thrummed. There was no desperation in the kiss, just a slow intensity, a deliberate taking that was somehow... more.

There was a weight to each of their actions that had every touch, each taste, and every kiss echoing in her bones. She pulled her mouth away from his, and her fingers slid down his shirt, slowly undoing one button at a time. Her lips followed after her fingers, tasting every exposed inch as she went.

She was so engrossed in him that she didn't notice they'd moved until the back of her legs were brushing the edge of his futon. Heat tightened in her belly, and her fingers slid under his shirt and around his torso until she could dig her fingers into the muscles of his back. She pressed a kiss to the center of his chest as she held him to her tightly.

She absorbed the feeling of his body against hers, every hard angle against every soft curve, burning it into her memory so she would never forget. Drew in his scent and drank in his warmth, even as her hands moved up... and slipped the shirt from his shoulders.

His hand at her jaw slipped down to curve around her neck, thumb stroking against the small scar there. The touch went straight to her core, heat building until she was squeezing her thighs together for relief. She saw his nostrils flare, felt the responding flicker of his heartfire as his empathy magic picked up what her scent was already telling him.

"*Fuck...*" he whispered, voice hoarse.

His lips were back on hers, and fire sizzled in her veins at the hard push of his erection against her abdomen. Her fingers found his jeans at the same time as he tugged her shirt up. She let him win the battle of wills, easing her arms up as he pulled the shirt from her and tossed it aside.

Her hands returned to his shoulders as he nearly bent her backward, arms locked around her middle as his lips found the swell of her breast above her bra. Clever fingers had the clasp coming undone, and he tugged the garment free from her body with his teeth, wringing a moan from her when his lips found her aching nipple.

She whimpered when he switched to her neglected breast, clutching at his shoulders as her back arched and wet heat pooled between her legs. He dragged his mouth up along her collarbone until his lips found the scars on her shoulder, and he sucked the skin hard as his fingers worked the clasp of her jeans.

"Slate," she moaned. Both of their breaths came uneven as she mirrored him, fumbling once again with his pants. Before she could free him, he shoved her jeans down, stepping on the material and forcing her feet out of them.

She nearly fell backward into the bed, but Slate twisted at the last moment, tumbling them both into the sheets.

She sat up, straddling his hips. She gave into the temptation to caress her hands over the scrolling tattoos on his torso before she returned to his jeans. A rumbling groan escaped him, and he wrapped his fingers into her lace panties.

The sound of ripping lace joined the sound of their panting. His apology was a wicked chuckle, which melted into a groan when she succeeded in freeing him from his jeans. His back arched and his hips thrust upward helplessly as her fingers fisted around the hard length of him.

"Oh *shit...*" he uttered it like a prayer, the muscles of his abdomen bunching. "Oh *fuck...*"

For a wild moment, she was certain he'd come right then. Her whole body flushed hot at the idea of watching him come undone underneath her.

He must've picked up a thread of emotion, because he pushed himself onto his good elbow. "What are you thinking?" he asked, his voice rough in all the right places.

She shifted just enough to yank his jeans down and off, and because she couldn't help herself, she stroked her hand up his cock again, gripping it good and firm. Satisfaction shivered through her as he hissed out another curse and tipped his head back.

"I want to taste you," she replied, throat absolutely bone-dry with sheer *want.*

His breathing hitched, and she watched his eyes take on that inner glow. "Gods, *yes.*"

She wasted no time, pulling his cock straight into her mouth. He groaned her name, sending a spear of heat through her, which only spiraled higher and hotter as he threaded his taped hand through her hair. She pulled deep and hard, one hand working in tandem with her mouth. She glanced up at him, and her heart jumped to see he was watching her, breathing hard.

"Dani…"

She devoured him, wanting every inch of him to fill her. She never wanted to be rid of him.

"*Daniella…*"

That's what she wanted, the heated agony in his voice just before he—

His hand tightened in her hair, and he was pulling her away. She gasped as he pushed himself up, and his taped hand shifted to span her throat, bringing her so close that their breath shared space.

"Not yet," he said. "I wanna come inside you."

Goddess, she wanted that too. She wanted him embedded in her blood and bones.

He kissed her. Deep, thorough, but unhurried as his tongue tangled with hers. She shifted, straddling his hips, encouraging him to lay back down. His cock slid between her slippery folds, the delicious friction pulling a gasp from her that he swallowed, tongue teasing hers as he rolled his hips in a deliberate motion.

What if she had lost him? What if he'd left her alone—

Dani pulled back, bracing herself against his chest as she angled her hips. Their eyes locked as he slipped a hand between her legs to fist his cock, lining it up with her entrance.

Time slowed, the rest of the world falling away in that one moment.

She held his gaze as he slowly filled her, her muscles stretching to accommodate. Didn't break that stare that somehow felt like their souls were joining together as much as their bodies were in that one moment.

A part of her knew he felt it too, that weight of something more that colored the air between them. He palmed her throat again, his fingers gentle in that familiar possession, and Goddess, she wanted him to possess her completely.

She pushed her hips all the way down until he filled her to the hilt.

It felt like he was filling all of her, the very essence of him inside of her, just as much as the very essence of her was surrounding him, twining together as their bodies twined.

It amplified the pleasure until she could barely breathe. He released her throat and tugged her hand from his chest, lacing their fingers together. He brought their hands up over his head until she was stretched above him. She rode his cock in a slow, languid roll of her hips.

His head tipped back, hips thrusting upward as a growl of pleasure rumbled from his chest. "*Fuck*, that's it, love, take your time..."

She did, letting him fill her to the hilt with each rolling thrust.

She braced herself with her free elbow by his head and found her lips on his throat. She kissed him, licked at the skin there as her hips picked up pace. The hand at her hip tightened, fingers digging in until it was no longer her moving, but his hips surging off the bed as he held her still for his thrusts.

Pleasure spiraled through her, and Dani felt each thrust through her entire body, relished the feeling as he filled, filled, *filled* her.

Until there was no room left, until he was in every part of her, and she was a part of him, body wrapped around his as she welcomed him into her heat, each thrust pushing her closer and closer to an explosion she didn't know if she could survive.

Dani bit him. There were no thoughts, no reasoning, just pure instinct as she sank her teeth into the flesh at the juncture of his neck and left shoulder. Bit him as his own teeth clamped down on her shoulder, over that little scar.

Slate's hips surged up powerfully, fingers spasming on her hip as he let out a savage growl. "*Harder*," he rumbled against her skin, and she felt his teeth break her flesh.

There was no pain, only a blinding pleasure as stars exploded behind her eyes. She cried out, the sound muffled against his skin, and she sank her teeth deeper into his shoulder. Until the coppery taste of blood coated her tongue.

"*Daniella!*" Slate nearly roared, and suddenly the world spun, and she was flat against the bed, Slate above her, holding her steady with one hand under her ass as he thrust madly into her. She wrapped her legs around his hips and held on, riding the tidal wave of pleasure as she felt the hot spurts of his seed deep inside her as he came undone.

His cock pulsed with every rush of semen as his hips continued to drive into her, and Dani cried out his name, head thrashing against the pillow in overwhelming pleasure, aftershocks rippling through her.

The entire world stilled, hips slowing to a stop as Slate sagged above her, spent. He kept himself from crushing her with his good arm, pulling his head back until Dani's wide eyes locked with his. Red tinged his lips, his teeth, as he panted above her. A lingering pleasure and a feeling of sudden and deep *rightness* pulsed through her.

Her heart felt like it was going to gallop right out of her chest, and she couldn't catch her breath. There were no apologies from Slate this time, no guilt or anguish over hurting her, only an intense satisfaction that was an echo of her own.

Without a word, he eased himself to the side, careful of his injured arm as he tugged her body into the curve of his. A small part of her was terrified by whatever had just been forged between them. Terrified, but also... overwhelmingly happy.

The only sound came from their ragged breaths slowly evening out as they watched each other, faces close enough that her nose nearly brushed his.

"Did you mean it?" The words popped out of her, inspired perhaps by the stillness around them. "What you said last night."

Right before he'd pushed her into a portal.

He didn't look away, but she felt the sudden stillness in him, a tense caution. Finally, he released a slow, silent breath. "Uh... yeah. I did. I mean. I do—"

She reached up and stopped him with a fingertip on his lips. The wary tension in him had her instincts bristling with annoyance, because he was doing it again, stifling himself in fear of scaring her.

"I'm not afraid of your feelings," she told him softly. "I don't want you to do what you just did," she murmured, shaking her head a little. "That backpedaling thing you've been doing with me. I don't want you to hold yourself back."

A heartbeat passed, his eyes flickering back and forth between hers, searching. Cautious. Wary. The fact that *she* had caused that wariness was a burn in her throat. The Slate that made her blood heat and her heart dance didn't walk on eggshells, and she wanted that man back.

After a moment, he nodded slowly.

She dropped her fingers from his lips to curl them against his chest. "I'm not going to run or hide. I'm... tired of it." She crinkled her nose at him. "So don't hold back to spare my feelings. I want whatever is between us to be real, all the time. I want the real you, all the time."

He shifted his hold until he could cup his hand around her nape in a possessive hold. "I just... didn't want to scare you," he said, his voice no louder than a breath of sound. "I didn't... I don't want to give you a reason to walk away."

"I'm not, though. I meant what I said, too." That she would stay. She'd decided—and probably decided a long time ago—that he was worth it. All the trouble, all the chaos. *They* were worth it.

Again, he watched her, as if he were searching for the truth. Or rather, searching for a lie. He might be a shit liar, but she didn't forget that he could sense them easily. But she wasn't lying, and yet the wariness didn't completely abandon his cerulean gaze.

"Don't hold back, right?" She offered him a small smile. "Talk to me."

He hesitated a moment, but she gave him a pointed look. His lips twitched into a wry smile, and he let out a breath. "I've been in love with you since the minute I met you, I think." His words started slow, but soon they were pouring out, like he'd been dying to say them for some time now. "And I knew it for sure when I caught you outside the studio that night in the pouring rain. And I knew... I *knew* you didn't feel the same way, but I was willing to do anything to keep even a piece of you. Still am, probably." His gaze skated away. "Even if that means... scaling back a bit."

I want what you want.

Words from that night, burned in her memory, because she'd known it then, too, that he'd wanted more. Because he'd always been a bad liar. But she'd wanted to believe his words so badly, and she hadn't been strong enough to face the truth.

So he'd been willing to shove his own feelings aside and box away pieces of himself in a colossal effort *just* to make sure she was comfortable...

She couldn't stand that. Whatever was between them... it would be true, and honest, and equal. She would give all of herself, and demand the same in return.

"I, uh... I also figured out that you might not have the best... history with the fae," he said carefully, and her stomach tightened.

She'd have to tell him soon. About Kat... about her abduction after her parents' death... lay it all out, be honest with him the way she expected him to be. Not now, though. She wasn't... *prepared* to do it now. But she *would* tell him. Soon.

So she nodded, once. A confirmation and nothing more.

She was grateful when he didn't pry, just feathered a thumb against her neck. "And... you know. Here I am, all fae and shit. High Fae Royalty, no less." His tone shifted, almost bitter, and it occurred to her in a rush—maybe part of why he resented that piece of himself was because he thought it meant she wouldn't want him.

"I didn't wanna rush you or coerce you into something you didn't want," Slate continued. "A lot is different now, and until very recently, you've always had one foot out my door." He winced a little at his own truth. "And I didn't want to give you any reason to put the other one out too."

When he put it that way...

Dani sucked in a slow breath, knowing that they would never get anywhere if they clung to the past. She nodded, then looked him straight in the eyes. "I'm not going anywhere. Both feet are firmly planted inside the door, I promise. So... don't hold back with me anymore. Please."

She knew he was assessing her again, this time both with his eyes and his magic. She let him. Wanted him to see and feel the truth of her commitment. She meant it. She wanted to stay with him. It was a choice, and it was all hers.

"Alright," he replied.

"I mean it," she insisted. "Promise me."

Once again, there was a beat of pause. But he nodded. Once.

Satisfied with his answer, her eyes strayed to where she'd bitten him, just on the juncture of neck and shoulder. It no longer bled, but the sight of it drew her gaze like a magnet. It was instinct to want to apologize for biting him, but the apology felt wrong, especially considering how he'd urged her to bite harder. Absently, her own fingers brushed at where he'd bitten her, and it was not lost on her that they now had matching marks. A scar that seemed more than just a scar...

He noticed the shift in her attention, and she was convinced a hint of pink tinted his cheekbones as he reached up to brush at the mark on his neck, gaze sliding away from hers.

"I'll be right back," he muttered, rolling out of the bed.

She watched him as he strolled out of the room, biting her lip at the way the muscles in his back shifted and bunched. As he disappeared from view, she was surprised to find the bite on her shoulder was already scabbing. She didn't understand why, but she had the feeling what they had just done, the sex between them, it had changed the dynamic between them.

Permanently.

Nerves fluttered in her belly, a knee-jerk reaction in the face of commitment. Old Dani would've rolled out of the bed and disappeared then and there, but she wasn't that person anymore, and she didn't want to be. She'd made her choice. She'd chosen happiness above safety, and with a rush, she realized she didn't regret that.

"You can have a life, or you can have a life led by fear. Make your choice, Daniella."

Safety and security—her old life, Old Dani—had felt like living in a cage. A cage she'd placed herself in after losing both her dearest friend and her parents, because she'd been afraid to feel the pain of losing someone she loved.

Someone like Slate—

He was right, though—his life would never be *easy*. It would not be easy, being the girlfriend to the future king of the fae.

Queen consort.

Zeyphar's words lingered in her mind, but she shut them down. She wasn't ready to consider that yet. Even though '*girlfriend*' felt strangely lacking in what they shared, it was much more manageable of a term than *consort.*

Slate reappeared, a wet washcloth in his hands. He crawled across the mattress and gently swiped the cloth over her neck and shoulder, over the mark. His own had already been wiped clean.

"It doesn't hurt, right?"

"No," she said. "It..." she blushed a little, feeling flustered and odd about the admission, "it actually felt really good."

A little grin pulled his face, then he slipped the cloth down her belly and between her legs, igniting a spark of heat that was mirrored in his gaze. But his movements were gentle and efficient, before he lobbed the cloth into the laundry basket across the room—a perfect shot. He settled down beside her, tugging her close to his body once more.

Curling into his frame, her softness against his hard planes, and the way he shifted to accommodate her as they settled together... they felt like two puzzle pieces, finally fitting together. She wondered if he was having that thought too, as his good arm tightened around her, tucking her under his chin. His lips brushed her brow, and warmth bloomed in her chest. Smiling, she snuggled into him, laying her head over his strong heartbeat.

She wanted this. Him. The good and the bad, the ups and the downs, because moments like *this* were worth it. Dani uncurled her hand to press it flat against his chest, savoring the heat of him. "Slate... about what you said last night... I..." she faltered for a second.

"It's unconditional, you know."

Dani shifted in his hold until she could angle her head to look up at him. He tightened his grip on her, like he was afraid she'd fly away. "What I said last night. I didn't say it because I expect anything in return," he told her, meeting her gaze.

She smiled, something settling inside her. "How are you such a good person?"

His lips curled. "I'm definitely not *good*, love." And the wicked look he gave her had butterflies curling low in her belly once more. "Though I suppose I'm good where it counts, *ne*?"

Dani let out a little laugh, shaking her head. She slid her hand up his chest until she could rest her palm against his face. "I love you, Slate

Melisande." She nodded definitively. "And that's the truth."

Dani definitely *felt* him stop breathing this time. His eyes widened a little, surprise darkening them to the underside of an iceberg. She leaned up to kiss him, a gentle brush of her lips against his. She felt his heartfire flare, then bank abruptly.

"No, it's fine," she said, sharing breathing space with him. "You can peek. You can share with me, too, if you want."

The more times she felt his empathy magic, the more she became familiar with it. In fact, the sensation had shifted from something that caused her stomach to knot up to something that made her melt with warmth. She relished the feeling, wanting him to bask in her love in any way he could. After all he had gone through for her, she would not deny him even an ounce of her feelings for him.

He shifted, holding her closer, and gingerly shifted his bad arm until he could slip his fingers around her nape, thumb brushing over the healing mark on her neck. "I love you, Daniella O'Callaghan."

The intensity of those five, singular words surged through her. She could see in his eyes, in the lines of his face, in the sharpness of him. A lightness filtered into her; a smile slowly spreading wide across her face. Dani's hands moved on instinct, one curling around his neck, fingers brushing against the scabbing mark where she'd bitten him, while her other palm pressed flat against his chest, over the strong beat of his heart.

An assurance. A certainty. That he'd never leave her.

Never alone. Ever again.

LIGHTS AND STARS

... interesting phenomena in which predatory packs will often control large territories and allow non-predatory or smaller predatory packs to co-exist within the territory given they recognize the true regional alpha and defer to...

- Gherald Schmidt, Faerloch Historical Archives

"Did you know they rebuilt the arena?" Dani asked.

The day had bled into a mild early afternoon, and they decided to walk along the river on their way back from shopping. Dani had a drawstring bag from the Apple Store over her shoulder, holding some gadgety Christmas gift for Roger, and Slate could feel her victory thrumming through her, bubbling and popping like a glass of bright champagne.

Her emotions were crystal clear to him, clearer than he'd ever heard anyone's before.

Because the *mayting* was complete.

He tried not to think about it too deeply, lest he give himself a raging hard-on, both physically and emotionally. The pure lightning that had jolted through his nerve endings as her mouth had trailed over his neck, mixing with poignant arousal so intense, he'd been certain he was going to pass out...

Then she'd bitten him, and his entire world had clicked into place like long-lost puzzle pieces.

It'd been an intense exercise in self-discipline to let her crawl out of his bed this morning. He'd failed no less than three times before she'd finally grabbed his face and demanded a breather and some breakfast. The part of him that wanted to wrap her in care and luxury won out over the horny, post-*mayted* fae male side.

But only by a little.

There had been a moment over breakfast and tea, where he'd opened his mouth to tell her about the whole *mayt* business. She'd been sitting on the barstool in an oversized cotton *yukata*, her bed hair twisted over one shoulder. The lapel of the robe drooping to one side, one hand scrolling her phone, and she'd looked exactly like the future he'd always wanted. Exactly what he wanted to wake up to every morning for the rest of his life. He'd taken a breath to start the conversation when she'd interrupted him. *"Ooh, the Apple Store is open this morning! I need a gift for Roger—"*

And he'd dropped it, a piece of him faltering. If he dug into his own emotions churning in his stomach, he recognized it as fear. Or maybe a cousin of fear, closer to anxiety, fed by the memories of her leaving him—at the Den, at the arena, at Kari's house. Despite her assurance that she was staying, despite the finality of the *mayt* bond, he couldn't quite bring himself to word the coming conversation correctly.

As if there were a single perfect way to tell her to prevent her from bolting out his door. As if there was a combination of words he could spin that wouldn't make her feel *trapped*.

"I did," Slate replied. "We contributed a sizable donation to the re-construction."

"Oh?" She peered up at him. "Have you gone back to see it?"

"Yeah. The new facility is beautiful."

The streets along the river were loaded with fancy condos and town-homes and shops and cafes, and the trees danced with Christmas lights and festive decorations. Around them, small shops were closing up for the holiday, but they weren't the only people out for a stroll despite the fact it was Christmas Eve.

"Do you ever think about getting back in the ring?" Dani continued, swinging their interwoven hands slightly.

Slate chuckled darkly. "I'm in a ring all the time, love. I don't have the luxury to miss fighting with mortals anymore."

A little furrow creased her brows. "Who do you fight now?"

"Soldiers." He sucked in a deep, wistful breath. "Though, now that you say that... there's definitely something about the spirit of the competition I miss. And the winning. I used to win a lot more back then."

"You like to win."

He grinned, sharp and wicked. "I do like to win."

"You were on your way home from a fight that night, weren't you? When we... met?"

Slate glanced around, taking in the short, wide streets and the ritzy condos and swanky shops. "I was. I was last on the card that night and I'd missed the bus. I used to walk through here all the time on my way home from fights. Usually with the twins. There's a cafe up here where we'd get drinks—"

It hit him in a rush. He stopped dead on the sidewalk.

The cafe.

The Lights and Stars cafe.

The barista, Andreyas...

"Another fight tonight?" The gentleman beckoned him to the counter. Slate guessed the man was older, but he didn't necessarily appear that way. His longer platinum hair was pulled away from a distinguished face that seemed young except for the eyes. He had old eyes, but Slate couldn't explain why he thought so.

His feet were moving before he processed the conscious thought to move, his hand gripping Dani's and tugging her along.

"Slate?" She stumbled after him. "Slate! Wait a second—"

He palmed open the door to the cafe, the little bell tinkling above his head. The scene was so familiar. The coffee bar along the left wall. Tables along the right. A door leading into the back, covered with a gauzy, floating curtain. A handful of silvery-blonde patrons...

And there, behind the counter, stocking inventory, was an older gentleman with platinum hair tied back away from his face. A male with a distinct magical aura that Slate could now sense with his own magic. Moreover, he heard—and now understood—the whispers of the patrons in the back of the cafe as they gossiped in Faerish behind furtive hands.

Andreyas met Slate's eyes, and the male stopped, a carton of soy milk in his hands.

Slate felt Dani's emotions swell with unease as she realized the cafe was full of fae, but her anxiety dissipated quickly as she squeezed his hand, tickling a sense of pride from him. She glanced between him and the male behind the counter.

"Andreyas," Slate broke the silence first.

Gently, the milk carton touched the counter, and without taking his eyes off Slate, Andreyas addressed the patrons. "*Please excuse us*," he said in Faerish.

One by one, the patrons darted away, slipping through the gauzy curtain into the back. Slate watched them go.

"I wondered if I'd ever see you again," Andreyas continued. "The young male with the bright blue eyes. *Titania* blue."

"You sound as though you knew something." Slate dragged his gaze away from the curtain back to the barista.

"We had... suspicions. More wild speculations and unfounded hopes, really." Andreyas gestured behind him to the wall of teas and spices. "Shall I make us some tea? Perhaps you and your..." His attention shifted to Dani, nostrils flaring, and Slate bristled, shifting his grip from her hand to her hip to urge her behind him—

"My name is Dani," she said, thwarting Slate's attempt to shield her by stepping forward and offering a small but bright smile. "I'm Slate's girlfriend."

Andreyas nodded, expression softening a little. "We are well-met, Dani-*tana*." He looked back to Slate. "I swear on the life of our late queen, I mean you no harm. Please, sit. I shall make us some tea."

When the male turned toward his collection of tea leaves, Slate turned his body to shield her from view with his shoulders, slipping a palm along her neck as he searched her face. "You okay?" he whispered.

She nodded. "I'm fine. I was just startled, that's all. You rushed in here like you were ready to do battle."

"Sorry... it popped into my mind and..."

She stared at him with curiosity and spoke in a quiet voice. "You realized the people in here might be fae? You came here a lot, right? Before?"

Slate nodded, his eyes sliding back toward Andreyas. The male obviously had some sort of glamour disguising his dominant fae features—like his tipped ears—but Slate knew from experience that even the best glamours couldn't hide everything. The eerie grace of the fae, the platinum hair and gray eyes, even the lilting accent he'd never been able to place. The cafe always had a strange vibe, one he'd found interesting, and now he knew why.

The fae turned back to them then and gestured to a small table. Slate sat next to Dani, facing the glass windows, knowing Kallen would likely catch up with them soon. His professional babysitter didn't take kindly to Slate dashing off the beaten path, so to speak.

Andreyas poured three cups of tea and placed the steaming kettle in the middle of the table. "By what name do they call you now?"

Slate shifted his attention to the older male, one arm draped over the back of Dani's chair. "Slate is still my name. But many of the fae call me Zlaet, which is also fine."

"Prince Zlaet."

The title still left a terrible taste in his mouth, but he didn't let on, instead leaning back in his chair a little.

Andreyas inclined his head. "I was familiar with your mother. Princess Aredhel. *Queen* Aredhel."

"Were you?" Slate had always liked Andreyas, and even now, he was getting an honest, genuine vibe from the male. The buzz of unexpected shock was still fading in his emotions, but there was also delight and a strange mix of bittersweet relief and victory, as though he'd found the final piece to a puzzle and the whole picture made sense.

But Slate had learned the hard way not to trust people he met. *Especially* fae.

"Indeed. I come from a long line of artisan spice merchants. We had a contract with the castle in the Silver Valley. We delivered tea leaves and other spices. The princess was a familiar face around the wagons when the merchants made their deliveries." Andreyas smiled as he sipped his tea.

"How are you here and not in the Silver Valley?" Slate changed the subject. If he'd learned anything about living with the fae—and growing up in his father's household, in fact—it was that most conversations were hardly more than half-truths, wordplay, and circumnavigating questions with more questions. Slate had learned never to show his whole hand, and never to expect straight answers out of anyone, including himself.

He hated the subtlety but the culture of communication amongst the fae was convoluted at best.

"Ah..." Andreya drummed his fingers against his mug. "We fled during the Great Burning, when Zeyphar burned down a great part of the Silver Valley and the castle, including the homes of many merchants and middle-class faerfolk. We did not make it to the summer retreat village and came here instead, to Faerloch. My *mayt*'s family owns this small plot of land here along the river, and..." He gestured around. "Over the years, we converted this building into this shop, and a few apartments upstairs. With some special accommodations, of course."

"Accommodations?" Dani asked. She had two hands wrapped around her mug of tea, her body tilted into Slate, their thighs touching. Just that small touch anchored him.

"Yes. The building is constructed with as little iron as possible. It makes city life more tolerable."

"Not interested in going back to the Silver Valley?" Slate asked.

Andreyas' face hardened, jaw tight. "Not as it is now, I'm afraid. We barely escaped with our lives back then, and I don't wish to be involved in Zeyphar's tyranny over our people."

"How do you know I'm not in Zeyphar's pocket?"

Andreyas shrugged. "You've visited my shop many times over the years. I've come to understand a little about you. I cannot be certain, but you don't strike me as the type to play Zeyphar's games."

Slate nodded slowly, satisfied with his answer. He slipped his palm around Dani's nape. "You're right. I'm aligned with the fae in Titan's Fen these days."

"I thought you might. After the Great Burning, we'd heard through the faeries that the princess had made it to Titan's Fen with the help of her companion... a young human man of Mystic origins. Years later, I had learned of Queen Aredhel's death, and not long afterward, you appeared in my shop, with your Mystic features and your Titania blue eyes... and I thought... *we* thought..." He waved his hand to encompass the unseen people who had disappeared behind the curtain. "We prayed, hoping perhaps the queen had left the fae a parting gift, and hid him with his mortal father."

"You thought right."

The fae male's eyes slipped to Dani, then back to Slate, and he smiled. "We are blessed with a bright future, then—"

The door to the shop opened with a soft tinkle.

Ah. There he was. Kallen.

Andreyas twisted to glance over his shoulder. "By the Goddess. If it isn't Guardsman Ewyt."

Kallen stopped dead, letting the door shut hard behind him. "Andreyas."

"It's been a long time, friend."

Kallen was silent for a handful of heartbeats. Slate had never seen that expression on the lieutenant's face, as though he'd just come face-to-face with a fucking ghost. Kallen cleared his throat and inclined his head. "I searched for you for weeks. I assumed you for dead after the Great Burning."

"We live, by the grace of the Goddess. It took us many months to navigate out of the Forest, to settle into the city here."

"Your Breena?"

"Breena as well. Myself, Breena, a few others—"

Kallen *definitely* looked like he was about to faint there on the spot. So much so that Slate felt a flutter of concern echoing through Dani's grid. Kallen's voice was tighter than Slate had ever heard it as he said, "Iris?

Did Lady Iris come with you?"

Andreya's emotion grid lit up with sadness as the male's expression fell. "No. We have heard nothing."

Slate could've cut the tension in the room with a rusty butter knife. He glanced sidelong at Dani, threading a little emotion to her—curiosity, discomfort, alertness. Her own mind vibrated with similar interest.

"I'm not surprised to see you at Slate's heels, my friend." Andreyas rescued them from the awkward interlude. "Always trailing our late queen like a shadow."

"I take the safety of our people and their future very seriously," Kallen replied after a pause, inclining his head. "Have you been here this whole time, Andreyas?"

"Yes. As I was sharing with our prince—myself, Breena, and several others escaped the Great Burning and fled here."

"There is a home for you in Titan's Fen," Kallen offered. "Away from the city."

Andreyas pressed a palm to his sternum in gratitude. "I thank you, but we are happy here."

"Zlaet," the lieutenant turned his heather purple eyes to Slate, "I shall find you and Tanyiel-*tana* another time." With a final press of his palm to his chest, Kallen slipped out the door so silently, the bell didn't even tinkle.

Very interesting, considering Kallen was a relentless babysitter. Concerned curiosity trickled through him, but Kallen's mental wards were ironclad as always. Slate hadn't been able to glean anything about the lieutenant's emotions.

"Who's we?" Slate asked after a pause, turning back to Andreyas and pushing aside the weird vibe he'd picked up through that entire interaction. "You talk like there's a lot of people here."

"There are quite a few, yes. Fae who've fled the Silver Valley over the years, ending up here in the city. As I said, we have a few rooms and apartments above us on the upper levels, so we house as many fae families as we can."

It struck Slate then. "Refugees."

"Yes, more-or-less. We are the lucky ones. There are plenty of others who are... less fortunate. Many dwell in the northwest corner of the city, near the cliffs above L'el."

"It's nothing but slums up there," Dani said, frowning.

"Indeed. The best place to house the desperate. Being so near the Forest gives many of them peace. It's familiar. Not all fae can tolerate so much iron in the inner parts of the city. Many less can afford the luxury it would require to reside in custom iron-free dwellings."

"How many?" Slate asked. He *rarely* saw City Fae. Andreyas was not wrong—Faerloch wasn't hospitable to fae. Slate's impression was that the fae families still living here were those vestiges left over from the First Fae War when there was a disagreement between the High Fae noble houses. House Druidhil and House Taernach defected from the city, supposedly settling somewhere up north in the UK, and the other noble houses followed House Titania into the Forest and established the Silver Valley, leaving Faerloch to the humans. All history that happened *several* centuries ago.

And he only knew that because Galyn had insisted Slate learn as much as he could about the history of his people.

Andreyas' eyes were sad. "The northwest corner has quite a few. They are more-or-less self-sustaining, but very poor. And extremely nervous of outsiders, part of why they haven't accepted much help from me."

Slate sat back in his chair, eyes wandering around the shop. Some emotion churned up through him, and he narrowed it down as *bothered*. It bothered him, that there were fae out there struggling, and he hadn't known.

"Who's Iris?" Slate asked after a moment.

"She was a cousin of my *mayt*, Breena. She worked closely with your mother, and as such, shared a friendship with the guardsman as well."

"Huh..." Slate mused. "And he's a lieutenant now."

Andreyas nodded slowly. "A deserving promotion. Kallen has always been duty-bound and loyal, even as a faeling."

Slate smiled faintly. "Yeah. Yeah, that he is."

SUNLIGHT AND SHADOWS

... several years, during which Marius Cassius Romano disappeared following the death of Rowan Fafnir. The talks were instrumental on an amendment to the vampire Highest Law, which stated...

- Gherald Schmidt, Faerloch Historical Archives

Roger materialized in the shadowy corner of the martial arts studio. For a few heartbeats, he kept himself hidden, watching the lone male on the training floor. A heavy punching bag swayed with each strike of a wrapped hand, and two more lay on the floor a few feet away, lifeless, stuffing flowing out of them like lifeblood.

It had taken a great deal of self-control not to confront Slate before this with concern to the High Fae attacking Daniella's home. The darkness in his soul had demanded the *faeling*'s blood after seeing the ruins of Daniella's house and knowing how close she'd come to harm. It had been an incessant roar in his veins, the desire to find each and every fae who had threatened her and make them pay for the trauma inflicted on her.

But Slate had taken care of that himself, and Roger had known better than to confront Slate before he had himself well and truly in control.

Daniella wouldn't be happy if he slipped and accidentally ripped Slate's head from his torso.

He'd had every intention of confronting Slate like a civilized being at Madeline's Christmas Eve Party, but the prince had simply dropped Daniella off and left to attend to another matter. Roger's sharp nose had caught a whiff of Daniella's scent shortly after the *faeling* had departed. Her bright scent—sunshine and flowers and grass and morning dew—had been blended into something new. Like a meadow freshly coated with frost and ice.

The darkness inside him had bucked, and he'd decided it'd been best for Daniella's wellbeing that the *faeling* had not stayed at the party.

Roger had had much of the afternoon and evening during the festivities to sit with the knowledge that Daniella's scent had imparted on him. To temper the aggravation in his blood and bones, to temper the appetite of the shadows inside him that sensed his turbulence and sought to rise from the ashes inside him. *She does not belong to you.*

He'd known this moment was coming, had seen the preview of it the night Daniella had been brought to him in a state of shock from a blown-up arena, her neck marred by more than just a blade nick. Then there had been that look on Daniella's face three nights ago when the prince had been carried through the door of Karisi's home, half-dead from his fight to protect Daniella and her home. He'd seen the forces at work, the Goddess's plans for those two laid out before him like paved cobblestones leading to one, singular destination.

Mayted.

There was a piece of him that was... happy. Perhaps *happy* was not the word. Satisfied, mayhaps, that the Goddess had not chosen a blubbering, weak-willed male for Daniella. Slate Melisande was many things Roger did not like—he was dangerous, an empath, a prince in the middle of a civil war, with a volatile temperament, and too little self-control. He was *young*. He was in over his own head.

However... he was strong. There was no denying Slate's father had done the best he could to raise a fighter, a champion in every mortal right. And he was an ambitious male. Not easily startled. Spine of steel. He was independent, strong-minded, and he certainly cared for Daniella, that much was evident. He certainly tried to put her needs ahead of his own.

There were definitely worse choices for a *mayt*.

... he still didn't like it.

The moment he made himself flesh and blood behind the shadows, Slate's hand snapped out and stilled the heavy bag.

His senses were sharp, Roger would give him that.

"We have to stop meeting like this," Slate called out. "People are gonna talk."

Roger let the shadows slip off his shoulders like a silk cloak. Hands in the pockets of his slacks, he glided across the waiting room, stepped into the studio, then leaned back against the wall opposite of Slate, hands curling in his pockets as he detected Daniella's sunshine entwined in Slate's frosty scent.

"I trust you were the one who slipped the garlic into my Christmas gift from Daniella?" Roger drawled.

A wickedness pinched Slate's eyes. "I thought it was a nice touch. Loving, really."

Such boldness... typical *faeling*. If not for his sour mood, Roger might have laughed.

Maybe.

His gaze flickered over Slate's taped-up right arm. "I assume the witch-doctor is ensuring you heal?"

Slate's gaze narrowed. "Why do you care?"

Roger didn't. But he had several burning questions for the *faeling*, and he supposed at least one question should be lighter. Social niceties and all.

"The *mayting* is completed." He probably could have tried harder to keep the edge from his voice, but the tone came out razor-sharp nonetheless.

This time, Slate's eyes widened, a shot of intense fear sharpening them to a light, clear blue. The boy's pulse jumped, a tempting song to Roger's bloodlust. He truly almost smiled then. So easy to read. So easy to *manipulate*.

That would have to change.

Slate sucked in a near-silent breath, and a cool anger slipped over his whole body, the air between them chilling noticeably. "Why is that any of your business?"

Interesting. Interesting and alarming, little red flags firing in Roger's head. He thought of the burning cold scent marker left behind at Daniella's house, at a similar acrid scent he'd detected earlier that same day, when he'd fetched the boy for Daniella. This cold... this ice...

He'd tasted it before. A madness lived in Slate, like many male empaths before him. Like his uncle, though not nearly as devolved. A madness that could be dangerous, and it had its claws in Slate.

Like calls to like, sometimes.

"I make it my business to know what Daniella knows..." A pregnant pause. "Goddess forbid I let something *slip*."

Slate's aura pulsed, and the tattoos visible around his tank top guttered, darkening. "You wouldn't *dare*."

"No, I wouldn't, only because I do not wish to cause her undue stress." A pointed look. "You, however, must make it your business to tell her. *Soon,* if it pleases his highness."

He knew he'd struck a nerve when the boy's muscles tensed up, a hint of tangy fear wafting off him. Jaw clenched, the male used magic to manipulate the heavy bag off the chain connected to the ceiling, and with a wave, shoved all three heavy bags across the floor. A touch too aggressively.

Good. The boy *should* be afraid of the consequences of keeping secrets from his *mayt*.

"You're not here to give me relationship advice, vampire," Slate snapped, some of that icy temper showing. "What do you want?"

"Indeed, no. I am here to... *discuss* the situation at Daniella's house the night after Solstice, three nights past." His tone lost any attempt at false friendliness, becoming hard and flinty.

Slate's dark brow cocked up, and from the look on the male's face,

Roger suspected his eyes had gone red from the bloodlust thrumming in his ancient blood. "*Discuss?*" Slate nearly growled.

"Indeed," Roger murmured, and the word fell between them like a gentle threat, one he allowed to simmer in a taut silence before he continued. "If you continue to be so careless—"

"Careless? What the fuck—" Hot words from the male as Slate took an aggressive step toward him.

It made Roger's bloodlust stir to a roar, an eagerness for the fight that he kept under tight control as he continued to lean casually against the wall, hands in the pockets of his slacks. "Let me *finish, faeling*—"

"No," Slate said, his tone rising. Roger's mouth thinned into a hard line. Slate pushed on, holding Roger's stare and earning a modicum of respect from the vampire—beings far older and more powerful than Slate had withered beneath his stare. "No, I'm fucking tired of being talked to like I'm four years old. I'm not a *child*. *You* sent me to Dani that night, and—"

"I *expected* you to take precautions, to not track—"

"Precautions? I took precautions. They didn't track *me*, vampire."

Roger stilled. Down to the blood in his veins and the beats in his heart.

"Explain yourself." The words came out as a bitter whip, and he finally straightened from the wall to his full height.

Slate stopped, staring at Roger for several long, agonizing seconds. Roger dug deep into his well of self-control to not launch across the training floor and throttle answers out of the male. He knew he wasn't entirely successful, could see shadows curling around his shoulders out of the periphery of his vision.

Slate didn't flinch, but there was a vigilance about him that was wiser than Roger gave him credit for. Finally, Slate lowered his chin, but kept his eyes locked with Roger's. "You think the High Fae followed me there, don't you?"

Roger's eyes narrowed. "A fair assumption, considering your *history*, wouldn't you say?" he hissed, his control fraying.

Slate winced, and Roger *almost* felt bad, but not when it came to Daniella's safety. "That's fair," Slate rasped, but the male dragged in a breath and shook his head. "But no... that's not how it went down."

There was a fury in Slate that had nothing to do with Roger's antagonism, and it stilled Roger's rage more than anything. His silent stare demanded more from the *faeling*, and Slate sucked in a breath, clearly an attempt to calm himself.

"No," Slate continued. "They... they followed *her* home. They weren't there for *me*." There was a bitterness inside the rage of Slate's tone that Roger wanted to relish, but he couldn't, not with that information.

Roger's face became a frozen mask as he struggled against the suddenly roiling darkness snapping and howling at him to find, find, *find* those who had tracked Daniella to her home and smoked her out like an animal.

Find them, and tear them to shreds... over the course of a decade.

A shame they were already dead.

"I overheard them speaking. They followed her home after her *chat* with Zeyphar," Slate spit the words out, and Roger's fingers curled inside his pockets, nails lengthening into talons. "They knew the house was hers, but her house is warded, so they couldn't sense her inside. Or me, for that matter. And they couldn't enter without permission, so... the fae attempted to smoke her out."

"And were greeted with a surprise from their prince." Roger barely checked the savagery in his voice, his normally refined tone now guttural with the fury he wrestled with.

"I killed them. And Gelayeth is in our custody." Slate flexed his injured hand, knuckles turning white with force. "I'd thought about sending his head back to Uncle Dearest, but I'm not that kinda person. But the thought was satisfying." A muscle ticked in Slate's jaw, and his sapphire eyes had lightened to a frosty, icy azure. "I hate that guy."

"I can help you with that," Roger said with deadly softness.

"Oh, I know you can," Slate said with a short, humorless laugh. "But we're gonna see what information we can get out of him first."

Roger could almost envy Slate's innocence. Because he'd not have hesitated to pull Gelayeth apart piece by piece, divesting him of all his secrets... until only the head remained, and he'd have sent the head to Zeyphar, wrapped with a lovely ribbon.

Hate seemed a tame word for how Roger felt about 'that guy.'

"Not that I owe you shit for shit," Slate said, crossing his arms over his chest, "but if it makes you feel better, I didn't want this for her."

"Yet you were too selfish to tell her the truth, to let her walk away," Roger stated flatly as he continued to wrestle the darkness down inside him.

"Maybe. But so are you." Sharp words from the male with a pointed look, and for the barest of a heartbeat, Roger felt seen. Seen by someone who, for that heartbeat of time, looked far older than Slate's 31 years, with too much knowing in his eyes.

There was a beat of silence, the shadows inside Roger roiling and writhing, annoyed and aggravated that this *whip* of a creature had the audacity to hold up a mirror. To call attention to Roger's deep *need* for the brightness of Daniella's aura, the sunshine she gave off that chased away the shadows and sins that lurked in every dusty, dark corner of his aged soul.

"You know, in another life, perhaps you and I would've been good friends," Slate broke the silence first. He stalked toward the entryway to the waiting room, not pausing as he strode past Roger. His sharp hearing told him when Slate stepped into the small studio office off the waiting room.

"Perhaps..." Roger didn't follow after Slate, still trying to process what to do about the fact that Daniella had been personally approached not once, but *twice* now by High Fae.

"Yeah." Slate didn't raise his voice from the other room, displaying a shred of awareness for Roger's hearing capabilities. "You piss me off, but I could see myself liking that quality about you, given some time."

"You enjoy being angry?" Roger turned and slipped out into the waiting room, the darkness inside him sufficiently throttled, and moved to stop in the doorway of the office. He propped one shoulder against the doorframe, hands relaxed in the pockets of his slacks, studying the half-fae male.

"No. I enjoy being *aggressive*. That's why I like to fight." Slate shook out a fresh t-shirt and switched out of his sweat-damp tank in favor of the fresher cotton. "Perhaps we can still be friends, seeing as we both have similar interests in the same woman."

The barest trace of a frown came to rest between Roger's dark brows. "You seem unconcerned by this."

"Why would I be? If you *really* wanted Dani romantically, you would have made your move sooner, and truthfully, if you wanted me out of the way for that? No one would find my body."

That was true.

And yet, here the *faeling* stood. Whole. Breathing.

Because it would kill Daniella if something happened to him.

Slate's words sank into his shadow-drenched soul.

He... *hadn't* wanted Daniella romantically before Slate had come around. He'd been content to simply bask in her sunshine, with no ambition to make anything more of it.

And yet Slate had come around and become a threat to that sunshine, and his darkness had reacted to that threat. Had seen how Slate could take away his light and... adapted to that. His possessive urges, the inexplicable desire to kiss her all those months ago...

He realized now it had all been a twisted sort of chess game to keep his Daniella from being taken away. He could vividly recall the way he'd felt when he'd looked at her sweet face, vulnerable from the emotional wreck the explosion at the arena had caused. He'd wanted to kiss her, but he hadn't felt *lust,* only a calculation of how he could take advantage of the mess Slate had made, to secure his spot in the sunlight.

Though he kept his expression carefully neutral, the realization had him reeling. He *was* selfish, just as Slate had claimed. He'd been willing to play dirty to keep that sunshine and happiness in his life.

Slate studied Roger, head tilted and eyes narrowed. "You do know this isn't some 'Slate vs. Roger' thing, right?" he offered. "Dani won't just abandon you because she's *mayted* to me. You're her best friend. There's no competition there."

Roger locked gazes with Slate. There was an understanding there, and it made Roger's spine straighten. Slate had seen right past his cruelty and selfishness, and seen to the core of it. Perhaps the boy was more clever than he gave him credit for.

"We're all adults here. She has room in her life for all her relationships, past and future," Slate said with a quirk of his lips. "She's a fierce and loyal friend, *ne?*"

Roger knew that. He'd *known* that about her. And yet... in his fear, he'd forgotten a basic truth about Daniella O'Callaghan. She was kindness and sunshine embodied, and no matter who she was with romantically, she would never leave Roger behind.

He might have a few millennia on Slate's three or so decades of life, but just then, he suddenly felt very young, and very foolish.

Continuing as though they were merely discussing the weather, Slate dumped his broad, long body into the office chair and spun it around to face him. "Seeing as you haven't killed me yet, I'll take that as a good sign for a future friendship." The male dared to grin as Roger remained motionless in the doorway. "I plan on living a long time, pending, of course, my crazy fucking uncle doesn't separate my head from my shoulders before this civil war reaches its peak."

"I will do whatever is in my power to make sure that does not happen." The words jumped out before he could stop them. And even as the words drifted in the space between them, he knew them to be true.

Because as Slate breathed, so did Daniella. And he would do everything in his power to make sure she was alive and well for a very, *very* long time.

Slate's cocky grin faded as he stared at Roger. Studied him for a long, breathless moment. Then, he nodded. "I won't read into that statement any further than what it is."

Roger's expression finally shifted from the forced neutrality he'd set it in as one corner of his lips curled up wryly. "Oh, you are not that important, princeling. It is merely in Daniella's best interests. Regardless of my feelings toward you, the fact remains that your well-being is now in her best interest. *Mayts* do not live long without each other." The last sentence hung like a drop of blood on the edge of a knife.

Guilt chased through the male's eyes, a tension shimmering over Slate's shoulders. "I'm aware."

"The increased presence of High Fae around Daniella concerns me deeply. What are you planning to do about it?" Roger raised a brow.

"Short of sewing her to my left hand?" A restlessness settled over

Slate. Roger watched as he leaned back in his chair and traced his gaze around the office, as if the walls held the secret to the solution of their mutual problem. "She's taken some time off work, and she's staying here. I already asked Jian and his father to add an extra level of warding on the building. Kallen too. She's safe here. Relatively speaking."

Roger nodded once. A fortunate element of Daniella's character was—while she was friendly enough—she didn't *trust* easily. She was conservative about her own safety and too smart to take uncalculated risks. She would stay where she was safest. And with whomever made her feel safest.

Roger studied Slate. "If she were lured to the Silver Valley, what would you do?"

Murder danced in Slate's eyes, the temperature in the room dropping several degrees. An appropriate reaction, as far as Roger was concerned. In that moment, he relished the hint of cold madness in Slate.

"Would you follow her?" Roger pressed.

"Without hesitation."

"I should inform you—if either of you end up within the wards of the Silver Valley, I cannot come to you. The ward is specially crafted to repel vampires, per an ancient treaty long before your time, to maintain peace between the Goddess' two most powerful factions. There is a twin ward around the vampire stronghold that repels fae."

"Duly noted."

"I shall keep an ear in the shadows, but I am forbidden to get my hands truly dirty in your war, *faeling*. Lest I tempt forces that would make dear Uncle Zeyphar look like a sniveling babe weaning from the breast."

"What about that magical loophole there? About guardianship over people or something. Dani's your ward, isn't she?"

Roger lifted one eyebrow. "She is *mayted*, boy. The 'loophole' no longer applies."

"I see..." Slate mused, leaning back. "And don't call me 'boy.'"

"Compared to me, you are barely more than an embryo. You should be thankful I've promoted you to 'boy'."

Slate snorted, like he found that amusing. "Well, whatever, but just because I'm here now doesn't mean she stops needing protection. Parents are still *parents* to their married children." Slate rolled his eyes. "It's not like the responsibility disappears overnight."

Roger's lips thinned. "Do not compare me to a *parent*." That comparison seemed... wrong to him, especially when he'd considered kissing Daniella only months ago. "My relationship with Daniella is far from *fatherly*."

"Hmm. You're right, you're more like... you give *senpai* energy," Slate offered him a lopsided grin.

Roger's brows knit together. "Excuse me?"

"Like an older mentor. You know what? Nevermind." Slate waved a hand. "The *point* is, why should the whole... *mayt...* thing change anything about you being able to protect her?"

Roger sighed, closing his eyes and pinching the bridge of his nose for patience. "Let me be quite clear, *faeling*; the Vampire Council does not care. Legal responsibility for Daniella's well-being, according to their admittedly archaic laws, has shifted from me to you, and they exist to *uphold* these *laws*."

"Huh. That's super sexist, but alright. I guess it's hard to adapt to the modern world when you were born in the stone age." Slate sighed, rubbing at his face.

Roger cocked his head to the side, studying Slate once more. He looked... tired. Roger forced himself to remember that this young male was dealing with politics far beyond his age, and handling them, admittedly, fairly well. So his voice softened, if only the merest fraction, as he said, "I will continue to do what's best for Daniella. She will have both of us to protect her, but you must also mind your own health. And you must *tell her soon*." He made a point of glancing at the mark at the juncture of Slate's neck and shoulder. "Do *not* invite another reminder from me, *faeling*. The next one won't be as pleasant." He bared his teeth to make his point, knew his fangs had elongated and blood likely swam in his eyes.

Without waiting for an answer, Roger melted into the shadows.

Roger stepped from the shadows and into his penthouse condominium.

He had a lot to digest, about his feelings for Daniella, about how he'd come so close to sabotaging everything because of his insecurities. Unbidden, the memory of how his entire life had shifted so drastically came back to him then, as he dropped into one of the chaise lounges and closed his eyes, head falling back against the lounger.

"Please..."

The word was so quiet compared to the din of the London night, but he heard it nonetheless. He wasn't sure what had possessed him to walk back to his apartment that evening, but the urge had been there and the night air had been sweet.

Roger paused at the mouth of the side street, peering down toward the source of the quiet plea. His vampire eyesight pierced the shadows of the alley to discern two tall males with pointed ears. One of them held a young girl—a teenager—up by the elbow.

"She needs rest," one of the fae hissed.

"Bitte..." the teenage girl stumbled, knees buckling under her slight frame. "Bring... mich nach... Hause..."

The words were slurred. As though she'd had a touch too much to drink. But he did not scent alcohol on her, nay, but rather the bitter tang of chemicals and the sultry sweet scent of herbs.

Drugged.

At that moment, Roger considered walking away. He did not want to meddle in the business of the fae. He lived by his own code, by himself, involved in nothing and with no one. Lately, he had been contemplating ending his existence, the weight of millennia suffocating him. He had lived long enough.

So why should this female matter? He could not possibly save every mortal woman from the fancies of other lorebeings. Goddess knew the fae from the Silver Valley still enjoyed the occasional sport of humans...

... but he was not in Germany. This was the UK. The fae culture here was different. Wildly so. The Tuathe De *did not endorse the kidnapping of mortals for slavery or human sport.*

Something was amiss.

As fast as his shadows, Roger was down the side street, and he snatched the teenager out of the hands of the fae, plucked her from their grasp like a daisy.

The two fae jumped back with a startled gasp. "Vampire!" one of them hissed.

The girl hung from Roger's grip like a ragdoll, knees weak under her, hands clawing for purchase in his forearm. Up close, he could see she was clad in little more than pajama pants and an old t-shirt. As though she were snatched from her very bed.

This close as well, he could smell her. Behind the scent of chemicals, she smelled of sunshine and meadows, of greenery and morning dew...

It was... amazingly calming.

"Now what would two fae males need with this girl, hmm?" Roger said, scooping the small female up as if she weighed little... because she didn't, not yet fully grown as she was.

One of the fae—braver than his companion—took a step forward. "She is the property of the Tuathe De. *Hand her over, vampire."*

Roger peered at her again. Her ears were rounded, with red hair in a loose, messy braid over her shoulder. Green eyes that couldn't seem to focus on anything, pale faerie-face with a sprinkling of freckles, cheeks still round with youth, though she was close to adulthood. "She is a mortal child."

"She belongs to us."

Once more, Roger floundered. What was it to him, the life of this teenager? What was it to him what happened to her?

But her scent... it called to him, somehow... soothed him. The shadows inside him writhed like waves, ebbing and receding, intimidated by the scent of such sunshine.

"She belongs to no one, least of all you," Roger said calmly, and stepped back into the shadows. He heard the girl cry out, heard the sound swallowed up by the inky darkness that was shadow travel, but then they were in his living room.

Roger set the girl gently on his settee. She was shaking like the last leaf of autumn. "Bitte... ich will einfach nur nach Hause..." she said. Please... I just want to go home...

Interesting.

"What is your name, child?" he asked in the same language.

Her eyes were huge, framed with wine-red lashes tipped blonde. "Dani."

"And where do you live, Dani?"

"Faerloch."

"And how old are you?"

"Sixteen." She reached out and gripped the lapel of his jacket. "Please, please, take me home." Tears welled up, spilling over her freckled cheeks, the scent of sunshine and morning dew even more powerful. "Please. I just... I j-just want to g-go home."

Something about her, about the warm, calming scent of hers, the desperate look in her eyes, the innocence... the combination of it all spoke to him. He'd seen that exact combination in a rare handful of people across the ages of his life. Rare people who struck him to the core of his old, beating heart, and invigorated him with new life.

He wrapped his long fingers around hers. "I will take you home."

Roger sighed, opening his eyes and staring at the ceiling. Daniella had been a gem in his life ever since, a single ray of sunshine. She'd known nothing of the Lore, of magic, and over the next few days and weeks as he'd checked in on her well-being, he'd revealed the secrets of the magical world to her. He'd learned of the death of her parents, that she lived alone for the most part, and she had a rare gift to speak to animals. A lorekissed mortal.

And she was... struggling. She'd had many unpleasant emotions she'd battled with, seemed barely held together by her elderly neighbors who helped her where they could. And Roger remembered thinking it would be such a waste if someone as bright and radiant as she was were to fade away. So he'd taken her under his wing, so to speak. Brought her to the Den, kept the fae away from her—and the weres as well, who had a strange attraction to her—and introduced her to Madeline.

He'd declared her his ward, made it known to the representative from the vampire stronghold of Thule, and had spread the knowledge to others in the Lore within the confines of the city. He'd offered a blood bond for her safety, and she'd agreed without hesitation. As the months had bled into years, he'd simply basked in her light. And pitied any fool who threatened to block out his ray of sunshine.

Roger's penthouse was wide and open, with sweeping views of Faerloch. He strolled over to the refrigerator, intent on filling a deep-bellied glass with bloodwine. The front of his fridge was covered in pictures—at Madeline and Daniella's behest—of various adventures the three of them had participated in over the years.

When had Daniella become so integral in his life? She wasn't the first person to touch his soul this way, but her timing? Before that fateful night, his darkness had become an ever larger beast he'd struggled to keep under control, and his life had been empty of meaning, making it even more difficult to control the monster inside him.

He might have saved her, but truly, she had saved him. He'd been considering ending his existence when she'd restored purpose to his life. Over time, that purpose had become... happiness. He'd begun to look forward to events, had formed new and deeper friendships, like with Madeline, when before he'd had no drive to form any new bonds.

His love for Daniella had transformed his life, and Slate had threatened that slice of happiness. Undoubtedly, Roger had striven to ensure Daniella was happy and healthy, but now he wondered if he'd done that for himself more than her. Had he selfishly ensured her happiness for the sole purpose of ensuring his own?

He remembered the first night she'd brought Slate to the Den. Roger had watched them, and for the first time in as many years, he'd felt real fear. Not only because of Slate himself and the strangeness of his scent and the fluctuations of his aura and the fae on his heels.

No, it was fear caused by how Daniella had responded to him. Unlike anything he'd seen before, unlike how she'd behaved with anyone else before, including himself or Madeline. And Roger had watched as the two of them drifted closer and closer together, like magnets unable to fight the inevitable pull of the other. Every touch, every glance, and the dread inside him had grown at the realization that there was someone out there who could take his ray of sunshine away.

Quite suddenly, Roger had found himself... jealous of Slate. Found himself aggravated by how the male made Daniella laugh without effort. An emotion akin to *desperation* clawed inside him when her attention shifted, and the number of her daily texts to Roger dropped off.

He'd become someone he didn't recognize around Daniella—a spurned lover, as if he desired Daniella romantically.

Yet no other male who had vied for Daniella's affection had bothered Roger. He'd known she shared her body with others, and it hadn't ever been a concern.

Those she dated hadn't held her attention for long.

He filled a deep wine glass, then dropped himself back into the chaise lounger. Slate's pointed comments tonight had been eye-opening, because he realized now his jealousy hadn't been about wanting Daniella romantically. He'd simply been loath to lose the person who meant the most to him, and if she wanted a romantic, charming partner, could he not also be that?

But such a subconscious plan was flawed, because it didn't matter how he changed himself or acted. He wasn't Slate Melisande. And there would be no one for Daniella but him. The Goddess herself had declared it.

Despite this, Slate had been right... Daniella would not abandon Roger now that she'd *mayted*. His fear of losing her had clouded his judgment, and it was like that fog had finally dissipated from his mind.

He pulled his phone out of the pocket of his slacks and checked the clock on the screen. Slate should have had enough time by now to portal to Madeline's and back.

Roger dialed his top number.

"Hi!"

Roger's eyes slid shut at her bright, cheerful voice, illuminating his soul even from miles away. "You did not text me when you arrived back to the Eastern District," he drawled, that bright voice filling him up, awakening within him a joy that had his lips curling into a soft smile.

"You didn't give me time! Geez, Roge, we *literally* just stepped over the ward boundary. Give a girl a minute, would you?"

Roger heard Slate's growl, but didn't quite catch the words. Based on the way Daniella gasped, he could only assume it was something foul. Roger smirked, and his voice was paper-dry as he said, "I never did thank your prince for the garlic."

"Slate Melisande!" Roger heard Slate roaring with laughter and heard Daniella tip the phone away from her face. "You did *not*. I told you not to do that!"

Roger's smile grew as he imagined her whacking Slate with her hand, a crinkle across her freckles, knowing the male would do little more than fend her off playfully.

The smile slipped, agitation replacing it. The *faeling* better tell her *soon*, because he feared the fallout would be explosive. And when it was, *if* it was, he would be there to catch Daniella on the other side.

Always.

CHAPTER TWENTY-NINE

ALL MANNER OF FOLK

... known as the Great Faeries, these mystical women reside in the deepest sector of the Forest and are purported to reveal destinies to those who...

- Gherald Schmidt, Faerloch Historical Archives

Dani could tell something was bothering Slate.

She had her head pillowed against his bare shoulder, tracing her fingertip over the sharp strokes of his tattoos on his chest. He was so quiet, she would've bet he was sleeping, except for the finger twisting a strand of her hair; a nervous habit of his.

He'd picked her up from Maddie's Christmas Eve Party and they'd come back to his apartment, where he had an expensive bottle of sake waiting for them. Beside the sake bottle had been a little gift wrapped in exquisite paper with a silk ribbon, so beautiful, she hadn't wanted to rip it open.

"Kari said you don't have this one yet." Slate handed her the gift, his typically sharp grin missing all the edges. "And before you ask, yes, she wrapped it too."

Inside was the newest Pokémon game, and she grinned in delight. "It's perfect! Thank you. This is weird, but, uh…" She bit her lip as she reached into her backpack, and pulled out a wrapped present. "And Jian said you don't have this one yet either."

Laughing, Slate tugged the wrapping off, and his smile regained all its sharp wickedness as he read the title of the cheesy martial arts Blu-Ray in his hands. "Nice. Excellent. Perfect background noise."

"Background noise?"

"Yeah. For later, when I show you my appreciation in my bed."

Needless to say, the sake came with them into the bedroom. And he'd made good on the 'later' part.

Now, she propped herself up and looked down at his face, finding his eyes slightly unfocused with inward thoughts. "Alright. What's eating you?"

His gaze snapped to hers. He blinked at her before his face pinched into a little grin. "Nothing." He detangled his hand from her hair and traced a line down the center of her face, over her nose and down to her lips.

She snapped her teeth at him, and he pulled his hand back, his grin widening a little. Dani resisted the urge to kiss him and wrinkled her nose at him instead. "Liar."

His face faltered a little, and his other hand slipped over her bare back. "I dunno. I can't stop thinking about what Andreyas said yesterday. About the refugees in the Northern Slums." His gaze wandered around his room. "Just… fae political stuff."

"Tell me." She leaned down to press a feather-light kiss against the hard line of his jaw. He studied her for several heartbeats, to the point where she questioned whether or not he was going to share. If he was going to backpedal or not. "Tell me," she repeated. "I want to know."

Slate huffed out a breath. "It bothers me. It bothers me that I didn't know. Because… you know, it's supposed to be my job to take care of these people. Well. My future job, I guess."

She laid her palm against his sternum. "You couldn't have known. You've been a fae prince for what? Seven months?"

He snorted derisively. "Feels like longer." His eyes tracked around his room again and his fingers returned to her hair once more, twirling a lock of red-gold over and over. "Still... I wanna help them. Even if people think it's a calculated political move, I still wanna do it. Zeyphar is *fucked up*. I know for a fact the Silver Valley is in heaps of shit right now. And there's no place for the faerfolk to escape. Titan's Fen is tricky to find at the best of times, and almost impossible for those completely unfamiliar with it. Means fae have to brave the Forest or the city. Both of which can be hostile environments for them..."

Dani nodded, a shot of pride going through her. To have such compassion for a people he didn't even know existed a year ago showed exactly what kind of leader he would be. "That's really hard. But you have to remember—Faerloch is a magical city too. It's not like there's a shortage of magicfolk here... they live in small pockets all over the place. Most magicfolk dwell in pockets with other like-folk. Witches covens. Were packs. I know Southside is controlled by a local were-leopard pack. There are pockets of magic everywhere for people to find."

"I know. I know." He shifted, nudging her to the side so he could sit up. He ran his palms over his face and his head, threading his fingers through his hair. Stress bled from his pores; acute and so sudden, she could taste it in her throat. Was he projecting his emotions with his magic? No, because she didn't see his heartfire flare. He was just easy to read.

"And I know I shouldn't really think about it too much either." Slate scowled. "I got enough shit to take care of between Titan's Fen and here."

That's what she was afraid of too, for him. Burning the candle at both ends.

"But you know... what if you have nothing?" He laced his fingers together on top of his head. "No family. No community... brand new to a foreign city? Fae families are *small*. Those with more than two children are considered *blessed*. So they rely on community. Fae are super communal."

Dani realized she was woefully ignorant about the customs and culture of fae. City Fae were so rare, and if she were sitting here spilling her own truth, she hadn't bothered to learn much about them. Other than how to avoid them.

At least, that's how she'd thought of fae before Slate.

Now? Perhaps... perhaps it wouldn't be so bad to learn a bit more about them.

"And," Slate continued, "I can tell you for a fact that almost none of the faerfolk civilians in Titan's Fen have seen a human other than my father and Jian."

Surprised, she cocked her head to the side, nose crinkling. "Really? They've never seen a human?"

"Most of them? Never. They don't leave Titan's Fen. They don't need to. The village is completely self-sustaining. Same with the Silver Valley. My mother? Never saw a human before she met my father, so I've been told. Imagine never seeing a human before, then suddenly you're dumped into a new city and a new culture *full* of humans, and you have *nothing*. No home. No clue. You don't even speak the language." He dropped his hands suddenly, letting out a breath. "I wanna help them... because I've *been* them."

Dani's heart lodged into her throat. Suddenly, she was five years old, going to kindergarten in Faerloch when she didn't speak German. Then she was sixteen and thrust head-first into the magical community. And now... she was here, literally just thinking about the fact that she knew nothing about the fae, yet was committed to dating their future king.

Future queen consort—

"Me too," she nodded. "I've been there too."

"Refugees of war never crossed my mind, even though Titan's Fen is literally full of them." He scooted to the edge of the futon and shot to his feet, making laps around the small room, naked as sin. "What if... what if there was some kind of refugee housing, just for fae and magicfolk. Right here in the city. Some place we can... I dunno.... protect? You know, sanctioned or something."

"Seal of approval from the Zlaet Titania, fae king?" She offered him a small smile, propping her head up with one hand as she lay on her side.

She watched him, trying not to be distracted by the way his muscles slid beneath his skin.

"Yeah. Like that." He shot her a little grin. "Does something like that exist in the city already? A magical... a magical district, maybe?"

"Something exclusive? No... not that I'm aware of, at least. The Dark Arts Market is the only place I've ever been to or heard of that's *exclusively* magical. No mortals allowed kinda thing." She shook her head. "It's full of seedy business and underground trade. Some of it is legal, by lorebeing standards, but a lot of it isn't. I definitely wouldn't call it a magical sanctuary by any means."

Silence fell. She could practically feel his mind whirling. "Imagine a community where all magical folk could just... be themselves, you know? Some place where... all manner of folk could come. Live. Do business. Go to school."

She beckoned him with her hand. He was instantly in her face, hands planted on the mattress on either side of her, and she sucked in a breath at his fae speed. She smiled and placed her hands on either side of his face. "I'm one thousand percent convinced that if you want it that badly, you will make it happen."

He grinned. "You think so?"

"I know so." Her grin widened. "Because you don't like to lose."

CHAPTER · THIRTY

THE LONE SAMURAI

Little is known about the quiet and elusive Shamanistic magic branch, which allegedly spans from the farthest reaches of Canada down to the tip of South America. Their scarcity is often attributed to the brutal treatment of their people when the mortal Europeans arrived and...

- Gherald Schmidt, Faerloch Historical Archives

"Go on, everything you got. Right here."

Dani gave him a look, a smile flirting with the edges of her mouth. "What if I hurt your arm?"

Slate chuckled. "It's cute you think you can hurt me." Her look hardened into a little frown, and he quickly amended, "Physically, I mean."

"I think that's worse, that you said that," Dani said, frown shifting into more of a pout.

Slate grinned, wide and cheeky.

They were in the studio, on the training floor. Slate had come downstairs to do a little physical training, testing out the recovery of his arm. It seemed to be healing swiftly; he had almost full range of motion and he could support his own body weight with it now. Besides a little stiffness, and some aching if he pushed it, his arm felt good as new.

Which, considering how fucked up it had been a few days ago, was a miracle.

And magic, of course.

It was the day after Christmas, and Dani had disappeared for the morning to go have a little date with Kari. She'd returned sooner than he'd expected, and all of Slate's big ambitions to train for the day petered out into some playful instruction. So far, he'd shown her how to make a proper fist.

And because she kept dissolving into laughter, that was about... well, all they'd done.

"Come on, love. Give me a good punch."

She laughed again and tapped her fist half-heartedly against his hand.

"Wow. I can't decide who hits harder—you or the faeries."

More of her laughter lit up his insides, and she looked at her hands. "Hey! I never learned to fight with my hands. I just rely on Sellie and my gun."

"You should learn. You might not always have your gun." He gave her a look, brows raised.

Her response was another cheeky grin. "Why? I have you."

That threw him for a second. "Oh... well. You just... you should. You should still learn."

She pressed her palms against his chest, sweeping her hands out and over his shoulders and down his arms. All his nerve endings stood right to attention. "I mean, I'm not a damsel in distress or anything, but I'd not say no to being rescued by you." She glanced at him through her lashes. "Especially when you wear the martial arts uniform."

He palmed her throat gently, possessively. "You like to be rescued by a man in uniform?"

"What can I say? Something about the black-on-black look does it for me." Her irises began to shimmer, the outer edges brightening to an iridescent emerald. She slipped her palms under his tank top and up his stomach.

Slate leaned forward, closing the space between them. "Do I need to go change?" he whispered against her lips.

She smiled. "I have a pretty decent imagination…"

He kissed her, tugging her in closer to him. Her hands slid around to his back, sharp little nails digging into his skin. He shifted his hand from her throat to her chin, tipping her head a little so he could devour her properly. A small sound escaped her, and his tongue was in her mouth, tasting her—

The door to the studio opened with a squeak and a suction of air.

Slate swiveled his head with a small growl—the studio was closed for the holidays, so students shouldn't be here—and made eye contact with Ronin through the glass dividing the waiting room from the training floor.

The kid stopped dead in his tracks, dark eyes widening. Several heart-beats passed in total silence. Ronin's eyes dragged over Slate and Dani, from where Slate held Dani's chin, down to where her hands were shoved up his shirt.

"Didn't… didn't think anyone would be here, sir." Ronin broke the silence first, flushing from his neck to the roots of his dark hair, his voice pitching nervously. He stared at his feet.

"Well, seeing as I own the building, kiddo…"

"Oh. Right."

"What do you need? Classes are canceled for the holidays."

"I uh… I wanted to get a little patterns practice in."

Slate waited an additional heartbeat before he eased away from Dani, giving his body a second to recover. She stepped back smoothly, shuffling her fingers through her hair.

Ronin picked his eyes up, bouncing them from Slate, to Dani, then did a double-take back to Dani, eyes sharpening on her in recognition.

Slate pinged his eyes from Dani to Ronin. "You two have met."

"The other day. Briefly," Dani said, offering Ronin a smile. "Probably not my finest moment. I'm Dani, Slate's girlfriend."

Girlfriend.

Slate's brain short-circuited around the word, nearly missing the exchange from Ronin. "I'm Konoe Ronin. Um, Ronin's my first name. I'm... I'm a student here."

"Nice to meet you for real, Ronin." Dani smiled brightly, and he noticed Ronin relax a shade. "Slate's talked about you before. Says you're a great student."

"Thank you. I have a great instructor."

Dani smiled again, and she laid a hand against Slate's chest. "I'll go upstairs and check on Dash and Sellie." Leaning up on tiptoes, she brushed her lips against his jaw, then she breezed off the training floor and around the corner. Slate heard the door shut and her soft footfalls up the stairs.

Every bone and fiber in his body screamed to go after her and pick up where they'd just left off. But now that Ronin was here, in the flesh, Slate remembered he'd been meaning to talk to the kid for a few days now.

Slate strolled off the training floor and dropped his body into the chair across from where Ronin was standing.

"I noticed you've been hanging around the studio a lot more lately." Slate rocked his chair back on two legs.

Ronin's attempt to look casual was a valiant one, Slate would give him that. The shrug was almost convincing... if Slate couldn't hear his heart racing and taste the anxiety roiling over him. "Part of my responsibility here, sir, for the internship."

"I told your parents I would take up 15 hours of your time a week. Last week... I clocked you at nearly *forty* hours spent here." The security cameras didn't lie. Slate had noticed that Ronin would come to the studio directly after school, teach the classes, and linger long after the last student had left. The footage showed him working on his own martial arts training or doing homework, but more days than not, the kid was here until long after midnight.

Rinse and repeat. Even on weekends.

Another almost-casual shrug. "I like it here. If it's a problem—"

"Look at me."

Ronin dragged his dark eyes up to Slate's.

"You being here is not the problem. It's never a problem and it will never be a problem. The problem is what you're telling your parents, and why you're avoiding your house."

"My parents don't care where I am…" The words were bitter, venom leaching into each syllable. "But they think I'm in a study group."

"What's wrong at home?"

"Nothing… I mean. Not really…"

Slate leaned back in his chair again, letting Ronin have his silence. Slate knew his student—he'd talk when he wanted to. Kid kept a lot close to the chest, especially about his home life. Slate knew just enough about what went on in the Konoe house to want to take Ronin home with him and keep him. Ronin's parents were older, and their oldest daughter, Mariko, was the perfect poster child of a dutiful Japanese daughter. Married young to a successful businessman who was closer to Slate's age than to Mariko's, and already had a baby.

And Ronin's parents were both weirdly strict where it counted and hands-off where it counted more. They set their only son up for success—the best education, great family vacations, extracurricular camps, all the opportunities, but…

Slate remembered when Ronin had started coming to the studio. Ronin's mother had brought him one day to Slate's Little Dragon Program—the one designed for 3-5-year-olds. It had been obvious pretty quickly that she'd wanted a place to put her son so she could do errands alone a couple of days a week.

And Ronin had shown up for every single class since. Slate hadn't seen such commitment to the art since he, Kari, and Jian had come up through the ranks.

It'd been a no-brainer to choose Ronin for the Internship Program Slate offered through the studio. In exchange for teaching, the studio offered a scholarship to cover living expenses for students enrolled in the University of Faerloch for the first year.

There'd been a lot of talk and tension in Ronin's family over it—they'd wanted him to put martial arts on the back burner and focus on graduating and getting into a top university. They were pushing Ronin to be a doctor or a politician or some sort of top-level executive. In fact, Slate and Kari had to fight to get Ronin's parents to allow him to take the martial arts internship.

The deal Slate and Kari struck with Ronin's parents was that if Slate would agree to shift the scholarship to whatever school they wanted Ronin to go to, they would allow Ronin to continue his martial arts career.

The kid had sobbed when Slate told him. Slumped into a chair in the waiting room and just cried.

"I got some early admissions letters," Ronin said, voice barely above a whisper.

"Oh?"

He nodded, unzipping his backpack with deliberate steadiness. He reached inside and pulled out three thick manila envelopes and laid them on the table.

Slate frowned and reached forward to shuffle the envelopes, reading the addresses. Cambridge. Kanazawa Tech. Oxford. "Paper copies?"

"I requested them."

"Why?" It wasn't a secret that Ronin was severely dyslexic, so it was an unusual request for him. His parents refused to admit there was anything *different* with Ronin, though, so he never got the help he needed. Plus, Ronin attended to private school, and from what Slate understood, special education resources there were extremely limited.

It was a direct testament to how much work Ronin put into school to maintain top marks without any accommodations.

"I didn't want my parents to sneak onto my online account and look at the responses," Ronin finally admitted quietly after a long pause.

Slate studied the teenager, heart tight in his chest. It had always bothered him how much Ronin's parents didn't *see* Ronin for who he was, and instead who they wanted him to be.

Slate would've considered himself *blessed* to have a kid like Ronin.

Finally, he held out a hand. "You want me to read them?" His tone held no room for judgment, only simple understanding.

"Please."

One by one, Slate opened the letters. One by one, each said the same thing: *We are pleased to inform you that your application to our program has been accepted...*

When he finished reading the last one, Slate placed the papers carefully on the table. "Is this why you've been avoiding home?"

Ronin nodded, still staring at the table. "My parents know admission decisions are coming soon. And I just... I don't wanna talk about it with them. I don't even want to go to college." Ronin swallowed hard. "School is hard enough now. I can't be a doctor or a politician. I can't *read* well enough for that."

Slate nodded. He knew, without a shadow of doubt, that Ronin could be whatever he wanted to be. He was smart and articulate and resourceful.

But he wasn't wrong about his self-assessment of his education. Slate couldn't even imagine how hard school must be for someone who struggled with reading. The lack of independence. Having to constantly readjust your workflow to make your own education accessible to you. And to volunteer to do *more* of that for something you weren't even interested in?

"What do you want to do?" Slate asked. "Where do you picture yourself in five years?"

Slate could guess, of course.

Ronin shuffled through the letters absently. "I dunno. Probably in business or something. I could pay someone to do the paperwork piece and handle all the reading for me."

"True. What about outside of a job? What kind of life do you want?"

Ronin was silent for a few moments. "Something simple. Something different. Honestly? I've always kinda admired your life, sir. Just... teaching martial arts, doing your own thing, going at your own pace. I feel like a lot of people probably expected you to get married young and get a wife to take care of Grandmaster Melisande. And... you didn't care what people thought."

"Still don't."

"I like that. But my parents would disown me if I didn't go to college. If I deviated from their 'plan' for me."

Slate had a lot of opinions about Ronin's parents, but he held his tongue. "Listen. I'm gonna give you some really adult advice."

Ronin nodded, still keeping his gaze locked on the table in front of him.

"Fuck what your parents think."

The kid's eyes flashed to Slate's, wide and shocked.

"I'm serious. I know that's terribly hard to grasp as a teenager, but the sooner you can shed the weight of whatever expectations they've loaded you with, the better you'll be," Slate continued, rocking in his chair. "You were not brought into this world just to fulfill generational expectations and blindly follow whatever path is already pre-paved for you. Some people like that, and that's fine. But if you want something different, you gotta rough it a little. And that's scary, I get it. Your existence doesn't have to boil down to legacy and posterity."

Ronin frowned. "Sir?"

Slate rocked back in his chair. "Basically, fuck what people think, *ne*? But it's hard because it's attractive to look down a pre-paved path and know everything will be done for you. Mindless, but would you be happy? Or would you only be content? It might not be easy, but sometimes, the right way, the way that leads to true happiness? It will fit. You'll feel better. Does that make sense?"

Ronin hesitated before nodding slowly. "How... how do I do that? How do I even start that?"

"Well... are you going to college or not?"

Ronin stared at the letters again. He threw them carelessly back onto the table. "No."

Slate gathered all the letters, and without a word, he shredded them. Ronin's dark eyes grew wider and wider, jaw dropping as Slate sprinkled the paper pieces onto the table like snow.

"What am I gonna tell my parents?" Ronin whispered.

"You say nothing until they ask you," Slate replied, standing and striding over to the office. He snatched the trash can and came back to the table. He swept the paper pieces into the bin. "And when they ask, you stick to your guns. You say you are not going to university. And when they ask what you plan to do with your life after you graduate... you tell them I'm turning your internship into a job."

Ronin stared at him, jaw slack. "What?"

"You heard me. I'll put you on my payroll. I have... other responsibilities that take me away from the school sometimes, and those times, I'll have you here to take over." Slate grinned, shrugging.

"Are you gonna give me your school?" It came out like a cautious whisper.

Slate chuckled. "You're 17. I'm not giving you *anything* except a job. We can re-evaluate after you've had some think-time outside of the academic setting, and when you get out from under the thumb of your parents, deal?"

Ronin stared at him like he was still playing mental catch-up. Finally, he licked his lips and cleared his throat. "Deal."

Slate's lips hiked into a grin. "You're nervous."

"I'm terribly nervous, sir, if I'm being honest," the boy admitted, rubbing at the back of his neck. He looked down at the trash can, then back up at him, meeting Slate's stare. "But... I think I feel better."

"Good." Slate nodded.

Ronin let out a breath that sounded like he'd just released months of anxiety from his lungs. Finally, he grimaced. "My father's gonna have an aneurysm when he finds out I'm not going to university, and I'm working for you instead. He thinks you're part of the *Yakuza*."

Slate laughed, full and deep. "Good. Let him."

Ronin looked at him cautiously, then asked, "Are you? Sir?"

"What do you think?"

The kid gave him an assessing look, eyeing the tattoos on his arms. "I think... it's better for me not to speculate."

Slate's grin was a little too wicked. "Me too."

A REPRISE IN TITAN'S FEN

... an unexplainable sentience. The Forest's shifting locations were once considered random, however after reviewing the logs of Herr Orlan of the Deephaven Dwarves, it has become clearer that the whims of...

- Gherald Schmidt, Faerloch Historical Archives

Dani lifted her head from her Nintendo Switch when the sound of the roof door opening interrupted her Pokémon battle. She was sitting in Ebisu's rooftop garden, her back nestled against Sellie's flank as the griffin dozed, while Dash slept curled against her thigh. A thread of happiness tainted with a hint of anxiety that wasn't her own filtered through her, subtle enough not to be overwhelming. Slate's smile was immediate when he spotted her, but it dimmed slightly as that anxiety peaked.

She wondered if he did it consciously or not, feeding her his emotions whenever he was nearby. Dani figured it was his way of leveling the playing field, since he had access to her emotions whenever he wanted, though somehow she never felt like he was invading her emotional privacy.

Not anymore, at least. Not since she realized she didn't have anything she wanted to keep from him, emotionally. It helped, too, that if she asked him not to read her, he'd close himself off to her at once.

Slate angled his way toward her, and as he passed the flowers, faeries darted out to assault him, bringing a smile to her face. She remembered Slate telling her how much the faeries loved gossip. *"They love to spill the tea over everything,"* Slate had said. She heard their tiny, high voices chattering at him, and Slate responded softly to them in Faerish.

Sellie stirred from her sleep, a deep rumble vibrating up Dani's back, but after opening one luminous blue eye to peek at Slate, the griffin returned to her nap. Dash didn't even stir.

"What's wrong?" she asked when he crouched down next to where she was sitting. "Everything alright with Ronin?"

"Oh yeah. He's fine. That kid is the least of my problems."

"He doesn't know about you, right? The whole magic thing?" She didn't think Slate would have said anything, but confirming didn't hurt. Besides, maybe the teenager had Mystic origins.

"Nope. Not a clue. And I plan to keep it that way. He doesn't need to know and I won't drag a kid into my shit."

She reached out and touched his face. "So what's bothering you, then?"

He was silent for a heartbeat, watching her. "I... I have to go," he hedged, "to Titan's Fen."

Titan's Fen. His fae town.

Panic tried to lodge its way up her throat, but she shoved it back down and forced herself to suck in a slow breath. She had to remind herself that she'd made a decision. She'd decided to be with Slate, really *be* with him, and that meant taking everything that came with Slate. She wasn't about to chicken out already.

Besides, half of that panic was about him saying he had to leave, which *was* something she had control over. She could worry about the other half of her panic later.

"For how long?" Dani finally asked, aware Slate had given her the time she'd needed to process what he'd said, and grateful to him for it.

He didn't answer right away, looking hesitant, so she shut off her game and cocked a brow at him. "We're going to break this bad habit of yours eventually. Talk to me, please." She reached out to touch his arm, a gentle caress that had his eyes drifting shut for a moment, like he was savoring it.

"Well..." he started slowly, eyes opening and locking with hers. "I typically spend a lot of time there now. I come back here occasionally to teach at the studio, or to see people, but..." He hesitated again, a wariness in his eyes, and she scowled at him. He let out a strained chuckle and nodded. "Sorry. Honestly? If I'm here in the city, it's not usually for more than a night. Two at *most*. I have a lot to do over there, and..." he made a face, "if I'm gone too long, people... talk."

"Talk? Like, gossip?" She frowned at him.

"Yeah. The faeries get their love of gossip from the fae. Very curious. I walk into a new rumor about myself *daily*." He shrugged. "And the people get nervous if I'm not highly visible. Bad for PR if their long-lost prince is a shut-in."

Right. He was a prince. It was so easy to forget because, well, to her, he was just Slate. She hardly noticed the fae part of him anymore, and in the last couple of days, she'd grown accustomed to Kallen shadowing them everywhere if they left the Eastern District. She had forgotten it was because of Slate's noble status.

"Alright." She nodded slowly, running her fingers through Sellie's fur. The griffin let out a soft purring coo but continued dozing.

This was it. This is what she had control over. Slate had to leave... but she had control over whether or not she went *with* him. She just wouldn't think about *where*, exactly, she was going.

One step at a time.

She sucked in another breath and smiled at Slate. After all, if she was with him, she could handle almost anywhere, even a town full of strange fae. "When do we leave, then?"

Slate blinked at her. "... we?"

Her smile widened and she took her hand from his arm to reach up and cup the side of his face. "Yes. We. I told you—I go where you go."

Slate stared at her, as if he hadn't heard her correctly. He opened his mouth, closed it, and then reached up to take her hand in both of his. "You're serious?"

Dani chuckled, raising one brow. "Yes, I'm very serious. I meant what I said, you know. I wasn't just pulling your leg." Behind her, Sellie stirred again and raised her large head, clicking her beak twice as she filtered images into Dani's head. With a laugh, she stroked the griffin with her free hand. "Yes, I'm sure you can come too," she assured Sellie, feeling the first tickle of excitement.

This was starting to feel much more like an adventure and less like a nightmare. It wasn't like anyone was going to sweep her away and kidnap her to some mythical faerie realm when she was with Slate. She was safe with him.

Slate glanced between her and Sellie, still holding Dani's hand like it was a lifeline she'd thrown him. A different kind of nervous energy slithered through her, distinctly Slate's.

"Why are you nervous?" she asked, actively pushing against his emotions so they didn't spiral hers into something larger.

He shifted until he was sitting cross-legged in front of her. "I dunno."

It was an honest answer, at least, without any of the hesitation that preceded all his words lately. She'd give him that. "Should I not come with you?"

"No, no, that's not it. I want you there. The town itself is beautiful and magical. I think you'll like it. It's just... I have to be someone different there." He grimaced slightly. "I'm treated differently, and it doesn't always feel natural to me."

Dani cocked her head to the side. "Different how? Because of your status?"

"Yes." He shrugged, still studying her face intently, like he was waiting for her to change her mind. "And you might also be treated differently, because of me."

Dani was tempted to let her imagination run away from her, but she knew she'd just be causing unnecessary worry for herself and for him. So she smiled. "I'll gauge it for myself. When should we leave?"

He didn't answer right away, eyes pinging back and forth between her own like he was still trying to decide if this was real. She rolled her eyes at him and tickled his palm with her fingers. "I'm serious. When should we leave?"

A slow smile spread over his face, lighting up his blue eyes until they shimmered with that iridescent glow behind his irises. "Tonight. The town gets quiet after sundown."

She nodded, grateful for his foresight. She wanted to believe she could handle a town square crowded with fae, but in reality, the idea made her nauseous. "Less people around to gossip about us?" she teased, breaking up the nerves inside her chest.

He frowned, tugging at her hand until she crawled into his lap. Dash protested with a sleepy yip before he curled tighter against Sellie. Slate wrapped his arms loosely around her and pressed his forehead into hers. "I won't let people talk about you. They can all mind their own fucking business."

Dani crinkled her nose, breathing in his wintry scent and letting it soothe her. "You know that won't happen. You said so yourself—the fae love gossip. *You* love gossip. You love to watch people."

Slate chuckled. "Given that I'm half fae, that does track."

"And I'm sure your love life is a highly-discussed topic."

His expression darkened a little. "In a lot of different ways, unfortunately."

"So it's just something we have to deal with." She stroked her hands over his shoulders, trying to alleviate the tension she could feel in his muscles. "It'll be alright. Listen, I have a lot of experience with gossip. You would not *believe* how judgy rats are." She offered him a cheeky grin.

"Naturally. Probably because people are judgy about rats." Slate answered her smile with one of his own, and the tightness in his shoulders lessened. She slipped one hand up until her fingertips brushed the scar on his left shoulder. She loved that scar. Like, an insane amount. It was a little out of character. She often found herself touching his, touching her own... and any time they had sex, she found herself magnetized to it.

Goddess help her, the way he would groan her name when she nipped him there...

She wasn't a sadist, though. Scouts' honor.

It was just something about it.

"We have some time before sundown..." she mused casually, pulling her eyes away from his scar to look up at him as heat curled through her belly.

He was still sharing his emotions with her, and she felt those emotions pitch hotly into arousal, any lingering nervousness vanishing instantly. Her own emotions spiked in concert, the heat in her belly building into a small inferno.

"You know..." he murmured, a hint of a growl in his voice as his focus dipped to her lips. "Not many surfaces left around here that we haven't fucked on."

"Bet you can still think of one. Or two." Her fingers curled against the mark on his neck, fingernails digging in gently.

His breath hissed out between his lips, and her position on his lap told her just how much it affected him. He palmed her throat, a wicked grin sharpening his face.

"You bet I can."

Slate portaled them to the ancient stone bridge in the middle of the Forest of L'el, Dani's bag slung over his shoulder. Dani stepped out of the portal and took a cautious look around, arms wrapped securely around Dash. Her eyes widened as she took in their surroundings, and she spun slowly in a circle, sucking in a breath.

"I've never been this deep in the Forest before..." She turned back to Slate, and he saw that the edges of her irises shimmered with that verdant green glow, ever-so-slightly. His empathy could taste her nerves, but also a hesitant, bubbling excitement that soothed his own worries about this introduction to a place that was slowly becoming a second home to him.

"The Forest is loaded with latent magic. It can be..." he drifted off, noticing her skin was pebbling, fine hairs standing straight up along her arms, "... it can be a little unsettling if you aren't used to it."

"I love it," she stated, a smile tugging at her lips. She let Dash jump from her arms and turned her face up into the tall foliage above them. Slate followed her gaze, and noticed several eyes on them as critters gathered in the low branches, curious animals no doubt drawn by Dani's magic. "There are so many little animals... I can feel all their little heart-fires. So many more than in the city."

As if on cue, a tawny owl drifted down on silent wings, and perched on the arm that Dani held up.

The owl ignored him completely, and Dani stroked the plumage of its chest with a murmur of appreciation. Instinctively, Slate's eyes zeroed in on the impressive talons wrapped around Dani's jacket sleeve, but the material remained intact. There wasn't a scratch on it when the creature flew away a moment later.

She glanced at him with a smile. "So... now what?"

He took her hand, threading his fingers through hers, and pointed down to the bridge they stood on. "This bridge? It's the anchor point for Titan's Fen. The Forest..." he paused, frowning. "How do I explain this... The Forest shuffles the location of Titan's Fen around, same for the Silver Valley. Like rafts in an ocean current. This bridge is the anchor point, a fixed tether between the town and the Forest. One side of this bridge always connects to the town, but the other end?" He pointed toward the dense forest. "It leads to a different part of the Forest every few days. Apparently, the Silver Valley also has a bridge like this."

Dani cocked her head to the side, studying the Forest just beyond the bridge. She twisted to look in the opposite direction, which appeared quite similar. "But... both directions look the same."

Slate smiled. "Yeah, there's a glamour—it keeps the entrance hidden. Can't glamour the bridge, though, or no one would ever be able to find it once you leave."

Nodding slowly, she looked back at him. "So... why does it do that? Shuffle the location?"

Slate shrugged. "I dunno. Kallen's theory is that the Forest is sentient. And when it breathes, everything just... moves. Honestly, I tune him out when he starts getting too deep about it. It's all just magic to me," he admitted with a laugh, rubbing the back of his neck. "I don't care about the little details of it."

Dani smiled, gaze darting back to the trees around them, so tall it felt like being deep underwater. "Well, I can agree that this place seems... alive."

Slate tugged at her hand and pointed to their feet. "See here?" He nudged a stone inlaid in the bridge, nearly directly in the center. Unlike many of the stones, it was large and perfectly square. "The moss on this stone only grows on the side of the bridge leading to Titan's Fen." He jerked his head in that direction, and Dani followed his gaze, fingers tightening within his. He felt a hint of trepidation shiver through her.

"We don't have to do this, you know," he murmured.

Dani squared her shoulders, facing the direction of Titan's Fen with her chin up. "No, I'm fine. I'm ready." Without waiting, Dani took a step, tugging at his hand. Pride filtered through him, and a smile curved his lips.

The moment they stepped off the bridge, the scene in front of them changed. The trees were replaced by a narrow mountain pass heavily guarded by a 30-foot stone wall with archers patrolling along the parapets at the top. Upon seeing Slate, the guards pressed their hands to their sternum in a fae greeting. He noticed they all gave Dani a careful assessment and a searing shot of possession clawed up his throat.

He should've told her about the whole *mayt* thing before they came here. Someone was going to spill the beans on him, he could feel it. He needed to be the one to tell her first.

Fuck, he was nervous about it, though.

He would. He would tell her. Soon.

One of the guards yelled to open the gate, and Slate was very aware of Dani as her gaze pinged around to take everything in. Her nerves were a tight wire around his heart as she eyed the strange fae soldiers warily. Once again, he was reminded that something had poisoned her over the fae. She hadn't moved since the scene had changed, and as the large, thick gate eased open, he made no move to urge her forward.

He wouldn't rush her. Not with this.

And… there was Kallen. Like clockwork. Or a fungus. But Slate was actually grateful for the lieutenant's predictable appearance as Dani's emotional grid evened out a bit at the sight of a familiar face.

"Do you ever sleep?" Slate growled, gently squeezing Dani's hand.

"And allow you to run amok unsupervised? Never." His attention shifted to Dani, and he offered her a gallant bow. "*Tana.* Good evening. Welcome to Titan's Fen."

"Thank you," she laughed, "but you don't have to bow to me or anything. I'm not the royalty here." She glanced at Slate with a little crinkle to her freckled face, which was lucky, because she missed the way Kallen glanced at him with a raised brow.

As his *mayt*, Dani was as good as royalty, as far as the fae were considered. She was *Tana*. Consort to *Titania*. A veritable queen, once he was crowned, of course.

He was seriously going to have to talk to her. Post haste.

She turned back to Kallen. "Is the village far from here?"

"It's a little bit of a walk. There are wards in place to prevent portalling directly into the town proper, but once you are within the boundaries of the town, Zlaet can portal you as you please." He offered Dani an encouraging smile.

She smiled back at the lieutenant. "Thank you, Kallen." Her eyes flipped back to Slate, and her smile widened a little, hiding her nerves from everyone but him. "I'm ready," she announced.

Kallen bid them farewell with a tip of his chin and disappeared back into the gatehouse. Slate squeezed Dani's hand, tugging her along the beaten path. Ahead of them, Dash darted around the path, sniffing madly and gekkering at the trees.

"What does *Tana* mean?" she asked as they walked. "Is it a title? Kallen keeps calling me that."

Slate nodded, sucking back the alarm that tightened like iron bands around his lungs. "Yeah. It's a title of respect."

She nodded thoughtfully, watching Dash as the fox rushed forward to inspect something. The fox returned to her, gekkering excitedly. "I figured," she finally said, after sending Dash off with a chuckle. "He seems like a pretty traditional guy."

"Very," Slate agreed. "Follows everything by the book. He grew up in a family of scholars before he entered into the service of the Titania House."

The path opened in front of them, the cliffs and trees abruptly ending, and they found themselves at the top of a hill, the path continuing downward into the valley that housed Titan's Fen. Twilight had settled over the valley, laying a rose-tinted darkness over the village like a cool blanket. Twinkling faerie lights flirted and danced along the roofs of houses and along the shore of the slender, babbling river that ran through the valley, illuminating the streets in a gentle glow. From here, they could see the market square, where figures were packing up their stalls and wares, now that darkness was falling.

Rising on the opposite end of the valley was a path leading to the elaborate Eas Manor, the once summer home for fae royalty. Next to the manor, a thin plume of a waterfall plunged from the mountains above and into a small reservoir, before three more, much smaller waterfalls plunged into a small pond. From there, the crystalline water curved around the entire settlement in a slender river. More faerie lights danced around the manor, with large clusters in the gardens surrounding it.

Beside him, Dani was staring with wide eyes and an open mouth. "Oh... oh *wow*," she breathed, then turned her gaze up to him.

"Beautiful, right?" He grinned at her.

"That doesn't even begin to describe it..." she murmured, turning back to the scene before them. "You live here?"

He chuckled. "Part-time, I suppose."

"Wow..." she murmured, still staring at Titan's Fen with a look of wonder that made him look at the town anew.

He tugged on her hand to continue, but she didn't take her eyes from the sight, trusting him to lead her as she continued to gawk. Slate felt the shiver of the next two wards they passed through, each several yards apart from the other. Once they were clear of all three wards, Slate portaled them straight to the manor, landing them on the bridge that connected the manor's property to the town

They strode toward the manor, which had no real door, only a large archway that denoted the entrance. Stepping inside, Dani's head was on a swivel, her hand squeezing Slate's as she took in residence—the polished stone floors, the large, sweeping stairway along the back wall that led up into the higher rooms and suites, and the trees that snaked up the walls, growing right along the stone, as if they had married the space together, rather than competing for it.

There came a soft shuffle of footsteps. Slate wasn't surprised to see Autymn floating down the stairs, carrying an empty basket under her arm. Her honey-blonde hair was braided in a fishtail along her spine with tiny flowers embedded throughout. She was clad in a simple silver dress that pooled around her feet, looking like the faerie-tale rendition of some young medieval maiden, except with tipped ears.

Sometimes he still thought his life was some kind of fever dream.

She paused when she caught sight of them. "My lord." Autymn smiled demurely. "Good evening." The willowy girl bobbed in a curtsy before her caramel eyes shifted to Dani, and she repeated the gesture. "The faeries spoke of your arrival with a guest," she said.

Slate gestured between them. "Autymn, this is Dani, my girlfriend. Dani, this is Autymn. She's... well. She's one of my attendants, I guess."

Dani's brow rose, and she glanced from Autymn to Slate and back. "Attendant? Like..."

Autymn offered her a polite smile. "I care for Prince Zlaet's rooms and other minor tasks."

"Oh." Dani blinked. "Right." She laughed, and Slate could feel some of her anxiety easing; Slate wasn't surprised—Autymn was probably the least intimidating person in the entire town. "Well, it's nice to meet you," Dani said with a smile, stepping forward and holding out her hand.

Autymn glanced at Dani's hand, then quizzically at Slate.

"It's customary to shake hands in Faerloch when greeting someone," he offered quickly.

Dani dropped her hand, casting him a glance of panic. "Oh, I didn't realize—" She was interrupted when Autymn stepped closer and delicately took Dani's hand in both of hers and—with a glance up at Dani—shook the hand gently.

"It's lovely to finally meet you, *Tana*," Autymn murmured with a smile.

"You can just call me Dani," Dani said, her responding smile open and friendly, relief sliding through her grid.

Autymn inclined her head with a smile, and she released Dani's hand to turn to Slate. "My lord, I freshened up your quarters and left some tea for you and your *Tana*."

"Thank you."

Autymn shifted her attention to Dani. "Tani-*tana*, I shall bring you some amenities. Will you require clothing? I can arrange for the tailor to come and fit you?"

"Oh... um..." Dani glanced at Slate, and he just shrugged at her, leaving the choice in her hands. "I'll be okay for now. Thank you. I packed some stuff." She gestured to the bag Slate carried for her.

Autymn nodded. "Please, do let me know if you change your mind, my lady."

"We'll be fine tonight, Autymn, thanks," Slate said.

The fae inclined her head again and pressed her hand to her sternum. "Good night," she murmured, looking between them, and with a last smile, the young female drifted down the hallway and disappeared around the corner.

Dani stared after Autymn, then turned back to Slate with raised brows. "I knew you were royalty, but I guess I didn't think about you having *servants*."

"She's an *attendant*. It's different," Slate said with a laugh.

Dani's brows rose impossibly higher.

Slate huffed a breath. "I know. It's weird. It took some getting used to. But she chooses to be here and she's compensated generously for it..." he paused, a flush crawling up his neck, "and I have two attendants. Autymn and her older cousin Rhylan."

"You have *two* attendants?" Dani's lips curved teasingly.

"Yeah... it's..." Slate rolled the words around in his head. "The fae think it's a great privilege to be involved in the royal family. Autymn's been here since she was small. She has a magical affinity with plants, and she was handpicked by Aredhel to help in the gardens sometimes."

"She was close to your mother?" Dani tilted her head to the side.

Slate nodded. "Very. She can't talk about her without crying."

"Oh. Poor thing." Dani glanced back after Autymn as she slipped her hand back into Slate's.

"Yeah. She and Rhylan are the only ones I allow in my rooms. They've earned my trust to remain discreet." Slate shrugged. "I like them both. I don't see Rhylan too much, though. He used to serve my father when he was—"

Slate froze, catching his words before they left his mouth.

He used to serve my father when he was Tana.

"What?" Dani asked, an alertness sparking through her.

"When... when my father was here. With my mother. So I told Rhylan to make sure my father is always comfortable," he recovered swiftly.

Dani's brows creased in a tiny frown, but she nodded her head, glancing back once more in the direction Autymn had disappeared to. Guilt prickled under his skin, and he decided then and there that he wouldn't keep anything from Dani once he'd told her about their *mayting*.

"Shall we go?" he asked, tugging at her hand and angling his head toward the stairs.

Dani turned back to him and smiled. He led her up the stairs, and at the top, he took them down the hall to the door at the very end. He waved his hand and the door opened at his command.

"And these... are my rooms..."

HAPPY AND SAFE

... experimenting with mortals, and is one of the earliest accounts of lorekissed beings kidnapped by fae to satiate the fae's natural curiosity. Da Vinci himself escaped the same fate, and this is often attributed to his astounding character and strength of mind.

- Gherald Schmidt, Faerloch Historical Archives

Dani felt like she was walking through a dream.

She'd been worried a fae manor would overwhelm her with its opulence, but she was delightfully surprised by what she'd found. It was certainly magnificent, but it was so interlaced with nature that it was impossible to feel imposed by it. It was inviting and rich and elegant.

Dani found the trend continuing as they entered Slate's rooms. The sitting room they stepped into featured several luxurious armchairs, a fireplace, a sofa along one wall, and a small Japanese table like the one Slate had at his apartment. Atop the table was a tea set, steam curling up from the spout of the small but beautifully painted teapot.

A balcony was visible across from the sofa, and from her vantage, Dani could see that the balcony extended past the sitting room and along the bedroom beyond. A set of intricately carved double doors separated the sitting room from the bedroom, which Slate pushed open for her before stepping aside to let her pass, her bag plopping to the ground at his feet. The bedroom was elegant and warm, but minimal, much like how he kept his apartment in the Eastern District. She could see pieces of him in this room; a sweatshirt on a luscious armchair, a phone charger plugged into what looked like a solar charger by the balcony, a couple of martial arts magazines on the table, a cotton robe—he called it a *yukata*—hanging on a peg next to a door that led to the bathroom.

In the center of the room was a massive four-poster bed, but the posts were living tree trunks, all four of them rising into leafy branches that spread out along the ceiling. Dani was certain she spied small faeries flitting about from branch to branch. Gauzy white curtains hung from the branches, pulled back and secured to reveal a rich white bedspread, embroidered with tiny flowers.

Dani brushed her fingers against the soft gauzy curtains as she peeked through the archway leading into the bathroom. She spied dual sinks, a spacious closet for the toilet, and a large sunken tub carved into the marble flooring. On the far side of the tub, the wall was cut with an arched opening, allowing for an uninterrupted view into a private garden while bathing.

The grandest feature of the bedroom was the series of open archways that led out onto the huge, sweeping balcony that spanned both the bedroom and the sitting room. Airy curtains fluttered on a light breeze as she stepped through one archway and into the night. To the left of the balcony, she could see the same private garden she'd noticed from the bathroom, but straight ahead was a stunning view of the village square. The colorful market stalls were quiet and empty for the evening, and faerie lights lit the space in a soft glow. She spotted a few fae lingering in the streets, and from up here, they were just... people. People going about their life, rather than the boogeymen fae she'd grown up believing them to be.

She turned to see Slate watching her, his shoulder propped against one of the bed posters, arms crossed over his chest. There was something predatory and male about the way his eyes trailed over her, observing her with an intensity she felt in her stomach.

"It's warm here..." she commented, unsticking her words from her throat.

"Kallen's warding magic," Slate answered. "His wards sorta... trap the heat in here, like a greenhouse. It keeps the village temperate so the faerfolk can grow food year-round."

A call came from high above in the sky. Dani peered upward, smiling as she made out the shape of Sellie as the griffin glided through the skies above the village.

"Kallen's going to let her through the ward, right?" Dani asked, glancing away from the circling griffin to see Slate had moved to stand in one of the archways leading to the balcony.

Slate nodded, eyes locked on the griffin. "Yeah, when I called him earlier, he said he would tie her into the ward so she can come and go as she pleases."

"Good." Dani smiled, watching as the griffin made one more circle, before Sellie's wings snapped close to her body and she dropped. Dani wondered if the griffin had sensed when she could get through the ward because she met no resistance. She snapped out her wings and glided to a graceful landing on the wide balcony next to Dani. Ruffling her feathers, the griffin snapped her beak, head swiveling as she let out a series of irritated chirps.

Need nest, Sellie's clear voice came into her mind.

"Sellie would like to know where she can make a nest." Dani turned back to Slate, who stepped out from the archway of the balcony to stand next to her.

He made a thinking noise in the back of his throat, and he pointed to the part of the massive balcony closest to the private garden. "How about over there?" He turned to speak directly to Sellie. "That area is covered by the overhang, so you'll be protected from the rain."

The griffin let out a sing-song whistle.

"She said it's perfect, and she doesn't mind a little rain." Dani reached up and stroked the spot where feathers and fur mingled along Sellie's neck. "Should she go find Kallen? So he can tie her into the ward permanently?"

Slate nodded. "He should be expecting you," he said to the griffin. "You should be able to find him by the front gate. He'll only need a minute."

Sellie's head angled as she glowered at Slate, clicking her beak haughtily and rumbling her annoyance at having to subject herself to someone in order to have freedom. However, she sent district impressions of reluctant respect for the violet-eyed lieutenant, so Dani didn't think she minded too much.

"Once you're finished with Kallen, avoid the north side of the village," Slate said. "Titan's Fen shifted locations recently, and we're near a griffin nesting ground now. A male, two females, and a couple of juveniles, I think. The male is a golden griffin, so he's a big fucker. He hasn't bothered us because we haven't bothered him, but I'm not sure how he'll react to a new female near his territory."

Sellie blinked one eye at Slate, then the other, swishing her tail back and forth.

Dani laughed. "She said she will go make friends. She'll introduce herself. But..." Dani crinkled her nose, "she doesn't want to mate, so she'll be cautious."

The griffin took off again, soaring high and heading toward the gatehouse to find Kallen, and Dani watched her go, gaze drifting once more over the small settlement nestled within the encircling mountains.

"So..." Slate started. "What do you think?"

Dani smiled faintly, fingers brushing the marble balcony. "It's... really beautiful here."

"Do you want me to take you back to the city?" Slate asked her. She turned her head to see he had propped his good shoulder against one of the archways, a little furrow between his brows. His heartfire swelled gently, and he tipped his head a little. "If you're uncomfortable—"

"No." Her breath jammed in her lungs at the idea of going back to his apartment and being alone. "No, I really want to be here... with you." She looked at her fingers on the marble railing. "Do you remember... when I first told you about magic? In the studio that day?" she asked softly.

"How could I forget? You changed my life that day."

"And you asked me why I bothered to tell you any of it? You were a stranger to me, and you asked me why I cared." Her fingers curled on the railing.

"I remember that too." His voice was soft, but she heard him clearly. "You said... you said 'I was you once'."

She drew in a long breath. "I was. Once. The fae grabbed me from my bed when I was 16 years old."

Silence behind her. She twisted her head just enough to see that Slate hadn't moved from his position, watching her. He said nothing, but she could see every part of him was cued into her, a vibrating tension to him, sapphire eyes burning like hot ice.

She gazed out over the town again, twinkling in the darkness. "They put a rag over my face, knocked me out with some kind of chemical or magic or something..." Air felt stuck in her lungs. Behind her, she heard Slate mutter a curse, and it suddenly felt a few degrees colder. With a shiver, she swallowed and continued. "I barely remember it. I... I remember seeing them, hearing them talk... and they were speaking English, which... which my brain had a hard time shifting to, at the time. Roger rescued me, actually. That's how we met."

She swallowed the tightness in her throat, sucking in a deep, shaky breath through her nose. "My parents had just... a few weeks before that, I'd lost my parents. I was a disaster. I can't—I don't even know that I remember what I did. I suppose I went to school. Saw a therapist. Spent lots of time with the youth welfare office. My neighbors agreed to become my guardians, but I was allowed to stay in my house. I was alone there when the fae came."

"Daniella..." Slate's voice was hoarse, and she sensed him step toward her. Dani glanced over her shoulder at him and shook her head, knowing that if he offered her comfort now, she'd lose it and never be able to finish. He froze, and she glimpsed his hands flex into fists before he nodded and stepped back to resume his vigil in the archway.

Dani dashed a hand at her eyes and pulled in another fortifying breath. "That... that wasn't the first time I saw the fae, though..."

This.

This was the hard part. Maybe it was because she'd received therapy over the death of her parents. Maybe it's because she knew death was permanent, so she had closure. Maybe it was because she and Kat had been just children, the terror of the moment so much larger to such a small girl...

"I had a best friend growing up." Her voice was shaking hard, a thick sock in her throat. "Her name was Kat—Katarina. She lived a few houses down from me, and even though she was a year older, we played together because... because she had magic too." She turned around and leaned back against the railing, wrapping her arms around herself. "She was telekinetic. Like you."

"Oh shit..." Slate's voice was barely a whisper. Dani couldn't look at him, not if she wanted to get through this. She trained her gaze on the floor between them.

Her throat burned with the effort it took not to break down and sob, Kat's laughing face fresh in her mind. "We understood we were special, so we stuck together. She came over for a sleepover one night during the summer, and we snuck out to go see the new fox cubs that had been born a few days earlier." She glanced at Slate and smiled sadly. "Dash's ancestors, actually."

She sucked in a deep breath, looking away once more as tears overflowed her eyes and began tracking down her cheeks. "She... the fae appeared and lured her away. And she just went with them. No—no resistance. She just *went* and I spent a long—a long time wondering *why*. Why did she leave? Where did she go? Who were those people?"

She scrubbed at her face with her hands. "No one believed me and for a while, I thought maybe I made it up. But it didn't *feel* made up... and after the fae came for me and I learned about magic, and I learned that some fae have the ability to manipulate the emotions of others... I knew in my *heart* that's what had happened to her.

"And I spent a long, long time thinking about it and worrying if the fae were going to find me again. I warded my house. I changed the spelling of my last name from Ceallachán to Callaghan and added the 'O' to the beginning, just to hide." She shrugged, hugging herself tighter.

"And that's what I did. That's how I lived. And I didn't intend to do anything to change that... until I stumbled across you that night in the street."

Finally, she looked at him. He'd been silent this whole time, listening intently.

"Thank you for telling me," he finally said, his voice quiet.

Her smile was sad and watery. "You deserve to know. My past has had... an influence on our relationship. Now you know why."

More silence stretched between them, and Dani found she couldn't read his normally expressive face. The temperature remained frosty, and there was a tightness to Slate that told her he was deliberately containing his feelings.

"What are you thinking?" she asked hesitantly.

"I'm..." He paused, huffing a breath as though he were carefully picking out his words. "I'm... grateful you shared all that with me."

Her arms tightened around herself, and she eyed him nervously. "Are you... angry? That I kept all that from you?" she asked, eyes skating over the furrow in his brow, feeling the chill lingering in the air.

"*No.*" His answer was immediate. "I'm... I'm *violent*. It's so unfair, all that shit that happened to you. There's some... instinctual piece of me that wants to fix it all for you. Go out and kick the shit out of some people or something."

She almost laughed, releasing her arms from around herself to anchor them against the railing at her back. "Very on brand for you."

She felt it then—his emotions leaching out of him and into her. It was a swirl of violent injustice mixed with something like guilt. And fear.

"But..." he said, pushing off the stone arch and taking a step toward her. "I also feel like a selfish prick, dragging you into my life." He gestured out toward the town. "It's... it's a lot. This is a lot. Is it? Is it too much for you? I would understand if it is."

She shook her head, tipping her face up as he came into her breathing space and rested his hands on the railing on either side of her. He was a presence around her; warm and large and masculine.

"No," she murmured, holding his gaze. "It's a lot, but I'm okay."

"I'm a little concerned you'll bolt now." His brows furrowed together as he stared at her.

She laid her hands against his sternum, laying her palm directly over his heart to feel the strong beat there, and it steadied her. She could feel the slow burn of his heartfire rising, and some part of her mind or her magic knew he lingered at the threshold of her emotions, listening at the door. Just listening.

"I'm not going anywhere," she said. "Promise."

She felt raw and torn open and so, so vulnerable… but with him next to her, she also felt *safe*. Wholly safe. As if she could crumble into tiny pieces right here, right now, and he would carefully scoop her all up and patch her back together.

There was also a sense of relief, a lightening inside her, as if exposing her nightmares to him had somehow stolen some of the horror from them.

Slate didn't look convinced. She slid her hands up until she could slip her fingers over his jaw, trying to ease the tension in him. "I'm fine, Slate. I'm still a little uncomfortable, but I want to be here because… because I want to be where you are. And you deserved to know the truth about my past." She returned her fingers to his chest, fanning her fingers out to touch as much of him as she could all at once. She crinkled her nose at him. "It's just going to take me a little bit to get used to being here, surrounded by the fae. I've spent half my life hiding from them… and now I'm literally in bed with their *prince*."

Slate gave her a wicked little grin. "I hear he's a good lay, at least."

She laughed, tension easing from her shoulders. "He's okay," she teased.

"Just okay?" Slate's eyes danced as he raised a brow and put on a show of looking hurt. Before she could say anything, he moved with inhuman speed to sweep her up. Dani let out a startled squeak, her heart jumping into her throat, but she laughed when he grinned down at her, delight and mischief brightening his gaze.

He dumped her in the bed and crawled over her. Dani laughed again, reaching up to wrap her arms around his neck as he lowered himself over her. At the feel of his heavier, harder body pressing into hers, she instinctively wrapped her legs around his hips and held him tightly. He tucked his face into the side of her neck, and Dani's eyes slid shut.

They stayed like that for several minutes, the only sound their breathing.

"You make me feel really safe, you know?" Dani whispered, opening her eyes to stare up at the intricate branches flaring along the ceiling.

Slate pulled his face from her neck, brows raised. "Do I?"

A smile tugged the edges of her lips. "You also make me feel like... like I could do anything or tell you anything, and you won't think I'm stupid or childish." She finally met his gaze, smiling at him. "If I told you I still sleep with that stuffed fox you won me at that arcade over the summer, you wouldn't think that was dumb."

He chuckled. "I think it's cute, actually."

"Or that I like ketchup on my eggs."

He made a face. "That's weird, but I'm not here to yuck your yum, I guess."

Her smile widened into a grin. "Or that I feel like I never really 'met' you... but instead like I've been... *waiting* for you. I feel... complete, for the first time in... well, maybe forever. That probably sounds really corny, right?" She crinkled her nose again.

Something shimmered through his emotions, a ripple of something powerful, deep, but also with a hint of... was it guilt? Unease? But before she could grasp what it was, the emotions fed to her from his magic slithered away from her mind. He lowered his head to brush his lips over hers. "Not at all..." he murmured. "I feel like that too."

CHAPTER — THIRTY-THREE

THE MAYT-BOND

... almost extinct in Ireland, but thanks largely to the conservation efforts of Clan Mac Tíre Bán, the wolf population continues to thrive in secret, and those few mortals who...

– Gherald Schmidt, Faerloch Historical Archives

Dani woke up with the sun streaming across the stone floors of Slate's suites. She was ridiculously comfortable, snuggled in the lush blankets, the curtains of the four-poster bed drawn around them, isolating them from the rest of the room. According to Slate, there was some kind of magic that let her see out through the sheer material, but no one could see in.

Her first instinct was to check on her animal friends, so familiar with their mental paths that it was the work of a minute to assure herself Sellie was asleep in her new nest on the balcony, with Dash tucked comfortably under her wing like an obedient chick.

Dani shifted gently, turning over. There was Slate, still sleeping, little more than dark hair and a glimpse of a bare shoulder.

Residual nerves mixed with tentative relief shimmered through her. She'd unearthed all her raw, naked history for him, and he'd... taken it exactly as she'd expected. Better, even. But there was still a piece of her that hummed with anxiety over her revelations to him, and watching him now, she realized that it had nothing to do with how he might think of her or her past.

The real reason was because there was nothing left now. No more secrets. She'd officially handed him everything she had and everything she was... and there was still a piece of Old Dani that worried that if he left, she'd have nothing left of herself. She'd be destroyed.

She reached across the mattress and gently slid her fingers up his shoulder, brushing her fingertips over the scar nestled against his neck there. Something about it bothered her, yet reassured her at the same time. The mark satisfied some... instinctual part of her that was restless over him, yet at the same time, a tendril of suspicion curled around her at the implications of it. A normal scar wouldn't draw her so much, and for them to have near-identical scars now?

The scar had to be something *more*. But what?

A deep inhale had her snapping her hand away with a start. He shifted, peering over his shoulder at her, one bright blue eye heavy-lidded.

"You okay?" His quiet voice was rough with sleep.

"Sorry..." she replied with a small smile. "I didn't mean to wake you."

He responded with a sleepy smile of his own, and turned back over. She watched him paw blindly for his phone, glance blearily at the screen, and groan.

"Something wrong?" Dani asked, rubbing the sleep from her eyes.

He sat up and mimicked her, scrubbing at his face with his hands. The sheets pooled around his hips, showing off his bare torso and all the sharp brushstrokes of his tattoos. Dani bit her bottom lip as her stomach fluttered at the sight of all that taut flesh.

"Kallen," he sighed. "I'm being *summoned*."

"Right now?" Her fluttering stomach tightened at the thought of him leaving her alone, but she tramped it down.

He speared his fingers through his hair and pulled the thick dark mass away from his face. He gave her a little look, and a swell of emotions slowly threaded into her—a hint of annoyance and a simmering heat as his gaze swept over her prone form. "Well," he tossed his phone to the side and shifted to crawl over her, lips curving into a slow smile, "maybe not right *now...*"

She opened her mouth to tell him to kiss her, when the sound of a door opening echoed from the sitting room. Dani froze, and Slate's head whipped to the side to glower toward the sound. A little rumble escaped him, so low she only heard it because he was pressed against her, sending a shiver of vibrations through her.

A soft knock came on the connecting door that separated the sitting room from the bedroom.

He growled again, then turned his head to kiss her, a thorough kiss that had her bones melting against the sheets beneath her. His tongue stroked hers, and she couldn't help the little moan that escaped her as he settled his hips into hers.

"Later," he said against her mouth, and she felt the promise down into the pit of her stomach.

"Later," she agreed in a breathless voice.

He rolled off her and over to the far side of the bed, pulling the curtains back. Dani watched, a little wide-eyed, as Slate snatched the *yukata*, swung it around his very naked body, then reached for the second robe that had been left hanging next to his. The material seemed finer than any silk Dani had seen, and it was a rich sapphire blue that echoed Slate's eyes. He tossed it toward her with a wink, and she reluctantly dragged herself out of the bed to pull it on. The material slithered over her skin like water given solid form.

"Come in," Slate finally called, and when the door swung open, he tipped his head in greeting. "Morning, Autymn."

"Good morning, my prince." Autymn placed a hand over her heart and dipped her head deeper than Slate had. Slate flashed a smile at Dani, then disappeared through the doorway into the bathroom.

Autymn repeated the gesture with her hand and her chin at Dani, offering her a warm, serene smile. "Good morning, Tani-*tana*. How was your first evening in Titan's Fen?"

Dani smiled back, finding herself surprisingly comfortable with the slender fae female. Then again, she couldn't imagine anyone being unsettled by the sweet-looking Autymn. "It was fine, thank you."

"Does the robe please you, my lady?" Autymn asked, gesturing toward her. "If it isn't to your liking, it would be a small matter to find another."

"Oh no, this is great, thank you. It's so soft," Dani marveled, stroking a hand over the buttery fabric.

"I have brought you breakfast, if you would like," Autymn supplied, gesturing with one long-fingered hand toward the doors leading to the sitting area.

Unused to being served, a flush heated her cheeks. "Wow, really? You didn't have to do that."

Autymn's smile widened, and her eyes danced with a hint of amusement. "It pleases me to do so, *Tana*. Please, help yourself."

Biting her lip, Dani glanced toward the bathroom, then padded toward the doors to peek through them. There was a spread of food on the low table in the sitting area, making Dani wonder how the small female had managed to bring it all up. She wandered over, eyeing the assortment of apples, oranges, grapefruit, and strawberries, as well as various breads and pastries. Next to the bread and pastries were what looked like whipped butter and fruit spreads.

"*Tana*," Autymn's soft, sweet voice came from behind her.

She turned and found the fae female holding out a steaming cup of tea. "Thank you," Dani said, taking it.

"I did not know what you prefer, so I gave you what Prince Zlaet prefers, if it pleases you?" Autymn tilted her head to the side.

Dani sipped it, the warmth seeping through her and melting away some of her trepidation. "It's lovely, thank you," Dani murmured. It was strange, having someone here in a private setting, handing her drinks, waiting on her. Dani studied the female, from her loose blonde fishtail braid to her tipped ears to the humble dress she wore. "I have to admit, I'm not used to being... served. Do you... is this what you do every day?"

The female smiled. "Not always. Prince Zlaet and I have an arrangement. There are times he does not wish to be disturbed or attended to. He's unlike his mother in that way."

"That's because I'm not a spoiled royal child," Slate called from the bedroom, and Dani glanced through the open doors to see him breezing out of the bathroom, dressed in cotton workout pants and a tank top, pulling his hair into a messy bun on the top of his head. He joined them in the sitting room, snagging an apple from the table.

A shadow interrupted the sunshine streaming in from the balcony. A soft coo drew everyone's attention as Sellie appeared from the far end of the balcony. In a very cat-like stretch, she pushed her front paws out in front of her and arched her back. While her back half wasn't visible, Dani knew her rump was in the air, her tail flicking with pleasure from the stretch. Her snowy owl wings spread a bit, before settling over her back, feathers fluffing.

Dani smiled. "Well, look who's decided to wake up. Sleep well?"

A sharp gasp cut through the serenity of the morning, followed swiftly by the sound of ceramic shattering on stone. Alarmed, Dani glanced back to see a pale-faced Autymn staring wide-eyed, hands covering her mouth as a string of Faerish came from her lips.

"Easy," Slate said to her, soft but firm. "That's just Sellie. Dani's friend."

"That, my lord, is a *griffin*."

Dani strolled out onto the balcony and stroked a hand up Sellie's beak and down her feathered neck. Sellie purred, but her eyes were sharply focused on Autymn. *Friend?*

Dani considered Autymn for a moment and offered the wide-eyed female a reassuring smile. *Maybe,* she said to the griffin. *I'm still feeling her out. Not sure yet... But she seems nice so far.*

Sellie clicked her beak, tail swishing back and forth, and angled her head regally at the fae female. *Plant smell. Small person. No threat smell,* the griffin enunciated, but sent impressions that she would eat the female if she threatened Dani. Stifling a chuckle, Dani stroked her friend again with a small shake of her head.

"Be polite and say hello," Dani heard Slate say to Autymn. "Selene is a lady, and she knows it."

Autymn recovered faster than Dani thought she would, but perhaps politeness was so ingrained in her that it gave her a platform to stand on. "I see…" Autymn pressed both her hands to her sternum, still a little pale, and bowed her head. "Good morning… Lady Selene."

Sellie cocked her head, blinking one eye, then the other. Mollified, she preened Dani's hair for a moment, then finally angled her head toward Autymn like a queen acknowledging a peasant. She clicked her beak at Autymn, but softer now, and inclined her feathery head. Autymn's eyes widened at that, but then the air from Sellie's wings nearly overturned the breakfast as the griffin took to the sky.

Dani watched her friend for a moment, then stepped back into the sitting room. Composure had returned to Autymn's gentle face, but her caramel eyes gleamed with curiosity. "You can speak to animals, Tani-*tana*?"

"Yep." Dani reached down to snag a pastry, smiling at Autymn.

Slate strode over to Dani, reaching up to stroke a hand over her jaw as he feathered his lips over hers. "I have to go. You gonna be okay?" His voice was soft, and in her periphery, Dani saw Autymn discretely step away and into the bedroom.

Anxiety choked her. "You're leaving now?"

Slate's eyes bounced between hers, concern etching his face and filtering into her from his magic. Dani wrestled with her own emotions, shoving them down and gathering calm around her while chiding herself. She was an adult. She could handle a few hours alone.

Frankly, it was the *alone* part that bothered her the most.

Slate's fingers slipped from her jaw to her throat, his thumb feathering over the mark on her neck, which instantly helped to calm her, for some reason. His voice remained soft as he murmured, "Listen, I'll just tell Kallen to fuck off and—"

"No." She pressed her palms into his chest. "No, I will be fine. You have things to do, right? I will entertain myself," she told him with more confidence than she felt.

He leaned his head down to press his brow to hers, meeting her gaze. "No one will bother you here." It was a promise to her, and a threat to others. He lifted his head and looked through the doors to the bedroom, and Dani spied the fae female straightening the bed. "Autymn," he called, and she paused, looking up. "No one bothers her."

Autymn nodded. Once. An understanding of the command just given. "I will make certain of it, my lord."

Slate gave Dani another look, and his thumb feathered over the scar on her neck once more. "I won't be gone long. Couple of hours at most. I'll be at the training facility, near the soldier's barracks. Autymn can take you there if you want."

Dani nodded. "I'll be okay."

He gave her another kiss, deeper now, turning her mind into jelly. "When I get back," he whispered in her ear, "I'm gonna lock the door and bend you over that bed." The wicked heat in his voice made her blood go molten, and she bit her lip to keep from whimpering with the sudden need twisting her gut.

With a final heated grin, he vanished through a portal.

Dani stood still for a moment, stitching herself back into a solid state, vaguely aware that Autymn continued to freshen up the bedroom, singing a song too low for Dani to catch the words.

Finally, Dani let out a breath and glanced out toward the sunlight streaming in through the balcony archways. Alone in a strange fae city... but the room smelled of Slate, and his heated promise kept her from feeling the chill of loneliness.

"Would you like a bath, Tani-*tana*?" Autymn's voice came from the doorway to the bedroom.

Dani started, images of Slate bending her over the edge of the bed and making good on his promise scattering from her thoughts as her cheeks heated. She turned to find Autymn standing just inside the bedroom, gesturing toward the bathroom. "Oh. Yes, that'd be great, actually, thank you."

The sunken bath was deep and warm, seeping into her bones and melting away any residual nerves she had. She heard Autymn breezing in and out of the room beyond the archway door, but the female fae didn't disturb Dani in the bathroom. She took her time, marinating in the water, washing her hair, and enjoying the light scents of the soaps and oils Autymn had laid out. After the bath, she pulled some jeans and a simple t-shirt from her bag, and slipped into them, not needing anything else in the warm Titan's Fen climate.

"Shall I tend to your hair, my lady?" Autymn asked.

"Oh, uh... I mean, you don't have to do that," Dani insisted, entirely unused to being waited on like this. She should be brushing her own hair.

"Certainly, but I would be pleased to do so. Your hair is so fiery and beautiful," Autymn admitted with a smile.

Dani hesitated because, in all honesty, the idea of someone combing her hair was too tempting to pass up. She relented and followed Autymn out onto the balcony, where the female had placed a chair. She had a lovely view of the town below, with the morning sunlight streaming over the mountains. The rest of Dani's anxiety bled away from her, especially when Autymn began to pull a comb through her hair.

"I'm grateful to have met you, Tani-*tana*," Autymn murmured after several minutes of silence.

"Why is that?" Dani asked, half in a trance from the combination of morning sun and hair brushing.

"Well, Prince Zlaet has spoken of you, of course, but... selfishly, I have never met a human female, even one kissed by the lore such as yourself."

"Really?" She was tempted to twist and see the female's face, but her relaxed muscles, along with Autymn's fingers in her hair, resisted the idea. Then again, she shouldn't be surprised. Slate had said as much the other night. The faerfolk here didn't leave Titan's Fen. Ever.

"Truly. I have never left Titan's Fen. Do you live in the mortal city outside the Forest?"

Dani smiled, unsurprised by the fae's curiosity. "Yes, I do. I live in a house all by myself."

"All by yourself? Do you work a trade, *Tana*?"

"A trade? Uh, yes, I suppose. I work with animals. I assist mortal animal doctors. It's a great life. I get paid to make animals more comfortable," Dani responded as Autymn continued to run the comb through her hair.

There was a pause of stroking, stirring Dani back to reality. Autymn's voice was contemplative. "That is a noble trade. What is it that humans do with their days?"

Dani let out a lazy chuckle, angling her head back a little to glance up at the female. "Well, that depends on the human."

Autymn, Dani found, was an insatiably curious creature, for all her quiet politeness. Dani answered all of Autymn's questions, from the mundane to the philosophical, a part of her blossoming open with kindness toward this innocent creature that knew of nothing of the world outside her small, magical town. She told Autymn about her job, what she did at home, how she'd met Slate, how cars worked, and that, yes, humans lived in large buildings made of iron without trouble.

Throughout, Dani noticed Autymn, too, called her *Tani-tana*, just as Kallen did.

"What does that word actually mean? *Tana*? I keep hearing everyone call me that..." Dani murmured aloud, long after Autymn had finished with her hair and had pulled up a chair alongside her. "Is it like Miss or Mrs?"

"*Tana*? It's your title." Autymn laughed lightly, sipping at a fresh cup of tea.

"Title?" Dani's brows crashed together in confusion.

Autymn studied her for a silent moment, then stood so fluidly it was like mist over rocks. She returned moments later and presented Dani with a handheld mirror.

Confused by the sudden gesture, Dani took the mirror and glanced at the reflection. Her lips parted at the sight.

Whatever magic Autymn had woven was *stunning*. She'd braided Dani's hair from the crown of her head all the way down in a beautiful, loose braid, and interwoven in the braid were delicate flowers and leaves, the tiniest stems green with lush buds. Dani turned her head from side to side, speechless. She felt like she'd stepped out of a Beltane festival of old.

Autymn twisted her fingers above Dani's head, and Dani watched as tiny branches grew right out of her hair, twisting and curling and threading across the top of her head, until it looked unmistakably like...

A crown.

Alarm made her heart skip a beat, and she lowered the mirror, glancing wide-eyed at Autymn. "Oh, I don't need a crown," she told her, trying to maintain a carefree tone.

Autymn's laugh was like silver bells as she reseated herself next to Dani. "Of course you do. You are *Tana*. Well," she paused, tipping her head to the side, "perhaps not yet. But once Prince Zlaet is crowned *Titania*, then you will be *Tana*. He will be king, and you will be queen-consort."

Queen-consort. The word stuck in Dani's head.

"You would make a stunning queen-consort..."

"Slate and I aren't married." She made a valiant attempt to keep her voice level.

Autymn blinked at her curiously. "Married?"

Dani's fingers of her free hand curled over the armrests of the chair. "Yeah, like... people in love who make a vow? To be bound together until death?"

"That is what being *mayted* is, is it not? You and Slate are *mayts*. Destined by the Goddess to be together," Autymn said with a happy, almost dreamy smile.

In the reflection of the hand-held mirror, Dani caught sight of the small mark between her neck and shoulder, the scar that had always felt like *more*. Panic shivered down her spine.

Mayts. Mayts. Mayts. The word clamored in her head.

She knew the term, of course. The concept of a forever partner existed across all races of magicfolk. Maddie's husband Tony was her life-partner, called a *tei enaid* among the witches. She knew Kari and Jian's parents were mated, called *tamashoko* by the Mystics. Hell, she even knew Slate's parents had been *mayted*.

She forced herself to take another deep, even breath. "And how can you tell when people are *mayted*?" Dani continued, impressed with how steady she sounded.

"Well." Autymn flushed, sipping at her tea. "It is in your scent, of course. But also..." Dani saw her caramel eyes flit over to Dani's scar. "The mark, yes? The fae believe it is the shape of two crescent moons, coming together as one whole."

For a solid minute, Dani couldn't speak. Autymn didn't seem to take her silence as anything but a natural pause in speech, for her gentle smile remained as Dani scrambled to pull herself together. "I see…"

The female fae sighed dreamily. "It is a privilege to be so blessed by the Goddess. *Mayts* are thought to be perfect for each other. Balanced." She rose to her feet and gathered the empty mugs. She glanced at Dani, a wistfulness to her features. "We should all be so lucky, yes?"

"Yes…. of course." Dani nodded, offering Autymn a smile. "Thank you for my hair."

"The pleasure is mine, Tani-*tana*."

Autymn left, leaving Dani alone on the balcony with her own thoughts. Which kept spinning out, one thought trailing to the next. *Mayts. Queen-consort*.

She still remembered it vividly, the sex in the tub that early summer night, in his apartment, after a wildly emotional week of not speaking. She'd begged him for something easy and light and casual and *fun*, and he'd promised to deliver.

He'd never been very good at lying, but she'd been in a pretty desperate place. She'd been willing to believe anything, if only for something to grasp in the sea of emotions she'd felt then.

Dani touched the scar on her neck, mind drifting as she recalled the orgasm that had blown her entire world apart when his teeth had sunk into her neck that first time. And how every time after that, her bones would turn to jelly when he touched it. Something had shifted between them that night, and if Dani was honest with herself, she'd known it then. Had known it for months afterward, when he'd disappeared and left her.

Had he known? Had he known what had started between them that night in the tub?

He must've. Someone must've told him, or he'd figured it out. He wasn't stupid by any stretch of the imagination.

Which meant he'd lied to her. Lied through omission, at least.

The mere idea of such a deep commitment sent a conditioned panic response to flood through her; scalp tightening, heart racing, goosebumps over her neck. But worse than that was the sickening notion that Slate *hadn't trusted her*.

He'd hidden something from her that was monumentally important, not only to her current life, but to her future as well.

He'd *promised*. He'd promised to be honest with her.

Dani's fingers curled around the edges of her chair, chest tight. Hurt, and something spicier, built inside her as her thoughts spiraled over all the little signs she'd ignored, all the little indicators that her relationship with Slate was something deeper than she'd known.

She suddenly felt very naive—she should've guessed. She knew the matching marks were significant.

Gasping for air, Dani shot to her feet and hurried inside. She was barely aware of her own actions as she reached for the small bag she'd packed for herself. Her mind kept swirling in furious, hurt circles, and her fingers trembled as she stuffed the few belongings she'd brought with her into the canvas bag.

She needed to leave.

CHAPTER · THIRTY-FOUR

UNEARTHED TRUTHS

The magicfolk amongst the indigenous peoples of the Americas are considered to be more in tune with the roots of magic from their inception, developing a deep spiritual connection to the land, and the animals. This is attributed to the youngest of the four gods of magic, the Great Spirit, and her ...

- Gherald Schmidt, Faerloch Historical Archives

Her mind was a furious firestorm of hurt, panic, and anger as Dani turned back toward the balcony of the suite, her bag hanging from her hand. She needed to call Sellie, have the griffin take her home—

A crash sounded behind her as she swung her bag over her shoulder, and Dani jumped, whirling around. Her bag had clipped the bedside table, knocking over a stack of magazines and Slate's phone.

A small, childish part of her felt a zing of satisfaction, but it was immediately drowned out by shame for such a petty reaction. Dropping her bag by her feet with a frustrated sigh, she crouched down to scoop up the magazines and the phone, hands shaking as she struggled with her own emotions.

Slate's phone screen woke at her touch, and she paused when she saw his wallpaper. It was a picture of the two of them, taking a ridiculous selfie with a Snapchat filter from one of their dates in the summer.

She lost her momentum, as if she'd tripped over a rock in the middle of a marathon. Her breath caught, and she found herself staring at the picture as if in a dream.

They looked so happy, and it pierced her heart in an entirely different way.

She was being a coward again, ready to run at the first struggle.

Running like she'd done her entire life, away from things that *could* hurt her. But she already knew how much it hurt to be without Slate. As she touched the screen to wake up the phone again, she suddenly felt foolish for her impulse to run.

There was no running from whatever existed between them, not when being without him had always hurt more than any of her panic or fear of commitment.

So... they were *mayts*. They were... forever, at least as far as the magical community was concerned. Wasn't that the same as what she'd told him, the night before? That since knowing him, she'd realized she'd been waiting for him?

It all made sense now, like complicated puzzle pieces slotting together.

But that didn't change the fact that he'd lied to her. Kept secrets.

Dani carefully replaced the magazines and his phone. Ignoring her bag of things, she headed for the door.

She needed to talk to Slate. Now.

Furious purpose burned through her mind, so much so that Dani didn't even realize she'd marched right out of the manor and onto the bridge connecting it to the village until the sight of a fae soldier had her steps faltering.

Normally, Dani wouldn't have it in her to approach to an unknown fae soldier, but the twisted hurt and spark of anger inside her fueled her. She straightened her spine, and stepped toward him.

"Tanyiel?"

A voice from behind her, one that had Dani halting. She whirled around and felt a mixture of relief and wariness at the sight of Kallen, his violet eyes sweeping over her with a concerned expression. His attention paused briefly on her hair, and she was suddenly deeply aware of the crown of flowers and branches still woven through the strands.

"I thought Slate was with you," Dani blurted, fists curling at her sides as his name burned through her chest. There was a knowing in the fae male's gaze as he approached to her, and when he got close, he effortlessly inserted himself between her and the small but growing crowd of curious fae that had noticed her from the nearby streets.

"Yes, but the matter no longer required my attendance." Kallen searched her face. "Are you well?"

"No," Dani answered honestly, voice tight. "Take me to Slate, please."

Kallen's brows shot up, and he studied her face for half a heartbeat before he inclined his head. "Of course, *Ta—*"

"Don't, please," Dani snapped, scowling as a spark of heat rose from that pool of hurt.

Kallen snapped his mouth shut, a sheen to his eyes that told her he knew exactly how deep into the hole Slate was at the current moment. He swept his arm into an unnecessarily elaborate bow, gesturing with one hand down the street, through the village. "I'm at your service, Daniella." He spoke her name deliberately, the D sounding odd with his lilting accent.

Her skin tightened over her bones at the idea of walking through the village, but she straightened her shoulders and followed Kallen anyway. She kept her gaze forward as they walked through the town and trudged back up the road she'd traveled the night before. Not far from the gate, off to the side of the road and nestled against the sheer mountain, was a large building. Beyond it was a collection of smaller buildings.

"The barracks," Kallen explained as he led her through a gate and around the main building rather than through. Dani could already hear the grunts and laughter of training soldiers. It was an unfamiliar sound, but enough to pull her from the firestorm in her head to steady her a little.

Slate was already looking in her direction the moment she rounded the corner, and she knew his magic had sensed her presence. He was standing at the edge of a large circle of packed earth with a group of similarly-dressed fae—soldiers, she supposed. Two soldiers were sparring in the circle.

Slate separated himself from his group, shoving their shoulders as they spoke to him with teasing edges to their voices.

"Zlaet!"

A female soldier called after him, a hardness to her voice, but Slate turned and gave a sharp shake of his head. The female flipped her attention between Slate and Dani, and after a beat, she backed off, shifting curious gray eyes in Dani's direction.

Two things became instantly obvious to Dani.

One—the nostrils of the fae soldiers closest to her flared with interest, and their immediate attention told her they could *smell* the secret Dani had only just uncovered.

Two—panic flashed through Slate so hard and so fast it was broadcasted by his magic before he could stifle it.

That spark lit up, fueled by the oil of hurt. Every single person in this place knew what was going on. News that was earthshaking and wild to Dani was so easily obvious to these people. All her thoughts blew straight out of her head.

"*You lied to me,*" she accused as tears pricked her eyes, advancing on Slate.

His legs ate up the distance between them faster than hers. She was dimly aware that the dozen soldiers behind him had stopped training, and instead had gathered in groups of twos and threes. They were gesturing and whispering as they watched. Even the female—who seemed to be in charge—barely seemed to be containing her curiosity.

"You *knew* we were *mayted*." Dani's fingers curled into fists. "You've known for a while, haven't you?" Her voice cracked, and she tried to harden her voice, to feed on that spark instead of the aching sense of betrayal.

He stopped abruptly several paces from her, as though her hurled words had pierced his feet to lock him in place.

"Tell me," she whispered, a part of her wildly hoping he hadn't known, that he hadn't been keeping something like this from her.

"Let's talk privately." His words came out fast, stressed, panicked, but spoken low, gaze locked on her face.

"It doesn't seem like much of a secret," Dani said, eyes burning as she blinked rapidly. "At least, not to everyone else here."

Slate shut his eyes, fists tightening at his sides, his entire body tensing in front of her.

Heartbeats ticked by in total silence. One. Two. Three.

She was a breath away from turning on her heel and walking away from him when he broke the brittle silence.

"Seven months."

Dani's breath caught in her throat. She couldn't have heard him right. Seven months...?

"That's how long I've known," he admitted on an exhale. "I wanted to tell you, but—"

Seven *months*. That was the entire time he'd been gone from her life and then some. He'd known... this whole time?

It rocked her back on her heels.

He'd been sitting on this information the entire time they'd been doing this 'dating' business all over again. He'd known. Every date. Every kiss. Every moment they'd spent together in the last month or so, re-learning each other... and he'd kept this piece of information to himself.

Instant doubt pressed into her heart. Was any of it real, then? Or was it just some sort of fae instinct thing for him?

She blinked hard, refusing to let her tears fall. "When were you planning to tell me then, *Titania*?"

He flinched as though she'd physically slapped him. "I was... I was working it out."

"Working... working it *out*?" Her voice pitched as a single tear overflowed, and the spark inside her flared. Dashing at the tear, she glared at him through blurry vision. "I told you *everything*. There is no part of me that you don't know now. I gave you everything, asked for everything back, and you *promised you would*. And you *didn't*."

He took a step toward her, and she could see he was shaking. The dirt around his feet trembled from the force of the telekinetic magic leaking out of him. "Daniella—"

"You kept this colossal secret from me for seven months. A life-changing piece of information." She sucked in a deep, trembling breath. "Is this a real thing between us? Or is it just some magical *mayt* shit?"

Some of the color drained from his face, his eyes lightening to a panicked ice blue. "Don't even think that—I can explain—"

He reached for her, and she fell back a step, jerking her head from side to side. "No," she whispered hoarsely. "I'm not ready for an explanation." Another tear tracked down her cheek, and he flinched again.

She turned on her heel. "I need to go. I need... I need some space right now." Her shoes crunched against the gravel as she started to walk away, her pulse pounding in her ears. She suddenly felt exposed and raw and fragile, and it all scratched down her throat and into her chest until breathing felt like effort.

She heard him take a few steps behind her, his footsteps picking up speed. She squeezed her eyes shut—if he touched her, she'd fall apart, even as her skin prickled with anticipation, craving his hands—

She sucked in a sharp breath at the sound of a body slamming to a stop, and she whirled to see Slate two feet from her, hands up and pressed flat, as if the very air was pushing back, a shimmer of magic evident where his hands put pressure on an invisible barrier. She watched as his bright eyes tracked to her, then past her, slipping instantly—frighteningly—from pure panic to pure murder.

Dani whipped her head around to see Kallen not half a dozen paces behind her, a single finger pointed at Slate.

"I believe my lady said she needed space," the lieutenant said.

A loud slam echoed from the barrier as Slate pounded a fist against it, drawing her attention. He glared at Kallen, and the temperature around them dropped several degrees.

"Let me out." His voice was definitely not human.

Kallen ignored him, turning his attention to Dani. "If you are ready, Daniella…"

Another slam came from the barrier, followed by a growl. And for a single heartbeat, some of Dani's ire faded as concern overtook her. Seeing Slate behind that barrier, as though he were someone she needed protection *from*, as though he were a *threat* to her, somehow…

It was that nugget of concern that had her closing the space between them until she was inches from the barrier, because no matter how angry she was at him, she wasn't afraid of him.

"I'll call you when I'm ready to talk," she promised in a soft voice, but she wouldn't look at him—couldn't, not when she felt so… angry and disappointed and sad. Some cocktail of all those emotions. She touched the barrier where his hand rested. The glimmering warmth of magic greeted her skin instead of his rough palm.

"Daniella, don't. Wait. Please. Let me explain." Panic laced his voice.

"No. You can explain when I'm ready to actually hear you. If you've any remorse for how hurt I am, you'll respect the space I need right now. I need time, and you need to give that to me. You owe me that much." With that, she turned on her heel.

"Daniella!"

She stepped up to Kallen, angling her head back to look at him. "Will you ask Ebisu to take care of Dash for me? Sellie will find her way to me when she wants," Dani spoke quietly, ignoring the pounding from behind her.

Kallen inclined his head. "Of course, my lady. He will be well cared for."

Dani nodded gratefully, and Kallen cast down a portal next to her. Without a backward glance, she stepped into it.

And vanished.

Several portals later, Dani found herself stepping out onto the rooftop garden of Slate's apartment. The brisk winter air was a balm against her flushed skin.

"24 hours."

Dani turned. "What?"

Kallen was standing in the middle of the garden, hands behind his back in a military stance. "I can promise I will keep Zlaet contained for 24 hours. It would be good for him to have time to cool off and consider his actions." He paused. "However, I am intimately familiar with who Zlaet becomes without Tanyiel, and I cannot in good conscience watch his slow decay into numbing madness again."

Dani's breath stilled in her lungs. It seemed like years ago, but it was only recently that Slate had described it to her—that 'cold numbness' he'd descended into upon killing the fae who'd attacked them and burned her house down. She'd felt it in him several times, an arctic chill that bled out of him.

"Is that...?" she asked hesitantly.

"It is known as the Malady, and it is the main reason there are so few male empaths," Kallen said. "They are prone to a type of psychosis... a madness, almost. Whether it is a side effect of their constant exposure to emotions not their own, or a symptom of the magic itself, we don't quite know. We also do not know why males alone seem to be afflicted, but if they are not able to control it..." He hesitated. "Well, they become a danger to themselves, and others."

The blood drained from her face. "Did Slate's mother...?"

Kallen shook his head. "Not particularly, no. She was gifted, yes, but she had greater control over the subtleties of the magic. She was a fine instrument compared to Zlaet's blunt force. More delicate, subtle..." a shade of a fond smile, "in all aspects of her life."

Dani swallowed hard, throat tight.

"It is not spoken of within the Silver Valley, but it is well known Zeyphar suffers the Malady," Kallen continued, "though with an uncanny control unlike any before. He is truly mad, and yet gifted in his madness."

The male shifted back on his heels a little. "We had hoped it would skip Zlaet, but his empathy magic is too powerful."

"Does that—" Dani's breath hitched, a different kind of panic wriggling through her. She thought of Zeyphar, the coldness to him, and how Slate's own emotions would also shift rapidly, and how the space around him became cold when he lost his temper...

Her gaze flashed to Kallen's. "Will he become like Zeyphar?" Her voice was tight, just like her entire body, poised on the edge of a horrible realization.

Kallen held up a hand, expression careful. "Not necessarily. Firstly, it does not always happen to Zeyphar's severity. Secondly, Zeyphar does not have a *mayt* to ground him. *Mayts* provide a tether to each other, a balance of the soul, and it may help Zlaet from being influenced by the Malady as much."

She'd always assumed the cold Slate seemed to exude when he was upset had something to do with his tendency to drop into a state of emotionless numbness, like when he used to fight in the circuit. Kari called it Slate's 'ice fight mode'. Jian called it a toxic coping strategy.

Yet to know that that numbness was a symptom of a... psychosis? And to know he could spiral into that apathetic, unfeeling numbness without her?

Whatever Kallen saw on her face had him hurrying to say, "Even without you, his father has trained him to have a strong sense of discipline, a tool that will assist him to remain level. He is not indefensible against the whispers of madness, and he has others to rely on as well, something else Zeyphar lacks in true form. Zeyphar does not have friends, only pawns."

There was a surprising bitterness to Kallen's tone. Dani stared at him, suddenly lightheaded. "Maybe I should go back—"

Kallen shook his head with a gentle smile. "I do not tell you this to make you reconsider your choice for space. I tell you this so you have all of the information, as a *mayt* should." A pointed look from the male, and after what she'd just told Slate, she couldn't really argue with that. Dani forced herself to draw in a steadying breath. "He will be fine for 24 hours," Kallen told her gently. "After that, you must decide how you will prepare. He is unlikely to keep his distance, not as a newly *mayted* male. His instincts will be riding him hard."

Mouth dry, Dani licked her lips, looking to where her fingers twisted together as she digested this information. The knowledge that Slate would be in pain was enough to make her want to return right away, but that wasn't the right choice. A relationship meant taking care of herself as well as him, and right now, she *did* need space. If she sacrificed her own sanity to save his, they would both still lose in the end.

So Dani nodded, meeting Kallen's eyes. "Alright. I'll be ready."

Ready for the possibility that Slate *couldn't* give her the space she needed, not because he was being a jerk, but because the toll it demanded from him was too steep.

Kallen nodded, a smile pulling at his face. "In full transparency, Tanyiel, he is not behaving differently than any fae would. Fae as a species are easily... riled up about their chosen partners. There is a piece of our hearts that remains truly bestial from our earliest inception at the hands of the Goddess. Seeing as you have a way with animals, I have faith you will handle Zlaet with grace."

Dani had to smile at that, a small unexpected laugh escaping her. "Are you saying Slate is an animal?"

Kallen shrugged. "Aren't we all?"

With a wave of his hand, a glowing portal reappeared on the roof. He bowed with a hand over his sternum. "Good luck, Tanyiel-*tana*." He stepped through the portal, leaving her to her thoughts.

THROUGH THE FAERIE CIRCLE

... do not all live within larger, multi-family packs. Examples include the solitary were-tiger and the elusive but powerful were-polar-bear. These were-beings usually oversee a smaller family unit...

- Gherald Schmidt, Faerloch Historical Archives

Slate stood shock-still as Dani and Kallen vanished right before his eyes. Nothing moved—not his blood, his breath, his heart.

Not even his mind processed what exactly had happened.

It was as though he were stuck in some feedback loop, a broken record inside his mind that just kept saying: *I need space. You lied to me. I need space. You lied to me. I need space...*

Is any of it real?

The ward around him faded, his hands falling. The world pressed in on his body, on his ears, dimming everything until all he heard was the sound of his own heartbeat and the sound of his own footsteps as he managed one, two, three steps.

And he was running.

Running, sprinting, out of the training facility and down the path that led out of the village, every instinct boiled down to pure survival.

Dani. Dani was his survival. He needed her. He needed to go to her.

He couldn't let her walk out of his life again. He *couldn't*. Physically. Mentally. Emotionally.

He'd fucked up. *Gods help him*, he'd fucked this up bad.

He hit the gatehouse. He didn't even get to the gate before he once again slammed into a ward. The magic shimmered over him as he felt the invisible barrier with his hands, slapping it until the slapping turned into his fists pounding it, pounding, pounding, *pounding...*

Until his hand was raw from the chaff of the magic, until his arm was throbbing, still trying to heal from being blown to smithereens a handful of days ago. Until his breathing was so staggered, his vision spotted around the edges.

Fucking Kallen.

He whirled, storming back up the path, mind dialing into a single purpose—talk to Dani.

Dani. Dani. Dani.

It felt like he blinked, and he was back in his suites. He scrambled for his phone, pulling up her contact information with quick efficiency.

Dani's voice echoed through the small speaker. *"Hi! This is Dani, I'm not here right now, so please leave a message after the beep."*

He paced his rooms, trying to wrap his head around words, around language, when all he could hear was a crackling inside his skull like fracturing ice.

Beep.

"Dani. Dani. It's me. Call me right now, *please.*"

He hung up and pulled up her texts, blasting some messages at her in quick succession.

And as the minutes ticked by, next to each one of the texts was a glaring little note: *unread*.

Unread.

Unread.

He roared in frustration and threw his phone on his bed and rubbed his whole face with his hands. He was going to climb the fucking walls. He couldn't explain it; he *needed* to go see her. He needed to see her, to... try and wrap his head around some kind of explanation, some kind of apology.

He couldn't breathe. He crouched down, pressing his palm to the floor to steady himself as his vision faded at the edges, and he attempted to suck in some deep breaths, filling his lungs to the point of pain.

The panic of her leaving edged away, leaving the sour, toxic taste of guilt behind. It speared through him like poison, leaving him mildly ill and jittery.

Goddess help him, the look on her face when he'd spied her behind Kallen...

The anger had been there, and that was bad enough, but it was the hurt behind it, so much heavier than the anger, that skewered him. Her feelings had been so *loud*, practically shouting across his mind, punctuating every word until she'd pierced him through like an iron knife straight between his ribs.

As if it fancied itself a dark knight sent to rescue him, the ice crawled over his mind like delicate filaments of frost, crackling, snapping. Tempting him with the blissful silence of snow-white apathy, a dark, empty promise of nothingness.

Slate sucked in another deep breath, yanking his sanity back. It was too easy to feel nothing.

If you've any remorse for how hurt I am...

He absolutely deserved it. Without question or debate, he deserved her ire and her hurt. Because he'd fucked *up*.

He'd fucked it up *hard*.

Dani didn't sleep much that night.

Slate's bedroom in his apartment had haunted her with the ghost of him, the wintry scent of him in every thread and fiber of the room. The scent had made her ache, made her lonely.

But she still wanted to be angry.

So after spending a solid hour gently untangling her beautiful hair, she'd ended up playing her Pokémon game in the living room until late into the night. The mindlessness of battling and leveling her team freed up her mind to think.

More than half a year, he'd known.

Had he found out after the whole fiasco with Zeyphar in the arena? Or had it been even earlier? What a thing to hold onto for that whole time...

Mayts were forever. It wasn't something to walk away from. It pulled people together, if anything. Dani wasn't entirely sure how it worked with fae, but she'd heard Maddie talk about the idea of being fated to someone, to find the one person the Goddess chose specially for *you*. Once you found them, it was nearly impossible to walk away from them. The soul couldn't fight it—didn't want to fight it. Fate pulled you together, and to go against that was to defy a magic older than magic itself.

"Maybe we can—do you... wanna date again?" he hedged carefully.

"Like, ten dates?" she asked.

"However many you want."

She hadn't specified a number, but she'd seen the resolve in his eyes, the way he'd braced himself for the possibility for her to say zero. She'd seen it throughout their entire rooftop discussion. If she'd told him she didn't want to see him again... he would have honored that. He would have vanished from her life to respect her wishes.

He would have defied the very fabric of magical law to make sure she was comfortable.

That meant something. It meant that she was more important to him than even his own instincts, didn't it? Had he not exercised every possible avenue to make sure she was comfortable? Had he not intentionally and carefully boxed away pieces of himself in an effort to calm her fears?

Was she, once again, letting her fear drive the narrative of her life?

The anger inside her petered out into an ache along her skin, tightening in the center of her chest. She couldn't fault him for keeping this secret between them. He'd told her he didn't want to drag her into the shit with him. He'd said he'd avoided her for all those months because he was scared. Scared of her possible rejection, yes, but also scared *for* her. He'd wanted to shield her from his life as much as possible.

If he'd told her then... would she have still chosen him?

She wanted to say yes, of course, she'd have chosen him, but the reality was she'd been scared too. Scared of how she felt about him, scared of the fact that he was fae. Not only fae, but High Fae, and royalty to boot. Future king. *Titania.*

She thought about the mark on his shoulder.

And she couldn't deny that she was *deeply satisfied* by the notion that just that tiny little scar made it impossible for him to leave her ever. She would never be alone again.

In a way, without his interference at all, she'd chosen him.

And a part of her was certain she'd chosen him a long time ago. On a darkened street at the threshold of spring, to the backdrop of a bullet and a failed kidnapping.

With these thoughts running circles in her head, she eventually fell asleep on the couch.

She woke up to her phone buzzing. She glanced at it, knowing it wasn't Slate. She'd muted all his calls and texts—to which there were a lot, but she wasn't ready to listen to his voicemails or read his messages.

When she finally mustered the energy to check her phone, she found a message from Caroline. It was an update on a new rescue dog with severe anxiety, and it was the excuse Dani needed to get out.

Technically, she was on vacation, and Caroline would never ask for her to come in, but Dani couldn't ignore an animal in need. Besides, she had a few other errands she could run as well. She needed to get out of this apartment and out of her own head. It didn't take her long to shower, throw on some clothes, and head out to her Vespa.

She checked on her house first, pleasantly surprised to see quite a bit of work had been completed on it in such a short time. The general contractor—a werelynx—informed her that she'd be able to move back in within a month. Her other errands took very little time, and she arrived at the animal clinic by early afternoon. By then, Sellie had found her and spent the entire last ten minutes of her drive scolding her for leaving without telling her, soaring high above Dani, easily keeping pace.

The griffin was still miffed by the time they arrived, but had accepted Dani's apology and grudgingly supplied that she'd reassured Dash for Dani too, to which Dani was grateful. She pulled her Vespa into the alley next to the clinic and turned off the engine. As she hung her helmet on the handlebar, Sellie flew up to brood in her rooftop nest above the clinic.

Still straddling her bike, Dani couldn't help it; she pulled her phone out of her backpack and found more messages from Slate. She pulled in another deep breath as she checked the time. It was quickly approaching the 24-hour mark Kallen had promised.

She should probably take care of the animal first, but instead, she opened up Slate's text thread.

Goddess help her, she did really miss him terribly.

Slate:

Dani. Call me.

Please call me.

Daniella.

Please.

I'm sorry.

Can we talk? Please?

Dani, you have to know I'm so sorry. I wanted to tell you. I did. I was scared. I know, it was stupid because we promised to be honest, but I was still scared. Please call me.

I can't sleep. Call me.

Daniella.

Daniella.

I love you.

That last message nearly did her in. She could almost hear his voice...

She pulled up his voicemails. All five of them.

She pressed play on the first one and put the phone to her ear.

"Dani. *Dani.* It's me—"

Strong arms locked around her from behind, so suddenly the wind knocked from her lungs as she gasped. Her phone flew from her grasp, and a long-fingered hand clamped firmly over her mouth, stifling her rising scream. The only sound in the alley was the crack and shatter of her phone's screen as it hit the pavement.

Panic surged, flooding her system with a shot of adrenaline. She kicked her feet and thrashed, knocking into her bike, but whoever held her was far too strong. They easily hauled her from the Vespa as the bike crashed to the ground.

Sellie! She reached for the griffin, roosting high above them, fear lacing her mental voice. Another person appeared in her periphery, and Dani recognized the armor and uniform of a soldier.

A fae soldier.

The last thing she heard was Sellie's shriek of fury from above before she was hauled backward. There was a glint of a golden portal around her feet, and Dani winked out of the alleyway next to the Kingstreet Animal Hospital.

LOST AND FOUND

... known as the Malady, in which those suffering are described as losing touch with all of their own emotions, succumbing to a stoic state of apathy. Interestingly, those suffering from the Malady report higher abilities to think rationally during moments of intense...

– Gherald Schmidt, Faerloch Historical Archives

Slate paced the balcony, watching as the afternoon sun began to sink toward the mountains. Anxiety punched through the icy numbness that had become his normal over the last... he checked his phone. 22 hours and 47 minutes.

22 hours and 48 minutes.

Anxiety surged over the thought of seeing her, over what he was going to say to her. How was he going to stuff this one back in the box?

22 hours and 49 minutes.

He'd tried and failed to use the *mayt*-bond inside his head to his advantage. Dani's emotional mind was always just a door over from his own now, since the *mayting* was complete. What had once been two doors connected by the path of his magic was now an adjoining door. Two minds joined, but separated from the rest of the world.

But when he stretched his empathy senses out, listening at the door of her mind, he heard... nothing. Perhaps they were too far apart—he'd never tested their range. Even opening the door between them yielded little more than an awareness that she was physically alright, that she was there but not there at the moment. It was infuriating and made him feel like he was missing a limb. Or an organ.

Waiting was not his strength. He was living on a razor's edge of sanity. He kept feeling ghost vibrations from his phone, and he'd yanked it out of his pocket so many times in the last day that he'd started simply holding it in his hand. Waiting.

"If you've any remorse for how hurt I am, you'll respect the space I need right now. I need time, and you need to give that to me. You owe me that much."

Kallen had given him a look upon his return from escorting Dani to his apartment over the studio, asking if he'd needed to keep the ward up, and Slate had shaken his head. But he hadn't been able to resist testing it himself, getting as far as the pedestrian bridge to the district, before he'd portaled back to Titan's Fen.

And commenced with waiting.

More like dying. Slowly.

22 hours and 51 minutes.

"Stop checking your phone," Jian drawled from where he sat on one of the balcony chaises, a sketchbook propped on his knees. His fingers were dark and smudged from graphite.

"Why are you even still here?" Slate snapped.

"Because I am a doctor, and you are a case study." Jian didn't look up from his sketchbook, his pencil working some minute details. He smudged the paper with his fingers. "I'm figuring out what, exactly, happens to you when that psychosis comes over you."

"I'm not crazy," Slate snarled. "I'm..."

In all honesty, he didn't know what he was. A jungle juice cocktail of mixed emotions.

"I didn't say you were crazy. But powerful male empaths are more prone to a magical psychosis as their own emotions eat them alive on the inside, so I want to keep an eye on you. And study you a bit."

"And what do you see?"

"I see your *chi* going ape-shit, thrumming, pulsing, and it's freezing. Most *chi* is warm, but yours isn't. It hurts me to touch it." Jian made some sweeping sketches, the pencil scratching the thick paper. "And you're angry—"

"Of course I'm angry!" Slate shouted. "Dani's upset with me, and I fucked it up big time, and I have no clue still how to fix it!"

"You're *only* angry." Jian's gray eyes flashed up to Slate.

Slate said nothing. Jian was right.

What Jian didn't see, though, was the ache Slate felt in his skin, down into his bones. It was intense, like this painful itch he couldn't scratch. It was desperation and need made into a physical ailment. And Dani was the remedy.

What was he going to say to her? He still wasn't sure how to phrase his apology to her, how he was supposed to frame his explanation. How was he supposed to explain that this whole thing, this blowout, this fight, was exactly what he'd been trying to avoid?

A shriek rent the air. Slate startled. Jian swore.

Slate whipped his head up, searching the skies for the griffin just as images hurtled into his mind. He sucked in a sharp breath, gripping the handrail of the balcony.

Sellie had communicated with Slate on less than a handful of occasions, but each time, it was alarming. Information assaulted him in a stream of images and impressions. Dani driving, the image of her clearly from an aerial perspective. Then settling into a nest on the roof. A panicked voice in Sellie's head—Dani's voice, calling for her. The alleyway next to the animal hospital, and a flash of three beings disappearing, too fast to identify them at all except for the fiery flash of red hair. Then... the alley was empty, except for a white Vespa tipped over onto its side.

And panic. Not his own. A more scattered panic, a nervous, jittery kind of anxiety, like an animal who suddenly had no bearing on where they were or what they were supposed to do. But it was all wrapped up in this fierce red-hot fury, so potent that Slate's own vision tinged red.

Slate's heartbeat roared into his head.

The female griffin was little more than a streak of white lightning, falling at a perilous rate from the sky. She screeched again, the sound piercing and agonizing. Slate slapped a hand over his ear right before a large body barreled into him, pinning him to the balcony floor. A beak clicked urgently in his face as large wings half-spread above him, obscuring Jian from his sight. Stunned, he stared up at the griffin as he tried to catch his breath, and Sellie nudged at his face with the top of her head, insistently, urgently. Her beak clicks became more aggressive as wave after wave of images and information blasted him. The same ones over and over again.

It took a second for his addled brain to put the pieces together, but once he did, he froze as still as death.

"What's wrong?" Jian demanded, leaning around the griffin to glance between Sellie and Slate.

"We have to go," Slate said, scrambling to his feet as Sellie backed off of him. He grabbed Jian by the collar of his shirt. "Right now."

He threw them both into a portal.

Slate and Jian materialized into existence in the alley next to Kingstreet Animal Hospital.

The first thing Slate saw was Dani's bike, lying on its side. Her helmet had rolled away. Her phone was nearby, facedown on the pavement.

He stooped and picked up her phone. The screen was cracked, rainbowed, and pixelated, but he managed to punch her code in. It pulled immediately to her voicemail box, and his heart jammed up as he saw that she'd been listening to one of his voice messages.

Ahead of him, he heard Jian lift Dani's bike upright. "What happened?" Jian asked.

"I don't know..." Slate said, voice raw. Icy claws scraped down his throat, down his spine, panic and fear driving up the icy madness inside him. "All Sellie saw was a flash of her hair, maybe some people... then nothing."

"Maybe we should ask inside—" Jian's voice stopped suddenly.

Slate's head snapped toward him, all of his senses on high alert. "What?"

Jian strode a couple of steps deeper into the alley, staring at a single spot amidst the dusting of snow. He glanced over his shoulder to Slate, and the look in his gray eyes was so stark that Slate found himself unable to move for several heartbeats. Jian pointed to the pavement.

Slate unstuck his feet and moved down the alley, every step agony as his mind predicted what he was going to find before he even saw it.

"Oh fuck..." he breathed, shooting out a hand to stabilize himself against Jian's shoulder as his whole world tilted.

There, on the pavement, was the faintest outline of a circle, the remnants of magic imprinted into the snow and dust and dirt of the city.

A portal circle.

She'd been kidnapped by the fae.

In the wealthy High Rise District, in the top penthouse of an impressive apartment building that sported a rare moat of greenery around it, Roger lifted his head from the neck of a young man. Seated on an elegant sofa with his latest companion, Peter, sprawled across his lap, Roger felt the shadows slither and whisper around in his ears.

Peter raised his head with a sleepy smile, but his expression melted into concern at the sight of Roger's face, and the vampire knew that red was likely overtaking his normally chocolate brown irises.

"Roger?" the young man asked, but Roger barely heard him, the shadows curling insistently over his shoulders. Roger's lips curled back from his elongated fangs, expression tightening into something he knew wasn't entirely human as Peter sat up from his lap, a hint of alarm in the young man's pale blue eyes. "Are you okay?" Peter asked hesitantly.

Roger's lashes lowered to shield the red from his eyes, and he forced himself to draw in a slow breath and school his features.

"I must go, Peter. I apologize for the interruption, but my attention is needed elsewhere." The hint of a growl in his tone sent a visible shiver through Peter.

It was an effort of will to relax his shoulders, to keep from surging to his feet and flinging the human from him in his rush to slip into the shadows as quickly as possible. Peter was a sweet man who had provided two years of companionship now—he didn't deserve to be frightened by Roger.

"Oh, o-okay, no problem," Peter said, pulling up a smile and reminding Roger why he'd kept him around as long as he had. He curled his legs under himself on the other end of the sofa. "I might head home soon, if I'm not here when you get back." Peter brushed a finger against the mark on his neck with tender fingers.

Roger was on his feet before Peter had finished speaking, but he took the time to reach down and brush the backs of his fingers along Peter's jaw.

"You may stay here, if you wish. I will be in touch." He offered Peter a small, tight smile before Roger stepped back and slipped into the shadows.

He had to find Daniella.

CHAPTER THIRTY-SEVEN

OF SHADOWS AND SNOW

...it is unknown how Rowan Fafnir and Marius Cassius Romano met. Their romantic relationship became public knowledge due to Rowan's position, and as conflict grew between the Fae and the Vampires, their relationship became...

– Gherald Schmidt, Faerloch Historical Archives

A familiar sense of apathetic dispassion colored Slate's entire being.

He felt nothing as he sat in the large council room in the manor at Titan's Fen. It was the first time he'd ever sat on the large, oversized throne at the head of the room, his back to the tall, arching balcony. He'd never called for an official gathering of his advisors before, and he was numb to the flurry of movement and voices around him.

His long body lounged almost casually on the throne, one elbow propped on the arm, his chin in his hand, gaze fixed on the door of the council room. Some distant, echoing sense of longing hoped to every deity he could think of that she would walk through that door and back into his life.

She wouldn't, though. Because Dani was missing.

The moment he and Jian discovered the portal, Jian had sedated him. Slate remembered nothing between seeing the shade of the faerie circle in the alley to waking up in his room in Titan's Fen. The ward trapped him in the village.

He'd been beyond reason.

He'd had to dig *deep* into the well of discipline inside himself to stay put. To stay and not detonate the ward, be damned the consequences, and head straight toward hell.

The Malady helped—in a masochistic, self-sabotaging way. The further he spiraled into the cold nothingness, the easier it was to detach himself from the aching desperation that clawed up his throat. Easier to see *reason* past the impulsive fae instinct to sprint toward his *mayt* and save her.

He could taste the appeal of staying like this forever.

Several people were in the room with him. He was aware that Jian kept watching him, the *manyeo*'s eyes flickering between Slate and the conversations around the large rectangular table in the center of the room. Kari too, kept eyeing him. Kallen, Saida, Galyn, and several other high-ranking lieutenants were positioned around the table, words flying back and forth.

"... gather the extraction team immediately..."

"... certain she's not in the mortal city?"

"... correspondence with Zeyphar..."

"... he will not negotiate..."

"... the team is more than qualified..."

Slate's gaze flickered from the door to the shadows as the darkness began to form in the corner of the room. His mind roared to life as Roger stepped out of the shadows, causing several fae in the room to step away in alarm, swords scratching against scabbards and curses flying.

Slate spoke for the first time in hours. "Roger."

A hush fell over the room, those unfamiliar with the vampire eyeing him warily and casting glances in Slate's direction. This is what it must be like to be king. To speak a single word and have a room fall silent to hang on your every whim.

Roger strode to the end of the long table opposite of Slate, ignoring the fae, Kari, and Jian as he leveled a red-tinged stare at Slate. There was a hardness to the vampire's jaw as Roger's hands rested on the top of the polished wood. When he spoke, his normally smooth voice had a rough edge to it as he addressed Slate directly.

"She's in the Silver Valley."

Somehow, the hush deepened around them. The temperature dropped a few degrees.

Slate didn't move. Didn't breathe.

Logic warred against the icy rage that began to boil inside him. He'd expected this, some part of him knowing that no matter how the narrative unraveled, this was always where they were headed. He'd known Zeyphar would find her, steal her away from Slate, despite the safety measures they'd put in place.

Why hadn't she stayed within the safety of the ward? Daniella was not *risky*.

He'd done this. Slate had driven her away. And his enemy—their enemy—had capitalized on that. He was responsible for Dani becoming *bait* in this deadly game he played with his uncle.

And damn if it wasn't going to work.

Slate stood swiftly. "Then we go. Right now. You and me. No one can stop us."

Roger shook his head minutely, focus still locked on Slate's. "Unfortunately, we cannot. Might I remind you, there is a ward around the Silver Valley that prevents vampires from entering the city." Roger's eyes slid to Kallen, and Slate caught the confirming nod the lieutenant gave the vampire.

"It is still in place. No vampires may cross the boundary, without exception," Kallen offered in a quiet voice.

Slate didn't take his eyes off of Roger, uncaring of the agony he spied there. "Fine," Slate said, voice deadpan. Emotionless. "I'll go alone."

Instant protests roared through the room.

"Out of the question—"

"We have a team designed for this exact purpose—"

"Zeyphar wants you—"

"You'd play right into his hand—"

That icy rage inside him boiled over, and Slate slammed his palms onto the table. A large crack split through the center of the wood, right down to Roger's side. "This is not a debate!" he snarled. "This is Dani we are talking about!"

"I'll go."

Slate flipped his gaze to his right. Kari was standing, one hip propped against the table with her arms crossed, a hard determination in her thundercloud eyes.

"I'll go," she repeated. "There is no one else in this room more equipped than me to sneak into the Silver Valley and scope out what's going on."

"Absolutely not. You will be caught instantly." Kallen shook his head. "The ward will recognize you as other and not allow entry to non-fae."

Kari reached behind her neck and pulled a rose-gold leaf out from under her hair. She touched it to her forehead. Instantly, there was a shimmer over her skin like thousands of fluttering ginkgo leaves, and in her place stood a male High Fae soldier, complete with Silver Valley armor, tipped ears, bright gray eyes, and platinum hair. Even her scent shifted to that of a fae.

She cocked a confident brow at a stunned Kallen. "Try me, lieutenant."

Murmurings erupted around the room. Galyn studied Kari's new form with curiosity. "We could add you to the extraction team—"

Kari's fae form dissolved, leaving her in her own natural skin. "No. I would go alone."

"Under no circumstances am I sending a *child* into the Silver Valley on her own," Saida said, voice hard. "Respectfully, of course."

Ghostly blue fire shivered over Kari's eyes, and blue-tinged *kitsune* fire shimmered over her body in irritation. "I'm a *kitsune*. A fox demon. My magic is illusion-based. Trickery. Lies. Stealth. I don't play well with others. A team would just hold me back—"

"No," Saida continued.

Kari shifted her stance, laying her palms on the table, claws digging into the wood. "Discretion is in my nature. I can find out what's going on... and if the gods favor us, I might even be able to get Dani out."

"You can't go alone," Jian snapped, scowling at his twin.

"I can and I will," Kari growled, meeting her brother's stare. Silence followed, but neither twin looked away, and Slate knew a mental showdown was taking place between them. After several moments, Jian huffed a breath and sat back in his chair, arms crossed over his chest, his eyes stormy.

"I'm going with you," Slate informed Kari, tone final.

Kari raised a brow at him. "You will do no such thing."

"Neither one of you is going," Saida said. "And that's final."

"Consider it an order from your king, then," Slate growled. "We. Are. Going."

"You are not yet king, Zlaet," Kallen chimed in. Slate slid his gaze to the lieutenant. "You are not going." He gave a gracious nod to Kari. "And while I appreciate your enthusiasm, the captain's logic is sound. You are young—"

Kari snarled.

"—but more importantly, you lack the depth of experience required for such a mission. You have no military experience, no war experience, and frankly, no formal training in espionage. With proper training and time, you can be a valuable asset to Zlaet's court, but not at the present moment."

"You are *grossly* underestimating me," Kari's voice was edged with feral anger. Two fox ears unfurled from her hair, and the red lines slowly appeared over her features, wrapping around her eyes, trailing down her nose, and framing her mouth. She looked positively savage. "This is what I'm born to do. I can *help* her."

Glances around the table, tension building. But there were more headshakes than nods, and Slate sensed Kari's anger ratcheting up.

"The answer is no," Saida said. "The extraction team is going. They can be ready by the morning. They are experienced and skilled, with firsthand knowledge of the Silver Valley and the castle. They will do as they have been prepared to do and extract Tanyiel."

Kari snarled again and slapped her hands against the table. She sucked in a deep, slow breath, her hands and features relaxing, the fox ears and facial markings vanishing.

"Fine," she said with furious, intentional calm. She turned on her heel and stormed out of the councilroom.

The tension in the room swelled. Jian rocked in his chair, fidgeting and tapping his fingers against his arm, eyes fixed on where Kari had vanished.

Slate slid his gaze away from his best friend. "I'm going," he said, turning his attention back to Saida and Kallen. "This is my fault—"

"You are not to blame for her kidnapping."

Slate's attention snapped away from Kallen to land on Roger, who now stood with his hands in his pockets. Slate stared at the vampire for several long heartbeats, his mind wrestling with how out of character that one statement was for Roger. He was usually quick off the mark to inform Slate of all his shortcomings, lest Slate's ego expand.

"You did not orchestrate her capture. You are both unfortunate victims of a war game you are both too young to play," Roger continued, voice deadly soft. He paused, and not a soul interrupted the vampire as he maintained eye contact with Slate. A flicker of red overwhelmed the chocolate color of his eyes, and despite the seemingly relaxed posture, Slate spied the tightness of Roger's muscles as if he were wrestling with his rage. "Zeyphar would have seized any opportunity to lure Daniella to the Silver Valley. Tomorrow, next week, next year. The timing and events preceding the kidnapping are irrelevant to the act itself."

"I promised I'd look out for her," Slate growled, every breath like ice shards coating his esophagus. "Promised *you* that."

Roger's eyes glinted. "Perhaps we are both to blame for our negligence."

Silence swelled in the room, thick and sticky, coating the room in uncomfortable tension. No one spoke, as though no one dared interrupt the two titans of the room volleying terse words back and forth with little more than a wooden table between them.

"Fine." Slate's voice was barely human. He dropped back into the throne, frost spidering out from where he sat. "Send the team. Gods help them if they fuck this up."

Kallen, Galyn, and Saida conferred on the details, the voices like insects buzzing against his ears. Slate tuned it *out* as he leaned back into his throne, once more resuming his previous position, content to spiral deeper into the numb nothingness inside him.

It wasn't long until the only people who remained in the room were Roger, Kallen, and Jian. The vampire met his gaze from where he stood next to the lieutenant, and although Slate's magic had never been able to spy on the vampires' feelings, he could read them all over his normally impassive face.

Roger was feeling as much guilt and rage as Slate was.

Words tumbled from him without thought, spurred by the knowledge that Dani wouldn't want Roger suffering. "There's a piece of me that knows, logically, that I should feel some kinship toward you right now," Slate spoke quietly, ice in his tone, "but I can't bring myself to feel anything except anger."

Roger studied him, and some of the red leaked from his eyes at whatever he saw. "The Malady consumes you," Roger murmured with a shrug. "It galls me to admit, but... for the first time, *I* need *you*. I cannot rescue her. I must rely on you and your people." Roger tipped his chin toward Kallen, before meeting Slate's gaze once more. "A true alliance between us is necessary, for Daniella's best interest."

Slate raised a brow. "Is it now?"

"We both have a vested interest in the same female. Civility is the least we can do. For her."

Slate said nothing, the icy rage inside him coated in the frosty shell of numbing nothingness. There was a piece of him that roared to life at the idea of sharing Dani with anyone, even in a platonic sense. She was *his*. His *mayt*. She belonged to him. It was an animalistic urge; a fae instinct he couldn't suppress.

But the more rational part of him—the part that was overwhelmingly Slate—understood one thing with clarity. He and Roger were bound together by the same female. Roger was not *mayted* to Dani, of course, but the stirring, frenetic madness inside Slate saw the darkness in Roger. As dark as Slate was cold.

Maybe even more so.

And sunshine was the antithesis of those plights.

Roger needed Dani as much as Slate did.

Slate understood this. He *knew* this.

And despite the numbness that enveloped him, Slate still felt a tickle of empathy. He didn't want to live like this forever, and there was a part of him that wouldn't subject Roger to the same madness by denying the vampire the taste of sunshine in his life. He'd said as much already to the vampire—Slate had assured him that Daniella would not leave him.

"I will keep my eyes and ears available to you," Roger said. "Should I come upon information that might serve you, I will make a report."

The shadows began to gather around Roger, and Slate's eyes flipped up to the vampire. "Roger."

The shadows slowed.

"I need you to promise me something."

The vampire raised a brow.

"If something... if something happens to her. To Dani... I need you to promise me that before you rage-fuck the world... you take me out first."

Kallen sucked in a sharp breath, eyes flicking between Slate and Roger. Jian whirled around to face Slate, slashing a hand to the side. "Absolutely not."

Roger's expression remained neutral, and his voice was soft as he spoke. "Oh?"

The room trembled a little as some of Slate's pent-up magic leaked out, the tattoos on his arms twisting closer and closer to a deadly red. "Because without her, no one else can stop me from turning this world into ash and rubble at my feet."

Roger regarded him carefully. The shadows picked up again, swirling around the vampire.

"I promise."

He vanished.

And Slate settled willingly into the cool embrace of numbing emptiness, until all feeling was obliterated.

CHAPTER THIRTY-EIGHT

THE SILVER VALLEY

The Oiche Gealach clan held fast in their beliefs, and with the support of other local clans, House Druidhil laid a curse upon Oiche Gealach as punishment for their crimes against humanity. For their punishment, the clan was deprived of their wolf skins except for one night during every lunar cycle...

- Gherald Schmidt, Faerloch Historical Archives

Zeyphar Titania lounged on his throne and cocked his head toward his Seneschal, Casphian. The male stood, back ramrod straight, as he delivered an update regarding castle maintenance, Royal Guard rotations, and which nobles were currently in residence.

He enjoyed keeping the nobles on a rotation, liked to keep them all close at least a part of the year. It was important they spend quality time with him, to keep their thinking in line with what mattered.

Zeyphar held up his hand, pausing his steward in the middle of his report. "Gwyn's family has been out of residence for far too long. Move her up the list," he interrupted.

Casphian bowed his head. "Yes, your grace. In addition, may I suggest—"

The doors at the end of the expansive hall swung open, the guards on either side stepping inside to flank the three figures passing through them.

"Let me go!"

The female cry went ignored by the two soldiers gripping her elbows, the male and female half-dragging his nephew's *mayt* between them as they guided her, blindfolded, deeper into the throne room.

There she was. Tanyiel.

Zeyphar leaned forward slightly, his interest piquing, and delight unfurled inside him as his magic sipped at the fear wafting off the redheaded female. His soldiers came to a stop before the raised dais and with a wave of permission, they tore her blindfold away.

Wild green eyes flared and rolled as her head whipped up and around, taking in her surroundings. That fear inside her billowed, and Zeyphar smiled as he twined his magic through it, savoring the delicious taste as her gaze finally collided with his.

She stumbled back a step, her face draining of pigment, and the soldier to her right pushed her forward with a short shove between her shoulder blades.

"Do not forget who she is," Zeyphar's voice cut through the room. "She is more valuable than the entirety of your kin, soldier."

"Of course, my lord." The soldier's face paled, but she recovered quickly, angling her head toward Tanyiel. "Apologies, princess."

Tanyiel's eyes widened, flicking between the soldier and himself, and Zeyphar smiled at her. How lovely, this lorekissed female, with her creamy skin, dusting of freckles, and fiery hair. It was truly a pity she belonged to his nephew.

He'd have much preferred to add her to his own collection of lorekissed females, kept safe in his playhouse in the mountains. He would have enjoyed bringing her there, would have enjoyed stroking that fear of hers until he could melt it with pleasure in a delicious twist.

But alas. She was, in fact, more useful to him here.

"There is no need to be afraid, Tanyiel," Zeyphar purred, pushing himself to his feet. He was aware of Casphian staring at Tanyiel, could taste the curiosity curling around the male, but Casphian's expression remained impassive.

It was part of why he favored the male.

He took his time stepping down from the dais, and Tanyiel's scent washed over him as he came to a stop before her. So alluring, so... warm. "You look bedraggled. I will have you shown to your quarters momentarily."

"What do you want?" Tanyiel's voice wavered only slightly, determination edging out some of the fear in her emotional grid.

"We have already discussed what I want," Zeyphar continued. He slipped a finger around a lock of hair by the side of her face, and he crafted his expression into a reassuring smile when she flinched away. "I want Zlaet in my court. And I want you to assist me with this." He wove a thin ribbon of pleasure through her emotions to accompany his words, the magic as simple as breathing. It would be best to start training her mind now to enjoy his suggestions.

Her shoulders relaxed, and his acute eyesight noted the dilation of her eyes, but it was a momentary slip before her eyes widened and fear rushed over her like a wave.

His patient expression twitched. He could sense her mind accepting the positive emotions he fed to her, so why was her fear more dominant? Irritation slithered through him, though he allowed none of it to show on his face.

Tanyiel raised her chin and glared at him. "I'm bait," she accused, and Zeyphar spied the tips of her fingers trembling.

He cocked his head. "Bait? Not at all, Tanyiel-*tana*. You are a revered guest. You will help Zlaet realize that this is where he belongs. When he sees how happy you are here, he will not be able to resist coming to join you."

He needed them both here, within his control. It would be easy to obliterate his nephew from existence and secure his own power over the throne, but then Zlaet would become a martyr. He would not risk the malcontents in his empire rallying over his nephew's death.

Tanyiel stepped back from him, her fingers curling into small fists. "Do you kidnap and blindfold all your *revered guests* before they arrive?"

Zeyphar followed her retreat, angling his head to look down at her as he lowered his voice to a soft caress, deliberately injecting an apology into his tone. "It was a necessary precaution, given your... unique magical qualifications." He tipped her chin up with his fingers. "I know your magic. I've seen it before. *Wild Fae.*" Obscuring her senses had been a precaution against mere animals getting in the way of his plans. He'd had all creatures but one removed from the castle, and he'd taken extra precautions to secure the creature.

Tanyiel batted his hand away from her chin and retreated once more. "Don't touch me."

A spark of something hot twined within the cold tendrils of fear in her grid. Stubbornness. Determination.

His irritation melted into interest. He had not expected such a will from a mortal.

But he could be patient.

He chuckled lightly, turning from her to face his throne. He addressed her as he slowly climbed the dais. "The castle is yours to explore, Tanyiel. I have limited your movements to within its walls, for your safety, of course. However, I do believe the castle has much to offer."

He fed her more of that subtle delight, that sense of satisfaction that simmered below the surface, so small as to be a nudge. It took precision to influence a person's emotional grid permanently, many delicate tweaks over a period of time. He would play hers exactly as he'd mastered all the minds within the council and nobility.

A mind might recognize large emotional shifts as foreign, but the small, careful whispers of his magic were much harder to discern.

"One final thing, Tanyiel-*tana*," Zeyphar called to her as he slid back into his throne, amused by the wary expression on Tanyiel's face as she watched him. "You will join me on the morrow for breakfast. I will be in the Silver Atrium. The servants will show you the way."

"And if I don't want to have breakfast with you?" she asked, her pert chin rising a notch.

"You are a guest, as I said. You are welcome to do as you please.

However, it would be a shame for you to miss an opportunity to discuss your future, and Zlaet's current predicament. I truly believe you and I can come to an amicable agreement that can benefit your *mayt* and his people."

He whispered more delight along her grid, and the skin of her arms pebbled as her eyes darkened to a rich pine. But to his surprise, she clenched her jaw and narrowed her eyes.

His smile slipped, interest and annoyance vying for dominance as he stared at Tanyiel. He wrestled the cold coil of temper into his control, fingers curling against the arms of the throne.

He must be patient.

It had been a long while since he'd encountered anyone with a strong enough will to stand against him. That it was a mostly mortal female was certainly intriguing.

Besides, it would be good practice before he bent his will against another empath. It would not be an easy task to manipulate Zlaet.

Tanyiel was staring at him as though she might refuse his offer for breakfast. A feral, vicious side of him almost wanted her to so he'd have a reason to punish her, but he dismissed the idea, wrestling his urges under a coat of ice.

Finally, she nodded reluctantly. "Fine. I'll be there."

"Very wise of you, princess." Zeyphar's smile slid into place once more. "I will see you on the morrow."

He flicked his fingers, and the soldiers showed the female out of the room. He watched her retreat, catching her gaze when she glanced back over her shoulder at the door. He wove in one last sip of pleasure, and he felt a thrill as her lips parted and she shivered visibly. Then she stepped through the threshold and out of sight.

Her body and grid reacted to his manipulations, and yet she seemed to pull herself back. How interesting. He wondered if perhaps—

Casphian's voice interrupted his savoring of this new challenge. "Shall we assign her a guard, my lord?"

Curbing the icy need to lash out at the interruption, Zeyphar cut his gaze to the male who remained standing next to the throne. Casphian was watching him, his face stoic and unflappable as always.

His Seneschal was loyal, perhaps more so than anyone. Casphian had been his first true success, oblivious to the careful molding Zeyphar had wrought on him since Zeyphar was young. He no longer needed to use his magic on Casphian, for he had well and truly crafted the male's thoughts and interests to align with his own.

"Indeed. Assign her two guards, but they are not to restrict her movements within the castle, with the exception of my suites and the sublevels. She may enjoy the central courtyard, but she is not to leave the castle proper." Zeyphar shifted his attention back to the doors his nephew's *mayt* had disappeared through. "Also, assign Iris to her as her lady's maid."

There was a beat of hesitation in Casphian. "My lord? Iris is most likely to sympathize with—"

"Precisely. The princess is to want for nothing, am I understood?"

"Yes, of course, your grace." Casphian pressed his palm to his sternum and bowed his head. "Your wisdom is beyond reproach. Forgive me."

Zeyphar's lips curled into a smile. Casphian was not as adept at these games as he, so he would forgive his Seneschal for his confusion. Yes, Iris was likely to sympathize with Tanyiel's situation, but she was also... fractured.

He'd learned that Tanyiel could not resist wounded beings. She was a healer, he knew she worked at a mortal animal healer ward, and Zeyphar was confident she would gravitate toward Iris' plight.

The cost of betrayal was steep, Iris had learned.

Tanyiel would want to help Iris, and that gave him leverage. She would be a tool he could use to ensure compliance. He couldn't rely solely on his magic to get his way, not when the stakes were this high.

Especially considering how resistant her mind seemed to be.

"You are dismissed." Zeyphar waved his hand, and with a final bow, his Seneschal turned on his heel and exited swiftly.

The *Titania* rose from his throne and strolled to the wide windows in the back of the hall, overlooking the sweeping vista of his city.

He smirked, satisfaction curling through him.

The next move on the chess board had been played.

BROKEN RAINBOWS

...rumors persist that Zeyphar Titania, especially, has a fondness for lorekissed females. Not much is known about the fate of these females, however it is believed they are not kept within the palace or even the Silver Valley itself, and...

— Gherald Schmidt, Faerloch Historical Archives

Dani was escorted by the two fae soldiers through lavish halls with marble floors and intricate gold and silver filigree on the walls. No one spoke. She was shown into an equally lavish set of rooms even larger than Slate's suites in Titan's Fen. The marble floors were covered with thick, ornate rugs, and green velvet curtains were swept gracefully back from windows overlooking a courtyard garden far below.

The door shut firmly behind her.

Dani whirled, lunging to test the handle. It opened readily.

Two fresh guards were stationed on either side of her door. Without a word, she shut the door and retreated inside, trying to control her breathing as panic rode her hard.

For one, wild moment, a strange sense of disconnect washed over her. Was this real life? Trapped in a castle with a crazy fae dictator who planned to use her to capture her... well, boyfriend no longer worked, not that it had ever felt comfortable.

Her *mayt*.

This is what Slate had been afraid of, what he had tried to protect her from by ghosting her for all those months.

And yet here she was.

Dani locked herself in the bathroom for the hysterics that followed. Fear and deep dread flooded through her, a hollow sense of failure, of grief, of a complete loss of control. Her emotions overwhelmed her, pressing in on her like walls closing in.

She was out of her element here. Could she escape on her own? Would someone come to rescue her? How long would she have to endure this? Endure Zeyphar?

She imagined Slate coming to get her, being captured by his uncle, and her hysterics started right back up, but stronger. He would do it, too. He'd come for her, and Zeyphar would ruin him.

Goddess above, their fight over the *mayt* thing seemed so insignificant now. She couldn't even bring herself to feel hurt by his secrets anymore—it seemed so unimportant when compared to the *war* they were entangled in.

Zeyphar had been inside her emotions. She'd seen his heartfire flare moments before foreign threads of delight and pleasure and calm had slithered through her mind. She'd felt them, felt her emotions respond to them, but she'd been acutely aware that they'd been *lies*.

What was it that Slate had told her? *It might feel like real emotions, but deep inside, you'd know they aren't yours...*

But Zeyphar's manipulations had been so small, so subtle, that she wondered if she'd have known if not for the visual reminder of Zeyphar's heartfire flaring each time. It was like seeing a waving flag each time her emotions shifted. It was a surreal, disjointed feeling, as if that visual warning had disconnected her mind from her emotions.

But Slate couldn't see heartfires. Would Zeyphar be able to play him, even though Slate was also an empath?

The idea was terrifying.

She wasn't sure how much time had passed, sitting on the bathroom floor, knees drawn up to her chest and her head tipped back against the wall. Her tears had dried, and she had slipped into a state of numb exhaustion when she heard a soft knock on the bathroom door. For an entire minute, she didn't move, eyes trained on the heavy wooden door.

Silence.

The knock came again, just as softly as the first one, and it took the edge off her apprehension. Deciding she wasn't helping herself or Slate by wallowing in the bathroom, Dani pushed to her feet and cracked open the door.

A willowy female stood on the other side, elegant and lovely in her simple dress of gray with blue threading along the hems. Her silver hair was braided in a coronet around her head.

"Good evening, my lady," the female murmured in a melodic voice, head bowed demurely. "My name is Iris, and I've been assigned to attend to you."

Dani's brow furrowed, and she pulled the door open fully. The female—Iris—glanced up, offering her a small smile that didn't quite reach her eyes. Eyes that immediately caught Dani's attention.

They were a unique starburst of purple, silver, bronze, and blue, with a different pattern on each eye.

"Hello..." Dani hedged, her voice rough from her bout of crying. Something about the name tickled her memory.

Iris ducked her head once more and stepped to the side, allowing Dani plenty of space to move by her. Slowly, she stepped out, shutting the bathroom door behind her. She glanced at the meal steaming on the table, and while it smelled fabulous, she found she didn't have an appetite. However, there was a teapot on the table, and her whole face felt swollen. Tea seemed like a nice idea, something to help get her head settled.

"It is past evening meal, so the *Titania* requested food be brought to your room," Iris informed her.

Dani swallowed the sudden gorge in her throat at the mention of Slate's uncle. "Thank you."

Iris clearly misread the apprehension on Dani's face, glancing between the food and her. "If my lady is not satisfied, I'm certain the kitchens would—"

"I think I just need some tea to start."

Iris nodded. "Of course, my lady."

Before Dani herself could take a single step toward the table to fetch the tea, Iris was already moving. Dani settled gingerly on one of the luxurious armchairs in front of the sparking fireplace, watching as Iris brought the tea tray over to the low table. She poured the hot liquid into a cup and held it out for Dani.

The movement revealed Iris' wrists from her flowing sleeves, and Dani's gaze locked on a series of silver scars, over a dozen little crescents clustering around her delicate wrists and scattering up her forearms.

They looked like someone had clawed Iris with blunt, human-like nails.

The moment Iris noticed Dani's stare, the porcelain cup wobbled, and some tea splashed onto the plush carpet beneath them. Dani hurriedly took the teacup, and Iris pulled her hands back, tucking them between the folds of her skirt as she bowed her head, not meeting Dani's gaze.

"Thank you," Dani murmured, wrapping her hands around the cup as she watched the fae female. Within a moment, Iris's face had composed itself, and she offered Dani a hollow smile. Her multi-colored eyes had a slightly unfocused quality to them that was unsettling when matched with the smile.

Another blink and Iris once more seemed a demure lady, nodding encouragingly toward Dani's tea.

Dani took a cautious sip, fortifying herself with the warmth, her skin tight as a sense of pity and worry overrode her previous anxiety. "It's Iris, you said?"

"Yes, my lady. I serve the Princess Aredhel."

Serve? It clicked in her so suddenly, Dani sucked back a gasp.

Iris... *Iris.*

Was Dani looking at *the* Iris that Kallen had spoken of? The one who'd made the lieutenant react so strongly at the mention of?

"I... don't really know what to do with a lady-in-waiting, I'll be honest." Dani traced a finger along the rim of her cup, mulling this information over in her mind. Was Iris a common name? It seemed unlikely for there to be two ladies-in-waiting named Iris.

Which meant this had to be the same person, and Kallen thought she was dead.

Clearly not.

"I can be anything you desire, my lady. Traditionally, a lady-in-waiting is assigned with tasks such as communicating messages, fetching items, accompanying you when you desire companionship, and even organizing your day." Iris handed Dani a biscuit from the tea tray. "Do you not have ladies-in-waiting where you are from?"

"No, not really. I mean, some people have personal assistants, but that's different." Dani nibbled the biscuit, more because it was in her hand than the fact that she was hungry.

For just a moment, a frown crossed Iris' delicate features. "You did not have someone to... *assist* you?"

"No. I'm..." Dani paused, remembering vividly how curious Autymn had been about her mortal life, how much the young female hadn't understood about humans. "I do everything myself at home."

"But you are a princess." Iris leaned forward and refilled Dani's mug. "Princess Aredhel has servants and ladies-in-waiting at her demand whenever she pleases. It is an honor to serve her."

It was Dani's turn to frown. "Wait. You mean *had*, right? Isn't she... she isn't still alive, is she?" Iris was alive, but she distinctly remembered Zeyphar speaking about Aredhel's death in the arena half a year ago.

Goddess, was Slate's mother still alive, somehow?

Iris froze, so completely that it was a little alarming. Then her head tipped forward, her voice strained as she jerked her head in a nod. "Of course. Had. Princess Aredhel had servants." Dani noticed the female was tapping a finger silently and repeatedly against her knee, as fast as a hummingbird's wing. It lasted for only a moment before Iris stilled once more, and she smiled serenely at Dani. "My apologies. It has been some time since I have spoken a mortal tongue."

"Of course." Dani nodded, but she had a feeling Iris' slip had little to do with a language barrier.

"Having servants to attend to a princess is expected, my lady," Iris continued smoothly. "You do not have staff at your home? You are *mayted* to Prince Zlaet, yes?"

Dani watched the female, unease blooming in her chest, before she nodded slowly. "Yeah, I suppose I am. But that's pretty recent. Never had servants in my life."

From the open doorway leading to the bedroom, the two maidservants emerged. Neither met Dani's eyes as they pressed their hands to their sternums and inclined their heads. After a moment, the one closest to them angled her head to the side, glancing at Iris.

"They wish for me to inform you that your bed is ready," Iris said.

"Oh, thank you," Dani said, pulling up a hesitant smile.

"They do not speak, my lady," Iris murmured.

"Oh." More of that unease spread beneath her skin like oil. "Well, thank you."

Both girls bobbed, before slipping from the suites on silent feet.

"Is it an injury?" Dani asked hesitantly, staring at the door they'd left through.

"No." Iris's voice was strained. She abruptly got to her feet. "I'm certain your day has been trying, my lady. Rest will be important."

Yeah, right, like she was going to sleep at all.

"I will take my leave." Iris pressed her hand to her sternum. "If the lady has any need for my assistance, let the guards know. However, I will be back in the morning to assist you before your meal with the *Titania*. He will expect you to be prompt."

Right. Breakfast.

Dani took another sip of her tea, watching Iris retreat to the door leading out to the hallway. At the door, Iris gave her another small bow. "I wish you a quiet evening, my lady."

"You can call me Dani, you know," she replied. "Or... I guess Tani or Tanyiel works. It's starting to grow on me."

Iris froze again, the way she had before, expression stark, but it was gone so fast, Dani couldn't be sure if she imagined it. Prismatic eyes flicked up to meet Dani's gaze, and the female finally offered her a real smile, one that bloomed hesitantly across her face. "I would like that... Lady Tanyiel."

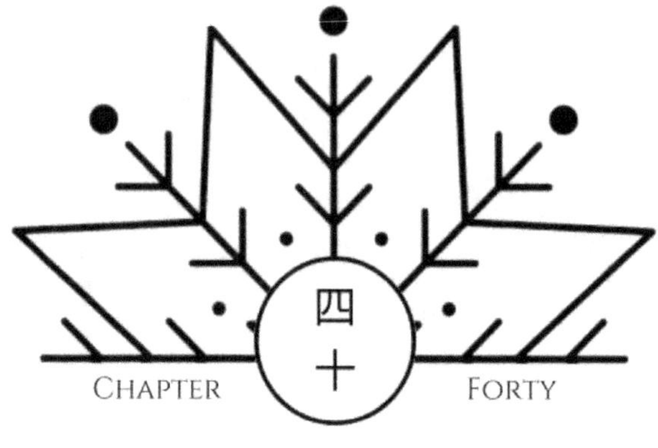

CHAPTER · FORTY

BREAKING FAST

... desired to live cohesively amongst the ever expanding mortals. The Vampire Council was supported by three factions of dwarves, two dryad, and five were-clans. Council Leader Theodora Justinia-Alucard spoke intensely on the need to control the human race...

– Gherald Schmidt, Faerloch Historical Archives

Dani found herself face-to-face with Zeyphar long before breakfast. The sun had yet to rise, and Dani wished it would, because the murky darkness of the witching hour made the dread in her chest heavier.

Laying in bed after Iris had left, Dani's anxiety and panic about being trapped in the Silver Valley had come to a peak. Feeling like a caged animal, she'd acted on impulse; she'd opened one of the second-story windows of her room and fed the drapes out. It had been just before three in the morning, so she'd hoped no other rooms that faced the small courtyard would notice her.

She'd shimmied down the drapes as low as she could go—which was considerably harder than the movies made it seem—then let herself fall the rest of the way. Her ankle still smarted from the way she'd landed, and her clothes were torn from the bushes she'd had to wade through to get out of the courtyard.

From there, she'd snuck around through empty hallways until she'd found a way outside, hiding in niches whenever she heard someone.

She'd made it outside and within touching distance of the outer wall before she was caught. Not that she'd had a plan for how she was going to scale the wall; she'd been hoping to find some stairs or maybe a crack.

Standing in the same throne room as before, Dani had to admit she hadn't been thinking clearly about her escape. She'd reacted in impulsive panic, and as she watched Zeyphar approach her with menacing casualness, she'd decided her hasty plan had been foolish.

"Princess Tanyiel," Zeyphar murmured as he finally came to a stop in front of her. He didn't look away from her face when he flicked his fingers, and the guards on either side of her retreated. "I'm disappointed in you."

The small hairs on the back of her neck rose, because the cold look in Zeyphar's eyes spoke of more than just disappointment. She barely restrained the urge to step back when her breath frosted the air in front of her face.

He wouldn't kill her. That much she was certain, since he needed her to get to Slate.

But Goddess help her, there were worse things than death.

Zeyphar watched her with such unblinking focus that her insides shriveled, and she had to lock her knees to keep them from shaking. When she didn't speak, he let out a sigh, glancing around the room. "Do you not find our palace to be hospitable? Have I not provided all you might need as we wait for your *mayt* to join us?"

She said nothing. What was there to say? Besides, she didn't know if she could get her tongue to cooperate anyway.

When Zeyphar's gaze slid back, there was so much arctic fury in it that her skin felt frostburnt, tightening painfully over her skeleton. "There are many who would die to be in your position, princess." He spoke softly, yet the words rang between her ears like a scream. It was a thinly veiled threat, and this time, she couldn't stop herself from retreating a step.

Zeyphar's hand clamped around her wrist. His grip wasn't painful, but the swiftness of his movement startled a squeak from her. Potent fear zipped through her, tunneling her vision. Instinct had her yanking her wrist, but he held firm, tugging her forward like a lover might, bending until his face was mere inches from hers. She forced herself to breathe so she didn't black out.

"Tanyiel, I worry for your safety. To attempt to leave my castle in the dead of night is dangerous and foolish," he whispered, and his thumb brushed over the sensitive flesh of her inner wrist, making her stomach turn over unpleasantly. "I must ensure your safety, for my dear nephew's sake."

He dropped her wrist and turned his back to her in a graceful pivot, and she swayed for a second before two hands landed on her shoulders. Pulse drumming, she glanced up to see the two guards had returned, flanking her as they urged her after Zeyphar.

"Come, princess," he called over his shoulder, almost cheerfully.

She didn't really have a choice, so she focused on moving her legs correctly as she was led out of the throne room after Zeyphar. Where was he taking her? Her mind raced from one possibility to the next, each more dreadful than the last. She barely noticed the portraits and tapestries they passed as they walked through hallway after hallway, down staircases, through arches.

Would he use his magic against her? Turn her brain into mush like he'd done with Slate at the arena? Dig around in her emotions until she was merely a puppet of herself?

Her fate rested on the whims of a maniacal king.

They came to a plain door. It was in a hallway like any other, though there were no windows and the light was faint. Two more guards flanked this door, and neither looked at Dani as they opened the door for Zeyphar.

It was a dark stairway leading down, with such little light that her heart stumbled. Zeyphar wasted no time strolling down the steps. The guards at her back gave her a little nudge, forcing her to take a few steps forward until her toes flirted with the top stair.

"Come along, Tanyiel," Zeyphar called from below, that cold note lingering in his otherwise gentle, chiding tone.

She did not want to go down there. Her instincts screamed at her to run, to put as much distance between herself and whatever hell awaited at the bottom of those stairs. She took a step back, but hands reappeared at her shoulders, then they slipped under her arms. The message was clear—either she walked on her own, or they would carry her.

Swallowing hard, Dani stepped into the darkness.

She kept her hands on the stone walls on either side of her as she walked, the light so dim she was certain she'd trip and tumble at any moment. By the time she reached the bottom of the long flight of stairs, her heart was pounding in her skull.

Zeyphar waited at the base, standing at an arching threshold, beyond which was another long hallway, dimly lit with faerie lights.

Dungeon. This was the dungeon.

She halted at the last step, legs locking. No. No way. He was going to throw her into a prison cell and let her rot.

What would happen to her down here? Torture? Rape? Starvation?

Zeyphar smiled in a horrifying mixture of encouragement and excitement. "Have no fear, princess. I merely wish to show you the lengths I will go to ensure your safety."

Anything that excited Zeyphar, she wanted nothing to do with. Behind her, she heard the light footsteps of her two escorts, haunting her like shadows. She forced herself forward.

She expected screams, or fire, or blood, but she heard and saw nothing of the sort. Instead, the long hallway was lined with open archways. There were maybe twenty thresholds, each as wide as a standard door, ten on either side of the hallway.

It was eerily silent save for their gentle footfalls. Zeyphar walked down the center of the hallway ahead of her, hands tucked behind his back, the picture of poise. "This is the most secure wing in my palace. If I must, I will keep you here for your own safety."

She passed one of the archways, morbid curiosity pulling her gaze around to peer inside. She held her breath.

It was... an empty stone room, the size of a cell, but with no bars or even a door. Her brows pulled together, and she glanced through the archway on the other side of the hall.

That one wasn't empty.

There was still no door, but inside the room was a person. They were pacing back and forth in an erratic, jerky manner that made goosebumps erupt over her arms. Their hands were raised in front of them, as if they couldn't see, and each time they reached the wall, they...

Dani frowned, stepping closer as she tried to understand what she was seeing. It was like they couldn't reach the wall, like an invisible barrier prevented them from reaching the stone a mere foot from the wall. The fae bounced off the invisible barrier, stumbled, then lurched for the opposite side.

She caught a glimpse of a face, and bile rose in her throat when she saw they had claw marks all over their face. What had...?

The fae bounced off the opposite wall, but instead of turning to resume their pacing, their face stretched in a scream she didn't hear, and they started scratching and clawing at their own face, blood welling and dripping down their chin.

"Ah yes, Fhuil. He also has trouble appreciating the safety and security I offer him," Zeyphar murmured, and she jumped, hand flying to trap her scream inside her lips as his words came right near her ear.

"W-why is he...?" Her voice came out hoarse, and she forced herself to look away from the male, who was now walking in tight circles and pulling his hair.

"A mystery, really," Zeyphar mused, and his fingers were at her elbow, urging her to walk alongside him as he continued down the hallway. "You see, these are special rooms. I designed them myself." The smug pride in his voice nauseated her.

She glanced into the next room they passed and saw a female inside. She appeared to be sitting in the center of the room, rocking back and forth. Dani could see her lips moving, but couldn't hear what she was saying.

She kept touching her lips, then her ears, head jerking with each touch.

"These rooms are havens, Tanyiel. No light, no sound, no smells, the walls are padded with wards to prevent the sensation of stone. Simply... nothing. The wards across the doorways are unique. My master warder is quite talented, you see. He has devised one-way wards that allow those outside of it to see inside, but not so the other way around."

Rooms of... nothing. The people behind the archways experienced... nothingness.

Oh Goddess.

Zeyphar stopped in the middle of the hallway. Dani peered around him to spot someone sitting cross-legged in the hallway, just to the side of one of the rooms.

Zeyphar smiled at her and gestured inside the archway.

Dani didn't want to look, but she had a feeling he'd force her if she didn't, so she reluctantly peered inside. A figure was floating in the middle of the room, and they were thrashing so hard she couldn't tell the gender.

"For some, the ultimate experience of *nothing* is necessary. Ghuill-haume here ensures they cannot even touch themselves." He gestured to the fae sitting cross-legged by the archway, whose eyes were closed. "It is a flawless system, really, to garner respect and obedience for even the most stubborn of wills. I am not above keeping you safe and secure down here, for your own good."

She could feel Zeyphar watching her, but she stared into the prison room, unseeing, her vision tunneling, hands clasped tight together in front of her. She didn't dare move. Or breathe. A tremor vibrated deep inside her—she knew it would shake her apart if she didn't keep all of her muscles locked tight.

Sensory deprivation. These were sensory deprivation chambers.

People went mad in those, and they were considered cruel and unusual punishment by most countries.

Zeyphar's dungeons had no screams, no blood or fire. They had... nothing.

He didn't need to torture his victims. They did it to themselves.

And he would keep her down here until Slate came for her. Days. Weeks. *Months.*

The little she'd had for dinner came screaming up her throat, and she retched onto the floor, dizzy. She threw out a hand to stabilize herself, her feet tripping on the floor, but an iron grip clamped on her elbow.

"Do you see how safe you would be down here? No harm can come to you in one of these rooms," Zeyphar purred at her ear, and her stomach heaved once more, but there was nothing left to expel. "Do you wish to stay here, or do you think you will stay safe in the suites I've assign you?"

Dani couldn't speak right away, lips trembling as she watched the person inside the room try to hit themselves on the head. The male sitting on the floor by Zeyphar's feet moved his hand ever-so-slightly, and the person's arm snapped straight out from their body.

A broken gasp escaped her as she caught sight of the person's expression, mouth stretched wide in a silent scream, eyes rolling wildly in their skull.

"What say you, Tanyiel?" His grip intensified on her arm. "Are you content with your suites upstairs?"

She nodded. Once. Call it self-preservation. Call it giving up. Call it whatever—she would not set one foot into those little chambers.

"Very good," Zeyphar murmured, voice pleased. Satisfaction and contentedness whispered through her, and she turned her head slightly to see his heartfire was burning brighter.

To feel any kind of positive emotion in this place caused a vicious repudiation deep inside her, but she still couldn't stop *feeling happy*.

She wished she had more in her belly to vomit out.

Zeyphar was watching her, and his brows flicked together for a moment, before he straightened and turned her, hand still firm on her elbow. "Now come."

He guided her back the way they'd come. Dani stumbled a few steps, but Zeyphar didn't break his stride, his fae strength keeping her upright as he escorted her down the hallway. The two guards who'd escorted her down were waiting on either side of the doorway to the stairs, eyes locked straight ahead and expressions blank.

Dani winced as she emerged from the stairway and back into the castle halls, eyes stinging in the much brighter lights. Zeyphar finally released her elbow, and he snapped his fingers.

A male appeared from seemingly nowhere, and it took a moment for her fear-drenched mind to recognize him as the male who'd been at Zeyphar's side when she'd first arrived to the Silver Valley some twelve hours ago.

Had he been waiting here for them?

"Casphian, rouse the servants. We will have breakfast now," Zeyphar commanded. "It seems the princess was all too eager to meet with me this morning, so I won't delay our meal a moment longer."

Dani stared at him, lips still crusty from the vomit she'd barely wiped from her mouth. It couldn't be past four in the morning; it was still *dark* outside. And he wanted them to have breakfast now?

"But—" she started.

"We will have breakfast together every morning, Tanyiel. And in the evenings, you will join my court for dinner. You are here now, it is morning, so we will dine," Zeyphar told her, his voice a whip of sound that had her skin tightening as her now-empty stomach lurched.

"Right away, my lord," the male, Casphian, said smoothly. His lips curved into a small smile as he flicked his gaze up and down her form. It wasn't the same sensation she got when Zeyphar watched her, but it was enough to raise the little hairs all over her body.

Without another word, Casphian turned on his heel and glided down the hall with effortless fae grace.

"Come along, Tanyiel," Zeyphar instructed and began walking once more. "I will show you to the Silver Atrium. It is where we will break our fast each morning."

"N-now?" Dani asked, glancing down at her clothes, dirty from her escape attempt, bits of bile clinging to her shoes and the front of her shirt.

"Now." Zeyphar's tone left no room for argument.

Feeling strangely disconnected from her own body, Dani followed after him, aware of the two guards still at her back. She barely registered the window-filled atrium they arrived in. She only heard the dull roar in her ears as Zeyphar held out a chair for her at a small bistro-like table in the center of the room.

The room might have been stunning, but all the windows were still dark from the early hour, giving it an eerie and suffocating quality instead of elegant and airy.

Zeyphar's smile was pleasant as she numbly folded her body into the chair. Out of the corner of her eye, she spied servants rushing around.

Breakfast was served within minutes, and it wasn't lost on her that those serving them had dark smudges under their eyes and pale faces. She could only stare blankly at the elaborate spread of food set before her, her mind shell-shocked.

What was happening right now? She felt like she was in a dream, watching herself from a distance, overwhelmed with both hollow apathy and the insane urge to shake and scream and cry and wake herself from this surreal nightmare she'd somehow wandered into.

Zeyphar was speaking. She peeled her gaze away from the feast of fruits and breads, watching him as he began chatting.

Chatting.

Like they were old friends catching up, expression pleased and relaxed as he buttered a soft pastry. A *pastry*. Like... food. Like he expected her to simply eat. Like this was all completely normal.

Like he hadn't just shown her people desperate to mutilate themselves just to feel *something*.

Was he... talking about the weather?

She stared at him, her mind struggling to process. *Was* this normal for him? For a wild moment, she questioned her own sanity—did she truly just see what she saw in the dungeons? Did he really threaten to lock her down there? The fear had been so real...

After a moment, he paused, attention sharpening on her.

"Are you not hungry?" he asked, eyes narrowing slightly.

Automatically, she picked up some food. She didn't even look to see what she grabbed; she just picked something up and put it in her mouth. Her jaw moved on autopilot as she dropped her gaze from his.

In her periphery, she saw his heartfire flare, and a sickening sense of pleasure wound through her as she forced herself to keep chewing. She wanted to smile. She wanted to laugh.

She wanted to scream.

"Good girl. It's delicious, is it not?" Zeyphar murmured.

When she didn't answer, more of that pleasure filled her. "Tanyiel?"

"Yes, it's... delicious," she mumbled, and her fingers trembled as she picked up a piece of fruit.

"I have excellent chefs," Zeyphar said, and he leaned back in his chair. He watched her eat, and each time she took a bite, she watched his heartfire flare, and more irrational enjoyment slithered through her.

Everything tasted like ash, but she kept chewing, her mind wandering away from the table and back to the dungeons.

Zeyphar smiled. He poured her a cup of tea and resumed his inane conversation.

And still she ate, her mind spinning out and spinning out and spinning... out.

HEART OF THE CASTLE

... often seen closely followed by a guardsman adept at portal travel, and a favored attendant with prismatic eyes. Princess Aredhel's ability to inspire loyalty is considered...

- Gherald Schmidt, Faerloch Historical Archives

Dani felt like a caged animal. She'd been pacing her new set of rooms for over an hour now, much like tigers do at a zoo, round and round, wearing a path into the carpets.

Zeyphar had immediately moved her to a new suite after their first breakfast together yesterday morning. She was now on the highest floor of the North Tower. The two exits were the long spiral staircase guarded by a pair of soldiers at both ends... or the windows with a drop at least 50 feet straight into the busiest courtyard in the castle.

She was effectively trapped.

Not that she was planning to make any grand bids for freedom any time soon.

Was she going to have to wait to be rescued? Relegated to these princess-like charades for Goddess-only-knew how long? The foreseeable future paved with breakfasts, emotional manipulation, and formal dinners?

The dinners...

She'd experienced her first one last night. And it had been, in a word, stressful. She'd been cinched into a corset, painted, pinched, and polished, and draped in a beautiful turquoise gown made of some kind of silk that sheered out the closer it fell to her toes. The front of her hair had been braided into a stunning coronet with the rest hanging down her back, and a sparkling tiara had been woven into the strands.

Her reflection had looked exactly like a faerie princess.

Despite the beauty of the gown, she'd still wanted to rip it off. She felt like a doll dressed up by Zeyphar.

But she hadn't, because the image of the fae in the cell, pacing and clawing at their face, haunted her. She kept imagining that person as herself, going mad inside that soundless and sightless chamber, consumed by the sheer nothingness.

She kept imagining Slate in there.

Would he hold out longer before succumbing to the desperate madness of deprivation? He was disciplined when he needed to be.

She'd been guided to a vast dining room on the ground level, lined with the same airy open archways she'd seen in Slate's rooms at Titan's Fen. A long table squatted in the center of the room, and by the time she'd arrived, every seat had been filled with fae nobles.

Every seat, of course, except the one to Zeyphar's right.

He'd stood the moment she'd arrived, a pleasant smile on his face. She'd seen his heartfire flare instantly, and she'd braced herself for the threads of pleasure, delight, and excitement that wafted through her. The smile that tipped the edges of her lips had not been her own choice.

"Princess Tanyiel," Zeyphar had introduced her, and like a perfect gentleman, he'd come to guide her to her seat at the table next to him, pulling out her chair for her, the picture of chivalry. "Is our princess not radiant? Prince Zlaet has chosen well for his future queen consort."

She'd suffered and smiled through several introductions over the first course, hardly touching her food, holding her wineglass because it gave her something to do with her hands. As the chatter had shifted to a more serious tone of politics and infrastructure, Dani had tuned the conversation out.

That is, until someone had mentioned Titan's Fen.

"Searching for that little backwater village is a waste of resources," Zeyphar said, his tone suggesting he would no longer entertain the conversation. "It is no longer a priority."

"My Titania, I would urge you to reconsider, given the recent disappearance of Gelayeth—"

"The commander's actions were unsanctioned. It was not my will to bring Zlaet back to the Silver Valley in chains. He is already suffering enough as a prisoner of the rebels—"

"Slate's not a prisoner," Dani said quietly, the words tumbling from her mouth in a rush.

The table silenced instantly.

"Did you have something to add, princess?" Zeyphar's tone was a silken threat, yet as his heartfire flared, tendrils of motivation wrapped around her. He wanted her to talk. Immediately, she fought to do just the opposite—to shut up, not say anything, not draw more attention to herself. Get in and get out, survive this dinner.

But the compulsion grew stronger and stronger with each beat of her heart.

"He's well taken care of there," the words continued to pour out of her. "He has a nice residence, and he works with their military, and he can come and go as he pleases—"

The look Zeyphar gave her was filled to the brim with artificial sadness. "It is his mind that is poisoned, princess. He knows nothing of the truth."

"He's not poisoned—"

He nodded slowly, placating her. Patronizing her. "Zlaet's mind is young and malleable, princess. As is yours. He has been groomed to be a martyr for their silly rebellion because they no longer have Aredhel to rally behind."

"If I may be so bold, Princess Tanyiel," one of the noblewomen on the other side of the table leaned closer. "It sounds like you have some unlearning to do as well. The Titania said you've agreed to come here to help bring Zlaet into the fold, but it sounds like you are having some second thoughts."

"Very normal," Zeyphar continued with all the airs of a doting relative, as if there were a soft and empathetic bone in his entire body. "It is difficult for mortal minds to unravel their own truth. We must be kind as we break down their reality."

Dani had zipped her mouth shut, flipping her attention from Zeyphar to the nobles. All of them were nodding, watching her with mixed expressions of pity and sadness, all while Zeyphar's heartfire burned bright enough that she suspected she wasn't the only one being fed emotions.

A tremor began inside her once more, a sliver of horror beneath the false happiness winding through her. Rage and fear and a hollow sense of helplessness beat against the bars of contentedness and delight that Zeyphar's magic wrought on her.

The nobles at this table were in Zeyphar's pocket, all of them. She could only imagine what she'd be like after years of this manipulation. This was how he'd stolen the throne from Slate's mother. Slate had told her as much, but it was another thing entirely to see it firsthand.

She was completely on her own here. There was no support to be had from the court.

A servant appeared at her elbow, gingerly placing a meal in front of her. "Thank you," Dani mumbled.

The servant—a young woman still round in the face with youth—gave Dani a slightly startled look before moving on.

Dani's pacing slowed, mind on the events of the evening before.

The servants...

Dani pivoted to find where Iris sat, contentedly stitching some elaborate embroidery into the neckline of one of Dani's dresses. Iris had done this yesterday as well, simply sitting with Dani in her rooms, keeping her company. She'd learned a little about the fae, though all of her stories seemed to be from before Zeyphar took power.

Dani ached to tell her Kallen was alive, but she wasn't sure the fragile female would take the news well. It had only been two days, but Dani had definitely noticed some strange quirks about the female that flashed red alarms in her mind. More than once already, Iris seemed to forget what time period they were in, going so far as to call Dani 'Ari' instead.

Occasionally, she would rub her hands over her arms and face, as if needing to touch her own skin or check for wounds. Other times, she would simply freeze, staring at nothing, and would continue to do so until prompted.

It was clear to Dani that Zeyphar had abused her in some fashion, or may even still be abusing her, though Dani never saw fresh wounds or bruises. Did he abuse the other servants as well?

There had to be a hundred servants here in the castle. If Dani had to guess, Zeyphar likely reserved most of his magic to manipulate the nobility, meaning he probably didn't waste it as much on the servants. Otherwise, he wouldn't need his chambers of silent hell in the dungeons.

The servants may not have been magically manipulated to believe the narrative that Slate was a prisoner of the rebels.

They might listen to her, even if the nobles wouldn't.

"Iris," she began, walking over to where Iris sat. "I'd like a change of scenery." She was careful with the words she picked, studying Iris' lovely face. "I didn't eat enough breakfast, and I'm a little hungry. Could we take a walk to the kitchens?"

The kitchens seemed like a good place for servants to gather.

Iris' brows knit together for a brief moment. "My lady, I can call for food to be delivered from the kitchens—"

"I would like to go there myself. Like I said, I need a change of scenery from my rooms, as lovely as they are." Dani smiled encouragingly at Iris, trying not to look too eager.

Dani didn't miss the way Iris' eyes darted around the room, as though she were afraid they were being watched. "The kitchens are not a proper place for a princess. If the *Titania* heard..."

"He would not want me to go hungry," Dani insisted, changing tactics. "Besides, Zeyphar said I was free to roam inside the castle. I want to go to the kitchens. I would be grateful if you could show me the way."

Guilt chased over her skin when Iris visibly paled at the mention of Zeyphar. Not for the first time, Dani wondered if Iris had seen the inside of those torture prisons.

A moment of silence passed, and Iris' fingers twitched before she started tapping her finger to her thumb, hummingbird fast. Finally, she jerked her chin in a nod as she shot to her feet. In a blink, all nervousness evaporated, and a somewhat dreamy smile replaced the apprehension on Iris' face.

The change happened so fast that the little hairs on the back of Dani's neck rose.

"Of course, Ari. I know you like your pastries." She smiled at Dani, a hint of mischief sparking to life on her face. "Perhaps we should fetch Kallen..."

Her words drifted off, and her eyes widened as the last of the color drained from Iris' face. Dani's heart clenched, and she gently reached out to take Iris' hands.

"You are not Ari," Iris whispered brokenly.

"No, I'm not. But we can still go get pastries," Dani offered, squeezing her hands gently.

Iris yanked her hands free, head snapping up as she quickly shook her head. "I apologize, Lady Tanyiel. I did not... It is just that—"

"It's alright. Let's just go to the kitchens, okay?" Dani offered with a small smile, and Iris gave a jerky nod.

Neither one of them spoke as Iris led Dani through the castle, winding down hallways and stairs until they reached a large double door at the end of a long passage. Beyond, she could hear the unmistakable sounds of cooking and chaos, reminiscent of what she heard in busy restaurants.

At the door, Iris hesitated, glancing back at Dani, then beyond her, gaze darting like she was looking for demons.

Or the *Titania*.

Finally, Iris drew in a breath and pulled open the door. "Come, my lady," she whispered to Dani.

Dani followed her through the doorway and stopped in her tracks. The room was enormous, and nearly two dozen fae darted around, engaged in preparing or cooking or cleaning, and the scent of food wafted deliciously from the several hearths blazing along the walls, varying in size and function. Wooden tables and countertops filled the empty spaces, and Dani could see other sets of doors leading out of the room, presumably to access other key points of the castle above. Another double door across the main floor was thrown open, leading outside, and she watched as a few people filtered in and out, carrying crates and barrels.

Loud laughter caught her attention, and she whipped her head over to the far corner to spot a few guards loitering around a counter, their leather armor distinct in the sea of plain gray servant colors. A young male kitchen servant handed them some bread and cheese, and with a few more exchanged words in Faerish, the soldiers disappeared through one of the many doors.

"Come, my lady," Iris urged again quietly.

"Is it always so busy in here?" Dani asked, drifting after Iris, unable to tear her eyes away from the scene.

"Of course," Iris replied. "A castle is only as good as its staff. And the kitchens are designed to be a central point. One can access the laundry, the wine cellars, and the cold storage from here as well. Come." She started walking past tables and scurrying servants.

Dani followed, her head on a swivel, watching as scullery maids arranged meals on trays and swept them away, and others attended to large cauldrons at the hearths. Servants glanced her way, giving her a double-take, some with wide eyes, some with narrowed expressions. She offered small waves and smiles to those whose gazes lingered, but that only caused them to look away with alarm, heads lowering. Dani had to actively keep a frown from settling between her brows.

A large female intersected their path, tall and imposing with broad shoulders and a stern face. Her blonde hair was swept back into a braid, a cloth band keeping any stray hairs from her face. Dani was immediately reminded of Loraine—this female was clearly in charge and not someone to be trifled with.

"Princess," the female said in perfect German, looking straight at her, "this is not a place for you." Despite the directness, there was an air of polite deference to her tone.

"My lady," Iris said to Dani, "this is Rhondae. She is the head chef here.”

"Nice to meet you," Dani said, offering a bright smile. "I was just hoping to get a little something to eat, maybe—"

The words had hardly left her mouth when Rhondae whistled sharply, snapping her fingers and speaking in quick, direct Faerish. A few servants instantly responded, startled into action, and within seconds, Dani was faced with a table spread with breads, cheeses, fruits, pastries, soups, and meats.

"Whatever you desire, Tanyiel-*tana*," Rhondae said, gesturing to the spread. "I will have the servants bring your meals to your rooms. There is no need to waste your time coming down here."

"This is lovely, thank you." Dani smiled again, looking over the assortment of choices, noticing how the servants all watched her with differing expressions. "But I'd prefer not to wait. I'm pretty hungry. I'll just eat real quick right here. I promise not to get in the way."

Rhondae narrowed her gaze at Dani, flitting her gray eyes over her, from her soft silk shoes to her elegantly braided hair, and Dani fiercely wished she could wear her own clothes. "My lady, your presence is a distraction to the staff."

Exactly what she needed, and while it pained her to do so, she needed to ensure she could stay. "Zeyphar said I may go where I please."

Rhondae froze, and her gruff demeanor shifted for a fraction of a second. Something haunted flitted across her expression, gone in a blink, but the female's expression remained strained. Dani's stomach turned over, guilt gnawing at her, because she'd offered Rhondae no choice. To send her out was what was expected, considering Dani's 'role' as a princess, but to deny the princess what she desired also put the female in a tricky position.

But Dani needed this. And maybe Rhondae did too, she just didn't know it yet. Dani could only hope no one would be punished for it.

Finally, Rhondae offered her a tight nod. "If you desire, Tanyiel-*tana*."

Dani smiled, bright with relief. "Thank you."

With a final nod, Rhondae turned on her heel and walked away, leaving Dani standing at the table with Iris. She wasn't really that hungry. She was always slightly queasy in this castle with fear hounding her heels, but she'd asked to be here.

So she slid onto one of the stools that lined the table and selected a roll. She took a bite, mind whirring around how she was going to do this. She was being watched, for certain, but the moment she paid anyone some attention, they avoided her gaze and busied themselves with their tasks.

"My lady…" Iris intervened softly, "it is not appropriate for a princess—"

"I've been a princess for less than 3 days, Iris. I'm just a woman. Who likes to take care of herself sometimes."

"I understand, but as the *mayt* to Prince Zlaet—"

"Listen. You have to know that Slate wasn't raised as a prince. He doesn't like to be treated that way, either. He's pretty laid back."

Iris stared at her, uncertainty on her face. "We should not discuss such… controversial topics," she whispered, and Dani noticed more than one fae within earshot had a tense expression.

Right. Slate was a sensitive topic around here, and from the resistance she'd encountered with the nobles last night, she needed a change in tactic. Insisting that Slate wasn't a prisoner of some so-called rebel group wouldn't get the reaction she was looking for.

Goddess, she missed him.

"This bread is delicious," she said with a smile, holding up the roll, speaking at a level that wasn't obscenely loud, but that she knew almost every sensitive fae ear in the kitchen would likely be able to hear. "I'm terrible at baking. I can make a nice Irish soda bread, and like, one dessert my mother taught me, but that's it."

Iris leaned her hip against the table, but Dani noticed that the female didn't so much as glance at the spread of food beside her. The female's eyes tracked over the kitchen distractedly, one finger tapping rapidly against the table. Gently, Dani reached forward and covered Iris' hand with her own, halting the nervous tapping.

"Did you know I have a griffin friend?" Dani asked, watching the female. "Her name is Selene, and she's a snowy owl and snow leopard breed mix."

Iris' eyes finally shifted to Dani, a small frown nestling between her brows as her gaze slowly focused. "A griffin?"

Satisfied that she had Iris' attention now, Dani nodded, smile widening. "Yes. A few years ago, I rescued her from an illegal animal trader..."

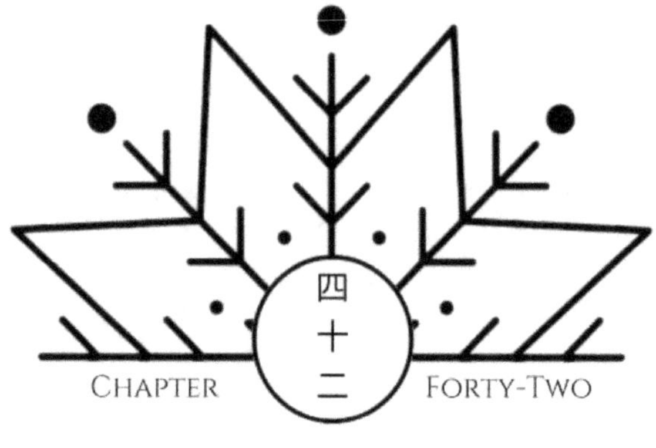

CHAPTER FORTY-TWO

PRINCESS OF SILENCE

Those with wild hearts are significantly more prone to becoming feral, and it is the responsibility of the alphas of each pack to ensure...

– Gherald Schmidt, Faerloch Historical Archives

For the next few days, Dani continued to convince Iris to take her to the kitchens following her breakfasts with Zeyphar, despite protests and warnings from the female. They would sit for a little while, and Dani would talk about her life. Of course, she really wanted to talk about Slate or Titan's Fen or something with more substance, but given she didn't know how long she would be trapped in this goddess-forsaken castle, she didn't mind keeping the topics light for now.

This morning, Dani had noticed a shift. More fae than usual seemed to linger near her in the kitchens while completing their tasks, and she'd even noticed a couple of guards loitering. She'd take it as a win.

The real win, though, was Iris. The female seemed more comfortable and confident, and Dani could almost catch what she hoped were echoes of who Iris truly was, who she'd once been.

There were moments, though, when the female's mind slipped through time more and more. She increasingly referred to Dani as Ari, and Dani didn't have the heart to correct her anymore. Just this afternoon, before they began their daily wandering around the castle, Iris had helped Dani into a dress of a pretty periwinkle, and Dani had asked for more dresses in the same shade.

Not that she wanted more dresses to wear, really. But she needed them.

"You are magnificent in blue, Lady Ari," Iris had murmured dreamily. "They match your eyes. I shall request them from the seamstress in the morning."

Iris had smiled at her, eyes unfocused, before saying, "If you are ready for our stroll, my lady, I shall fetch Guardsman Ewyt—" Iris had cut herself off, grief crashing into the serene rainbows of her eyes. Wordlessly, Dani had taken the slender female's arm, and they'd walked out together. Knowing Iris had needed a distraction, Dani had begun telling her about the Den, hoping stories of Loraine, her surly affection, and the colorful patrons would brighten her new friend's afternoon.

The daily walks had started innocently enough—Dani had needed something to do or she'd go stir-crazy and visiting the kitchens simply wasn't enough—but it also gave Dani a chance to map out the many hallways and rooms in her mind.

"If you have a mind for literature, Lady Tanyiel," Iris said, bringing Dani's attention around to the present, "the library here in the castle is quite expansive. Though, it's not as impressive as the one in the city proper."

Something snagged Dani's senses, like seeing movement in her peripheral vision. She tuned out Iris' idle chatter, focusing intently on what had caught her attention.

A heartfire, one that was wild enough to be a creature, as opposed to all the fae heartfires around her.

Dani froze, stretching her senses, closing her eyes, feeling, reaching—

A voice.

A tiny voice, but one nonetheless, of a creature within the castle. Dani's excitement bubbled in her blood as she scrambled to introduce herself.

"Tanyiel, we must go. It is time to prepare for supper," Iris said, a gentle hand tugging on Dani's.

"But..." Dani turned her head toward the heartfire.

"We mustn't be late," Iris insisted, and Dani reluctantly followed.

As they moved down the hallway, Dani gestured back behind them. "What's down that way?"

Iris glanced back, and her face paled. She turned her head to stare at her feet as they walked. "That is the *Titania*'s Wing. It is forbidden," she whispered, her voice brittle.

Dani's brows crashed together, but she said nothing. Interesting. What animal was Zeyphar keeping in his personal suite? It wasn't a dog or a cat or even a Familiar, that much Dani was certain.

"Come, Tanyiel," Iris insisted, gently guiding Dani around. "Let us hurry."

Needing to know more, Dani decided she'd ensure their wanderings tomorrow took them close enough to hopefully make contact.

It made dinner that night tolerable, as she mostly ignored the nobles and got lost in her own thoughts and plans. The presence of a potential creature ally, as well as her successes in the kitchen, took the edge off the long days spent here playing princess.

Things could certainly be worse.

A budding sense of hope simmered in her veins as she drifted off to sleep that night.

Zeyphar stared out over the midnight-blanketed city from his throne as he digested the news Casphian brought to him. In the five days since Tanyiel had arrived, she'd spent the last three visiting the kitchens around mid-morning. It was inappropriate behavior for one of her station, one he'd forgiven at first, knowing how little she'd eaten during their first two breakfasts, while her nerves had still been wrought.

This is what he reaped for his kindness.

"What has she been doing there?" Zeyphar asked softly, not looking away from his slumbering city.

There was a pause, then Casphian said, "She simply... talks. The guards attending her say she mostly speaks as if to herself. She eats slowly and talks for about an hour, before she leaves."

Zeyphar's eyes narrowed. "And what does she speak of?"

"Herself, it seems. Her life story, if the guards are to be believed."

An innocent enough topic, it seemed, however...

He normally paid the servants little heed, but he was highly aware of everything Tanyiel did. And this morning, she'd thanked the servant who'd brought her breakfast. She had done it before, much to his irritation, but this time, he'd noticed the female had smiled.

Just a little, just slightly.

But enough that he'd noticed. Then he'd noticed the glances. She was being watched by the servants now. He'd noticed it again at dinner this evening.

The nobility had no need to thank servants. Were they watching her because of that? Was it her mortal countenance? Faerfolk had little, if any, interaction with humans, so the curiosity was expected in that regard. Or did they watch her for these... stories?

"Tell me, do the servants speak of these stories amongst themselves?" Zeyphar turned his head to peg Casphian with his gaze.

Without hesitation, Casphian nodded. "Yes, my lord. It seems her stories have spread like wildfire amongst the staff, and even the guards as well."

Displeasure curled through Zeyphar. He should have expected his people would learn about the future queen consort, and yet... he had not expected the way they looked at her. There was an eagerness there, a warmth and a curiosity that was a threat to him.

He wanted to bring Zlaet and his *mayt* under his wing so he could mold them as he wished. Make them *his*. Now, some of his people were starting to look at Tanyiel the way they had once looked at *her*.

Aredhel.

Beneath his feet, frost spread like creeping vines from around the base of the throne, and Zeyphar's fingers tightened on the armrests until they creaked.

Casphian's breath misted the air before him. "What is your will, my lord?"

Zeyphar had expected Tanyiel to meekly sulk while she awaited his nephew's arrival, after showing her his silence rooms. After all, she had certainly become meek at their dinners, no longer attempting to convince his nobility of Zlaet's willingness to associate with rebels.

Apparently, she needed a stronger reminder that her behavior had consequences.

"Rouse the princess," Zeyphar murmured with a smile. "I wish to see her now."

Dani saw Slate in her dreams. She saw him laughing, teasing her, as they strolled the streets of Faerloch. She felt a sharp, poignant sense of happiness and relief to see him, but she didn't know why. "Slate! We should—"

Slate turned to look at her, and Dani froze. Slate had no mouth. Or eyes. Only gaping holes appeared there, with silent tears streaming down his cheeks. Horror gripped her, and she started shaking her head—

Wait. She wasn't shaking her head. *She* was being shaken.

Dani's eyes flashed open, a squeak of alarm escaping her. Disorientated, she instinctively shrunk away from the contact, blinking rapidly as her eyes adjusted to the dim light in the room. Someone loomed in the shadows, standing at the side of her bed.

Casphian.

He smiled down at her, a flash of white teeth in the darkness, but there was no warmth in his silvery eyes. "The *Titania* requests your presence."

"Now?" she asked, heart still racing and ribs tightening as fear curled through her. It had to be the middle of the night.

"Indeed. Come." Casphian straightened and stepped back from the bed.

She wasn't given time to change, and she shivered in her thin sleeping gown as she followed Casphian through the chilly dark halls, her two guards trailing them and making her nape prickle. She wrapped her arms around herself, eyes bouncing around as her brain began to slowly wake up.

What was going on?

Apprehension slithered through her, and it turned razor-sharp when they passed the hallway she knew led to the throne room, and they were nowhere near the Silver Atrium or the dining hall.

She'd only met with Zeyphar in one other place.

Oh Goddess. No.

Panic spiked through her head, tightening the skin over her whole body, collapsing her lungs. She froze, and when hands settled on her shoulders, she dug her heels in.

"Where are we going?" She didn't know why she bothered to ask.

Casphian said nothing, barely slowing his pace for her. The hands on her shoulders urged her forward, the strength in them leaving no room for argument. She stumbled, catching her momentum and walking.

Walking.

Walking.

When she balked at the stairs leading underground, she was practically carried down the long set of stone stairs. She was shaking by the time they reached the dimly lit hallway lined with sensory deprivation chambers. There, waiting in the middle of the hallway like a phantom, was Zeyphar.

This was it.

Zeyphar did not smile when she came face-to-face with him, directly in front of a room that was noticeably empty. She didn't breathe. Couldn't breathe.

"Princesses do not cavort in the kitchens, Tanyiel," he said by way of greeting, his voice as sharp as ice. "It is important that you understand your position. I have decided to give you all the time and quiet you need to consider the proper behavior befitting a future queen consort."

He gestured to the room.

Dani opened her mouth to protest, to tell him that *he* was the one who'd told her she could go where she wished, but there was a sharp shove between her shoulder blades. "Wait—"

The word cut off abruptly as everything winked out.

She froze. Pervasive darkness, an endless black, pressed into her eyes.

No. No, no, *no.*

She spun around, but all she saw was darkness. Heart hammering in her ears, she searched for an exit.

Searched for anything.

Panic pounded through her, and she held her hands out in front of her as she hurried forward. Or maybe she didn't.

She couldn't feel the ground under her feet.

Was she walking forward? She reached, reached, *reached* but felt nothing. Instead, she had the internal sensation of spinning, as though something repelled her backward and around. As though she'd been stopped.

It was like being stopped by nothing.

Nothing, nothing, *nothing.*

She tried to breathe, to capture and hold her own thoughts. She remembered the way the fae she'd watched before had bounced off the walls. The ward in here rebuffed her so smoothly, she didn't even feel it. She couldn't even touch the walls to orient herself.

She whimpered. Or did she? She heard nothing. Her fingers flew to her throat, trying to feel the movement beneath her flesh as she tried to scream.

But she couldn't touch her throat. Or her skin. It was nothing. Where her throat *should* be, there was nothing. No skin sensation. No pressure. No visual to aid her. Exactly like magic was stopping her, pushing her hands back, guiding her away, preventing her from closing the distance between her fingertips and her skin.

She remembered the telekinetic fae, sitting cross-legged in the hallway outside these chambers.

Her panic escalated, and she could feel her lungs laboring hard against her ribs, expanding and contracting in short, staccato bursts. She reached for her own body, for her face, for her arms, but there was nothing. Nothing to ground her. Nothing to focus on. She was drowning—drowning in a sea of dark nothingness.

Like she no longer even existed.

Nothing. Nothing, nothing, *nothing*.

Even though she couldn't hear it, even though she couldn't even *feel* herself doing it, Dani screamed.

And screamed.

CHAPTER · FORTY-THREE

THE WAITING GAME

> *... and the use of chi in medicinal remedies. Their theory is further supported by the practice of using one's own chi against them, with recorded instances of manyeo controlling individuals akin to puppetry, regardless of the magical or non-magical nature of the being...*
>
> *— Gherald Schmidt, Faerloch Historical Archives*

Had it only been a few days?

Some moments, it was as though Slate blinked and time marched forward. Others, it was as though he'd endured a thousand nights instead of just a handful.

He rested his hands on the banister of the balcony outside the council room, staring at nothing. For a moment, he was a thousand miles away in the barren wasteland of emptiness inside his own head. The lack of sunshine and summer and warmth was pervasive around him. Nothing but frost and snow and winter.

Waiting around for updates from the extraction team was murderous. Sleep eluded him. He'd prowl his suites, the halls, the balcony, at all hours of the day and night, unable to keep his body still.

Through it all, a numbness gripped him. In the frozen cavern in his mind, a massive wall of ice separated him from his emotions. He knew the anger and the fury were there, just beyond, boiling and frothing, but he watched it with a sense of detachment, like one does a vicious animal behind a cage. Sometimes he fought to pierce the ice and reach for that anger, to feel anything, but the numbness always swept away his efforts.

He was rarely left alone. His father pushed his physical limits and mental discipline every morning in the studio space here in the manor, and Saida continued to abuse him at the training facility. The physical distractions were welcomed, gave him something to do besides dwell on the ice-coated sea of rage stretching within him.

Behind him, he could hear Jian from where his best friend currently sat at the long table in the center of the room, flipping pages from textbooks and making notes in his own journal. Jian had been following him like a shadow, constantly finding something to do in Slate's presence. Slate pulled himself from his frozen numbness enough to notice that Jian looked a little haggard around the edges. Not gaunt like he'd been right after the arena exploded all those months ago and the witch-doctor had used nearly every ounce of his own magic to keep Slate alive, but tight lines had appeared around his eyes, and a faint smudge of darkness bruised the hollows beneath.

Come to think of it, Slate hadn't seen much of Kari lately—he supposed she was in the Eastern District, keeping the studio afloat. He wondered if the separation was causing some strain between the twins.

He heard the soft tread of leather boots against stone. Heard Jian pause his writing and page-flipping.

"My lord."

Slate shoved himself away from the balcony and turned. Kallen stood at the entrance to the council room, hands behind his back, a soldier's position. Not a speck of emotion drifted off the lieutenant, but there was a tightness to his shoulders and a rigidness to his spine that made up for the placid neutrality of his features.

"What?" Slate demanded, stalking into the room proper and leaning his palms against the table.

It creaked from the force of his touch, and frost limned the surface where his fingers dug into the heavy wood.

The lieutenant sucked in a slow breath. Blew it out. "The extraction team has failed."

Slate's breath hitched, stalling out in his lungs. Something cracked inside him, an echo in the frozen stillness.

He'd heard Kallen's words, but somehow, the information short-circuited through his brain. "What does that mean, *failed*?"

There was another crack, one that wasn't just inside his head. Slate stared dispassionately at the table beneath his hands.

A deep fissure split the table nearly in two, fractals of ice lining the edges.

A shame. They'd just repaired this table.

Slate straightened, fingers curling into fists as he forced his lungs to move, to suck in air. Failure was *not* an option. The purpose of the team was to retrieve his *mayt*. It was crafted out of experts, experienced soldiers who'd been handpicked for exactly this purpose.

"Two dead, two injured. They were unable to retrieve Tanyiel-*tana*. The healers are seeing to their needs, and they were able to give a short report. The castle is heavily warded—"

Slate stopped listening, Kallen's words echoing hollowly in the icy chamber in his mind: *They were unable to retrieve Tanyiel-tana.*

His ears heard Kallen speaking, heard Jian's clipped and clinical response, but Slate's head filled with static. The words echoed over and over in his head, pinging around that glacial cavern in his skull in a sinister, agonizing loop. *They were unable to retrieve Tanyiel-tana.*

Oxygen instantly became scarce as a tidal wave of panic overwhelmed him, but it was quickly swallowed by a veritable tsunami of icy, frigid anger, bursting through that wall of ice and overwhelming his system.

His breath was visible in the sudden chill that surrounded his body. Without a word, Slate pivoted, the broken pieces of the table vibrating as he stepped past them, his tattoos pulsing with contained magic.

He made it halfway across the room before Jian intercepted him, his hands locking down on Slate's shoulders.

"Slate, you need to wait—" Jian's tone was low, insistent.

"No." Slate snapped, feeling like a hurricane, too much for even Jian to contain. "All I've *done* is wait. I'm *done waiting.*" Frosted fractals edged out from beneath his feet, the temperature around them plummeting swiftly. "I'm going after her *now*," he hissed in Jian's face, teeth bared.

He stepped back from Jian and threw down a portal, thunder in his ears as his entire being screamed at him to go after his *mayt.*

His foot was halfway to the portal when Slate's body completely locked up. As if the very blood that coursed through his veins had frozen, stilling his body mid-animation. "What the fuck—"

Jian came around into his line of sight. His best friend's hand was raised, and Slate could see the muted orange glow that emanated from Jian's palm.

"What are you doing to me?" Slate snarled, willing his limbs to move.

"*Chi* manipulation. Slate, you can't *just go*. You. Will. Die. And then what?" Jian snapped, ginger brows furrowed together.

"I'm going after my *mayt.*" Slate bared his teeth, straining against the hold. "You can't hold me forever. You aren't strong enough."

Something slithered through Jian's gaze at that. It was there and gone, and Jian closed the distance between them, meeting him eye for eye. "You need to stay here."

"Fuck you."

Jian traced the tip of his finger on Slate's forehead. "Time for a nap, Slate-*kun*." A final tap from Jian's finger... and Slate's world disintegrated into darkness.

CHAPTER   FORTY-FOUR

OUTFOXED

... created this weakness in kitsune as a balance against their incredible magicks, including teleportation via fire, illusions, shapeshifting, and eidetic memories.

– Gherald Schmidt, Faerloch Historical Archives

It took Kari five days to get from the Forest of L'el to the long and heavily guarded road leading to Zeyphar's castle.

Getting into the city proper of the Silver Valley had been the easy part. She'd disguised herself as a fae merchant, stolen a small cart, and pushed herself right through the West Gate. It had been as effortless as breathing, just as she'd promised Kallen.

She'd spent the first day scouting the city, taking on different disguises and listening in the busy marketplaces. Fae were curious gossipers by nature, and she'd learned much by simply loitering in congested places.

On the surface, life seemed fine in the capital city of the fae. But Kari paid attention, and she caught the strong undercurrents of unhappiness, fear, and a simmer of anger that pervaded many of the people she'd observed.

It seemed they paid a high price for the supposed 'freedoms' they enjoyed in the city—not in taxes or anything so pedestrian, but in labor and in bodies. Kari had gathered that families were often torn apart, forced to cooperate with the whims of the leadership because they had loved ones in service within the castle. Faerfolk were going missing without explanation. Minor magicks weren't taught in school anymore. Anyone who displayed larger gifts was conscripted into servitude or the military. A military the fae hadn't needed in hundreds of years.

It made them question if a war was coming with the so-called rebels.

The information was useful, but it wasn't the main reason she'd let herself linger so long in the city. She'd needed the time to plan the escape route she'd have to take with Dani. It would be much harder getting her out than it would be for Kari to get in.

She'd also needed to learn more about who traveled the road between the city and the castle, how often patrols moved, and which guise would best allow her to accomplish what she needed. It was difficult, ignoring the instinct to get to Dani as quickly as possible, but she was never alone in her own mind.

Slow is smooth and smooth is fast, Jian had reminded her through the twin connection. *Don't try to rush your way in.*

So she hadn't. It was on the fourth day of her mission that she'd finally picked the right merchant. The cart was always led by an older fae male, old enough that age actually seemed to touch the almost-immortal. He minded the lovely elk who pulled the cart, and a younger fae male always sat on the back of the cart. They made deliveries every morning, their cart carrying various fruits, vegetables, and other farm goods.

And always, before they started up the long road to the castle, they stopped at a small local market in the city to part with some of their goods. It was in the chaos of that morning market that Kari managed to knock out the younger male as he stepped into the latrines to relieve himself. With Jian whispering in her mind, she hit the right pressure points to take him out with nothing worse than a headache to look forward to when he woke, which would be hours from now.

Then she'd taken his place, a perfect replica of the male.

Perched on the back of the swaying cart, Kari struggled to control her heart rate as she moved ever closer to the imposing castle at her back. As the cart lumbered on, she studied the guards she passed, making note of at least five faces she may need to assume within the castle itself.

The cart began slowing, and she peered around to see they were near the top of the road. A mixture of excitement and anxiety shot through her. This is where her mission became dangerous, and every movement she made would need to count.

She sent a quick prayer to Inari, the goddess of foxes and industry, and hopped off the cart. Just as she rounded the cart to walk alongside it, something shimmered over her skin.

Something that smelled like *miko* magic.

She didn't break her stride, even as she cast her senses for the source of the Mystic magic in the heart of a Lore stronghold. She felt Jian in her mind, his presence sharpening just as she heard the voices.

Voices that rose not with the normal barking of orders, but in alarm.

She still didn't break her stride, not until she noticed the stares. She froze, catching sight of rose-gold hair in her periphery.

She was in her own skin.

The *miko* magic had melted her illusions.

Get out of there, Jian growled in her mind, a panic in his voice that was twin to her own pulsing through her.

Her gaze flashed up, caught sight of half a dozen guards who'd broken from their own shock, and started moving toward her. Weapons came up, shouts ringing through the misty morning air.

Kari regarded the castle, with its parapets and high walls, and for a moment, she couldn't make herself more. *Dani's still in there!*

And she won't be getting out if you get caught or killed. Move, *Kari*, Jian boomed in her mind, his panic reverberating in her skull now.

Kari tried to bring her magic back up, but just when her form began to shimmer, the magic faded, as if it were being canceled out. The guards were closing the distance, and she had two choices now—either fight them all off... or run.

Fighting them presented its own set of complications. She was out-numbered, for starters. And their shouts would put the entire castle guard on alert, making her already difficult rescue mission an exhausting uphill battle. Her success rate for retrieving Dani was dropping expo-nentially.

You don't have choices, Karisi. Get out of there!

Kari let out a snarl as guilt became a sharp stab to her chest. She didn't want to. Leaving Dani behind when Kari was so close drove fury through her. Part of her wanted to say fuck it, desperate to forge ahead and simply... burn it all down. Pull as much magic out of Jian as she could, demand he pull from the very earth itself to fuel her, and simply set the entire city ablaze. Be damned the consequences.

What did it matter to her, these people? What did she care about pol-itics and thrones and war? Her friend was trapped in that gods-forsaken castle. And Kari was a *kitsune*. She was fire and magic, a living, mortal piece of the Goddess Inari, the purveyor of success and industry... failure was not an option.

But she had failed.

An arrow shot past her head to embed in the side of the cart, making her start.

Run! Jian roared in her mind.

And Kari ran.

By the time she left the *miko* ward, she was already changing into her full *kitsune* form. Four paws ate up the dirt as she shot down the road the cart had traversed.

Hot fire exploded in her haunch, and Kari skittered from the force of the arrow. With a savage growl, blue fire raced over her fur, incinerating the arrow from her flesh, but red blood stained the white of her coat as she forced herself to pick up speed.

Another arrow grazed her ribs as she sped through the city, aiming for the gate closest to the Forest. She felt no pain now, not with Jian in her mind, and she forced herself to move *faster*. She couldn't risk the bridge, so she pushed herself to punishing limits to vault the river.

She didn't quite make it, her body splashing into the water mere feet from the opposite bank. Her muscles screamed, but she thrashed her three tails and flailed her legs, making it to the Forest side of the river several yards down from where she'd plunged into the icy depths. She dove into the trees, soaked to the skin. It wasn't long before she felt the tug of the enchantment she'd lain in the fireplace in Eas Manor, right in the councilroom.

Reaching inside herself for the fire at the core of her being, into the deep essence of who and what she was, Kari dissolved into flames, winking out of the Forest in a flash of brilliant fire.

The suites of the *Titania* in Titan's Fen were dark. The moon had long set, the night creeping into shades of charcoal that came between the witching hour and dawn, where the shadows were as deep as the secrets were long.

Kari lay on one side of the enormous bed, arm tucked under a pillow, watching as Slate slept on the other side, his breathing deep and even from his enchanted sleep.

She didn't remember what her life had been like before Slate; a testament to their long history together given she had a *kitsune*'s eidetic memory. She remembered the countless hours sparring together, frightening the rest of the students with their intensity and drive. She remembered stealing his clothes when puberty hit her like a freight train and she'd spent years hiding herself in his loose clothing.

Kari didn't have many friends. She didn't need friends. She had Jian and Slate and that had always been enough for her.

Then Dani showed up.

And while her appearance had been the catalyst for much chaos over the summer, Kari had seen the shift in Slate. It wasn't something as dichotomous as positive or negative, but rather a metamorphosis. Dani's presence had transformed him, chipping away at the shell around him until someone more focused and level-headed emerged, despite the dysfunction around them at that time.

Kari had promised Slate that she would keep an eye on Dani. What had started as a simple favor had blossomed into a friendship. The love Kari felt for Slate boiled over and covered Dani too, until that woman had wormed her way onto Kari's very short list of people she would die on the sword for.

Frustration spiked through her before it quickly siphoned away to guilt and shame.

She had failed to rescue Dani.

A small part of her felt the sting in her own pride—she hated failing. She hated losing. A trait she shared with Slate; this intense, crippling sense of competitiveness. She always had a plan, a counterplan, a counterplan to the counterplan. And not bringing Dani home made her feel like an utter failure.

Which, in turn, made her feel like a shit friend, focusing on herself when Dani was likely being tortured at the hands of Slate's crazy uncle.

Both feelings are valid, Jian whispered through their bond. If she rocked back into the recesses of her mind, where their twin bond connected, she could feel his presence, his emotions, his thoughts, his actions. He was currently in his workroom down the hall, writing some new spells and enchantments into his grimoire. *Feelings are complex and intertwined and rarely follow a logical rhythm.*

You should've been a shrink, she responded.

Absolutely not. The inside of my own head is dark enough for me, thanks.

Across the bed, Slate's breathing changed, and he shifted. She stilled, watching as he slowly came out of his magically-induced rest. Jian had filled her in—apparently, they'd received news about the extraction team not long before Kari had burst into the fireplace, bleeding and breathless. Slate had already been transferred to his rooms, and after Jian had patched her up, she'd come straight here. He'd slept all day and night, getting some much-needed rest.

Slate sat up like a shot, pinging his gaze wildly around the room. His attention landed on her, and he started, stilling for a moment before letting his breath out in a long exhale.

"Not the redhead you were expecting in your bed, *ne,* Sailor Scout Slate?" she said softly, teasing him.

He scrubbed his whole face. Let out another breath. He flipped his eyes back to her, his attention sharpening. Even in the pervasive darkness around them, his gaze tracked over her, lighting on the bandages on her ribs peeking out from under her sports bra. The heavier bandages around her left thigh were concealed by the cotton martial arts pants she wore, but she saw his nostrils flare.

"You smell like herbs and shit. What happened to you?" His voice was deep and raspy and laced with concern.

Kami, she didn't want to tell him. She didn't want to see the agony in his face when she explained where she'd been and what she hadn't been able to accomplish.

He rubbed his hands together and from his palms, faerie lights materialized. They floated to the ceiling, nestling between the branches of the tree that grew there and casting a warm, soft light over them. "Kari."

"I went to the Silver Valley."

He froze. "What?"

She pushed herself up to a seated position and pulled her legs in, crossing them and smothering her wince with a shrug. "After the council meeting, I took matters into my own hands." She flipped her braid over her shoulder but paused and inhaled deeply, forcing the mask of false bravado to dissolve. "I wanted to bring Dani back," she said softly, dropping her gaze. "And I was so close, Slate. But Zeyphar has some kind of Mystic-ward around the castle that disables illusion magic, and I was spotted. I would have fought through them, but there were too many."

His gaze dropped back to the bandages, and she saw his jaw clench. "I had no idea... I thought you were in Faerloch."

"I left a shadow clone there to cover my tracks in case Kallen came snooping."

Silence stretched taut between them.

"You should've taken me with you."

She frowned at him. "Absolutely not. We wouldn't have made it through the wards if I'd taken you along."

"You could've used your magic to disguise me. We could've just rage-fucked through everyone. Hell, the two of us could probably bring this war to a real quick conclusion if—"

"Stop. Stop, stop, stop." She grabbed his hands, forcing them down and keeping his attention centered on her. "Pull your head out of your angry ass for a second and think clearly. What do you think Zeyphar would've done if he had a single whiff that you were in the Silver Valley? He'd squirrel Dani away and use her well-being as bait to coax you right into his palm. That's *exactly* why I couldn't... why I couldn't continue forward."

There was no telling what Zeyphar would've done to Dani before Kari got to her. The fact that he knew enough about Kari and her magic to commission a ward tailored to her specific brand of magic brought her to the uncomfortable conclusion that Zeyphar knew a lot more about her than she knew about him.

Which was an unforgivable disadvantage in the world of espionage.

Slate leveled her a hard look. She gave it right back.

With a growl, he released her hands and shoved himself off the bed. He paced furiously around the bedroom, fingers flexing. "It's infuriating. Doing nothing. Sitting around on my fucking hands. There's this... irrational urge inside me to just... sprint headfirst into the Silver Valley and absolutely obliterate anything between me and her."

Kari understood that. Kami only knew what unspeakable acts she'd perform if something were to happen to Jian. Unlike Slate and Jian, she'd never taken a life before, but nothing was too morally black when it came to the safety and security of her twin. Some bonds simply existed beyond a moral compass.

"But I can't." There was a haunted agony around the edges of his voice. "I mean, I could. It would be so easy to just... slip into the depths and be a mindless killing machine. But I *can't*. I can't let myself be like that. For me. For her. For everyone. And Jian's right—I'd kill myself trying."

He didn't have to explain it to her. She knew. The Malady made it easy for him to be ruthless. The complete separation between himself and his emotions allowed him to act swiftly with calculated callousness. She'd seen parts of it in him her whole life through the lens of martial arts. If

Slate thought for a single moment that Dani was in physical danger, there wasn't a ward that Kallen could build around him that would keep him contained.

Or, kami forbid, if Dani died... all bets were off. Kari didn't want to see what *that* would even look like.

She did not envy these feelings for him. It broke her heart to watch him in this kind of agony, knowing she'd been so close to fixing it for him.

"I'm sorry," she finally said, her tone soft. "If I could've blazed through the Silver Valley and gotten her out safely, I would have. I failed you. Failed her."

"Failure would've been death."

"Death is irrelevant."

If you died behind the ward... Jian growled at her, and she felt his blood pressure tick up a little as memories haunted him, *we'd be fucked and you know it. Collecting the fire would've been...*

Tricky, she finished for him.

That's a word for it.

Slate frowned at her. "Not to me. Or Dani. And probably not to Jian either. I don't wanna know what happens to him when you die."

She said nothing, and a beat of silence fell between them.

Slate blew out an agitated breath, and resumed his pacing. "What are we supposed to do now, Kari?" he finally asked, a hint of vulnerable desperation shivering in his eyes.

Kari smiled grimly. "We do what we always do when life throws shit at us... we adapt and overcome."

CHAPTER · FORTY-FIVE

THE ENDLESS DARK

... at their core animals who can assume human skins at will, unlike their counterparts in other magical cultures who use magic to assume an animal form...

- Gherald Schmidt, Faerloch Historical Archives

Dani slept.

Or maybe she didn't.

She couldn't tell when she was awake, or asleep. For a while—hours, days—she simply existed. She felt tired, and then wired, and then tired, so perhaps she slept, spurred by the sheer exhaustion of her initial panic.

Thoughts drifted into her mind, intrusive thoughts coupled with rational ones.

Was she dead? No, she wasn't dead. She knew she was in one of Zeyphar's hell chambers, and this was sensory deprivation.

Time stretched, her mind becoming a blank slate, and no matter what, she couldn't get herself to mentally fill that chalkboard with thoughts.

Time.

So much time, crawling by like a weight she couldn't feel, and yet couldn't ignore.

How many days had passed? It was hard to tell. She tried to count. Tried to keep track of the seconds, but her mind teetered off not long past a hundred.

How long would she have to stay? Her mind had no answer to that. Her life was at the whim of an irrational king.

Would she be fed? How long could she survive without food? Without water? Days... maybe a week...?

She felt hunger clench her insides, but the sensation didn't last long, her body giving up on the idea of eating. Perhaps she had to pee, feeling the pressure of her bladder, but once more, the sensation floated away.

Had she soiled herself? Probably.

Boredom found her eventually, when her mind was exhausted from panic. It grew and grew, until boredom threatened to suffocate her. Her mind ran in circles, desperate to alleviate the tedium. She'd read about people who choose to shock themselves rather than endure boredom, and she'd never understood that until now.

The little hairs on the back of her neck rose as she remembered the fae who'd been scratching their face. Had they felt this maddening sense of ennui?

She needed to get out of here. She needed... she needed...

Her breathing sped up. *Existing* didn't feel like anything anymore. She only knew she still existed because of her pounding heart and expanding ribs with each breath.

She started to cry, but she didn't feel the chilled wetness of the tears on her skin, the temperature of the room exactly the same as her skin, dulling any sensation.

Was she crying?

Where was the air? She couldn't breathe. She couldn't...

She attempted to rub at her face, to touch the tears that must be running down her cheeks, but she couldn't feel her skin. The knowledge of the fae sitting outside these hell rooms was slipping from her mind, and it was becoming more difficult to remember that she wasn't being allowed to touch herself.

Instead, it was like touching herself didn't exist anymore. *Touch* didn't exist.

Nothing. Nothing, nothing.

She screamed. Screamed and screamed. Was she screaming? Her thoughts flew apart. Was she dead? Was she—

No. She couldn't be dead. Slate's Malady would eat him alive if she died.

She would *not* die. This was *not* death. The erratic beating of her heart, her gasping breaths, were pieces she could cling to. Breathe. Beat. Breathe. Beat.

Those thoughts slipped through her fingers, her mind fragmenting as she struggled to string her thoughts together.

Her mind was liquid, thoughts bleeding out and scattering like ink in water. Fear combined with panic. She was trapped here forever. She would never get out, never see her friends again, never see Sellie or Roger or Slate—

Slate.

She clung to that thought like her life depended on it.

Because Slate's life might depend on it. She was bait to lure him here to the Silver Valley. If he came for her, Zeyphar would throw him in this room. Zeyphar would try to break him.

She couldn't allow that. She wouldn't.

It took all her willpower, but the thought of Slate helped her cast a net around the floating bubble of her mind, reining it back in. If she let go of her sanity, she would never be able to get out of here, and Slate might end up in one of these rooms.

She forced her mind to trace the lines of his face, his body, the scars on his palms from the iron wires that had bound him during the spring. She tried to remember the way his fingertips caressed her skin, the sound of his voice in her ear, tried to live in the sensory experience of her memories and allow them to fill the darkness around her.

His laughter, the wicked smile, the shape of his eyes... he looked a lot like his father... Dani looked like her father too... but he was dead...

Was she dead?

No. Slate.

It was exhausting, pulling on the reins of her thoughts time and again, to find where she'd left off and continue her recollection of him. He was the reason her mind didn't drift away completely.

Slate. Slate... Slaaaaa... Sla...

Her head snapped up. Or did it? She wasn't sure, but it took monumental effort to wrench her thoughts back.

Slate.

She needed to focus, to *think*. What color were his eyes? Blue. No. Sapphire blue, with that hint of light shining from within. What did he smell like? A winter wind, with a sharper—

Light blinded her.

She felt a jolt, then rough stone under her palms, her forearms, pain blasting from her knees. Dani cried out, the sound deafening, vibrating her skull. Her ears buzzed with the sound, and her eyes stung, tears blooming to protect her corneas as she threw up her hands.

Hands. Hands. Her hands.

What—?

"Tanyiel."

The whisper boomed. Dani covered her ears with a whimper. There was so much noise. So much light.

Where was she? What happened?

Hands slipped under her armpits, the touch abrasive and almost painful but so grounding.

She was hauled to her feet, and she leaned into the touch of the unfamiliar hands, relishing the contact as a garbled gasp slipped past her lips.

She savored the sound.

The stone hallway outside the chamber was blindingly bright, even though her mind remembered it as dim. She relied on those unknown hands to keep her upright as she stumbled, hands flying up to cover her eyes once more.

"Tanyiel," Zeyphar's voice slithered around her, too loud, too grating.

She blinked watering eyes to find Slate's uncle smiling down at her. "I've provided you plenty of time to consider carefully the proper behavior of a princess. Are you ready to resume such an important role?"

A princess?

Right. Right. She was playing princess. A hostage. She was a hostage.

"Yes," Dani gasped. She might have said yes to just about anything right then.

"Good. Are you ready to return to your room?"

"Yes." Anything to get as far away from that endless nothing.

Zeyphar snapped his fingers, the sound abrupt to her still-sensitive ears, then he turned and began walking toward the staircase. She was dragged along, her legs wobbling underneath her, her balance compromised like a colt just born. Her vision tunneled, a cold flush zipping through her head. She was so far past hunger, her body didn't even recognize the pain in her stomach anymore.

"How long?" Dani rasped, her throat scratchy and raw, her saliva thick. She was parched, her thirst driving her mad.

"Hmm?" Zeyphar looked back, one foot on the bottom stair.

Dani cleared her throat, trying to pull her thoughts together as they slipped like a sieve through her mind "How... how long was I... ?" She could feel the slime of dried sweat coating her skin, and something that was probably dried urine between her thighs.

It must've been *days*.

Had Slate tried to come for her? Was he here, trapped in this castle with her?

The idea jolted her system, resuscitating her brain as she sucked in a deep breath.

Zeyphar smiled slowly, cruelty glittering in his eyes. "Twelve hours."

Dani stopped moving, staring at Zeyphar as everything inside her simply... ceased functioning. Only when her lungs started burning did she gulp in some air, feeling dizzy again. "Twelve?"

Twelve hours.

Twelve.

That couldn't be right. That was... that was impossible. Not even a *day* had passed?

She suddenly felt sick, but she had nothing in her stomach to throw up. Thick saliva filled her mouth, and she swallowed it hard.

"Come, Tanyiel. There is time for you to rest before dinner this evening," Zeyphar urged, and a whisper of delight wound around her. She saw his heartfire flare, burning brighter, and more delight filtered through her.

No. There was no way he could spin this in a positive light. It was *wrong*.

And yet... pleasure and happiness loosened her shoulders as Zeyphar said, "I will make sure there are plenty of choices at breakfast for you tomorrow as well, so you will not be hungry throughout the day."

Her sluggish brain picked up on what he wasn't saying.

She would not be going to the kitchens again.

Hands gently urged her from behind, and like a lifeless automaton, she let them guide her after Zeyphar. Her mind still felt fractured, and she struggled to pull herself together, struggled to feel something other than the pleasant warmth that Zeyphar was feeding her.

But she was a hollow vessel, empty of even her own horror, as Zeyphar played with her emotions like a cat with a mouse.

CHAPTER · FORTY-SIX

PUPPET PRINCESS

Dani was a ghost at dinner that night. She felt empty, hollow, and yet Zeyphar kept filling her with emotions, marionetting her reactions, and she had no energy to fight it.

She smiled and laughed, but it wasn't *her*. He was the puppeteer, and she was the puppet.

She was struggling to refill her mind with *herself*.

Sleep that night following the dinner was much more difficult than the crash she'd experienced after Zeyphar took her out of his hell chambers. Then, her body had simply shut down. Now, however, closing her eyes led to a terror that had her bolting upright in bed.

When she closed her eyes, the darkness swallowed her.

Eventually, she must have passed out from sheer exhaustion, because the next thing she knew, watery morning light was spilling past the curtains, and Iris loomed above her, a gentle hand on Dani's shoulder.

Viscerally aware of the last time she'd been woken up, a whimper escaped her as she scooted back before she realized it was Iris, and not Casphian, leaning over the bed.

Worse, rather than confusion or contrition, a mask of solemn horror flashed over Iris' expression at Dani's retreat, the dainty fae female freezing as if caught in her own flashback of hell.

Neither of them spoke as Iris helped Dani prepare for breakfast with Zeyphar, even when Dani lost her nerve right before they left the bedroom and froze. Iris simply waited patiently, but Dani was aware of Iris' fingers tap-tap-tapping against themselves.

Understanding dawned through her. Since Zeyphar had pulled from all the nothingness, Dani found herself picking at her skin or simply touching her face, just because she *could*.

Just as Iris did.

Iris left her at the doorway to the Silver Atrium, as she always did, but Dani wished she hadn't. She didn't want to be alone with Zeyphar. She still felt... empty. Like she'd lost a piece of herself in that darkness.

And yet Zeyphar acted as if this were any other breakfast. His smiles, chuckles, and cheerful conversation were razor blades across her skin.

And his emotional manipulation was poison in her blood.

But she had no resistance today. Her mind kept retreating from the way her emotions were responding without her consent.

The world was slipping into a monotonous gray around her, her mind disassociating from a body she was mechanically fueling with food she didn't taste.

Until she heard the one word that brought some color back into her life.

Zlaet.

Dani blinked and wrenched her focus back from the numbness she'd settled into. With a start, she realized another person had entered the room. Had she been *that* out of it? She struggled to pull her mind together.

Casphian was speaking to Zeyphar, but as she focused on him, he was already turning away from the table to stride across the smooth marble floor. Dani's gaze flew back to Zeyphar, who was watching her.

"I expected your *mayt* to have joined us by now, seeing as it has been a full week since your arrival. I will be sending another missive, to remind him how dearly you wish to be reunited," Zeyphar told her. His smile sent chills down her spine. "I am doing everything in my power to bring you together again, my dear."

A flare of Zeyphar's heartfire accompanied the tickle of pleasure that rippled through her, but his words had ice crystalizing in her veins. As Zeyphar stared at her, her mind conjured images of a different set of sapphire eyes, the darkness of the nothing rooms swallowing them until that inner glow within Slate's eyes winked out of existence.

If Zeyphar arranged a meeting with Slate and used her as leverage… Slate would go. He would go for her sake, and throw away his whole life if he thought for a second it would guarantee her safety. He'd been willing to do it before, at the arena. He would do it again, and Zeyphar would get his hands on his nephew.

Panic was a vise around her heart, and Zeyphar's shiver of false excitement inside her did nothing to thaw the chill winding through her insides.

She couldn't let that happen.

"You will accompany us when we negotiate with my nephew. He will be reassured of your happiness and well-being, and he will join us here in the Silver Valley, where he belongs," Zeyphar murmured, delicately cutting a piece of sausage.

Unsticking her tongue, Dani cleared her throat. "W-when?"

"I will propose that we meet on the full moon in five days' time," Zeyphar responded. "He cannot refuse to meet on an evening sacred to the Goddess, not without insulting her."

Five days.

She had five days to get out of this place. She couldn't risk putting Slate in a position where Zeyphar could use her as leverage to get him into this city.

She needed to pull herself together. Slate's sanity was on the line. Her *own* sanity was on the line. She could not even begin to imagine what kind of hell their lives would be like together under Zeyphar. Used against each other as cooperation. Ruined, wrecked, and redrawn in Zeyphar's image.

She had a deadline. She needed to get her mind right, stuff her trauma from Zeyphar's dark room deep down, and resume her mission.

If she was successful, it could change the narrative for more than just Slate.

Even as determination buzzed through her, she couldn't ignore the shrinking in her stomach as she looked at Zeyphar. He might throw her back in those silent rooms, but she knew he couldn't keep her in there longer than five days, not if he wanted to bring her to the meeting with Slate.

Twelve hours had felt like an eternity, so she couldn't imagine what five days would feel like.

But Slate was worth it. She would do what she needed to do, for him.

Dani's mind raced with everything she needed to accomplish in the next five days. It was daunting, but having a goal helped keep her mind off the fact sleeping had become a new form a torture since the silence room. The jolting panic every time she closed her eyes left her exhausted during the days.

Since the kitchens were now off-limits, Dani was forced to walk much more of the castle to be heard by as many of the servants as possible.

In a twist of fate, Dani found herself glad rather than daunted when she noticed the number of guards roaming the castle had gone up. She wasn't sure if this was in response to her time in the silence rooms, or from something else, but it meant more ears to hear her stories.

So she made the decision to throw caution to the wind, and she began speaking about Slate, ignoring Iris' initial disquiet. She needed as many people as possible to know what kind of man Slate was, and that he was clearly not a prisoner of the rebels.

Speaking about him felt good, even if it made her ache with missing him. She had been gone a little more than a week now, and she worried about him. With a voice loud enough to carry, she spoke about the way he made her feel, the adventures they'd had, and even her anger at him for disappearing for half a year.

They made laps around the castle, Dani mostly speaking to herself as she told story after story. She knew she was reaching fewer servants this way, but the two guards who were her constant shadows heard every word. She could only hope they gossiped about her stories to others.

With each lap they took, Dani studied their surroundings carefully. She noted which hallways had balconies, where various guards were stationed. They made enough laps that she even spied on a few guard changes, and noted what time it was when that happened.

Most importantly, with each lap, Dani brought them closer and closer to Zeyphar's wing.

Until finally, she managed contact with the animal the maniacal fae king was keeping in there.

Since she'd discovered that Casphian asked Iris about what they do together, Dani worked hard to keep her excitement from her face. She didn't think Iris would deliberately betray her, but she didn't want to put the female in a position where she'd get in trouble.

The conversation between her and the creature took place over a few different laps, and with each exchange of words, hope bloomed through her.

A plan was beginning to form inside her mind.

One that relied on that little creature. Which meant she was going to need to find a way into Zeyphar's wing.

Two days after Dani learned about Zeyphar's planned meeting with Slate, Iris didn't show up to prepare Dani for breakfast, like she had every morning. The lady-in-waiting didn't appear after breakfast either.

When Dani tried to leave her rooms after breakfast, the guards blocked her, saying they'd been instructed to keep her in her rooms for the day.

The male and the female stationed today were guards she'd had before, and neither looked particularly happy to share that news with her.

Nerves wracking her belly, Dani nevertheless had a mission. Sitting near the door, she began talking about Slate. The guards outside would still be able to hear her, even if none of the other servants in the castle would. Unless Zeyphar gagged her, he wouldn't keep her from spreading what information she could about the true heir to the Silver Valley throne.

Every word could mean a difference for him in the future.

By the time she needed to get dressed for her nightly dinner with the nobles, Iris still did not appear. Worry gnawed at her insides. When she opened the door to ask her guards about Iris, she was informed that Iris was unavailable to assist.

Dani hadn't missed the grim expression the two guards exchanged at her question.

Skin too tight over her bones, Dani chose one of many dresses she'd collected and got dressed for dinner alone.

The walk to the banquet hall was one she'd made every night since she'd arrived, but this was the first time she'd done so without Iris' company. In less than two weeks, she'd grown close to the soft-spoken female, despite the times she lost touch with reality. There were times when Dani got a glimpse of the steel spine Iris must have had once, but even when Iris struggled with reality, she was always kind and considerate. She'd kept Dani from feeling so utterly alone during her time here.

She hoped Iris was alright.

"The prince is truly warrior trained?"

Dani nearly missed the softly murmured words from the guard to her right, the Faerish accent thick as he carefully pronounced German. She turned her head in surprise, meeting the pale gray eyes of the tall male she'd seen on more than one occasion. She'd been so concerned about Iris, she hadn't noticed earlier that this guard, in particular, was one she'd seen lingering in the kitchen when he wasn't on duty with her.

Listening to her stories.

Dani smiled, full and bright, and saw the guard's brows rise. "He is! He's been involved in martial arts since he was small."

A small furrow between pale blond brows. "Martial... arts? I don't understand."

"Right." She paused, trying to succinctly describe a topic she wasn't particularly knowledgeable about. "He knows how to fight. And he's very good at it, if I'm honest."

There was a deliberate throat clearing, and Dani glanced at the female, who was scowling at the other guard. The male's face paled, and he returned his eyes forward, mouth pressed tightly together.

Though her mind was still consumed by Iris and her whereabouts, Dani couldn't waste this opportunity. She started talking about everything she knew of Slate's martial arts training. How he used to fight in the professional circuit, the classes he taught, what she understood about the ranking system... she even threw in a couple of extra details that may not have been completely accurate.

Neither of the guards seemed to pay her any mind, but more than once, she could swear the male was watching her out of the corner of his eye.

Not wanting to get them in trouble, she ceased speaking before she got within earshot of the dining room, and her thoughts drifted back to Iris. Had Dani gotten her in trouble? Was she being punished for Dani's defiance?

Being punished for her own actions had been difficult, but at least she was responsible for her own choices. If Iris was being punished because of Dani...

Her stomach turned uneasily, and she curled her fingers into little fists, hidden in the folds of her dress as she stepped into the dining room. She struggled to slip into the numb emptiness she strove for at these dinners, but Iris' fate continued to be a pebble in the shoe of her mind.

Zeyphar was watching her as she moved to the chair she'd been assigned to his right. He smiled evenly when she slid into her chair, and before she could even open her mouth to ask about Iris, the false king leaned forward to peg her with a stare.

"A princess must learn that her actions affect her people. Choose the wrong actions, and the people suffer for it. Until you learn to make the right choices, your people will suffer." Zeyphar's words were whispered for her ears alone, dripping with the frost of displeasure as he stared her down.

And unlike usual, he did not feed her pleasure. Instead, he amplified the horror that was already budding within her, until she was gripping her skirts so tightly, her fingers tingled with lack of circulation.

She suddenly knew why Iris had been assigned to her, and not one of the servants loyal to Zeyphar. Iris was a tool, one Zeyphar planned to use against her now that Dani had come to learn and like the fae female.

The horror Zeyphar had been amplifying in her ebbed, draining from her as his heartfire banked, leaving her as desolate and void as she'd been when she'd left that room of silent hell.

A room she now had no doubt Iris was occupying.

She wasn't able to eat much that night, and every second Zeyphar watched her with that smug coldness, her dread slowly shifted to something hotter. The petty and useless chitter of the nobles around her slowly faded under the increasing roar of anger in her ears.

Zeyphar played with the people of this castle like they were clay dolls, to fit and mold as he pleased. And when someone didn't toe the line, he used his magic or his silence rooms to emotionally brainwash those resistant until they fell in line.

It had been horrible when it had been her, but it was intolerable when it was someone she had come to care for. Someone who had already been through enough pain, someone who seemed too fragile to fight back.

Dani prided herself on helping those who couldn't help themselves, and she wasn't about to step aside and let him continue to abuse, manipulate, and torture her friend.

Fury simmered in her veins, but she had no choice but to smother it, deprive it of all oxygen until the fire suffocated as she strove for numbness. She wouldn't give Zeyphar any satisfaction, nor any hint toward her plans.

She shut it all down, until she became the shell Zeyphar wanted her to be.

What he expected her to become.

OUT OF TIME

... smaller than often depicted in traditional mortal lore. Indeed, the Forest Dragon subspecies more closely resembles Asian depictions, with long and powerful serpentine bodies that allow for higher maneuverability through the canopy of L'el. This agility, combined with their chameleon-like ability to...

– Gherald Schmidt, Faerloch Historical Archives

It was nearly impossible to sleep that night. Nerves chewed on her ribs. The little shut-eye she did manage to achieve was interrupted by vivid nightmares where she was trapped in a doorway, unable to move as Iris clawed her own eyes out until nothing but bloody, gaping holes remained.

Or worse, when her nightmares replaced Iris with Slate.

Eventually, she gave up and opened the heavy armoire against the far wall.

Inside were dresses, the ones which had been in here before her arrival as well as the *many* she had requested to be made.

Smiling grimly, she tugged them out, one by one.

And began tying them together.

Each knot fueled her determination as she mentally prepared for what she would have to do. She'd wanted to wait one more night to cement her plans, but her conscience wouldn't allow it.

She wouldn't allow Iris to suffer for another twenty-four hours.

She was officially out of time, and she had to make do with what she had.

An hour later, the bed was completely stripped, the sheets and duvet added to the makeshift rope that was now coiled beneath the window, one end tied to the corner of the bed. It was late now, and her task had taken her longer considering she'd had to move quietly and carefully to keep the guards from picking up any suspicious sounds.

She inched the window open with such silent slowness, she wanted to scream. When it was finally wide enough for her to squeeze through, she slowly fed the rope out the window, watching to make sure it didn't bump against either of the two windows it would pass on the way down.

And down...

Her room was six stories up, but she wasn't aiming for the ground.

Once the rope was set, she spent a few minutes tugging and pulling on the end tied to the bed to ensure it wouldn't come loose on her way down. One of the gowns had become her anchor, with the sleeves tied tightly around the post four times over.

She had to hope that fae seamstresses were good enough to keep the dress from being ripped apart by her body weight.

Finally, there was nothing left to do but tie the skirts of the simplest dress she could find, secure her vibrant hair under a scarf, and slip out the window.

The slipping out the window part wasn't as easy when you were as high up as she was.

It took several seconds before she could gather the gumption to dangle her legs over the edge of the window and into the open air.

She could do this. She had to do this.

She froze as her self-preservation instincts screamed at her to return to solid ground. For a precarious moment, she hung, half in, half out, as her heart hammered in her ears and her breath sawed from her lungs.

"Iris needs me," she whispered to herself, barely a breath of sound. "Slate needs me to get out of here. I can do this."

Dani squeezed her eyes shut, gripped the bedsheet rope, and slowly shifted herself over until she was on her belly. Carefully, she eased herself out and down from the window.

Then she was hanging in the open air, six stories up, with nothing but a knotted bedsheet keeping her from plunging from her death.

"Maybe don't think that way..." she muttered as she huffed out several steadying breaths. She wiggled her legs until the rope was loosely wrapped around one ankle with the other braced against the stone wall, and she slowly started to shimmy her way down the rope.

It was slow, and she'd only made it one story before her arms started aching. Dani gritted her teeth, desperately clinging to her determination as she kept moving, one hand over the other. After what felt like an eternity, she dared to glance down. Her target was a narrow ledge located on the third story.

It seemed like a million miles away still.

When her arms began to shake, she tangled both of her legs in the rope and clenched her thighs together to give her arms a rest. Sweat poured down her face and between her shoulder blades, and her lungs burned from the effort it took not to gasp too loudly as she struggled for breath.

Goddess help her, the movies made this seem so easy. Princesses and teenagers effortlessly escaped on bedsheet ropes all the time. She was neither a princess nor a teenager, but she wasn't a slouch either.

She could do this.

Dani shifted her hands to continue her descent. One fist. Then another.

And she was falling.

Falling, falling, a moment of weightlessness. Her stomach jumped into her brain, her hands clutching the rope desperately—

A hard tug. A bounce. Her shoulder scraped hard against the stone of the castle as her body swung. She bit her lip hard to stifle her scream.

But she wasn't falling to her death.

Heart hammering somewhere in her brain and tasting blood on her lips, she glanced up. Horrible enlightenment filled her.

A seam must be giving way in the dress tied to the bed.

She had to hurry.

A whimper escaped her as she forced her screaming arms to move. Her hands burned, but the threat of death and the adrenaline in her system were enough to let her ignore the throbbing pain in them as she moved, hand over fist, down the rope. She sacrificed stealth for speed, desperate to reach that ledge.

Ten feet.

Five.

She touched the ledge with her toes. It was just wide enough for her to get her feet on, but she still needed the rope for stability. She glanced upward, silently commanding the threads to hold, as she wobbled along the ledge. One hand gripped the rope to keep herself upright, while the other pressed flat to the stone, leaving a smudge of blood behind.

Ahead of her, just outside of her arm's reach, was a balcony.

Anxiety tingling through her veins, she *reached* for the balcony's banister.

Her fingertip brushed the marble just as the rope gave way. A strangled gasp escaped her, and she lunged for the balcony, throwing herself at it desperately as she heard the quiet thump of the rope hitting a bush in the courtyard three stories below.

Her fingernails cracked and skin split as she scrambled at the balcony, one foot slipping against the marble as she clung to the railing. Slowly, with arms trembling so hard she could barely move them, Dani hauled herself up and over the stone banister, then collapsed in a heap on the other side.

She did it.

She allowed herself a minute to catch her breath and recover. She glanced back up the way she'd come, the height somehow less daunting from below than it had seemed from above.

Any pride she had for herself was immediately snuffed out, drowned out by the knowledge that she was far from safe. This was only one step of many she would need to take tonight, and it wasn't even the riskiest one.

She had to keep going.

Dani shifted into a crouch, then peered through the doorway to the hallway. As expected at this time of night, she saw no one. Carefully, she hurried past the glass doors to the other side of the balcony and braced herself once more before she climbed up onto the railing, arms shaking with the effort.

The ledge on this side of the balcony remained as wide as the other side had been, but she had no rope this time. Instead, an ornate carving of a stone tree speared between this balcony and the next. Several more of these decorative trees dotted the wall, punctuating the space between this balcony and the next. Dani was careful to keep a tight grip on the balcony railing as she slipped her legs over to carefully position her feet on the narrow ledge. She took a deep breath... and lunged for the tree.

Her heart splashed into her belly when her fingers slipped, but her other hand managed a firm grip. For a wild moment, she windmilled her free arm to keep her balance as she clutched at the stone branch. Finally, she righted herself, clinging to the handhold the tree offered as she slowly shimmied her way along the wall.

She continued this way, aiming for the other end of the courtyard, heart pounding, body aching. Fear and adrenaline kept her focused and alert, and there was no way she could forget that she was still several stories above the unforgiving ground. She might not die on impact, but there was no way she'd walk away after a fall from this height.

She kept her eyes forward and forced herself to push forward at an unhurried pace.

After what felt like a lifetime, she ducked into one of the balcony doorways and into the silent hall. She gave herself another couple of moments to regain her composure, but momentum was the priority. Holding herself close to the wall, she hurried along until she reached a specific corridor she and Iris had walked many times.

She was about to round the corner when she heard the near-silent tread of footfalls. Sucking in a breath, she backtracked and pressed herself behind one of the curtains hanging on either side of the closest window.

Despite the fear flushing through her, it was not lost on her that this was a ridiculous hiding place, more fit for a cartoon than her current reality.

Desperate times called for desperate measures, as they say.

She held her breath, pressing herself back against the wall, and thankfully, the footsteps passed. She waited another minute or two before peeking out. All was quiet again, and she resumed her careful trek. She traveled along two more hallways before she spied the doorway she'd need.

She crept through a dark sitting room, and out onto its balcony. The night was still dark, the shadows and pervasive quiet a blessing from the Goddess. Moving to the edge of the balcony, she peered up at another carved stone tree. Rather than using it to get to the next balcony over, she would need to climb this one.

Her fingers throbbed at the thought, blood now seeping from the sores on her palms. She'd torn off a part of her dress to wrap them, and it would ease some of the sting for this next climb, but not all. She gritted her teeth and swung her legs over the railing. The stone branches gave her the grip she needed to scale the wall, but her body was tired and aching, and it took her far longer than she liked to reach the balcony on the fourth floor, one up from where she'd come from.

You comes?

Dani froze, crouched on the ground of the balcony, as the creature from Zeyphar's room whispered into her mind.

Yes. I'm almost there, she promised him. *We're getting out of here tonight.*

There was no response, but she could sense the heartfire now, could feel the quivering excitement in the bond she'd barely managed to form with him in the few times they'd communicated. She'd been amazed when she'd realized the creature understood German, and she was even more impressed when she'd realized how young it was. Sellie and Dash were the only creatures she'd ever communicated with words instead of impressions, and that was after years of picking it up from living with Dani.

The excitement she felt slowly tainted with something heavier, more jittery, as he sent her impressions of nervous fear.

We can do this, she promised him, and she rallied herself for her next action.

She had one more stone tree to climb.

Dani felt the moment she moved through a ward, like a shiver over her skin and a slight pressure on her ears once she'd passed. She'd experienced this kind of ward before, in the city. In the Dark Arts Market, many stalls used this kind of warding to prevent others from sensing the magical qualities of the items. It also kept people from sensing the auras of the individuals within the ward. In a sense, it was like a magical tinted window.

A slow smile curled Dani's lips. Zeyphar must have assumed her magic wouldn't be able to sense the creature past the ward, but she didn't sense magic with her abilities. She sensed the wild heart within all living beings.

It wasn't something that could be stopped with wards, which was why she'd always been so successful at freeing illegally obtained animals in the Dark Arts Market. No magic could hide animals from her.

She hadn't been able to map out this part of the castle, with it being so close to Zeyphar's rooms, but at this point, she was following the heartfire to get to where she needed to be.

Which happened to be a large and lavish balcony one over from the one she was currently perched on. It made sense, given its grandiosity compared to the others. It seemed like the balcony the king of the castle might have.

Dani didn't make the crossing to the final balcony right away. Instead, she wedged herself against the balustrade, hiding herself in a little niche, away from any casual glances.

I'm here. Tell me when Zeyphar is gone, Dani whispered into the creature's mind.

In response, she got an impression of confusion, and Dani had to remind herself that she was dealing with a child. She sent an impression of what Zeyphar looked like, and in response, the creature showed her the image of a bed, with a figure laying flat on their back with their eyes closed.

So Dani settled in to wait, leaning her head back against the stone to rest. She couldn't risk sleep, not when she was keeping herself in place with locked muscles, but she could preserve her energy.

She was going to need it.

A DASH OF PEPPER

... blend into their environment, their magic making them invisible to their prey. Forest Dragons hunt similarly to a jungle panther. For this reason, their wings have developed less prominently than the plains or mountain dragons...

- Gherald Schmidt, Faerloch Historical Archives

As the witching hour gave way to a watery rose, Dani opened her eyes, wishing she could see the sunrise, but it was on the other side of the building from her. Still, she watched the sky lighten, as blue slowly overcame the rose. She heard sounds coming from the bedroom on the other balcony, but it wasn't until the creature had confirmed the room was empty that Dani forced her stiff muscles to move.

Shooting pains like pins and needles tingled over her muscles as she dragged herself over the banister, across the narrow ledge once more, and onto the balcony. Her body begged her to lay flat and rest, but she had no time to lose. Zeyphar would be expecting her for breakfast within an hour, and she needed to be well away from this room by then.

The weak morning light was the only illumination as Dani's gaze swept the room and landed immediately on the cage set on top of an elegant table on the far side of the room. It was hard to miss, the way it was so obviously on display.

Of course Zeyphar was the type of being to gloat over a captured animal.

Suppressing a growl, Dani hurried across the room and peered into the cage, a square, gilded contraption slightly longer than her arm.

Jewel-like eyes peered back at her, shifting from a cautious orange to a yellow-tinged green as the small serpent-like forest dragon huddled against the back of the cage.

An *actual* forest dragon.

She could scarcely believe she was seeing one.

The small dragon reminded her of dragons of Eastern Lore, but miniature, his body long, narrow, and serpentine. His head was more like a viper's, though, pointed and triangular with multi-faceted eyes like a dragonfly. The dragonette's body was a little over a foot long, with another foot and a half of a slender tail, tiny ridges running from between its eye ridges to the end of the tail.

Two thin membranous wings were plastered to the sides of its body, perhaps too small still to carry him in flight.

Dani smiled, wrestling down her amazement at seeing such a rare creature in order to convey a sense of calm and safety.

"Hey little guy... nice to finally meet you in person," she whispered aloud so the creature could get used to the sound of her voice. She held her hand up to the cage.

It took longer than she'd like for the little dragon to approach her hand, but she wasn't going to rush him. Forest dragons were notoriously shy and reclusive, and this one had been through quite an ordeal. Dani let none of her impatience show on her face or on a mental level as she slowly fed reassuring impressions, until finally the dragonette peeled itself away from the back of the cage and sniffed at her hand.

Dani smiled at it. She switched to a mental voice, not wanting to risk being overheard. *Are you ready to get out of here?*

The dragon cocked its serpentine-like head, studying her. A forked tongue tickled against her palm as he licked at her. *Go home?* Images of a canopy filled Dani's mind, sunlight filtering through leaves.

Yes, I'll take you home. Is your mum in the Forest? Dani asked, gaze sliding from the creature to study the cage.

Sadness, enough to make Dani's heart clench, filtered from that creature, and the cage vanished from her mind as the dragon fed her a vision.

No, a memory. Dani was viewing a scene from the perspective of something... small. The trees were monoliths, giants that soared around her, with leaves as big as her whole body rustling on the branch next to her.

A sudden screech wrenched the air, and the branch beneath her shook violently. Verdant colors flashed past her as she fell, a pitiful cry escaping her. She landed on something soft and warm and wet. Skittering to her feet, she twisted around, the comforting scent of her mother fresh in her nose, but also something... coppery.

She looked down, and saw red. More red than she'd ever seen in the Forest. She nudged her mother, wondering why she was so red. She opened her mouth to cry to her, but strong hands grabbed her, and she was shoved into a small dark space.

The scene changed, time passing. Dani immediately recognized where she was. Sellie had described the back room of Dagby's Creature Emporium, where captured animals were brought to be sold in the Dark Arts Market.

"I think you will like what we have for you, Titania," a voice in German said, a new language she was learning slowly.

The front of the cage was wrenched open, and Zeyphar Titania was staring at her, a greedy gleam in his eye as a slow, pleased smile curled his lips.

Dani's free hand shot out to catch herself on the edge of the table as the vision faded from her mind. Her own sadness rose as the dragon's faded from her, and the fingers on the table curled into a tight fist as she wrestled her temper down.

Zeyphar had officially become the worst person she'd ever met, now that she could add animal cruelty to his long list of offenses.

I'm going to get you out of that cage, then you're going to help get me and my friend out of this castle, okay? She spoke slowly, accompanying each of her words with visual impressions. The dragonette watched her for a long moment, then finally gave her an affirmative impression with a little shake of its body, much like a dog did, as he got to his feet.

Dani smiled, and she reached between the bars to tickle the creature's chin. *So very brave. What's your name?* she asked, shifting to study the cage once more.

The small dragon whispered a name into her mind, and when Dani tried to pronounce it back, the dragonette wrinkled his muzzle and blew out a puff of fire, barely the size of a candle flame.

Dani suppressed a laugh. *Can I call you something else? My clumsy human tongue can't make that sound.*

The dragon considered for a moment, his multi-faceted eyes shifting from green to yellow to purple, then back to green. Finally, he gave a grudging acceptance.

Inspired by the fire, and because of the way he looked with his little legs all tucked close, she proposed, *How about Pepper? Like a Jalapeño pepper.* She sent an impression of the spicy pepper. *It's hot, makes your eyes water if you eat too much.*

The dragon was delighted by that idea, another lick of flame appearing to dance around his tiny teeth.

Pepper it is then. You can call me Dani.

The small dragon got up with a small trill, and made a happy lap around the cage, and Dani's attention snagged on the small engraving on the bottom that had been concealed by the dragonette's body.

Jackpot.

The mark was about the size of a small coin, a paw print overlaid with the symbol of talons, with two scratches across the mark. Though it felt like years ago now, it was really only a few weeks ago that Zeyphar had found her in the Dark Arts Market District of Faerloch.

Right near Dagby's Creature Emporium, the same place she'd rescued Sellie from. Dagby, a vile witch without a coven, sold magical creatures for high prices. He *also* sold the means to keep those creatures contained for their new masters. Since Dani regularly patrolled the Dark Arts Market in the hopes of rescuing any of his unfortunate wares, she had become intimately familiar with many of the cages and ward enchantment products that he sold.

It also helped to have a powerful witch friend who could explain how witch enchantments worked.

When are you fed, little one? Do you know where your food comes from? Dani leaned down until she was at eye level with the dragon.

Images filtered into her mind; Zeyphar holding a silver tray, setting it down next to the cage as he teased the creature about being hungry. Dani turned full circle, and found a small table across the room with a silver tray. It was located next to the small discreet door she assumed the servants used.

Panic licked her insides. She had no idea what time the servants came to attend his rooms.

Spurred to action, she hurried across the room to the tray. Most likely, the servants delivered the food to the tray every day. She couldn't imagine a control freak like Zeyphar allowing others to feed his prized pet.

"Let's hope he likes convenience..." Dani muttered as she examined the tray. She carefully lifted it to look beneath, but couldn't find what she needed. Frustrated, she turned to survey the room again, and her eyes landed on what looked like a jewelry box next to the enormous bed. Keeping the servants' door in her peripheral for any signs of movement, she investigated the box.

It was silver like the tray, and when she tipped back the lid, it was lined with sapphire velvet. Inside was a small coin, gold like Pepper's cage, with a pawprint, talons, and two slash marks on it. Elated, she snatched it up, but as her fingers closed over the metal, a shiver raced along her arm and down her spine.

She'd just triggered something magical.

Trying to stay outwardly calm, Dani hurried over to the cage as she studied the coin. There was Dagby's symbol on one side, and a simple open circle on the other. One side to lock, one side to open. Fumbling with it as she reached the cage, she peered around the back until she spotted another of Dagby's symbols, in the center of an indentation the same size as the coin.

When she pressed the circle side of the coin into the mark, the latch opened, and Dani wasted no time in opening the small door and reaching a hand inside. *Hurry, my friend.*

She needed them out of here as soon as possible.

Pepper hesitated, investigating her fingers, and Dani stifled the urge to just grab the dragonette. She couldn't rush trust, but she also needed to get them moving, before trust no longer mattered. *The bad man might come back soon, so we have to hurry.*

Pepper let out a snort of flame, a trickle of smoke wafting up from the cage, and the two-foot-long dragonette shot forward and up her arm, scrabbling his way to her shoulders. His long tail wrapped around her throat, and Pepper perched on her shoulder, his small body trembling slightly.

I'm going to need you to do what we talked about before, okay? Dani was already moving as she murmured in the creature's mind, hurrying to the still-unmade bed. She ripped the sheets off, then flung the duvet back over the bed to hide the fact that the sheets were missing. She tied them together, the fine fabric trailing on the floor as she moved toward the balcony.

A sense of urgency churned in her gut, as if a countdown had started. Sensing her anxiety, Pepper let out a low purr that came from fear rather than happiness as he huddled close to her neck, his tiny talons digging into her skin and the fabric of her dress.

Moving to the corner of the balcony she'd come in from, Dani tied the sheet to the banister. With any luck, the sheets wouldn't be immediately noticed by anyone coming into the bedroom, buying her a little more time.

Hold on tight, little one, Dani urged Pepper, feeding the little dragon impressions to cement her words. She winced as little talons dug into her flesh, but he said nothing as she swung a leg over the banister, then the other. Sliding down on her belly, she curled her aching fingers around the bedsheet just as she heard the sound of muffled shouting coming from beyond the bedroom, followed by the slam as a door was shoved open hard enough to bounce against the wall.

Dani froze, hanging from the bedsheet as she held her breath. Against her neck, Pepper shivered and let out a small whimper, but before she could mentally comfort him, heavy footsteps sounded from above them as someone walked out onto the balcony.

She squeezed her eyes shut and tried not to move, even as her fingers pulsed and burned from the effort of holding herself in place.

The footsteps approached their side of the balcony, and fear flashed through her as she peeked upward. A face appeared over the edge of the balcony, a guard she didn't recognize, with a deep scowl and searching gray eyes.

Dani opened her mouth to say something, anything, to defend herself, but the words died in her throat when the guard seemed to look straight through her, then he was gone, his heavy footsteps echoing from within the bed chamber. Distantly, she heard him say something in Faerish.

Startled, Dani looked down at herself, and saw... nothing. She was so surprised she nearly let go of the bedsheet.

The one she could no longer see.

Are you hiding us? Dani asked cautiously, slowly letting herself start to move down the bedsheet, going by feeling alone. As she started to move, she could see the shimmery outline of her hands and the bedsheet, both blending into the stone behind it seamlessly. If she didn't know her hands were there, she'd not even see them.

There was a chirp of confirmation next to her ear, and with a shimmer like the surface of water, she could see her hands again. *How long can you hold it?* she asked.

The answer was one she'd expected from a baby creature who didn't understand the concept of time, so Dani prodded the dragon with impressions and suggestions as she carefully maneuvered them down to the balcony beneath Zeyphar's.

This is what she'd been counting on. Forest dragons had a useful ability much like a chameleon's. It wasn't strictly invisibility as much as projecting what was behind an object to be in front of it, creating the illusion of invisibility. In the books she'd read, they'd been able to disguise entire glades while hunting, so Dani had hoped Pepper would be able to disguise her as well.

But Pepper was young, and she'd have to use his abilities sparingly, because it seemed like he wasn't able to hold it for long at once. He was her key to getting out of this place, and she'd go as slowly as she needed to ensure they got out of here safely.

Once she reached the floor beneath Zeyphar's, Dani knew she could no longer move along the outside walls like she'd been doing. Her hands were officially shredded, and she spent precious seconds re-wrapping them as Pepper crooned comfortingly in her ear.

For a baby, he was surprisingly aware and intelligent. She'd been expecting to engage with much more coaxing for this harrowing escape, but Pepper understood what she needed from him quicker than even Sellie would pick up on, especially at such a young age. She supposed the intelligence of dragons wasn't overstated.

Once she'd wrapped her hands, they began the slow process of creeping through the halls again. She cautioned Pepper against using his ability too much, but there were two instances where she had no choice but to rely on the dragon as guards hurried past them in the hallways.

The tone of their voices and the movement of their bodies indicated that her absence had been noticed. Her stomach clenched as fear slithered through her. They would be actively searching for her now, making her progress that much harder. She began preparing Pepper for what would be the most difficult part of their journey.

It took a while, but finally, Dani and Pepper reached the hallway that led to Zeyphar's nothing dungeons. *Are you ready?*

Ready, Pepper whispered back in her mind, and she was struck again by how clear Pepper's voice was when he used words. Sellie had been through adolescence before she'd started using words instead of impressions.

Dani reached up and stroked the little dragon. *Now*, she whispered, and watched as her own hand vanished.

Dani moved quickly and quietly, hurrying toward the guard standing at the top of the stairs. Unable to see Pepper, but feeling the warmth of his little body, Dani gently wiggled her shoulder. He hesitated a moment, then slithered down her right arm, which she lifted to be parallel to the ground.

The moment her hand got within a foot of the guard, Pepper lunged, fast as a viper, and Dani nearly dropped him, but the little dragon wrapped his tail tightly around her wrist. The same moment she felt the dragon drop, dangling from her wrist like a yoyo, the guard dropped too. Dani reached out with her free hand and grabbed the slight female, easing her down to the ground as Pepper scrambled back up her other arm and around her throat once more.

Dani wasted no time checking on the guard—Pepper was a baby, and his snake-like venom wasn't likely to last longer than ten minutes at most against an adult fae. Pepper hadn't even known he was venomous until Dani had explained it to him, likely because his mother hadn't gotten to that part of their hunting education before the poacher had ended her life.

Each time she used Pepper as a weapon against the three other fae on their path to the dungeons, Dani felt a sick twist in her stomach. Manipulating animals for her own gain made her feel no better than the poachers and illegal traders, but she had no choice if she wanted to get all three of them out.

As the final fae—the one who levitated people in these hell rooms—slumped to the floor, Dani hurried over to the same chamber she'd been put in. As expected, she spied Iris inside, struggling on the floor as if she'd just been dropped there. Tentatively, Dani attempted to slip her hand through the doorway, and when she met no resistance, relief surged through her.

Despite the need for speed, Dani forced herself to eye the space between the door and where Iris lay, knowing she could only see Iris right now because the room functioned like a two-way mirror.

I'll need to follow your voice to get out, Dani instructed the dragon, and gently set the creature on the floor outside the dark room. Pepper hissed unpleasantly at the touch of the cold stone and curled into a ball, but he gave a mental affirmative to Dani.

Taking a deep, fortifying breath, she plunged into the room.

Darkness swallowed her, and for a moment, Dani froze. Fear wrapped around her throat and whispered in her ear that she'd never leave. She could neither see nor hear Iris, and the sudden stillness brought her nightmares back in full swing.

Hurry hurry, Pepper whispered in her mind, breaking her from her paralysis. Time was ticking, and the guards would wake soon. Sucking in a breath she couldn't feel or hear, Dani slowly counted her steps, then crouched down to where she hoped Iris would be. Her left hand encountered a body.

Fingers clawed at her arm, scrabbling for contact, and Dani's heart flipped at the desperation in which Iris clung to her, not even aware of who Dani was, but Dani knew any sensation was welcomed at this point. Tugging Iris to her feet, Dani reached for Pepper with her mind.

Here! Pepper's mental voice rang out, and Dani angled herself appropriately, half dragging Iris with her.

Dani nearly sobbed in relief when they emerged into the dim light of the dungeon hallway, but Iris didn't hold back. A wailing sob escaped the female, and Dani had no choice but to slap a hand over the her mouth.

"Shhh, Iris!" Dani whispered urgently. "We need to be quiet."

Iris' eyes squeezed shut as muffled cries escaped Dani's fingers. Dani's heart tightened for this female, but they didn't have time for hysterics. Keeping one hand over Iris' mouth as best as possible, Dani pulled her into a tight hug, letting her feel the press of a body, the scent of another person. "Iris, I know this is hard, but I need you to pull yourself together," she whispered in Iris' ear.

Tiny claws caused pinpricks of discomfort as Pepper scaled her back, his tail wrapping around her neck in a tight hold that made her gasp, before he loosened it and burrowed against her. Iris noticed the dragon, and while she didn't make a sound, her brows lifted.

"Listen carefully, Iris. We're getting out of here. We're going to leave this castle and this city, and you're coming with me, okay?" Dani didn't take her hand away from Iris' mouth just yet, and she was justified when Iris tried to let out a cry of denial and shake her head. Dani smothered the sound, and gently gripped Iris' chin.

"Iris, do you remember Kallen Ewyt?"

Iris froze, and her eyes widened even more, then narrowed as if in betrayal. Dani lowered her hand, and Iris's voice came out quiet, but heavy with despair. "He is dead."

"He is *not* dead. If you come with me, you can see him again." Dani stared at her, even as a timer in her brain started screaming at her that this was taking too long.

"You lie, he—"

"He has the prettiest purple eyes I've ever seen, and he's got more manners in his little finger than I have in my entire body."

Iris's mouth fell open, and what color she had left drained from her face, her body swaying. "But... but he—"

"He doesn't know you're alive, and if you want to tell him yourself, you're going to listen to me, do what I say, and help me get us out of here, okay?" Dani's voice was harsh, but she needed to get them *moving*.

When Iris still didn't move, Dani leaned in close. "Would Ari want you to stay here and rot while her son and Kallen need your help?"

The fear and the shock evaporated from Iris' eyes as her mouth snapped shut. Wordlessly, Iris tried to get up, and Dani helped her. Iris glanced at the dragon, then toward the guards. Uncertainty clouded the determination in her eyes. "How are we going to...?"

"Iris, this is Pepper. Pepper, this is Iris. He's a forest dragon, and he's going to get us out of here, right?" She glanced at her shoulder, and the serpentine dragon blinked one eye, then the other, before puffing his little chest with pride, a trickle of smoke leaking from between his lips. "That's the spirit." Dani held out her hand. "Iris, you need to hold my hand, and not let go. His magic will keep us hidden, but we need to be touching for it to work for you too, okay? He's too young to camouflage without contact."

Iris gave a sharp nod, and Dani wished she had time to ease the terror and anxiety clear on the female's face. Instead, Iris wove her lithe fingers firmly with Dani's, and Dani tugged her toward the stairs just as one of the fae at their feet began to stir.

A whimper escaped Iris, and Dani tightened her grip on the female's trembling hand as she urged her up the stairs. Right before they reached the hallway, Dani whispered in Pepper's mind, and glanced behind her to confirm that Iris, too, had become invisible. Iris must have noticed the sudden invisibility, because a squeak of surprise left her, and she loosened her grip on Dani's hand.

Dani clutched her tighter, giving her hand a gentle squeeze in assurance. Relieved that Pepper's magic did extend to both of them, Dani slowed enough to peer out into the hallway as they reached the top of the stairs. The fae there was groaning, hand over her belly and propped against the wall.

Hoping that Iris would remain silent, she hurried them past the guard and down the hallway, moving as quickly as she could without making too much sound. Pepper's magic wouldn't conceal sounds or scents, so they had to be careful.

"Where are we going?" Iris whispered as they hurried down an empty hallway.

"The kitchens. I'm hoping we can slip out that way," Dani whispered back. She was hoping the small service entrance where supplies were delivered was less heavily guarded than other, more obvious entrances to the castle.

"The kitchens are very busy..." Iris said nervously.

"Exactly," Dani muttered.

The journey to the kitchens was difficult and slow. Guard patrols had started roaming the castle, likely because they were searching for her. Every now and then, a fine tremor vibrated under her feet, like something was shaking the entire castle, and she wondered if it was Zeyphar's doing.

A shiver raced through her. She needed to move them *faster*.

They reached the hallway leading to the kitchens when Dani caught sight of her arm flickering into existence in her periphery. At the same time, she heard a small whimper right next to her ear.

What's wrong? Dani asked, trying not to let her alarm bleed into her mental voice.

Tired... Pepper responded, and his little body tightened around her neck for a moment as a tremor passed through him. Pepper was still young, and holding a camouflage for this long was taking its toll.

Can you go a little longer? Dani asked, injecting encouragement and soothing assurances into her mental impression.

A little puff of smoke warmed her neck, and Pepper gave a rallying affirmative.

"What's wrong?" Iris whispered, likely because Dani had slowed their hurried pace.

"Nothing," Dani whispered. There was no point in creating more panic in the female. "Ready? Stay close to me, we need to move fast." Dani squeezed her hand as they approached the kitchens door, the raucous sounds of breakfast preparation echoing out into the hallway.

"Ready," Iris murmured, a thread of steel in her voice, and pride swelled in Dani's chest. She tugged Iris close to her, stroked Pepper's flank with her other hand, and plunged into the chaos of the kitchens.

Over the few days she'd spent in the kitchens, Dani had done more than talk. She'd also paid attention to the routines of staff and servants, and from which doors people came in and out. She'd studied the traffic of the room, what parts of the kitchens were the busiest, and plotted three different routes she could take through the kitchens if she needed to move fast.

Almost immediately, her most promising route was ruled out by a mass of fae gathered around what looked like a wild boar. She still didn't have a grasp of Faerish, but it seemed they were about to cut the dead beast up.

Pivoting, Dani hurried them toward her next best route, which took them through the heart of the kitchens. Several times, they had to pause or change trajectories to avoid colliding with people, so Dani held Iris as close to her as she could.

Sweat trickled down Dani's back, and her pulse sounded in her ears when a group of guards stormed into the kitchens. Iris let out a squeak of alarm, but the kitchens was loud enough to cover the small noise.

Voices rose as the guards called out in Faerish, and while she couldn't understand their responses, the intonations of the kitchen servants were a mixture of fearful denial and irritated dismissal as they hurried to complete their breakfast duties.

"They are searching for you," Iris breathed in Dani's ear.

Dani's heart rate jacked up. She mustered a deep breath.

Her courage would not fail her now.

Dani and Iris were almost to the door, and soon they would be mostly out of sight from the rest of the kitchens, in the short but wide hallway connecting the bustling room with the double doors leading outside.

They were currently closed, but hopefully they would be able to slip out when someone opened them.

She hoped Pepper's magic lasted until then.

Even though Dani knew they were invisible, relief slithered through her when they moved out of view of the guards and into the receiving hallway for the kitchens. Even still, Dani glanced behind them, watchful of the corner in case the guards came around it.

Pepper let out a squeak of alarm in her ear a split second before Dani felt the jarring impact of her body colliding with another. Alarm blared through her, and from her periphery, she saw her body flicker into existence.

Dani tightened her hand around Iris' as she looked up and found Rhondae, the head chef of the kitchens, staring down at her. Or, where she used to be, since Pepper had pulled his magic back around them, his tiny body quivering against her neck.

Dani held her breath, holding herself still and hoping Iris did the same as she gave the female a warning squeeze with her hand.

Rhondae didn't move for a long moment. Then the female drew in a long breath. She looked up from where she'd spotted them and called out in Faerish, a bark of an order that had all the little hairs on the back of Dani's neck stand up straight.

Fear twisted Dani's gut, and her muscles tensed with the need to flee as she looked behind them, waiting for the guards to come running.

But Iris tugged at her arm, her body pressed to Dani's back as Rhondae turned on her heel and approached the double doors. Grumbling words that Dani didn't catch, and likely wouldn't understand even if she did, the large female yanked one of the doors open and shifted away from the gap provided by the door.

"Go," Iris' voice whispered from behind her. "She has opened the door for us."

Trusting Iris, Dani surged for the gap. She was halfway out the doorway when she heard Rhondae murmur in German, "Good luck, *Tana*. Take care of Iris."

Heart clenching, because she wished she could save all of these fae from Zeyphar, Dani tugged Iris along after her as they rushed out into a small courtyard. The cobblestones had been worn from countless carts, and Dani followed the wheel grooves out of the courtyard and to a gated archway guarded by four fae soldiers. A cart waited on their side of the gate, stopped as though the gate had come down before it could get through.

The driver of the cart was speaking heatedly with one of the guards, gesturing at the gate, then back at his cart. Dani watched impatiently as the exchange took place, acutely aware of how Pepper's breathing had started to pick up.

The dragonette was nearly panting in her ear from the effort it took to keep the magic active.

Finally, the guards relented, and moved to search the man's cart. They did a thorough job, investigating each empty crate and even under the cart itself, before they finally backed off from the cart.

Dani waited for the noise of the gate as it started moving upward before she tugged Iris toward the cart.

And found the female wouldn't budge. Dani couldn't see her, but she could feel the trembling in Iris' body. "For Ari's son, and for Kallen, remember?" Dani whispered desperately, eyeing the gate as it ascended.

Another moment passed, and Dani bit her lip to keep from screaming her frustration, but Iris' feet stumbled forward. Relieved, Dani hurried alongside the female as they rushed to the back of the cart as quietly as possible.

They'd just managed to perch on the back when the wheels creaked and the cart started moving. As the cart rolled under the gate and past the guards, Iris' shook so hard that Dani slipped an arm around her shoulders and pulled her in tight.

They were past the guards and onto the main road connecting the castle to the city when Pepper gave a whimper and sagged against her shoulder. The camouflage broke, and Dani tugged Iris down until they were lying in the cart, the sound of their shuffling masked by the clatter the wheels made against the stone road.

As quietly as possible, she urged Iris to take shelter between two empty crates, and Dani settled herself across from her, cradling an exhausted Pepper in her arms.

Dani inhaled her first real, deep breath in hours as they left the castle behind them.

CHAPTER · FORTY-NINE

THE WEST SQUARE

... a topic that was hotly debated before the Fae Civil War by House Druidhil. Their stance on Fae-Human relations, being in favor of building a relationship as opposed to a strict separation of Human and Fae, has led to...

- Gherald Schmidt, Faerloch Historical Archives

They were out.

They'd left the palace.

Across from her, Iris made a small sound, and Dani knew she was crying. This was the first time the female had left the palace in decades, and Dani knew those tears were happy ones as the female sucked in a deep breath of the fresh morning air.

"We did it..." she whispered, voice hoarse.

Dani smiled reassuringly. They were far from safe. They still had the city to navigate.

Knowing a forest dragon would stand out, Dani helped the exhausted Pepper slip down into the bodice of her dress to keep him concealed, his tail wrapping around her waist as he settled against her belly and between her breasts. He was barely conscious, but his little body fit snugly between her breasts, and it wasn't long before she sensed he was asleep.

The cart reached the bottom of the hill and turned into the city proper. Peeking out, she noticed marble houses and estates—the wealthy district. Dani ducked back down, and waited until the quiet and well-mannered streets were behind them, until they were on a street bustling with business and bodies. When the sounds of the streets were loud enough to cover their movements, she tugged Iris behind her as they slipped out the back.

She quickly fixed her head scarf and brushed her hands over her filthy dress, pausing to untie the bottom skirts. Worry jangled through her as she assessed Iris' rather haggard appearance, knowing she herself was no better.

They turned the corner and tried to blend into the crowd. Dani held Iris' hand tightly and kept her head down, praying no one would notice or comment about them.

Two streets over, and shock rippled through her as they passed not one, but a handful of clearly disheveled fae begging on street corners. As Dani eyed the crowd around them closely, she realized her worry had been for naught—many faerfolk were hustling from place to place wearing dingy, faded garments.

Iris, too, seemed surprised by the number of ill-fed and ill-clothed fae on the streets, and Dani wondered what the city had been like before Zeyphar took control. She'd always heard that the Silver Valley was an idyllic city. A magical paradise where the people wanted for nothing—not that she'd ever considered a fae city as a paradise for herself, but still. She'd always heard of its beauty and splendor, streets overflowing with flowers and lights and sparkling fountains and beautiful architecture.

There were fountains, and the buildings were beautiful, but between the elaborate structures were abandoned shops, unmaintained homes, and unkempt market stands. The beggars on the street distracted from any beauty that had been maintained, not to mention the less-than-pleasant odor that no flowers could mask.

"Iris. Do you know where we are?" Dani asked quietly.

Iris was staring around them with wide, sad eyes, and reluctantly dragged her attention away from a female fae and a bare-footed child trying to sell flowers half a block down. She gave Dani a solemn nod.

"Can you navigate us out of the city?"

Iris hesitated, looking around again. "There will be guards at all the gates," she hedged, fear creeping into her voice.

"Then we should go to the busiest exit, so we can try to blend in with the crowd," Dani murmured, tugging at Iris' sleeve to draw her deeper into an alley as she spied a patrol of guards who were walking the street and scanning the faces of those they passed.

"The gate next to the West Square, then. The square is very busy almost all hours of the day, especially with the market in the morning," Iris whispered, her voice trembling as she noticed the guards and huddled closer to Dani.

"We can do this, Iris. We just need to move carefully and slowly," Dani encouraged, offering her a smile she didn't feel. Between her breasts, Pepper wriggled, and she mentally urged the dragon to stay hidden.

"This way..." Iris pointed down the street, and they both waited until the guards were out of view before they began moving.

It was slow going. Dani's stomach gnawed with hunger and the sun peaked toward midday by the time they made their way to the edge of the square. It had taken them longer than Iris predicted because they'd needed to stop and hide so many times. Almost every street had guards roaming them, likely searching for them.

Iris slipped her hand into Dani's, voice thready as she looked around. "The West Gate..."

At the far end of the square, past the hundreds of bodies packed into the space, an entire squad of guards stood in front of the closed gate.

"Is that gate always closed?" Dani asked quietly.

"No," Iris whispered, face pale.

Dani drew in a deep breath and squared her shoulders. They'd come this far already, and crowds had helped to obscure them. They could do this.

Trying to bolster her own confidence, Dani squeezed Iris' hand and tugged her into the square. She didn't walk them in a straight line, but meandered and wandered her way through the market, occasionally stopping at stalls as if admiring the goods.

A guard somewhere nearby shouted something in Faerish, and Dani resisted the urge to look, keeping her head down as she fought not to break out in a sprint.

She was so focused on looking inconspicuous that she didn't see the fae who stepped right in front of her until she was already barreling into them. The tall fae flailed, and Dani was knocked against one of the market stalls.

Her scarf snagged on something on the stall, jerking her head back. Dani scrambled to keep it in place, losing her balance and stumbling to the ground.

Her hair spilled out from the scarf, shining a fiery red in the bright midday sunlight.

There were gasps around them, and more than one pair of wide eyes stared at Dani's hair as she desperately tried to shove it back under the scarf. Murmurs and conversation spread like a wave, with them at the epicenter as Iris cast nervous glances around them.

"They have heard of the female with fiery hair who is *mayted* to their lost prince," Iris hurried to whisper as she helped Dani up from the ground.

Dani stilled, glancing around as more and more fae stopped to stare, some openly pointing, others calling and gesturing. Dani shook her head, trying to secure the scarf back over her head, but her fingers were trembling too hard. "No, I'm not. I'm just—"

More gasps and murmurs raced through the crowd, and she clamped her mouth shut, panic crawling up her neck.

She'd spoken in German. Not Faerish.

The mutterings of the crowd increased, and she thought she might have heard her name a few times. They were gaining more attention than was safe.

More than one group of guards had noticed the commotion, and her panic transformed into adrenaline as the crowd began to shift to allow guards to pass through.

"Shit." Dani reached for Iris' hand and started pulling her toward the gate. "Iris." It was time to do the one thing Dani wanted to avoid, but knew she'd have to do regardless. "We need to run."

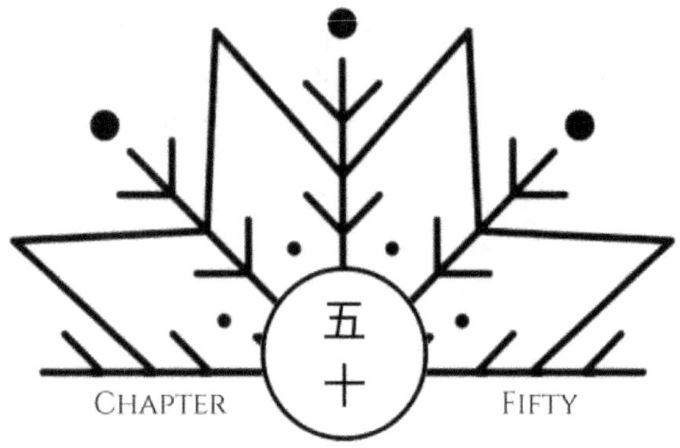

CHAPTER · FIFTY

FLIGHT FROM THE VALLEY

... have withdrawn the most from mortals—and even Lorekind itself—in recent years. Entire kingdoms, secure within mountains across much of Europe, have closed themselves to visitors. The highest number of surface dwarves can be found in Faerloch, where Dugan Stonecutter has organized...

- Gherald Schmidt, Faerloch Historical Archives

Dani pulled up short. She twisted to see Iris standing still, expression narrowed, all traces of her anxiety and fear gone from her face. The female appeared entirely in the present, with no traces of her normally unfocused or dreamy expression.

"Iris!"

Goddess help her, now was not the time to be standing around.

Determination sparked to life in her rainbow eyes, and Iris squared her shoulders. "If we leave this city, I can meet Ari's son? I can see Kallen again?" she asked quietly as she locked eyes with Dani.

"Yes, but we need to—"

Iris lifted her chin and shouted in Faerish. Her high, clear voice rang through the square like a bell, lovely and strong. She turned her head and met the eyes of many of the fae around her, continuing to speak loudly and insistently.

Dani didn't know what she was saying, but to her utter surprise, the group of fae directly before them parted, scrambling to either side and leaving a clear way for them.

Straight for the West Gate.

Dani didn't hesitate. She tugged Iris after her as they took off into the gap. Other fae began to press in, heads and bodies craning to try and spy Dani as they ran.

She heard hoarse shouting from the guards. Growing louder. Growing *closer*.

A panicked sob clawed up her throat, mixing with the breath laboring from her lungs as they sprinted. They were going to get caught. The guards were trained soldiers. Dani was a barely mortal woman with zero fighting skill, towing a malnourished, mentally unwell female behind her.

The odds were not good.

Panic surged, and something drove her to scrabble for her magic, as if she could sway these fae civilians like she could animals.

She knew she had absolutely no power over lore beings. Nothing mattered right then, driven by her desperate need to not fail, driven further still by her clawing, crippling desire to make damn well certain she escaped so she could save Slate from Zeyphar.

So she could save Iris. Save herself.

"Please move, please move," she begged, the sob ripping out of her throat, shoving the message with her mind as well as her voice.

Above them, birds took flight, scattering from the tops of stalls and buildings, flying *away* from Dani. She spied a nearby elk she hadn't noticed before, leading a cart, and the creature reared up, nearly tipping over the cart.

Maybe she could get the elk to...

Her thoughts disintegrated from her mind when she realized the fae before them were moving. Like a wave, the figures between them and the gate began to part, flowing away from them even as curious eyes continued to eat her up. Her senses were going haywire, and she could *swear* that she saw the heartfires of the fae nearest them ripple, like a wind had ripped through the square to make those inner fires dance.

Dani didn't question it, didn't think as she barreled through the open space, zeroing in on the West Gates, nearly twenty yards away. Iris was no longer being dragged by her, but now ran alongside Dani, still clutching her hand as she charged forward.

The guards were surging toward the gates, trying to shove past the crowd that lined either side of the now completely clear path to the gate.

Clear save for the five guards standing shoulder to shoulder directly in front of the closed gate.

"Please!" Dani sobbed, staring them right in the eyes as she rushed them.

A voice bellowed from behind them, enraged and commanding, no doubt ordering the guards to apprehend them. Panic drummed in her ears, and she squeezed Iris' hand as fear crawled into her skull.

Iris surged past Dani, as if she'd only now gained the courage or ability to tap into her fae speed. She dragged Dani's hand up, and shouted in Faerish once more, her words directed at the guards blocking their path as her expression blazed with determination.

Before them, pale eyes flickered, and time seemed to slow. It was the guard closest to her that moved first, swinging his body to the side and slapping a palm to his sternum.

"*Tana!*" he shouted, and he gestured toward a small door cut into the side of the gate, one used for individual passage when the gate was closed.

One of the other guards closest to that door broke rank and pulled out a ring of keys. Moving with the fluid grace that was inherently fae, he unlocked the door and threw it open before standing to the side of it. Like dominos, the other four guards shifted from their blockade until they'd formed a funnel for them.

All five soldiers, two on one side, three on the other, standing to attention with palms pressed to their sternum, flanking the door leading out of the city.

Dani couldn't believe it, her wild pace slowing as she stared at the guards who would likely be severely punished for this betrayal.

Iris tugged her forward now, her grip surprisingly strong as she rushed for the door, chin dipping in acknowledgment to each of the guards they passed.

"Thank you," Dani nearly sobbed, not knowing if they would understand her words but hoping they understood her intention. She met the gaze of each of them as they flew past, trying to convey without words her gratitude.

They offered her grim smiles in return, and the last one they passed said something in Faerish, but Dani caught two names.

Tanyiel-tana, and *Zlaet Titania.*

There was shouting behind them, angry and commanding, but the guards did not waver as Dani and Iris reached the door.

They shot through it, and Dani felt the shiver of a ward passing over her skin.

They were out.

They emerged onto a wide bridge separating the city from a meadow, behind which was the Forest of L'el. There were guards on this side of the gate too, but Dani and Iris' sudden appearance startled them, and the females shot through the guards before they could recover.

But they were fae, and the reprieve was short-lived before Dani heard their shouts as they gave chase, and they were bound to be faster than she and Iris.

"Run, Iris!" Dani commanded, eyes locked on the treeline beyond the small meadow and the Forest beyond.

If she could get them to the Forest, then there was a chance. Dani reached for her magic, desperately looking for wild heartfires she could call to aid. Anything. Anyone. Everyone.

Behind them, there was more shouting, and the sound of pounding footsteps in hot pursuit. A whimper escaped Iris, and Dani could see she was looking back over her shoulder.

Dani didn't want to know what she saw, trying to push her burning muscles to run faster. They were so close. Tears burned in the corner of her eyes, but she couldn't fail now.

"They're catching up!" Iris cried, and Dani's heart stumbled as fear rose like a *tsunami* cresting from behind.

They hit the other side of the bridge and bolted into the meadow, neither one of them daring to look over their shoulders now.

So close. They were so close—

A hand clasped around her wrist, halting her flight.

No.

"Iris! Run!"

TITANIA AND TANA

... direct result of a squabble for succession in the then-largest coven in Faerloch. Several mortals were accused of witchcraft alongside a number of actual witches...

- Gherald Schmidt, Faerloch Historical Archives

A missive from the Silver Valley sent Slate's council into a tailspin.

It wasn't the first letter they'd received over the last week and a half. The first had been an acknowledgment that Dani was, in fact, in the castle. Subsequent letters had been polite requests for Slate to join his *mayt* in the Silver Valley.

This one, however, had been a request for a meeting in an alternative location—Faerie Glen—in five days, with an assertion that Dani would be in attendance with Zeyphar.

"Yes," Slate had said immediately, not even reading the rest of the letter. He'd tossed it back on the table for Galyn. "Tell him I'll meet him right now."

"*Mai tatya*, this is a trap—"

"I don't care."

But his council cared, and so here they all were, four fucking days later, discussing plans and contingency plans and alternative plans and whatever else needed to be discussed.

It was maddening.

Slate wasn't even listening to the discussion anymore. He'd already long decided he was going to that meeting with his uncle, regardless of the consequences and regardless of what the council's consensus was. The chance of seeing Dani, of returning to her, was too agonizing a temptation to ignore anymore. The Malady was the least of his concerns—the physical symptoms of separation from his *mayt* were starting to impact him. His body was forgetting its own basic needs. Eating, drinking, sleeping... nothing happened with consistency anymore, his body so focused on trying to survive the touch starvation that he was starving in other ways.

The touch starvation was far more intense than it had been when he'd actively chosen to separate himself from her for several months, but then, the *mayting* had only been half-complete.

Slate paced the back of the room, too energized to stay still. Near him, Roger leaned against the wall, one hand in the pocket of his tailored slacks and the other cradling a small, worn leather book. For all the world, the vampire seemed consumed with his novel, but Slate knew he was listening intently to the conversations at the table. Waiting. Analyzing.

Just after Kari had returned from the Silver Valley, after the extraction team had failed, Slate had sought out Roger individually. The vampire had been a shadow at Titan's Fen for days, always lingering in the dark corners of meetings. He was never far, and Slate had found him one night on the roof of the manor, leaning against one of the pillars of the atrium situated there.

"At what point do we take matters into our own hands?" Slate had demanded of him. "How long do we sit here, doing fucking nothing? You're

a fucking vampire. *We have magic—"*

"As do they," Roger had replied. "Your thought patterns remain firmly fixed on your mortal mindset. Magic is not power when the enemy also possesses it. It simply is. And if used irresponsibly, it can lead to apocalyptic consequences. The systems in place are based on many millennia of history between magical beings to prevent cataclysmic events that shape the mortal world."

"So blowing up the Silver Valley will… what? Bring on the Dark Ages?" Slate scoffed, rage boiling through him.

Roger was quiet for a moment. "Every event in mortal history can be attributed to the irresponsible use of magic," he stated with infuriating calm. "Including the Dark Ages."

"How do you do it? How do you stand there, hands tied, refusing to do anything? This is Daniella *we are talking about!"*

"My hands are tied for reasons you cannot yet fully comprehend. It is not refusal. It is patience. Something you lack in spades. Daniella nor Zeyphar can remain tucked behind the safety of the ward forever, and when that time comes, I will make my move."

"And if she dies—"

"She will not, not when she is integral to your cooperation with Zeyphar. And if something should happen to her, I will not refuse you your revenge. That you can trust. Dark Ages be damned."

Saida slammed her hand on the table, anger clipping her tone. "Tanyiel won't even be there. I'd bet the entirety of the coffers on that fact. It is all lies, just like the last supposed meeting."

Galyn shook his head. "This missive is direct. And arranging the location to be hallowed ground on a blessed evening is a mark of good faith—"

"There is no faith between us and him," Jian spat. "Good or otherwise."

Slate paused in his pacing and leaned his shoulders back against the wall beside Roger with a frustrated growl. The vampire gave him a sidelong look before returning to his book and his cultivated image of detachment. Of *patience.*

There wasn't a patient bone in Slate's body.

"—bring the vampire—"

Slate checked back into the conversation.

Roger heaved a patient sigh. "I cannot engage in such a visual role within your war. The Vampire Council—"

Slate was watching Roger as the vampire stilled. His eyes unfocused for a split second before the book fell from his hand to thump on the marble floor at the same moment shadows thickened behind him, curling over his shoulders like snakes.

"Daniella nor Zeyphar can remain tucked behind the safety of the ward forever, and when that time comes, I will make my move."

And Slate *knew*.

He knew. The vampire could sense her whereabouts through their blood bond. She must be out of the ward.

"Roger." He grabbed the lapel of the vampire's sports jacket, crushing the luxurious material in his fist. "Take me with you." A beating, pounding need swelled inside him, starting in his ears, surging to his throat, his limbs. *Go, go, go. Go to her, go to Daniella.*

Roger's hand landed on Slate's shoulder, and the room fell quiet around them.

One heartbeat.

"Don't leave without me."

Two heartbeats.

An emotion flickered through Roger's mahogany eyes.

Shadows gathered with more urgency around the vampire, spiraling over him... and spilling over to Slate.

"Slate, *no*," Jian's voice was a whip behind him.

Kallen rose. "Zlaet, do not—"

"We will return," Roger said to the room.

The shadows swallowed Slate's vision... and they vanished.

Slate had never shadow-traveled before, and he decided he didn't particularly like it.

Unlike portalling—which was simply darkness between two points—shadow travel was more visual. It was like being on a raft piloted by Roger, on a black rushing river within a shadowy tunnel, moving far too fast for his liking. As they sped through this netherworld tunnel, Slate noticed indistinct shapes and light occasionally flashing past them. He realized they were exits, every shadow between Titan's Fen and the Silver Valley, egresses that Roger could take from this shadow highway. The lack of a focal point was nauseating.

Roger yanked, and sunlight bloomed around them as they dove from the shadows caused by the trees along the edge of the Forest of L'el. Slate's bare feet hit the tangle of undergrowth, and he stumbled forward a few steps from the momentum of the exit. He was just outside the Forest, on a wide strip of grass between the trees and a rough dirt road. Across the dirt road was a swath of river, providing a firm demarcation to the great, walled city beyond.

The Silver Valley.

It was his first time seeing the fabled city of fae, but its majesty was lost on him. Instead, he zeroed in on the wide stone bridge that connected the city to the Forest. Sprinting the last few yards of the bridge were two people, one as blonde as starlight and the other as fiery as the setting sun.

Dani.

Behind the women, soldiers raced over the stone, others following as they poured from the steadily opening gate. "There!" Slate shouted. Gods, they were never going to make it. The fae soldiers were too fast.

"Portal yourself," Roger commanded before shadows crawled over the male in a protective shield from the midday sun, but it was already too late.

A shriek echoed across the meadow as the soldier closest to Dani snatched her arm.

Rage boiled over as a snarl ripped from Slate's lips, one that echoed from the vampire next to him. Roger shot forward, too fast for the eye to follow. Slate threw down a portal, a cold focus slipping over him. He had one single-minded objective.

Get Dani.

He stepped through and in less time than a heartbeat, he was in the thick of the chaos. Around him, shadows exploded, a film of gloomy darkness disorientating the soldiers. Slate pivoted, wildly scanning the mayhem for a flash of red.

"Daniella!"

There. Slate's eyes locked on Dani's flaming hair, his focus narrowed to her even as Roger appeared at her side, ripping the fae from her arm and tossing the soldier over the side of the bridge with one hand.

In the chaos, none of the soldiers had yet discovered their prince was among them, and Slate shot toward Dani, Roger, and her companion. Through the shadows partially obscuring the vampire, Roger was nearly unrecognizable. Red eyes blazed like lanterns through the darkness, fangs and talons elongated to frightening proportions as he hissed menacingly at soldiers pouring over the bridge toward them.

"Rog—"

Dani's cry of surprise was cut off when something impacted the ground hard enough to make the ground quake under Slate's feet. He stumbled, catching himself as more than one soldier lost their balance. Shadows exploded around them like a bomb, and Dani screamed, grabbing her female friend.

Roger was gone.

Another explosion sounded, and Slate whipped his head to the side as a mass of writhing shadows appeared downriver, two figures locked in combat within the swirling darkness.

Holy *shit*, was that another vampire?

"Daniella!" Slate called again, pulling his gaze around as soldiers around them swiftly recovered themselves. The shadows surrounding them began to recede like the tide flowing out.

"Slate?" The feminine cry was filled with desperation, emerald eyes pinging wildly around as Dani clutched her companion closer to her.

Their gazes locked, and for a moment, the entire world faded away, time screeching to a halt as recognition crawled over Dani's face.

Slate closed the short distance between him and the females, shoving disoriented soldiers out of his way. His hands latched onto the women and he spun them out of the way as he slashed out a hand, a wave of telekinetic energy driving the soldiers back.

Frantic fingers clutched at him, and Slate pulled Dani against him, heedless of the female she kept a handhold on. "You okay?" he asked her briefly, sparing a breath to press his palm to her cheek.

She jerked her head in a nod, then gasped at a point over his shoulder. Slate spun around and planted a kick straight into the chest of an incoming soldier before twisting to lay out another with a deadly spin-hook.

This. Fighting. Something uncorked inside him, every long, desperate moment of crippling inaction over the last several days rushing through him, fueling him. He didn't think—he simply acted and reacted, countering blows, blocking, crushing through opponents indiscriminately.

Another explosion echoed, and Slate spared a glance downriver. The mass of shadows had collided with the Forest several yards down the river, and more than one tree felled like a giant's hand had smashed the earth. Roger went flying from the shadows, quickly followed by another figure, but Roger's feet hit the ward around the Silver Valley and he rebounded, fast and hard enough that he drove the other vampire back into the Forest, more trees falling as the vampires continued their fight.

Slate kept Dani and her friend at his back, flowing around them both effortlessly as he slowly retreated them toward the Forest while fighting off the fae, looking for a break in the assault to throw down a portal.

"We have to move!" Slate shouted, dodging a pair of wire bolas aimed at his shins. He relieved two soldiers of their weapons and plunged one blade into the hamstring of one before flinging the other sword, catching the soldier in his abdomen.

He didn't have time to feel anything close to remorse.

Dani's hand was on his back, her touch like a lightning rod to his blood, and the female with her clung close to Dani. More and more fae continued to pour from the gates at the other end of the bridge.

Slate threw out his right hand, blasting the closest fae back from them with his telekinesis, before he twisted and threw down a portal with his left, keeping his right hand up and a steady stream of force going to keep the fae at bay.

"Go!" he shouted, turning to urge the women into the portal—

A flash of golden light. A sharp object slammed into his outstretched arm, the impact jerking him around. His control on the telekinetic force field wavered as he twisted his stance to right himself, but his feet were trapped to the earth. He wobbled dangerously, windmilling his burning arm—an iron wire attached to heavy balls was tangled tightly around his right forearm.

Beneath his feet, a golden circle glowed, holding him firmly.

He didn't waste a second.

"Go!" he roared again at Dani, gritting his teeth as he fought to hold the portal open and keep his telekinetic blast going behind him, even as the iron leached the magic from his blood, his tattoos fading over his arms.

Dani's wide eyes locked with his.

He nodded at her.

She turned toward the portal. Relief filled him.

She would be safe. She *had* to be safe.

Dani shoved her friend forward, straight into Slate's portal.

"Kallen will find you!" she shouted.

The other female gasped, and Slate shouted, alarm ringing through him. "No, Daniella! Go with her! Now!"

"I'm not leaving you!" Dani blazed as she turned back toward him, determination plain on her face.

Slate snarled and the magic swiftly burned out inside him. The pale-haired female vanished along with the portal as Dani scrambled for the wire wrapped around Slate's arm.

Slate's heart rate jacked into his skull as panic gripped him. "No! Daniella, you need to—"

It was too late. His makeshift telekinetic force field died as the last of his magic winked out, and the fae surrounded them, overtaking their position, and before Dani's fingers could free his arm, she was wrenched away by two soldiers.

He whipped his gaze around, refusing to lose sight of her as he snarled at the two fae who pulled her back from him, holding her thrashing body between them as she screamed at them.

But she stood no chance against the strength of two fae soldiers holding her fast.

"I'll fucking kill you," Slate snarled, forcing himself to tunnel into his magic, forcing his body to push beyond the smothering of the iron. It was like trudging through cement and sand, pushing, pulling through sheer force of will. He could feel the movement of the soldiers' lungs, the beats of their hearts—

Slow steps crunched over the dirt at the end of the bridge.

"Well, well, well," Zeyphar greeted, appearing between two soldiers. "I could not have planned this better myself." He eyed Slate trapped in the golden circle, then shifted his gaze to Dani. "Thank you, princess, for helping to bring our prince home."

CHAPTER FIFTY-TWO

WILD MAGIC

... goes deeper than the empathy magic prevalent in the Titania line, superseding most forms of mind or emotional control and almost impossible to detect. Wild Magic can...

— Gherald Schmidt, Faerloch Historical Archives

Slate hadn't laid eyes on his uncle since that fateful night in the arena.

The scene felt eerily similar; Slate in the middle of a ring of fae warriors, unprepared and outnumbered, confronting the male who lived to make Slate's life as miserable as possible.

With Dani once again held hostage.

But she didn't look nearly as afraid this time around. A flush worked up her neck and across her face as she leveled a death stare at his uncle.

"I'll make my request swift," Zeyphar said. "You will return to the Silver Valley and behave like a proper prince should... or there will be consequences." His gaze flicked over to Dani, before returning to Slate's as a cold smile curled his lips.

"Fuck you," Slate growled. "And fuck your *request*." He'd just left a council room full of his best people. They knew where he was. And in the distance, he could still hear the distinct cracks and explosions from the two vampires locked in battle downriver.

Reinforcements were coming.

He just had to buy time.

Zeyphar's smile didn't waver, but those eyes, twin to his own, glinted with frost. The barest exhale of a sigh escaped the male. "Take her to the safehouse." He snapped his fingers. The two fae soldiers holding Dani nodded once, then one of them threw a portal down by her feet.

Panic gripped his ribs like a vise. "Wait... wait, what are you—Daniella!" He shifted, attempting to step toward her, but his feet were still trapped to the earth by the binding circle.

No. No, no, *no.*

This was happening too fast.

He needed more time.

"Let me go!" she screeched, digging her heels in and thrashing her torso. Her eyes glowed an iridescent emerald. "Slate!"

"Wait, wait, wait!" The words rushed out of him. "Wait—" His mind spun rapidly, swirling with panic. They were going to take her away again, to the gods only knew where. "Wait. I'll go. I'll go with her." He couldn't let her go through the portal without him. He needed to hold onto her. They needed to arrive on the other side together.

Wherever that was.

"No," Zeyphar said flatly.

A different kind of panic blazed across Dani's face, fury bleeding into desperation as the *entirety* of her eyes glowed a bright green. "No! You will *not* take him from me!" she shrieked.

Zeyphar tossed down a portal next to the binding circle and approached Slate.

"No!" Dani screamed, and the sound echoed in Slate's very bones, a reverberation that felt like the earth trembled beneath them.

Wait. The earth *was* trembling.

Soldiers shifted uneasily, a hesitation in the air as Dani's heaving breaths filled the space between them.

One breath.

Two.

Branches rustled, the sound growing rapidly until it drowned out all other sounds, a cacophony that vibrated through the earth right before the Forest exploded behind them.

Birds, rabbits, mice, owls, foxes, deer, and wolves poured from the trees like a wave of fur and feathers, snarls and shrieks rending the air as the creatures rushed the soldiers surrounding Dani and Slate.

Several fae scrambled back, alarm clear on their faces. Wolves and foxes ripped into the soldiers while rabbits darted underfoot, causing more than one soldier to trip. Deer wielded their antlers and bodies alike as birds dive-bombed from above, and mice scrambled up pant legs to bite sensitive flesh. The portal at Dani's feet vanished, along with the binding circle beneath him.

Zeyphar screamed with rage, and Slate saw his uncle blast a wolf that lunged for him with his telekinesis. The poor beast's crumpled body hadn't even hit the ground before Zeyphar charged toward Slate.

Slate tensed, his body prepared to fight, but Zeyphar never made it. A massive white body dropped between them, fur and feathers raised as a vicious hiss escaped Selene, wings spread wide in a barrier.

A savage cry mixed with the growls, calls, and screeches of animals. Slate whipped around, his body already moving toward the source of the scream. Dani thrashed in the arms of her captors, turning her blazing neon-green eyes on them. "Let. Me. Go!"

The reaction was immediate, both soldiers releasing her as if she were suddenly white hot, eyes wide as they backed away from her. Slate lunged, snatching her close to him.

"Do not let them escape!" Zeyphar shouted. Slate glanced over to see him dodging Sellie's beak and claws, attempting to parry against the female griffin with a long rapier sword.

Heavy wingbeats echoed through the air as more griffins descended on the scene. Dani frantically scrambled for the wire around Slate's arm, her fingers unwinding it from his flesh. Just as she got it free, shadows cascaded into the scene, adding to the chaos around them as darkness momentarily blinded everyone.

Slate shoved Dani behind him, the hairs on the back of his neck rising as a figure formed in the epicenter of the blackness. He held his breath, body tense, waiting to see who—or what—was going to emerge.

Red eyes and an elegant face he recognized appeared, and Slate sucked in a breath when he spied raw gashes that carved across his distinguished features. His tailored suit was littered with rips and tears.

"Go now," Roger said, his voice lacking any emotion. It was a directive.

And Slate was a good soldier.

In a whirling chaos of forest and fur, he threw down a portal, snatched Dani up, and fell back into it.

The last thing he saw was Zeyphar's red, furious face as he hollered in rage.

Then darkness closed around them.

CHAPTER · FIFTY-THREE

AFTER THE RAIN

... Bran Ewyt was key in incapacitating both the fae and vampire armies' generals simultaneously, working with Rowan Fafnir until his untimely death, which...

- Gherald Schmidt, Faerloch Historical Archives

The shadows had hardly stolen his prince away before Kallen was on his feet. Without a glance at the rest of the room, he threw down a portal and stepped in, so swiftly, it was as though he simply vanished with barely a glimmer of light. It was a matter of a few heartbeats to portal-skip through his various wards until he was at the gatehouse at the perimeter of the village.

He knew exactly where the vampire had taken Zlaet, and damn them both for going in on a whim.

Kallen barked some orders at the soldiers on duty along the parapet, then called for those soldiers within the gatehouse. He would put together a portal-capable team to support his prince, preparing for the worst.

He would not allow Zlaet to be a victim of Zeyphar.

Outwardly, he maintained a calm demeanor as he armed himself and shouted orders, but internally, panic gnawed at his insides like a feral beast.

Zlaet is not Aredhel, he tried to remind himself.

The prince was not incompetent—not that Ari had been either—but Zlaet was built for battle. Ari had been sharp of tongue and wit, but fighting and war were not elements that had come readily to her. She'd desired peace, unity, and love more than conflict, and in the end, her sentimental attachment to family had allowed her to walk straight into the lion's den and not return.

Zlaet was under no such nostalgic compunction for Zeyphar. Zlaet would slit the male's throat if he got the chance.

But that was cold comfort when the memory of his best friend's death still haunted him.

Mere minutes had passed since the vampire had vanished with Zlaet, but already a handful of Titan's Fen soldiers stood at the ready. He opened his mouth to issue the command to move out when shouts came from the top of the parapet.

"Lieutenant! A portal at the bridge!"

Jaw clenching, Kallen shoved his way through the small single-entry door built into the massive gate. Above him, he heard the light creak of bows as his soldiers readied themselves.

There, on the opposite end of the bridge connecting Titan's Fen to the Forest of L'el, a lone female stood. A glimmer of a faerie circle faded around her. She spun in a circle, looking lost and confused. From where she stood, Titan's Fen remained hidden by the glamour tied to the wards around it.

Kallen was already striding toward the female when she turned in his direction, and he caught a glimpse of rainbow-colored eyes. Kallen froze, the world around him ceasing to exist as his breath froze in his lungs.

Impossible.

It could not be.

He'd searched for days, weeks, in and out of months. Kallen had long since blacked out the memories of his frantic, suicidal searches. Eventually, he had heard from a reliable source that she had not survived the Great Burning. She was dead.

He had not wanted to believe it, had not wanted to cease his searching. He still dreamt about the day Ari had told him to stop. To allow himself the space and the grace to grieve, and to throw his agony at the Goddess and trust she would guide him out of it. It had been shortly before Zlaet had been born, Aredhel's womb swollen and full.

The presence of the baby, and the distraction little Zlaet offered, had been perhaps a blessing from the Goddess.

"Iris," he breathed her name like the very arrangement of sounds could bring him back from a waking death.

The female who couldn't possibly be Iris turned again, and he realized he was still invisible to her, still on the other side of the ward. Tremulous uncertainty filtered over her lovely face as she wrapped her arms around herself.

Just as she took a tentative step—in the wrong direction—Kallen forced his legs to move, forced his world to start again as he stepped beyond the ward.

"Iris?" he tipped it like a question, a mirror to his doubt, the name burning his tongue as he swallowed the painful hope clogging his throat.

The female spun once more, eyes widening when they landed on him, and he knew then. Knew without a doubt that this was *his* Iris. He'd long ago memorized the unique palette of each eye, how the colors mixed and blended. No one else in the world had those eyes.

"You really are alive..." Iris whispered, a broken catch to her voice.

Kallen opened his mouth to respond, not entirely sure what he was to say, but her eyes slid back into her skull, and he moved quickly to catch her crumpling form.

The reality of their current predicament crashed down around him, the moment shattering across the frosty ground like fragile glass.

Kallen cradled Iris to his chest, the warmth of her body a balm to his soul as he looked at her face, dirty and smudged.

Where had she been all this time? What had happened—

A shout from the parapets alerted him. Kallen whirled. There was a flare of golden light as a portal formed at the end of the bridge. Kallen shifted to shield Iris from any threat, focus locked on who—or what—might come through.

Zlaet and Tanyiel burst out of the glowing circle, stumbling to the ground, Zlaet absorbing the brunt of the fall as he wrapped his arms around Tanyiel. Angry red lines crisscrossed the prince's forearm, and Tanyiel looked as wretched as Iris, her hands wrapped in blood-stained fabric.

Zlaet recovered swiftly, shifting to his knees and tugging Tanyiel up until he could cup her face with both hands. "Are you alright?" he demanded.

She nodded rapidly, and that is when Kallen noticed her eyes. They glowed a vibrant green, which stood starkly against the paleness of her skin.

"I'm okay. Are you?" she asked, a frantic panic in his *Tana*'s voice as she gripped at Zlaet's forearms.

Zlaet did not even glance at his own arms as he released her face to tug her hands up, a ripple of rage darkening his expression as he gingerly inspected her wrapped hands. "I'll get Jian, he can—"

"Wait!" Tanyiel interjected, the glow fading from her eyes as they widened and her head whipped to the side, gaze searching, while one of her hands pressed against her chest, patting her bodice as if in search of something. "Wait! Iris! Iris?"

"She is here," Kallen said, surprised by the hoarseness in his voice as he looked down at the limp female in his arms.

She was *here*. In his arms.

"Thank the Goddess," he heard Tanyiel say, could hear them getting to their feet, but he couldn't look away from Iris' face. She was gaunt, pale, and far too thin. Though he betrayed nothing, a fury was building inside him.

At those who would harm her, and also at himself, for giving up on his search for her. Guilt rose through him like poison, seeping through his chest, through his blood, through his very heart.

He'd abandoned her.

Shadows coalesced behind Zlaet and Tanyiel. Zlaet shoved Tanyiel behind him, his body shifting into a defensive position. Kallen's heart skipped in alarm, and he fell back a step with his charge.

A tall figure manifested, and Roger stepped from the dark, though some tendrils of shadows continued to cling to him like a midnight cloak. Zlaet lowered his hands, a deep breath escaping him.

Had he been expecting someone else?

The shadows slowly peeled away, and Kallen sucked in a breath as he spied the vampire's face. Deep wounds like claw marks scored his pale flesh down the side of his face and nearly to his neck, the blood leaking down and staining the collar of his fine shirt. The edges of the wounds were stitching together, slowly healing.

Kallen's fingers tightened around Iris. Vampires could only truly be injured via a small handful of methods—silver, fire, sun... and other vampires.

And judging by the distinct shape of the injuries... Zeyphar must have a vampire ally.

The notion sent ice sluicing through Kallen's veins.

"Daniella," Roger murmured, the words soft and completely at odds with the lingering red that burned within the brown of his irises.

"Roger! You're face!" Tanyiel stepped away from Zlaet, reaching for the vampire's face.

"I am fine," Roger murmured, catching Tanyiel's wrists. He glanced over Tanyiel's head at Zlaet, and Zlaet tipped his chin in a small nod. Surprise had Kallen's brows rising as Roger tugged Tanyiel into an embrace, his long body bent to accommodate her smaller stature. Kallen could not see Zlaet's face, but he spied Roger's expression as the two males locked gazes over her head.

There was an understanding between them that Kallen could not fathom. To allow another male to touch his *mayt* after all that time apart? And a vampire?

Kallen's arms tightened reflexively around Iris, a protective urge rising that he deliberately shoved back down. He schooled his features once more, keeping his face impassive as he cleared his throat.

The vampire finally released Tanyiel, stepping back from her. Instantly, Zlaet tugged Tanyiel against him, and for good reason. It appeared his *Tana* was on her feet from sheer will alone.

"It is important this village remains a safe haven," Roger spoke as he slipped long fingers into the pockets of his slacks, gaze lingering on Tanyiel. "I will survey the situation outside the Silver Valley. If I uncover information that is pertinent to your efforts here," he slipped his attention to Kallen briefly, "I shall report them."

Kallen nodded. "Noted."

The shadows of the Forest thickened and spread around the vampire like an encroaching black fog. "Daniella."

She turned to him, body swaying slightly from the exhaustion written across her face.

"Be well, yes?"

She nodded and offered the vampire a tired smile before the shadows took him.

The moment the vampire vanished, the bravado leaked from Tanyiel's face. Zlaet scooped her up off her feet. She wrapped her arms around his neck, but not a peep of protest escaped her.

"Zlaet," Kallen beckoned softly, tipping his chin toward the village.

His prince nodded, and his crisp eyes bounced to the female in Kallen's arms, his expression unreadable. But he said nothing, instead leaning down to whisper in Tanyiel's ear something Kallen could not hear. But there was an agonizing tenderness on his prince's face that made Kallen look away.

He couldn't bear to see that, not now, not with Iris in his arms. He turned from them, giving his future king and queen their privacy as he strode toward the gate of Titan's Fen.

SAFE AND SOUND

... upon death, the kitsune's essence is reduced to a blue flame. Its mobility is limited, but if the flame can be returned to a known hearth, the body will be reformed over the course of several days. Should the blue flame be extinguished, true death will...

- Gherald Schmidt, Faerloch Historical Archives

Slate threw down a portal and scooped Dani against his chest, intent on taking her to Jian to be checked out. Between one portal and the next, he sensed her composure crumbling. Her emotions shifted from an adrenaline-fueled resolve into something fragile and exhausted, so he took them directly to their suites.

The moment he entered their rooms and shut the door behind him, everything inside her trembled. He waited, still as a held breath, but she held on like the last stubborn leaf of autumn. She sucked in a gulp of fortifying air and tugged at the bodice of her dirty dress.

"Pepper, this is a safe place," she whispered down at her breasts, and if he had anyone else for a *mayt,* he would have been surprised when a serpent-like head appeared from within.

Wait. Was that—

The small creature scrambled out of her bodice. No, not just a creature. A two-foot-long motherfucking *dragon.* It eyed Slate warily with its dragonfly-like eyes of a swirling deep orange, and a long, forked tongue flicked against Dani's cheek in a comforting gesture.

Slate closed the distance to the couch in the spacious sitting room, twisting his body to sit. The motion disturbed the little dragon, and the creature hissed at Slate before reluctantly scampering away. He heard it leap down from the couch, its claws scratching against the stone floors as it disappeared into the bedroom.

"Another member of the Pokémon team?" he teased gently.

A weak smile graced her tired face. "Where'd he go?"

Slate twisted his head around, scanning what he could see of their bedroom. "Bedroom. He'll be alright."

She nodded, and he sensed it in the heartbeat before it happened. Her emotions collapsed, and a sob tore from her throat. She covered her face with her hand, sucking in several rapid, hard breaths.

"You're safe," he said. "Let it out, love. I got you."

And she did. She buried her face into his chest, burrowing as close to him as she possibly could, her fingers latching onto his t-shirt. He shifted gently, cradling her closer to him until she was completely enveloped in the circle of his arms.

He stroked one hand up and down her spine, actively compartmentalizing his own feelings away as every thread she'd been holding onto came loose. Fear, stress, worry, exhaustion... it came out of her like one releases grief and pain, in great, heaving, senseless sobs he'd never heard out of her before.

"I got you, love," he murmured again as her body alternated between clenched agony and trembling exhaustion.

It was an act of severe self-control not to reach inside her mind and whisk away all her pain and replace it with happiness and joy and rest. He desperately wanted to fix it for her, to fight her demons for her, but her emotions weren't an opponent in a ring match. He couldn't protect her from her own feelings, and it spiraled a sense of helplessness through him.

She needed to get it out of her system on her own. That was the only way forward.

But she was crying like she was dying, and it was killing him, tearing him apart piece by piece. "Breathe for me," he begged quietly, lowering his face to press a kiss to the top of her head.

She tried, he could feel it, but her emotions were out of control, her body trying to accommodate them as she struggled to draw in even breaths.

He was going to kill Zeyphar. Not figuratively, and not metaphorically. He would slide a dagger right between his ribs and watch the life leave his eyes. Every scrap of fear, every thread of panic, every tear was another nail in the coffin for that bastard. Slate didn't enjoy the idea of killing people, but for Zeyphar?

He'd make a glorious exception.

Gently, Slate began to feed her threads of his love, his relief, his protectiveness. He wrapped those threads around her like a heavy blanket, a comforting weight to help ground her.

The sharpness of her emotions eased, and she took a couple of staggering breaths. "He c-can't ever have you," she gasped, her voice hoarse from crying. "N-never. You can never let him take you, Slate, he–he will completely unravel you until you don't know who you are anymore—"

"I know," he assured her, running his fingers through her hair, gently untangling the fiery strands.

"No." She pulled her wet, red face out of his chest and reached up to cup his face. "No, you don't know. He has these d-dungeons. Dungeons of *nothingness*. You go in, and you c-can't see or hear or feel anything. It's..." She shook her head mutely, fingers clenching against him.

Slate scowled, tamping down the vicious, cold fury that wrapped him in a swift vortex. "What?"

"He uses them to punish people—"

"Did he put you in that dungeon?"

She jerked her head in a short nod, and something haunted flickered in her eyes.

His rage trickled through his iron grip of self-control. Things around the room trembled, and the temperature dropped several degrees before he wrestled his emotions and magic into some semblance of control. His tattoos darkened in color as they absorbed the excess magic.

"He put Iris in there, too. Probably many times over the last few decades," Dani whispered hoarsely, shaking her head. "And others. They're all so afraid, the servants. I tried to help them. I tried to tell them all about you, tried to give them a little hope—" her voice cracked, breaking around the edges.

"Breathe."

She pulled in a few deep, shuddering breaths as she tucked her face back into his shoulder. They stayed like that for several long moments as he held her, until her crying subsided, her breathing leveled out, and her emotions settled down from their turbulent spiral inside her.

He sensed the moment she slipped into an exhausted sleep. Slate tipped his shoulder until he could see her face. She was out cold, breathing shallowly, her freckled face red from her tears. The skin beneath her eyes was bruised, her cheekbones too sharp, and where her face wasn't red from crying, she was ghostly pale.

She was drained, and while he knew some of it was from her time with Zeyphar, he was familiar enough with magical burnout to know it was a healthy contributor. The way she'd pulled the animals out of the Forest like that... he hadn't even known she was capable of that level of magic, to call so many animals at once.

It made him wonder if there was more to her magic than even she understood.

Slate pushed to his feet and carried her over to the bed, setting her down gently. He heard a chirp above him. The dragonling—Pepper, Dani had said—peered down from the branches that spread across the ceiling from the four posts of the bed. The faeries darted around him, chattering with excitement and wariness, especially when a thread of smoke puffed from tiny nostrils.

Hissing at Slate, the snake-like dragon scrambled over to the branches directly above Dani, then crooned softly at her, eyes shifting to a comforting periwinkle.

"Keep an eye on her, I'll be right back," Slate murmured to the creature, then strode from his rooms.

It didn't take him long to locate Jian. The witch-doctor had just
finished checking on Iris.

"You scared the shit out of us." Jian shoved his shoulder, his gray eyes
tingeing orange with his anger. "I'd say don't do that shit again, but I
know you."

Slate didn't have the capacity to feel guilt. "I need you to come look
Dani over." It went against his fae instincts to let anyone near his *mayt*
right now, but her health was paramount. He smothered them, reminding himself that this was Jian, his best friend, his doctor, and it was
alright.

"I was on my way to you."

They returned to Slate's suites. Dani was exactly where he'd left her,
but her breathing seemed to be easier and her face wasn't as red anymore.

Slate hovered annoyingly close as his best friend got to work, and he
hadn't even noticed he was growling until Jian flicked his nose. Hard.

"Growl at me again, and I will sedate you. Back up, and let me do my
fucking job, *ne*?"

To his credit, Jian was swift. He did a quick examination, then tended
to her shredded hands and a scrape on her shoulder that Slate hadn't
seen. Otherwise, Jian deemed her healthy, prescribed rest and a magical
tea to help her sleep, before Slate ushered him out of the room.

Dani continued to sleep. She didn't budge when Slate grabbed a wet
cloth and cleaned her face, nor was she disturbed when he braided her
hair and peeled her out of her dirty dress, trading it for one of his t-shirts.
She continued to sleep deeply.

So deeply that a part of him remained restless and on edge, despite the
fact she was safe in his bed. The utter stillness of her emotional grid felt a
little too much like the nothing he'd lived in for two weeks, and it grated
on him.

But he could be patient, now that she was here.

Sellie arrived not long after Jian left, and Slate knew better than to
get in her way as the griffin strode directly into his bedroom from the

balcony and curled on the floor next to the bed, her head resting on the mattress by Dani's legs. She seemed unharmed, though she was missing several wing feathers, and there was a gleam of rusty red on her talons.

Dash, too, soon found his way to Slate's chambers, having spent the better part of the last several days with Ebisu. Both the fox and Selene seemed wary of the dragon, but it went no further than that, all three creatures more focused on Dani than each other.

Slate watched her for a long moment as he sat on the edge of the bed, his palm resting on her hip. The physical contact was grounding, feeding the primal satisfaction that she was here, she was safe, even though their mental bond was quiet.

Gods, he felt fragile now too, like he might shake apart at any moment. He pressed his free hand to the center of his chest, something painful stuck behind his sternum. Perhaps it was his heart breaking into a thousand pieces over her. Only she could break him and mend him between one breath and the next.

His phone buzzed on his bedside table. He leaned over, tapping the screen.

Roger

In the atrium. At your convenience.

He bristled, instantly irritated at the idea of leaving her here, alone. But he needed to move, he needed the action. It made him feel useful, like he was helping, fixing, fighting. Something.

Slate eased off the bed. Instantly, Dash hopped into the spot Slate had just vacated, curling against Dani's stomach. He rested his little chin on her hip and whined at Slate. Slate scratched his ears before slipping out of the room. He glanced back at her one more time before he left, watching her chest rise and fall in slumber.

She was safe, and he was going to do everything in his power to make sure she stayed that way.

A DEAL WITH DARKNESS

... prevents vampires from killing each other. The Highest Law was implemented for multiple reasons, but topmost is the significantly lower birth rate than any other species in the lore, the price of being the longest lived of all lorekind.

– Gherald Schmidt, *Faerloch Historical Archives*

The sun had just dipped to the horizon by the time Roger slipped from the shadows and into the roof-top atrium at the center of Eas Manor in Titan's Fen. Exhaustion tugged at him, his skin hot and tender from overexposure to the sun and his healing wounds throbbed. He'd pushed himself to the limits today and would need to feed. He would likely require actual sleep soon...

His mind continued to whirl over the fact that Adeline was working for Zeyphar. He had not spared her a thought in decades, maybe centuries. But their long history had always seemed to find them on opposite sides of any conflict.

The first had been on Mensis Sextillis 18, 10 BC. The hot sun baked the bodies of those who'd resisted the occupation of the village of Moenus. It was the third Germanic village his legion had plowed through that summer.

But it had been the first to be the home of another vampire.

The first time he had faced another of his kind in true combat.

A moment etched in his mind for eternity, one of an immortal facing the first possibility of true death.

And also the moment Adeline had decided he was her enemy, in some kind or another, for encroaching on her territory.

Territory was something he understood, but to hold such a grudge over this much time?

And this wasn't the first time she'd found a way to oppose him, but for her to take it *this* far?

To risk the council coming for *her* over him?

Unfathomable.

And yet another threat he had brought to Daniella's door.

Roger's fangs lengthened in his mouth as he wrestled with the piece of him that grumbled and hissed over the fact he had spared Adeline a justified death. He'd wanted to rip her head from her shoulders, but that would only garner the attention of the Council more swiftly.

It was a fate he would forestall as long as possible, for both Daniella *and* Slate's sakes.

Quiet footfalls sounded, and Roger turned to watch as Slate prowled from one of the hallways that connected the atrium to his private wing.

Slate stopped when he caught sight of Roger, making no effort to close the distance between them. He might have been irritated at the boy for it, if not for the knowledge that every step away from Daniella right now likely caused him actual pain. Feeling gracious, Roger stalked the rim of the shadowy edges of the atrium, until he stood before the faeling prince.

Roger had not forgotten the heavy words that had passed between them the night of Daniella's capture. Assurances made, promises forged. It had changed something, turning whatever ripe and raw tension that had once thrived between them into something... less antagonistic.

Something that tasted like the rough beginning of a very long, very complicated relationship.

Acceptance. Tolerance. Respect.

"Silver Valley patrols are combing the Forest, but none close to the current location Titan's Fen occupies," Roger told Slate by way of greeting.

Slate's brows furrowed as a dark look passed over his face. "For now."

"Indeed. Also, not long after you escaped Zeyphar, there was a riot in the Western Square. It was put down brutally by Zeyphar's soldiers, but not before several groups escaped the city-wide lockdown into the Forest."

Surprise flickered across Slate's face, before his scowl darkened even further. "What kind of groups?"

"Apparently, people trying to escape Zeyphar's reign."

Slate nodded slowly. "I'll notify our scouts to be on the lookout. We will take as many refugees from the Silver Valley as we can." Slate paused, gaze snagging on the marks on Roger's face, which were not healing as fast as usual.

He needed to feed.

"So... do we have another vampire to worry about?" Slate asked slowly.

Roger's jaw clenched as he gave a sharp nod. "I have injured her severely enough that she will not be a threat for at least a week."

Slate's gaze narrowed. "She's still alive?"

"For the moment. To kill her would have brought the Council down on your head faster than you are prepared for," Roger murmured, his expression giving away none of the internal war he fought with the darkness.

It bucked and writhed for freedom, his blood singing for death, but he strangled it mercilessly until his entire body felt numb from the effort.

Perhaps he let out more than he knew, because Slate shifted uneasily as he studied Roger, before he finally nodded in understanding. Still, even as the wariness lessened in Slate's gaze, the male's shoulders remained tight, and Roger did not miss the way he continued to glance reflexively in the direction of his rooms.

"How is Daniella?" Roger asked, a question he had been burning to ask from the beginning.

There was a long pause. "She's asleep. A little banged up, but otherwise, she is fine," Slate answered.

Roger studied Slate's face, and read the rest of what he needed to know by what he saw there. Daniella's injuries went beyond skin deep, and the dark, silken voice within him whispered for murder, *mayhem*.

Though he kept his expression neutral, Roger felt his fangs lengthen as bloodlust simmered beneath his skin.

"The female she was with?" Roger asked, tone clipped.

Slate blew out a breath, hand rubbing at the hair shaved short at the side of his head. "She's asleep too, I think. Jian checked her out and said she was malnourished and exhausted, but otherwise fine. Physically."

Roger cocked his head, hands sliding into his pockets, at the dark expression that passed the princeling's face.

"He has these dungeons, she said. Almost sounds like sensory deprivation dungeons," Slate growled, and Roger's gaze flicked to the male's tattoos as they pulsed a darker color. "Zeyphar uses them to control people."

The darkness inside him coiled tighter, hissing through his blood in a song Roger could not afford to listen to, even now. "A cruel but effective tactic," Roger murmured, voice cool despite the violence stirring beneath his skin.

"He put her in one," Slate spat, shoulders tight. "I can't wait to kill that fucking bastard." He took a deep breath, making a visible effort to calm himself, something Roger was surprised to see.

While Daniella had been captured, the prince had either been implacable when upset, or unable to muster feelings at all, too deep in the grip of his Malady. Already, Daniella's presence was having an effect.

Roger watched Slate, watched the flicker of ice in the unusual blue of his eyes and the dark smudges beneath them. "Perhaps it would benefit Daniella not to wake to a half-dead *mayt*," Roger suggested dryly, despite knowing the answer.

Slate offered a half-shrug. "Can't sleep yet."

He'd expected that, could see it in the stubborn set of his jaw, this male who meant so much to Daniella. Roger surprised himself when he asked, voice unusually gentle, "Will you be alright until she wakes?"

Surprise banished some of the frost in Slate's gaze, and the male sucked in a breath. "Are you... are you genuinely asking me or is this an attempt at social niceties?"

"I am genuinely asking," Roger said smoothly, his amusement at Slate's shock dampening his own. "Daniella's well-being is tied to yours."

"I'm... yes. I'll be fine," Slate hedged, and he looked just as surprised by the seemingly honest answer as Roger had felt in asking.

He was sure that was a vast overstatement. No fae would be well if their *mayt* had been missing for nearly two weeks, but Roger was not the person to help with that. The two of them had already gotten as *cozy* as Roger was comfortable with.

"I have given it long consideration," Roger said after a moment. "I have decided that I wish to play a direct role in your war."

At Slate's silence, Roger looked back at him to find the *faeling* scowling, studying Roger as he crossed his arms over his chest. "Why? I thought vampires weren't allowed to get involved in other species' wars. You said it would be too great a risk."

"I did," Roger responded with an incline of his head. "However, the situation has changed. Zeyphar is unlikely to forsake Daniella as a target, and that is unacceptable to me. It is my belief that my assistance in this war will be a benefit to Daniella's safety—and your own— and therefore outweighs the risk. I will simply have to take care."

The scowl didn't lessen on Slate's face as he stared at Roger. "Does this risk mean we have to worry about vampires on our asses as well as Silver Valley fae?"

Roger's eyes sharpened, and his fangs lengthened at the thought of a vampire threat to Daniella. He knew the bloodlust was reflected in his eyes from the wariness that cooled Slate's gaze. "No. The risk will be mine alone to take. Previously, I would not have risked the wrath of the Vampire Council; not when doing so may have left Daniella unprotected against the dangers inherent in a life amongst immortals."

"And now?" Slate asked, voice deadpan.

"And now, I see that you are adequately equipped to protect her in my absence, considering the powerful allies you have surrounded your-self—and therefore her—with." The words rankled coming out, a part of him unwilling to admit that anyone could protect his light as well as he.

However, it was time to face the facts, and it was undeniable that Slate would do more than lay down his own life to protect Daniella. He would waste the world, if he had to. As was his duty, as Daniella's *mayt*.

"I'm not sure if Dani would be alright with you putting yourself at risk," Slate said after a long pause.

One corner of Roger's lips curled up, and he lifted his shoulders in a small shrug. "The risk is mine to bear. Besides, vampires are slow to act, even more so than the fae. It might be years before they rouse themselves in their frozen fortress to come to deal with me. Moreover, you are in desperate need of a proper spymaster."

Slate didn't answer right away as he studied Roger's face. Roger arched a slender brow, and Slate let out a breath. "I won't say no to more help. Especially yours."

Roger inclined his head. "I can also guide Karisi for your court. She is incredibly talented. With the right guidance and her particular magical talents, she could become an accomplished spymaster. I shall train her for you."

Slate's lips twitched into a semblance of his normal wicked grin. "She would like that. She's a voracious learner."

Roger shifted, the shadows unfurling around his shoulders as he straightened from the pillar to lock eyes with Slate. "There is another reason that has driven me to partake in your war..." he began. "I worry that you and Daniella are tempting forces greater than you understand, and I do not say that to be patronizing. You are a young half-fae prince in the middle of a war of succession, and it is the first time a half-blood like yourself has even had a claim to the throne. In addition to that, your *mayt* is a mostly mortal woman with magic long lost to the fae."

Roger inclined his head toward Slate's rooms. "Because of Daniella's relationship with Madeline, you have inadvertently allied yourself with the strongest witch Faerloch has seen in several generations. Loraine tells me the weres have begun stirring, becoming more aggressive with the increased fae activity, both in the Forest and in the city. Most unusual of all, you've also gained the undying loyalty of two highly unique Mystic beings. The twins are powerful. They are young, but I sense the otherness in them. And if I can sense it, it will not be long before other, greater powers sense their burgeoning becoming."

Slate's brows drew together. "Like who?"

Roger's lips curled into a smile with no humor. "The gods, Melisande. They are not tales, they are truth. The Goddess is only one of many gods who watch this world, filling it with magic. Too many strings are tying you and Daniella to old and new powers, and if that does not draw their attention, little will. I would be a woefully inadequate friend to Daniella if I did not stand beside her at the dawning of this new era."

"I have a healthy respect for the gods," Slate assured him, uncrossing his arms to scrub a hand over the shaved sides of his head.

"Hold onto that respect. You will need it." Roger tipped his head as shadows began to writhe and coil around his shoulders. "I shall take my place at your council table, princeling. To whatever end."

Slate nodded once.

Roger's form wavered like the shadows around him, becoming ethereal mist, but before he slipped away, he paused, and met Slate's gaze. "Thank you, Slate."

Once more, surprise flitted over Slate's features, and his voice was heavy with suspicion when he asked, "For what?"

"... for doing what I alone could not. You nurtured a single beam of sunshine into a summer sun. And I am grateful to bear witness to her warmth."

With that, Roger slipped away into the shadows.

NO MORE SECRETS

... distinct hierarchy within each pack, lending to a cohesive unit in combat. Because of this, werewolf packs are considered to be powerful and dangerous entities even within the Lore...

- Gherald Schmidt, Faerloch Historical Archives

Something startled Slate awake.

He opened his eyes, blinking and glancing around. The room was dark, a sliver of moonlight streaking softly across the lush rugs. The white mass that was Sellie still lounged on the floor by the bed. Dash, too, was still in bed with them. The little dragon was in the tree branches above them, as far as he knew.

Beside him, however, Dani was awake. She was sitting straight up, her breaths coming in fast puffs as she scrubbed at a damp face.

"Whoa, hey..." He sat up. "Daniella."

She flipped wild eyes his way. They were limned by that iridescent, magical glow. The moment she made eye contact with him, the color faded and a whimper escaped her. She moved at the same time as he tugged her to him, both of them coming together as she crawled into his lap. She buried her face against his neck, and her lips brushed the small scar there.

Despite the way her distress twisted through him, a calming warmth slid beneath his skin at the touch. "What's wrong?" he asked gently, resting his cheek against the crown of her hair.

After his talk with Roger, Slate had returned to his suites, stripped down to his boxers, and crawled into bed with his *mayt*. She'd continued to sleep like the dead, bone tired from her magic over-use and her experiences with Zeyphar. Slate had watched her sleep for a few minutes, listening to her breathing, but he too, had been exhausted, and sleep had found him swiftly.

"I was in that room..." she whispered against his neck. "The nothing room."

"Easy. I got you. It's just a memory."

"The dark makes it worse."

"Here..." He pulled back from her, freeing up his hands. He rubbed his palms together, creating tiny faerie lights that floated up to the tree branches, softly illuminating the room. The lights chased away the murky shadows in the corners, casting an ethereal glow through the branches. "Better?"

Her gaze tracked around the room before she nodded. "Thank you."

"Do you want me to make you some tea or something? Jian brought some valerian root and chamomile concoction earlier, but you were already asleep."

She rubbed at her face again, shadows still haunting her gaze. "That sounds nice." She hesitated, glancing down at herself, and her nose wrinkled. "Actually, I'd like a shower first."

He brushed his knuckles against her jaw. "Do you want company?"

Her eyes slid shut, like she was savoring the touch. "Yes, please. I'm not quite ready to let you out of my sight yet," she admitted quietly, making his heart clench.

They crawled out of the bed and into the expansive, open-floor bathing chamber. Dual sinks adorned one side, with a large closet for the toilet, but Slate bypassed these and headed for the shower adjacent to the tub. He'd once asked how such modern conveniences were built into a structure that was nearing two millennia old, but when Galyn had started to drone on about updates dating back to the 1800s and the origin story of running water and the convoluted history of human-Lore engineers, Slate tuned it out and simply counted himself blessed to have such luxury.

He turned on the faucet for the shower, divesting himself of his only piece of clothing before he turned and beckoned to Dani. She was standing in the doorway, gaze unfocused, her attention turned inward.

She stood so rigid, he was afraid a stiff breeze would shatter her.

He touched the *mayt* bond with his magic, feeling her emotions as easily as he felt his own. He could hear the echo of her terror from the nightmare, her lingering anxiety and panic from it still reverberating through her emotional grid. He crossed the space between them, gently tipping her chin up as he sought her faraway gaze. "Hey. You okay?"

She blinked away the shadows in her eyes, focusing on him. She nodded. Short. Once.

He shook his head. "No, you're not, and that's okay. You don't need to be okay yet," he whispered, cupping her face with both hands and bending down until he could press his brow to hers.

She let out a shaky breath, some of the stiffness draining from her muscles as a tremor racked her. They stayed that way for a few moments, neither of them moving even as silent tears tracked down Dani's face, each one a blow he absorbed without reaction.

He felt a shift in her, both with his magic and in the way she lifted her head. He slipped his hand down to take hers and tugged her toward the shower. Silently, she undressed and stepped into the space with him, face tipped up into the hot water.

He watched the fiery red of her hair darken to auburn as the water sluiced it back from her brow. His palms itched with the desire to touch her, but he didn't want to crowd her. Instead, he turned to study the array of glass containers lining one wall, searching for soap.

Different scents appeared every now and again, based on whatever flowers or herbs Autymn gathered from the private gardens. He had his eye on an iridescent pink one when the lightest touch interrupted his search. He sighed, savoring the physical contact as Dani pressed herself against his back.

"Touching helps," she murmured, her lips brushing against his skin. "In that room... I couldn't even touch my own skin."

The frailty of her voice ruined him. Carefully, he turned around and snaked an arm around her, tugging her close to his chest and he pressed a kiss to the top of her head. "Touching you is never a problem, love."

A watery chuckle escaped her, muffled against his skin.

His lips curved, sharp at the edges. "The problem is keeping my hands to myself."

She splayed her hands against his back, another ribbon of laughter escaping her.

She pressed herself impossibly closer, and he shifted them so the water kept her warm, running down her back. He could feel her emotions roiling and churning inside her, though he noticed they calmed the longer he held her.

"Do you wanna talk about it?" he asked quietly.

Her breath fanned across his skin as she let out a deep breath. "I..." she trailed off, and he waited, slowly slipping his hands up and down her back soothingly.

"It doesn't really matter," she finally said after a long pause. "Zeyphar tried to make me into something I'm not, tried to mold me into a tool to use against you, and he failed." She tipped her face back to look at him. "He failed because the thought of you anywhere near Zeyphar? I would never let him—" her voice broke, and she sucked in a breath. She held his gaze, and her next words were laced with steel. "My love for you is stronger than my fear of him."

Warmth at her words bloomed through him, diminishing the heat of his fury. He cupped her cheek, running his thumb gently over her lower lip. "I'm sorry," he said softly. "I never wanted any of this for you."

She gave a little shrug. "I know, but that's okay. *I'm* okay with all of it, because we are inevitable." She smiled, a genuine one that lit up her face. "That's what soulmates are." She released him with one arm and brushed her fingertips against the little scar on her neck.

His gaze zeroed in on the mark, a faster burn racing through him for a moment. He forced his attention back to hers. "I wanted you to feel safe."

He meant it. Gods help him, it was the fucking truth.

She held his gaze, her delicate fingers splaying across his chest. "Is that why you didn't tell me about the whole *mayt* thing? Because you were afraid something would happen to me?"

Slate didn't breathe for a moment, flicking his eyes between hers. He expected something else to rise to the surface inside her, like wariness or irritation or frustration, hell, even anger. But all he found when he gently touched her emotions was relief and love.

Such a strong love that it humbled him, made him weak at the knees.

"No more secrets, okay? Don't hold back," she whispered, raising one brow.

He shifted his palm to wrap around her throat gently, stroking his thumb over the *mayt*-mark. "I didn't know how to tell you without trapping you. This is not the life I would've chosen for myself, let alone for us. I would've chosen a quieter life as a martial arts instructor, and we could've had a house filled with animals and children and boring, mortal domesticity."

"How very normal," she said, smiling.

"I didn't wanna drag you into all this shit. It's so unfair, to take that choice away from you. And yeah, I was afraid something would happen to you."

And something *had* happened to her. Because of him and this fucking dangerous life he was trapped in.

She took his free hand and leaned back, pressing his palm to her chest. "Listen to me plainly. My heart made the choice a long time ago, even if I didn't realize it. I want *you*, Slate Melisande. Everything about you and your very un-normal life."

Releasing his hand, she pulled his face down to hers. "I do not regret a single second of my life with you," she murmured against his lips, and Slate's eyes slid shut. "Not *one*. You make me feel alive, and if I could go back to that night on the street when I first met you, I would do it all over again a thousand times if it meant I could have you. I'd endure Zeyphar all over again, because we are worth it."

She kissed him. Softly, the barest touch, but Slate felt it right to his toes.

"Again," he whispered when she pulled back, his eyes still closed.

She did, her lips easing over his. He slipped his palm around her nape and trapped her to him, angling her jaw to kiss her more thoroughly. He poured everything he had into that kiss, everything he felt for her—the love, the fear, the care. He mirrored it with a thread of his magic, letting her hear each one.

He felt her lips curve into a smile, felt the bubbling happiness in her grid that banished the lingering shadows of anxiety from her nightmare. Her arms slipped around his neck, her breasts pressing against his chest as she rose on her tiptoes to deepen the kiss.

Heat sizzled through his blood at the full body contact, skin to skin, so fucking good, it hurt. Along their bond, he sensed her emotions tip over, a ribbon of pleasure and arousal weaving through her.

His cock hardened against her stomach, and Dani arched against him, hips pressing forward as she slid herself against his suddenly aching erection. His breath hissed out of him, and in a single fluid motion, he hoisted her up. She took the cue and wrapped her legs around his waist, a little noise escaping her from the contact.

With one hand under her ass for support and the other curled around her nape, he used his telekinesis to turn off the water before he strode back into their room. She never once stopped kissing him, her hands in his hair, and good fucking god, the sensation was heavenly.

He dumped her in their bed, uncaring that they were both dripping wet from the shower. Vaguely, he was aware of Sellie and Dash vacating the room. His attention was on the feast of flesh before him. He chased water droplets with his mouth, swirling his tongue along her skin as he pressed kisses along her shoulder, up her neck, across her jaw until he could capture her mouth again. He slipped his hand over her ribs, thumb brushing over the taut peak of her breast, and she let out a moan, shoulders rolling.

He moved his fingers down her ribs, over the plane of her belly, and between her legs, slow enough that she was whimpering by the time he teased his fingers through her sex, finding her absolutely soaked, and not just from the shower.

She gasped into his mouth, her fingers clutching at his shoulders. "More," she whispered hoarsely.

He pulled away from her lips and offered her a wicked grin, before he kissed his way down her chin, across her throat, and between her breasts. He tasted every inch of her as he moved down her body, licking at the water droplets along the way. He kissed down her belly, shifting off the bed to kneel on the floor, before he feathered his lips over one hip.

Dani propped herself on an elbow, watching him, eyes rimmed bright green. "Go faster," she whispered breathlessly.

"Absolutely not." He tugged her legs apart, propping one over his shoulder and scratching his teeth against her inner thigh. She sucked in a sharp inhale, dropping back to the bed as her fingers curled into the sheets. Her hips rolled insistently, but he held her in place with his free hand, meeting her gaze. "I'm gonna take my fucking time."

He teased his fingers along the inside of her thigh, then slipped them between her folds. He reveled in the wet warmth he found there, rocking his hand against her until breathy gasps strangled from her lips. Grinning, he finally slid two fingers inside her at the same time as he dragged his tongue over her clit.

She cried out, head thrown back as her body writhed beneath his ministrations. He sealed his mouth over her, his fingers finding a slow, deep rhythm in time with his tongue.

This. This is what he wanted. He felt each shift in her emotions as if they were his own, her arousal pitching higher and higher, and he teased her, pushing her close to the edge only to back off and bring her back down just to push her higher again. It spiraled through him, jacking up his own pleasure nearly to the point of pain. She rocked her hips against him, like she was trying to ride his mouth. He locked his free hand over her hip once more, stilling her, and she whimpered.

"Slate, please..." she nearly sobbed.

Gods, he could come just with the sound of his name on her lips, spoken *just* like that.

He eased a third finger inside her, and her moan shifted to a gasping cry as her body rioted under him, her orgasm tumbling through her, her pleasure spiking so hard through her emotions, through his own, he nearly came right there with her.

She went limp, melting into the mattress. Slate pressed his mouth to her hip, eyeing her as she lifted her head to meet his gaze, her face flushed.

He gave her a sharp, wicked grin.

Dani laughed breathlessly, beckoning with a weak hand. "Come here."

He obliged her, gently removing his hand from her body and crawling over her. She scooted back toward the pillows, and he followed. Her fingers splayed over his chest, then slid over his shoulders until she was caressing his back. She pulled him down, and he supported himself just enough that he didn't crush her as he pressed his body into hers. The full body contact, her soft body pressed into his hard one, satiated the deep, crippling touch starvation he'd suffered. It was sensation overload, and he soaked it in like the frozen ground soaks in the first warm rays of sunlight.

He kissed her, tipping her face just the right way so he could properly pillage her mouth, tangling his tongue with hers, tasting every piece of her. He rocked his hips into hers, his cock sliding in a slow tease against her sex.

Gods, she was *soaked*.

She moaned into his mouth, her fingers digging into his shoulders like she could drag him closer, and along their bond, her emotions spiked hot, tipping toward desperate, pounding need.

He pulled his mouth away from hers and sat back on his knees, nudging her thighs farther apart. He fisted his cock, stroking himself once, hard, the pressure impossibly good, and her eyes zeroed in on him. Her arousal pitched hard, and his own breathing escalated to match hers.

Fuck him, he could probably come his entire skeleton just from her captive attention. He could *feel* how much she wanted him. It was entirely too tempting to stroke himself to orgasm just to feel her emotions jack up.

He wanted more. He wanted all her emotions inside his mind, until he couldn't discern where she ended and he began. It was a fierce, heady want, almost dizzying.

She undulated her hips, curling her toes. "I need—" she gasped.

"I know," he replied roughly. He rubbed the head of his aching erection against her entrance. Her arousal pitched higher, but this time, there was a tickling curiosity spiraling through her mind as well.

"Can you feel all my emotions right now?" she asked breathlessly.

He slowly eased himself inside her, the tightness maddening in its pleasure. "Uh-huh. You're very loud."

"Share with me," her words faded into a gasping moan as he pulled back and thrust forward again, working his cock into her. "Your emotions. Make us share. I want to know how you feel."

"Yeah?" He didn't mind sharing normal day-to-day emotions with her, but he'd held back during sex, cautious about overwhelming her.

"Please."

He started a slow, easy rhythm, driving deeper with each thrust. He leaned over her again, bracing himself on his arm, and he curled his palm over her throat. "Take a deep breath."

She did, and the moment she exhaled, he fed her all the threads of his emotions. The crippling arousal, the frantic desperation to touch and be touched, the intense desire, the addiction of the emotional highs...

And the love. Gods, the *love*. There was so much of it, it filled him completely, in all the space between his blood and his bones, and he shared it all with her.

Her eyes brightened, her magic responding to his. "Oh Goddess..." she moaned.

"Too much?"

She shook her head. "No. I want it all."

He gave it to her. He'd give her anything she asked for.

He captured her mouth in another bone-melting kiss, thrusting into her again and again in a lazy, rolling tempo. Her emotions ratcheted higher, climbing and twining with his own, both of them amplifying each other to new heights of pleasure.

She pressed her mouth into his shoulder, and anticipation had his blood roaring. "Fuck, Daniella, I'm gonna come *hard* if you do that."

She sank her teeth into his *mayt*-mark, and whatever edge he'd been teetering on, he launched right past it and into pure ecstasy. It was pleasure, it was pain, it was primal and feral and he came hard, shouting her name. He fucked her with total abandon, his emotions spilling into her with every piston of his hips.

He guided her mouth away from him so he could kiss her, drown in her, devour her. He tipped her head to the side and ran his mouth down her neck until he too, bit her. He felt her orgasm burst through his mind, and she screamed his name, digging her fingers into his back and arching into him. Until there was nothing left but a wild tangle of gasps and moans, feeding the touch starvation until it became touch overload. Just pleasure and love and contentment for them to soak in, limp against one another.

Slate kept a part of his weight supported by one arm, but let the rest of his body ease into her, savoring the warmth of her body against his. They stayed like that for a long time, until their heaving, ragged breaths leveled out, and the high of sharing emotions ebbed away like a drain pulled.

Eventually, he pushed himself up onto his elbows and kissed her—slowly, thoroughly, stealing her breath.

"I love you more than love itself," he said when he pulled back. "It's so far past love, I can't even explain it. I would fight death itself for you."

She smiled, crinkling her nose at him. "You like to fight, that's hardly romantic."

"I would fight death and *win*."

She laughed. "I don't doubt that for a second."

He gave her a wicked grin, starting another easy, agonizing pace with his hips. Her laugh shifted into a gasping moan, and his kiss promised a very long, very sleepless night.

CHAPTER · FIFTY-SEVEN

THE MAGIC WORD

... quality time, as dryads and nymphs are shy and reserved. The lack of touch between mayts (fae) and mates (were) can lead to detrimental health conditions. According to psychologists of the Lore, touch starvation is considered...

- Gherald Schmidt, Faerloch Historical Archives

"So. What are we, then?"

Slate glanced at her, a frown pulling between his brows. "What... are we?"

They sat at the bistro table in the sitting room, morning light filtering through the gauzy curtains over the balcony doors. Dani could see Sellie in her nest, and she even spotted a little orange fur and emerald scales tangled up somewhere in the mess of debris that made up the construct.

They'd spent nearly the entire night tangled together in one way or another; long bouts of sex punctuated by bursts of sleep. Dani felt surprisingly refreshed and relaxed, and she could tell by the cut of Slate's shoulders and the shape of his face that he was feeling similarly.

More Slate and less... cold.

Dani nodded to Slate's question, picking at the pastry on the plate in front of her, presumably left for them by Autymn earlier in the morning. She had her blue robe on, and Slate had donned his black *yukata* with the blue waves on it. "Yes, what does this whole '*mayts*' thing mean for us?" Dani asked, popping a piece of honey bread into her mouth. "You're a prince, future king. Am I a princess?" She thought about how the fae in the Silver Valley addressed her. "Does it mean I *have* to be a queen-consort?"

Slate set down the muffin he'd been about to take a bite of, studying her for a few moments. Finally, he offered her one of those smiles that melted her heart, because she could see how vulnerable he made himself with her. "So long as you stay with me, I don't care. You can be whatever you want to be."

Something in her chest warmed, but she raised a brow at him. "I'm sure it's not that simple."

"It is that simple," Slate assured her. He reached out and slid his palm along her collarbone and up her throat. "You hold all the power, always. Whatever you want, I will make it happen. You want to be a queen? I'll give you my throne. You want to be more behind the scenes? I will make sure that happens. You wanna watch the fae burn themselves to the ground in their own civil war, and we go hide in some obscure part of the world? I will make sure the gods themselves can't find us. I want what you want."

"Hiding from a civil war is tempting..." she mused in an effort to unstick her heart out of her throat.

"I'll admit, it's a top fantasy of mine."

She laughed, but she knew he was being totally sincere. Even though it went against a major part of who he was, he would turn his back on his people, for *her*. Would she want that? No, not when it would break something in him, but what *did* she want?

Would she be okay with stepping back, letting him handle the duties as *Titania* while she stayed out of it, happy as a veterinarian's technician?

To let him bear all that responsibility on his own?

She didn't want that. Being with Slate was more than simply being together. They were a team, and teams worked together and supported one another.

She'd made her choice. Happiness over safety.

But the other option... to be a queen? And not just any queen, the *fae* queen?

She thought about her time spent in the Silver Valley, thought about the servants and the soldiers who did not have an easy life under Zeyphar's rule. She'd been a princess to them, but to her, it was so much simpler than that. She was a person, just as they were, living and breathing and bleeding.

In a rush, she realized it didn't actually matter what the fae called her or what they thought of her, so long as she had Slate. Right next to her. All the time.

"I want to be next to you," she settled on. "So... equal. I guess. A matched set."

Something shone in the depths of his eyes, an ethereal shimmer as he studied her. "Are you sure? It's a lot... like, trust me, it's a *lot*."

Dani smiled. "I can handle anything with you."

That glow in his eyes intensified, and he gave a single nod. "Alright."

A hint of a smile tugged at his lips, but he was still staring at her, his eyes bright enough that he looked every bit the fae *Titania* right there.

"What?" she asked, when he still said nothing.

"I want you to marry me."

Her breath stuttered out from between her lips. She couldn't have heard him right. "What?"

"Marry me."

She was certain her heart stopped beating. He was still watching her, unmoving, and she knew from the slight flare of his heartfire that he was trying to get a bead on her.

She stared at him for several long, breathless moments. "Married? W-why? We're *mayted*, aren't we?" Wow, was that her voice?

"So? My mortal self still wants it, and even before all this shit happened with the fae, if you'd given me half an opportunity, I would've dropped to both knees and begged you to marry me." His gaze finally dropped from her face to the floor next to her. "Still will, if you want."

"You want me to marry you?" she squeaked.

Slate's eyes flipped back up to hers. "Yes."

"Like, husband and wife?" Her heart began to race in her chest.

"Yes."

"Like... a family?" Did her voice just crack?

Slate's lips slowly spread into a smile. "Yes."

He was serious. He was serious and... a flutter of nervous energy slithered out of him, matching the one pounding behind her ribs.

"Slate, are you—"

He surged out of his chair, and she sucked in a breath as both elation and panic bloomed in her chest when he dropped to both knees next to her.

"Oh Goddess..." she breathed, a flush crawling up her neck and filtering through her face. "Slate..."

"Daniella O'Callaghan, will you marry me?"

She covered her face with her hands as emotion overwhelmed her, tears pricking at her eyes even as happiness beat like a thousand butterflies inside her stomach. "Why should I marry you?" she asked him when he gently pulled her hands from her face.

"Because I asked nicely."

A wet laugh escaped her. She slipped her fingers over his jaw, cupping his face. "What's the magic word?"

"*Please.*"

She kissed him, and he dragged her out of her chair and into his lap, arms wrapping tightly around her.

"Is that a yes?" he asked against her lips.

She smiled. "That is a yes."

CHAPTER · FIFTY-EIGHT

FRESH BEGINNINGS

... and will co-exist within the territory of a larger pack, but they are law unto themselves. For example, wolves and bears share a symbiotic relationship in the wild and their werefolk counterparts will often...

– Gherald Schmidt, Faerloch Historical Archives

Although it was January, the temperature was mild enough inside the warded pocket of Titan's Fen that Dani and Iris went without jackets as they conversed together in private gardens three days after the debacle in the Silver Valley. Slate watched them from several yards away, shoulder propped against the stone doorway leading from the manor into the secluded gardens.

The entire town was in a tizzy over Slate and Dani's engagement. Gifts flooded the foyer of Eas Manor, and the two of them couldn't walk through town without being stopped every few feet. Slate wanted absolutely nothing to do with the planning part, leaving everything to Dani, Iris, Autymn, and the major-domo, Frieda.

Soft footsteps shuffled behind him, and Slate glanced back to see his father approaching him, a cup of tea in his weathered hand. Ebisu stopped beside him, his dark gaze tracking over the females. They crouched in the strawberry beds, picking the bright red fruits.

"Lady Iris is settling in well," his father murmured in his quiet, even tone.

"She was definitely a heady surprise," Slate replied. "The way Kallen talked about her, I figured she was dead."

Dani had told him Iris seemed more grounded here at Titan's Fen, though to him, she was quiet and nervous, like a fawn caught without its mother. He couldn't imagine living with Uncle Dearest for the last three decades had been good for her health.

"She has certainly changed from how I remember her," Ebisu commented, sipping his tea. "She refers to Dani-*san* as Ari occasionally."

Slate winced. "I'm sorry."

"It is not your fault. Her mind slips through time. I'm certain my presence is both a strange comfort and an aching nostalgia."

The barest glimmer of faerie lights across the garden caught his attention, hardly discernible from the afternoon sunshine dappling the greenery. Kallen stepped from a portal, his eyes sweeping the space until they snagged on the females.

On one female, if Slate had to guess.

After a beat, the lieutenant tugged his gaze away with seeming effort, and turned to walk over to Slate.

"I apologize for the intrusion," the lieutenant supplied in a quiet but urgent voice when he reached them. "There is a matter that requires your immediate attention."

Slate straightened. "What's wrong?"

The females were already approaching them, their idle chatter no longer brightening the air of the garden. Dani's brows were pulled together in worry, while Iris lagged behind, fingers twisting together nervously.

"Is everyone okay?" Dani asked, vibrant eyes flipping between Kallen and Slate. "Is it one of Zeyphar's patrols?"

Slate's uncle had flooded the Forest with patrol after patrol of soldiers after Dani and Slate's escape, combing the woods for any of Slate's people in what they assumed was an attempt at finding the current location of Titan's Fen.

Slate had issued orders to pull everyone back inside the ward except for the stealthiest of his scouts.

Slate glanced at his father, and Ebisu took his cue gracefully. "Lady Iris," he said, holding out his arm. "Shall we go inside? I could use some assistance preparing more tea."

Iris glanced at Dani, then at Kallen, before she took the proffered arm, gaze locked on her feet.

Dani watched Iris' face, and she gently placed a hand on the other female's arm. "Still want to go to the market together later?"

Iris hesitated, then jerked her head in a small nod, though she did not lift her gaze.

"Come then, my lady," Ebisu murmured and led her toward the manor.

They had gone three steps when Kallen blurted, "If you care for an escort to the market, I..." Kallen cleared his throat, the male's ears a vibrant shade of red. "I would offer my services."

Iris froze, and Slate held his breath. He couldn't read either one of them with any accuracy at all because of their mental shields, but gods help him, there was something electric between them.

Iris turned her head, but she never quite looked back at the lieutenant. Her lips parted, then closed, and Slate spied the way her delicate fingers dug into Ebisu's arm.

Without a word, Iris turned her face away from Kallen, and resumed her careful walk back to the manor, Ebisu patting the hand on his arm as he accompanied her.

"Lady Iris," Slate heard his father say to her, "let me tell you about the time when Slate was hardly more than a toddler, and he raced through Titan's Fen in naught but his skin..."

Slate watched his father escort Iris away, their voices shifting to Faerish and disappearing around the corner.

Slate eyed Kallen. For just a moment, Slate saw through the stoic facade—there was a desperate yearning in the lieutenant, an almost heartbreaking grief. Kallen's gaze lingered a moment longer before he finally shifted his attention back to Slate, all the heavy emotion evaporating from him.

"There have been no sightings of Zeyphar or his patrols nearby," he began, his voice a little hoarse. "However, one of our scouting parties found some faerfolk wandering through the Forest. They claim to have escaped the Silver Valley and are requesting sanctuary within Titan's Fen."

"Sanctuary?" Dani asked, raising her brows. She leaned into Slate, slipping under his shoulder and linking her arm around his waist.

"Did you bring them here?" Slate demanded, an icy shot of protectiveness barreling through him. He didn't need his uncle sending in a spy into his village, risking his people and Dani.

Kallen shook his head. "No. The scouts have them some distance from the bridge as a safety precaution. You should speak with them, both as heir apparent and as an empath."

"Ah." Slate nodded, understanding. He'd be able to tell instantly if the refugees were lying. He stroked his hand up Dani's spine until he could wrap his palm around her nape, leaning down to speak to her quietly. "Why don't you go see if Iris and my father—"

"Absolutely not," she interrupted him. "You go, I go. We are a matched set, right? We are a team, and that's how we are going to handle this."

The Malady instantly had Slate in a chokehold, a swell of cold barreling through him. He could see his breath in the sudden chill around him. "If something happens to you..."

"Nothing is going to happen to me," she assured him, resting her palm on his chest. The cold eased off as his empathy magic reached across their bond, the sunshine warmth of her determination and love thawing him out. "You and Kallen and a whole bunch of guards will be there."

Slate searched her gaze for a moment. Her stare was unwavering, but something in her emotional grid tapped against him, urgent and immediate. He turned to Kallen. "Go. I'll meet you at the gatehouse."

Kallen nodded once, pressing his hand to his chest before he vanished instantly.

Only the two of them remained.

"What are you afraid of?" Slate asked softly, reaching into her emotions once more and listening intently. There was a thin ribbon of fear in there, but he couldn't place the source. "You can stay here, it's alright, I won't let anything happen to you again."

She shifted until she could rest both her hands against his sternum. She shook her head. "It's not me I'm worried about. Part of me wonders if this is a trap for *you*. You know Zeyphar is after you—"

"Wait. You're worried about me?"

"Yes."

He caught his next words before they jumped out of his mouth. It was instinctual to assure her that he would be fine. Scripted, rote. He was a career fighter and a half-fae prince with untapped magical potential. All the trappings for reasoning to her that she had nothing to worry about.

But how easily and swiftly they were trapped by Zeyphar haunted him around the edges. The truth was, he felt as though he'd reset the last six months of brutal training, pushed back to zero. He spent the last three days punishing his body with fighting and training and magical exercises. Weakness was not a luxury he could afford for either of them.

He was still in over his head with all this war shit.

Her fear was as logical as his own.

Slate sucked in a slow, steadying breath. "We stay together."

She nodded, a smile stretching across her faerie face and crinkling her freckles. "We stay together."

He slid a hand over her nape, tugging her close to him, and pressed his lips to hers in a fierce kiss. When he pulled back, he threw down a portal. Together, they stepped into it and vanished.

Slate and Dani portal-skipped to the gatehouse just inside the large, reinforced wall at the entrance to Titan's Fen. Slate kept his hand wrapped firmly around Dani's as they approached, and his sharp eyes locked on an individual who peeled from the wall to approach them.

Basyl pressed his hand to his sternum. "Prince Zlaet."

Slate heaved an annoyed sigh. "Seriously. I kicked your ass this morning on the mat. Drop the formalities."

"Apologies, my lord." Basyl's attention shifted to Dani. "My lady, we've not been formally introduced…"

Dani smiled at the male. "I'm Dani, Slate's—" she hesitated, glancing at Slate. "Do I say *mayt* or… fiancée? Does it matter?"

"Whatever you'd like, love."

Basyl froze for a heartbeat, pinging his eyes back to Slate rapidly before returning to Dani. "Ah. It is a pleasure to formally meet you, Tanyiel-*tana*," Basyl responded with a delighted grin. "Last time we all saw you, you were a wrathful Goddess out for Zlaet's blood."

Dani laughed. "It was not his finest moment."

"I didn't kick your ass hard enough," Slate growled at Basyl.

They approached the single door built in the larger gate, and Basyl opened it swiftly for them. "Lieutenant Ewyt is waiting beyond the bridge. He will take you to where the scouts have secured the refugees. We found the group about a mile south of the bridge in a rudimentary camp," Basyl said. "They offered no resistance or violence when our scouts approached them."

"Civilians?" Slate asked. They exited through the door, heading across the bridge to where Kallen awaited them.

Basyl nodded. "Yes. Four adults, one adolescent, and two *faelings*. Though one of the adults is a soldier in a Silver Valley uniform."

"You left children outside in the winter?" Dani's voice was sharper now, and Slate almost felt sorry for Basyl as he floundered under the weight of her incredulous glare. She'd gone from a smiling sweetheart to a feral mother bear between one breath and the next, and he couldn't help the little seed of wicked pride that pulsed inside his chest.

The young male blinked, a flush crawling up his neck. "Apologies, my *Tana*. It's a safety protocol."

Slate didn't miss the way Basyl addressed Dani differently than he had just moments before, as if he'd realized he wasn't talking to a mostly-mortal woman, but his future queen.

"It's okay, love. Fae don't feel temperature the same way as mortals. They're fine," Slate assured her, releasing her hand to slide his arm around her shoulders, tucking her against his chest. He wasn't sure if it was to keep her safe, or to keep Basyl safe from her.

"My lady, the scouts have outfitted them with supplies and blankets. We are thorough, but we are not cruel."

Dani assessed him briefly, running her gaze over the young soldier from crown to boots. She smiled, and Slate saw Basyl visibly relax. "Thank you."

Kallen pressed his hand to his sternum when they approached him, and he had them portaled swiftly to a new location in seconds. They stepped out of the faerie circle into a small camp.

About a dozen Titan's Fen soldiers stood vigil around the camp, hands on weapons and bows loaded. Standing around the small fire in the center of the clearing was the group Basyl had described. Fresh blankets and cloaks covered their ragged forms, though it looked as though the one Silver Valley soldier had been stripped of his weapons.

Slate hesitated, a shiver of caution whispering through him. What if this was a trap? He doubted Zeyphar was above using children to further his own agenda. It would be so easy to bind him and Dani in a circle and portal them away...

Dani squeezed his hand, as though she sensed his wariness. "It's alright. Look at the trees," she said softly.

He glanced up, and he sucked in a swift and silent breath. All around the clearing, eyes stared down at them. Owls, songbirds, falcons, ravens... a veritable army of winged creatures watched the faerfolk, bright eyes refracting in the afternoon sunlight.

"Did you bring them?" Slate asked.

Dani nodded, eyes gleaming with a protective light when she glanced at him.

A shriek ripped through the air, startling everyone around them. Slate's gaze flicked up to spot Sellie circling above, sharp eyes on Dani as she descended. Completely ignoring all of the fae and their bows, Sellie landed gracefully behind Dani, ruffling and settling her wings. Soldiers touched their weapons, but hands fell away when Selene preened Dani's hair for a moment, purring. She even picked at Slate's hair, perhaps a little harder than necessary, but he considered it an honor.

And the message it sent was clear. Anyone who fucked with Dani or Slate fucked with a full-grown female griffin.

The crowd in the clearing shifted, turning to face Slate and Dani. The Titan's Fen soldiers immediately bowed, and when the refugee fae noticed, they too, followed suit.

A shiver of awkwardness raced through him. He wasn't sure he'd ever get used to this prince shit.

The soldier in the Silver Valley uniform stepped forward. "Tanyiel-*tana*..." the soldier greeted Dani first, pressing his palm to his chest. "Prince Zlaet."

"Do you speak German?" Slate asked in Faerish. He eyed the faerfolk. Behind the uniformed male, Slate spotted a civilian-dressed male and female pressed close to a baby held between them, another female with a toddler on her hip, and an adolescent *faeling* male. The female with the toddler had one hand on the teenager's shoulder, trying to hold him back despite the eager way the youth leaned around the soldier at the front of the group.

The soldier nodded. "Yes, my prince," the soldier replied in German, his accent thick and lilting. He gestured behind them. "They do not speak the mortal tongue. However, they understand a little."

Dani let out a gasp, startling Slate's heart into a rapid rhythm.

"I know you..." she said, attention trained on the soldier. "You... you were one of my guard escorts. You asked about Slate's fight training."

The soldier had the grace to flush. "Yes, princess."

"What's your name? I never asked."

"Cirdan, princess. Cirdan Leythia. I was in training during the time Princess Aredhel lived at the castle." He glanced at Kallen, who was stationed behind Slate. "And we all knew of Guardsman Ewyt."

"Lieutenant," Kallen corrected.

Cirdan nodded. "Of course, sir." His gaze shifted to Slate, brows rising ever-so-slightly as the fae took in Slate's fleece and athletic joggers, then over to Dani with her leggings and green sweater dress. "Tanyiel-*tana* shared many stories about you during her..." he seemed to flounder with the right word for a moment, "stay... at the castle. We have been looking for your small village, my prince. We are hoping for... safety."

"Did you escape during the riot?"

"Yes." He gestured to the others. "My *mayt* and two children, and my cousin and his *mayt* and child. We were fortunate to not lose one another in the madness."

Slate studied the group, flexing his empathy magic. Listening to emotions was almost as unconscious as breathing to him now, but those were just surface emotions, pieces that most people didn't bother to ward behind their mental shields. Digging into someone's grid for deeper emotions felt a bit like a violation of something vulnerable.

However, his *mayt* and an entire village depended on him to keep them safe. For them, he needed to be *sure* this wasn't some sort of trap from Zeyphar's.

From the soldier, he found surprisingly solid mental shields, but it didn't take long for Slate to pick the mental lock and crack open the door to his emotional grid. The fae had a rigid control over his emotions, but there was still fear there, as well as an uneasy sense of unfamiliarity.

Fear overwhelmed the couple with the baby, and he felt a similar, if more subdued, feeling from the female with the toddler. The teenage boy's emotions were spiking between fear and excitement, and Slate knew the kid was going to crash soon.

"Is it true you are a warrior prince?" the adolescent blurted in Faerish. "And Tanyiel can speak to animals? Is that her pet griffin?"

"Jhal..." the female shushed him, glancing nervously at Cirdan.

Keeping a tab on the soldier's emotions in case a curl of dark deceit made an appearance, Slate turned to Dani. "He asked if you can talk to animals, and if Sellie is your pet."

Dani smiled, and she reached back to smooth her fingers over Sellie's feathers. "No, she's not my pet. This is Sellie. She's my friend."

Slate translated for Dani and watched as the kid's excitement spiked, his fear dimming more and more in his grid. It was the icebreaker that was needed, and tensions in the clearing eased.

Dani invited the kid to come pet Sellie, who stood there with her chin tipped up like the queen she was, preening at the obvious admiration in the teenage boy's face as he let Dani guide him to gently stroke the spot where feathers and fur merged.

Slate watched the entire exchange, and from the emotions he picked up from the adults, he was pretty convinced they were exactly as they appeared. Only Cirdan's grid felt... off to him, but it was similar to how Iris' grid felt.

Traumatized, overplayed by his uncle.

Slate sucked in a breath and nodded. "Alright," he said in German, glancing at Kallen. "Let's pack it up, boys and girls."

Kallen inclined his head, and around them, the Titan's Fen soldiers began gathering themselves for departure.

"What's happening?" Cirdan asked, a spike of fear in his grid as he reached protectively for his son.

"We're leaving," Slate replied. "Going to Titan's Fen."

The soldier stilled, and Slate sensed a potent shot of anxiety that replaced the fear. "That's... all?"

Slate frowned. "Were you expecting something else?"

Cirdan glanced at his small group, then back to Slate. His son's wide eyes bounced between, trying to glean the meaning of the words he didn't understand. Cirdan placed a comforting hand on his son's shoulder, drawing the boy close to him. "Truth be told, my prince, we had assumed we'd be spending time in a dungeon of some kind until you deemed us trustworthy."

"We would never," Dani said immediately, indignant fury sparking through her. Slate knew her fury was for no one in this clearing.

"See, here's the thing," Slate started. "You can come with us... or you can simply go. We will hand you some supplies and send you on your way. Or portal you to the mortal city if you choose. It doesn't matter to me what you do, but you requested sanctuary, and I'm offering it. I don't need to manipulate you or force your cooperation or obedience. You come or you go. No tricks. No lies."

"But what if we are spies?"

"Are you?"

Cirdan's brows rose, and he shook his head sharply. "No."

"Do you plan to rage through my village and murder the civilians? Or burn my manor to the ground and attempt to slit my throat?"

Cirdan looked horrified. "No, my prince."

"Then what's the problem? I don't have time to manipulate or coerce everyone to like me. If you don't plan to cause harm, that's good enough. I don't care what people think about me. I've assumed the role of prince because that's what my mother left behind for me, and because Zeyphar started a fight with me. I don't start fights, but I sure as shit plan to finish this one. That's it." Slate shrugged. "I don't care about politics or power or the trappings of court. Either that's alright with you, or we can send you on your way. It's your choice. No harm will come to you or your group regardless."

Cirdan stared at him for several long moments, a wide-eyed surprise scrawled across his sharp features and his emotional grid, nearly overwhelming that... trauma hitch... that Slate could still sense in his grid.

Finally, Cirdan's attention shifted to Dani. "You spoke the truth," he said to her, a hint of disbelief in his tone.

She smiled brightly. "I told you. He's not his uncle."

"And I never will be."

Dani clapped her hands once with a wide grin. "Good! Now, let's all go get some food and rest." She turned to Kallen expectantly. "Lieutenant? If you could..."

He inclined his head with a small smile and threw down a large portal, enough for at least three people to step in at once.

A feat Slate had seen no other fae do with such ease and efficiency.

Kallen swept his hand out in a regal bow, gesturing to the portal. "*Tana.*"

For a single heartbeat, he saw her exactly as Kallen and the other soldiers did—a queen, dedicated to helping others, to leading these people with unrivaled compassion and consideration.

His queen.

Dani glanced back at him and held out her hand, her smile widening. "Are you coming?"

He didn't know why she bothered to ask. He'd follow her anywhere.

He slipped his hand into hers, tugging her close to press his lips to hers. "After you, love." Slate turned back to the small group of fae. "Let's go home, shall we?"

Then he stepped through the portal with his *mayt,* his love, his life, gesturing behind him for *their* people to follow.

CHAPTER FIFTY-NINE

LEGACY

"We should kill him," Slate announced. "Cut off the head of the snake."

Kallen huffed out a breath with a shake of his head. "My lord, I'm certain everyone in this room desires Zeyphar's death, but—"

"We cannot simply aim our meager troops at the Silver Valley and engage them," Saida snapped, blazing eyes boring right into Slate's. He didn't so much as flinch. "It would be suicide."

All the essential players were present and accounted for around the giant table in the council room: Galyn, Saida, Kallen, the squad leaders, Roger, the twins, Dani, and himself. Even his father had made an appearance, despite Ebisu's distaste for politics.

"He needs to die. It's as simple as that," Slate deadpanned, bracing his hands against the now-repaired wooden table. He offered Saida a wicked smirk that was more of a baring of teeth than anything humorous or kind. "Happy to do it myself, if there aren't any objections."

"We are not disputing that," Saida ground out, leaning forward in her chair. "His death is irrelevant if we are not sufficiently manned for not only the assault, but also to take control of the Valley in the aftermath."

"Forcibly removing a monarch can have... intense ramifications," Galyn added calmly.

Slate's fingers curled into the wood, and he opened his mouth to retort when a delicate hand on his arm stopped him. He glanced down to see Dani watching him, her expression grave but determined.

"I have an idea," she offered quietly.

Immediately, the room hushed. All eyes turned toward her. Dani smoothed her hand over his arm in a small caress, and the jittery aggression under his skin eased back. She turned to look at everyone at the table, and he slid his palm around the nape of her neck, his fingertips brushing over the *mayt*-mark on her shoulder. He shifted half a step back from the table, giving her center stage.

She hesitated for a moment before she cleared her throat. "We should continue the work I started in the Silver Valley. Our major problem is our lack of numbers, right? The more people we turn to our side, the better our chances."

"How do you propose to do that, *Tana*?" Galyn asked quietly, simple curiosity coloring his tone as he watched her with keen interest.

"Well... right now, the people in the Silver Valley are only hearing the narrative from Zeyphar's perspective. Our priority should be to change that narrative. If we can somehow infiltrate the city and create a different picture, I bet the city itself will do the work for us. Instead of trying to fight Zeyphar, we can help start a revolution right on his doorstep."

There was a pause in the room as everyone considered that.

"You're talking about espionage, *tori-chan*," Kari said, eyes narrowed in thought. "Spies to go in and sow the seeds of civil discontent." She cupped her chin in her hands and grinned, showing her canines. "I *love* it."

Saida considered Dani, head tilted slightly, before she slowly nodded. "If it's a game of numbers, the general population of the Silver Valley outstrips any military Zeyphar could enlist. We cannot underestimate the power of an angry collective."

"I agree with Daniella's idea," Roger's smooth voice came from behind Slate, where the vampire leaned against a wall as far from the sunlight as possible. "Zeyphar enjoys power, but above that, he enjoys control. He will not be able to turn his full attention to Titan's Fen if he is also dealing with discontent and rebellion in the city. He will want his city under his full control before he can amass troops to scour the Forest. The longer it takes him to control the city, the longer we have to prepare for his inevitable assault."

"This plan poses serious risks to the civilian population. They are not prepared for war," Galyn said with a grim expression. "There is the potential for heavy casualties. However, this could be the best course of action, given our other alternatives. Let the faerfolk know the truth of the male who leads them, and let *them* decide what to do about it. Provide them hope for something different."

Jian was already shaking his head. "No way. I don't like this. Sorry," he added to Dani. "This is some 'sacrifice people for the greater good' shit that doesn't sit right with me."

"That's because you're a doctor and you took an oath to do no harm," Kari said. "This is a war, *ji-ji*. People die."

"Karisi is correct," Roger added. "Death is imminent. From a political position, allowing the populace to spark the revolution will provide the people a sense of control over themselves, rather than seeing Slate as yet another oppressor coming in."

Slate pinged his gaze around the table. He hated this. He hated making plans and decisions like this, because it was easy to think about the fae as a faceless collective. Jian made a good point. Individual lives were meaningless so long as they *won*.

Along their bond, he could feel Dani's determination wavering as a little bit of that horror began to sink into her. He could tell she didn't want this, didn't want to ask innocent people to put their lives at risk.

But she also knew it was their best chance, both for him as well as for the fae.

For *them*. For their people.

He pulled her close to him, tucking her under his shoulder.

"It's a good plan," he said, feeding her confidence. "We can't control what Zeyphar does, but we can be there to pick up the pieces afterward. War is messy." He glanced at Jian pointedly. "We can't save everyone, even if we want to."

Jian pursed his lips together and huffed a hard breath through his nose. "Fine. Whatever you think is best."

Plans bounced around the table. A small team of highly skilled spies was created immediately out of fae Saida and Kallen recommended. They would be briefed and deployed within the week.

"Their mental shields are some of the strongest," Saida said. "Trained with Kallen themselves. As long as they do not tread close to the castle, they are more than capable of skirting under Zeyphar's knowledge. They need only find the right people and whisper the truth."

"I should like to inspect your team thoroughly, and if you are amendable, I will oversee them for you," Roger offered. His gaze shifted to Kari. "You will assist me."

She scoffed. "I don't take orders from you."

"But you take orders from me," Slate fired back at her. "And since when do you pass up an opportunity to spy and meddle? It's your favorite pastime."

She studied Slate, expression hard and calculating. He didn't listen to her emotions, but he knew she was thinking through the idea several different ways, and likely sharing her thoughts to her twin. "Do I get to go into the Valley again?"

"No," Jian growled.

"Yes, possibly," Slate replied evenly. He looked at Jian. "Listen, brother, you know she's perfect for this."

Jian shifted his attention back to Kari. "I hate this," he growled at her. "And I'm saying it out loud with witnesses."

Kari's expression lost some of its cool calculation for a moment, a swift softening that only those who knew her well would even notice.

Something else must've been said along the twin plane, because Jian sighed loudly and sat back, crossing his arms. But he nodded at her.

Slate turned a pointed look at Kari. "You're under strict orders not to get near the castle though, am I crystal clear? It's zero percent helpful if you die and send Jian into a breakdown."

There was a beat, then Kari grinned once again, foxy and devious. "Yes. Excellent. I suppose I will be joining you then, *partner*." She aimed her smile at Roger.

Roger's expression remained impassive, and for a wild moment, Slate would've paid good money to know what he was thinking. He wondered if the vampire realized what he was getting into when he offered to guide Kari's abilities.

"That leaves us with a final problem," Kallen said quietly, glancing toward the large archways that gave a view of the village of Titan's Fen. "As the revolution takes hold and people begin to flee, we will run out of space to house them."

Cirdan and his family were not the only refugees that were picked up by Titan's Fen's soldiers since Dani's escape. A pair of scouts found another group not long after; a small family of four, consisting of parents and their two children.

A few days after that, it was a handful of soldiers and their families.

Like Cirdan's group, all the refugees were found wandering the Forest by Titan's Fen scouts, and all were taken to the temporary camp set up away from Titan's Fen. Slate personally vetted each person, testing them with his magic, before he allowed them into the village.

There were bound to be more, especially if they planned to stoke the fires of this rebellion.

Kallen gestured toward the archways and village beyond. "The Silver Valley's population is almost ten times ours here in Titan's Fen. We cannot possibly house even a fraction, if we get more refugees."

Which was inevitable, at this rate.

"We'll need more space," Kari mused.

"It would take years to expand," Saida replied. "Carve out the mountains, expand the ward, build homes. We can't magically create more space in a matter of months."

"Wait," Slate said, mind churning. He glanced at Dani, and she sucked in a knowing breath, feeling his emotions and where his brain was going. "Wait... what if... what if we could?"

A week later, Slate and Dani found themselves on the desolate, icy streets of Faerloch, to the north of the Cliffs of L'el, the sun falling below the city skyline. A rippling of shadows next to them materialized Roger and Maddie, and yet another glowing golden portal blazed on the ground, and Jian, Kari, and Kallen stepped out.

Jian whistled low, sliding his hands into his pockets. "Slate, brother, when you said slums..."

"Okay," Slate started, "hear me out..." He pulled out his phone and pulled up a map of Faerloch, zeroing in on their current location. Everyone gathered around him, huddled together to watch the screen. "This street here..." He pointed to the street they stood on. "I'd say ninety percent of these are empty buildings. Some of them are for sale, but most are abandoned." He took a screenshot, then swiped until he opened his Photos app with the drawing tool. "I'm thinking we beg, borrow, and bewitch our way into owning the rights to as many of these buildings as possible, and we renovate them." He drew a circle around two blocks of the street, a reasonable amount of space they could possibly get their hands on. "And this becomes the new All-Manner District. Exclusively magical community. We catch the fae refugees from the Silver Valley, but anyone can live here."

He tucked his phone into his pocket and glanced at everyone. "Tell me I'm crazy."

There were several beats of silence. Slate reached for Dani's hand and squeezed her fingers, letting some of his anxiety and nerves bleed over to her.

"It's a marvelous idea, *cherie*," Maddie crooned. "Especially given the current climate with the fae."

"Fae wars do not resolve quickly," Kallen conceded with an incline of his head. "We should have the time to make this space viable for the refugees."

"Why hasn't something like this been done before?" Dani asked, turning her attention to Roger. "A magical district?"

The vampire shrugged, his hands tucked into the pockets of his slacks. "It's been my experience that while magical communities often overlap, they do not always overlap collaboratively. Historically, it draws too much attention from mortals. However, you have a unique perspective as being raised by humans. You have the potential to create this space without making it too... other."

"There are small communities in the city," Maddie interjected. "Many were-packs own entire buildings, and several covens also own spaces. But this would be much larger, and to offer it to all lore species? Quite revolutionary. Most in the Lore would not think to make a space shared with those who are not their own kind."

"Even humans do that," Kari said, brow furrowed. "That's why the Eastern District exists. Communities stick together and don't trust what they don't know. Fear creates racism."

Kallen nodded. "Precisely. Many fae would not consider leaving the Silver Valley or the other small forest communities when all of their needs are met without the discomfort of hiding amongst humans."

"Unless you have a mad king in charge, fucking up your city," Slate growled darkly.

"Who killed his own sister..." Jian added. "And is trying to kill his nephew."

"Are we living in a Shakespearean drama? This feels very Shakespeare-an..." Kari said.

"I met Shakespeare once," Roger said softly. "Interesting man. We attended a masquerade together."

Six pairs of eyes swiveled to the vampire, who raised a brow, expression mild.

"Roger!" Dani gasped. "Your age is showing."

"You slept with Shakespeare, didn't you?" Kari whispered gleefully.

"*Who* is Shakespeare?" Kallen asked, a shimmer of curiosity in his heather eyes.

Frustration mixed with a strange sense of agonized love seeped through Slate. He adored his friends, but right now...

He whistled sharply. All conversations instantly halted. "Hey! Focus!"

A rumble of muttered apologies colored the air from all but Roger.

Slate huffed out a breath. "I want a safe place for the refugees, a place that would be a pain in the ass for Zeyphar to mess with. The city makes it much harder for him to interfere. Here, they will be relatively safe, and they can help us renovate this place into a home for everyone."

"I think it's a great idea," Dani said, squeezing his hand. "And it would be nice to have a place for any magicfolk to come and just be themselves."

"I picture renovating these buildings." He pointed to the multi-level warehouses that bordered one side of the street. "We make them into apartments, with some shops at the bottom." He pointed to the center of the street, at the intersection between the two blocks he'd circled on his phone. "And here, at this junction, a huge community garden."

"We could make a community center," Kari said, pointing to a shorter warehouse on the other side. "A hub of sorts. We can put together some meeting rooms, set up some entertainment, a park, a place for classes or something, maybe a training facility for soldiers—"

"A school would be beneficial to the community here," Roger murmured.

"A clinic," Jian said, nodding. "A small hospital."

"An animal clinic!" Dani gasped. "Can we have an animal hospital?"

"Anything you want, love."

"You would need a market as well. Many fae are artisans," Kallen added.

"We would need to hook into the city's resources..." Kari mulled.

"We need to ward this place as well," Kallen mused, glancing around at the buildings curiously. "If you plan to have this many magical beings in one place, you cannot have mortals wandering in unwittingly."

"I can help with that," Jian said.

"I have witches who can help as well," Maddie added. "And we have our ways of navigating the city resources for power and water."

Slate nodded, slowly filling with elation. "We're gonna need some money..."

"We can pull from the coffers at Titan's Fen," Kallen said. "We are not without some wealth, however meager it might be compared to the coffers of the Silver Valley."

"The coven will help as well," Maddie said with a smile at Dani.

Dani turned a big smile at Roger, who let out a sigh. After a moment, he leveled Slate with a stare. "If you are unaware, princeling, I am quite proficient in real estate dealings. I will be able to assist."

"I bet our parents would be willing to pitch in," Jian hedged. "And there are a few in the Mystic community who would likely be interested in investing in this, I bet..."

Kari scrolled on her phone. "I know people who would probably want to invest in something like this, too. Loraine is having a meeting with the were-alphas in the area tonight. I can pop over there. I'm... friendly with them." She said it with a coy smirk, as though she were a bit more than friends with some of them. "I know the were-leopards are happy down south, but there are small clans of weredeer and werewolves I know who would love to be closer to the Forest."

"I want you to head this project for now, Kari," Slate said to her.

"Me?"

"Yes. Put that business degree to good use. You're a boss at managing projects. And you have a way with people to get what you want."

"It's called magic, darling." Kari smirked, tossing her rose-gold hair over one shoulder. "I mean, I suppose... I'll have to run it by my new boss first." She gave Roger a pointed look, raising her brows and linking her fingers together. "Roger-*senpai*."

Jian howled with laughter.

Roger's eyes narrowed, lip curling, but Dani burst out laughing, and Slate watched the shadows in Roger's eyes flee as the vampire cast her a startled look.

"Roger, it's like from one of those... cartoons I was talking about," Dani spoke through her laughter, waving a hand at him as she leaned into Slate.

The vampire's gaze back to Kari, even as the corner of his lip twitched upward. "Karisi, our espionage is the priority, but we will not be able to rush our expedition without risking lives. We will divert what time we can, but no more."

Kari's smile tightened, and even without hearing her emotions, Slate knew she'd slipped out of one mask and into another—this one more observing and shrewd. "Of course. I'll defer to you. *Senpai*."

Roger raised a brow. "Daniella, you must explain this word to me again. Soon."

"I can pick up the slack when Roger or Kari are busy, *mes amis*," Maddie interjected with an amused glance toward Roger. She turned her gaze to Slate. "If that's alright, *cher*? My coven will enjoy a little project."

Slate nodded. "Of course. That's why I wanted you here."

A soft silence fell around them as everyone glanced around the street, as if imagining its future.

"How will you govern this community?" Roger asked, breaking the quiet. "It will need guidance."

Slate dragged his eyes down to look at Roger, before he looked back down the street, the one that could very soon look wildly different. "I guess I imagined it would be self-governed... I don't imagine I'll have the ability to be the sole leader here. And frankly, I don't wanna be. The idea of being a fae king someday is exhausting enough between the Silver Valley and Titan's Fen."

"A council, then?" Maddie offered. "Representatives from the major communities who reside here?"

"Faerloch was once governed by a diverse council," Kallen said. "Before the First Fae War, over a thousand years ago. Overseen by the fae and the *Titania*, but also witches, werefolk, dwarves, vampires, even mortals, all had a seat at the table."

Slate nodded. "Then that's how we do it here. We go back to the basics, to the foundation. Strong foundations build steady homes."

He noticed Kallen watching him closely, a rare hint of a smile tipping the lieutenant's mouth. "What?" Slate asked.

Kallen shook his head slightly. "Nothing." His eyes bounced between Slate and Dani. "The Goddess has blessed us with an incredibly bright future, that's all."

Slate frowned, sensing there was more to it than that, but just as he opened his mouth to press the issue, Kari clapped her hands once. "The Goddess is about to bless me with a freaking drink," she declared. She circled her finger in the air. "Let's wrap this up, Sailor Scouts. The Den has a pint with my name on it."

An affirmative mumbling sounded through the group, and people began to peel off.

Until only Slate and Dani remained on the chilly street, hand in hand.

"You really think we can do this?" Slate asked her, gazing around at all the buildings until his eyes settled on her.

She nodded. "I think it's selfless of you, and it showcases how you're more motivated to take care of your people than Zeyphar is. You're committed to them, to their well-being and needs. And..." she paused, a thoughtful furrow crinkling her face, "Roger told us a long time ago that the Titania line was chosen to be leaders because they always put the needs of the faerfolk ahead of the nobility, right?"

"Right."

She gave him a little shrug. "Maybe this is the beginning of your legacy then. Not Aredhel. Not Zeyphar. *Slate.*"

He slipped a palm along her jaw and down to encircle her throat. And when he leaned down to kiss her, she met him halfway, tasting like sunshine and summer and warmth.

Emotion surged through him. Something that tasted like pride, mixed with a healthy dose of something too strong to be simply *love*. Because what he felt for this woman was so much headier than love. It couldn't be contained by four small letters. What he felt for her could start wars, end civilizations, and stitch together universes.

It was the beginning and the end. Cyclical and infinite.

Two halves, one whole.

"*Our* legacy," he said against her mouth. "Slate and Daniella."

She smiled. "*Titania* and *Tana*."

Always together. Never alone.

Just as it was meant to be.

EPILOGUE

Tierney Faolain, alpha of the werewolf clan Mac Tíre Ban, tossed his glasses on his desk and dug the heels of his hands into his eyes.

He huffed out a long breath and dragged his fingers down his face. He was absolutely knackered. Another long day of meetings and spreadsheets.

A ping from his email. He glanced at it, already prepared to put it off for the morning, but his golden gaze sharpened.

An alert. From a search he'd flagged ages ago.

Adrenaline spiking, he clicked on the alert. It pulled him through to a registry in southern Germany. Brows knitting together, he clicked on the PDF that triggered the alert.

It was a marriage certificate.

He scanned it. A marriage between a male named Slate Melisande and a female named Daniella O'Callaghan.

O'Callaghan?

But that name wasn't the one that triggered the alert. It was the name of the lass's parents, a required piece of information for marriage licenses.

Elizabeth Ceallachain and *Magnus Ceallachain.*

Tierney stopped breathing. Goddess, it'd been a long time since he'd seen that name. *Magnus Ceallachain*. Magnus Ceallachain was dead, along with his *mayt* Elizabeth.

Daniella O'Callaghan.

Impossible. After the death of the Ceallachains, their child Tanyiel Ceallachain had disappeared without a trace. Vanished into the wind. He presumed her as dead as her parents, as dead as Tierney's hope of finding an end to the curse on his clan.

Could it be that she survived?

He pulled up a records search and typed her name into the browser: *Daniella O'Callaghan.*

He waited, resisting the urge to drum his fingers against the desk. Seconds ticked by.

No results.

Tierney speared a rough hand through his white hair, growling under his breath. He typed another name into the search bar: *Slate Melisande.*

A plethora of surface-level information appeared. Male. 31 years old. Born in Faerloch, Germany. Parents were listed as Ebisu and Ari Melisande. Mother was deceased. Grandmother was listed as Sachiko Melisande, widowed. He attended high school in the city—Tierney briefly hacked into the database to peek at his high school transcripts and hummed a little approval. Boyo was right smart, apparently. Top marks. Owned a flat in the Eastern District in Faerloch. The website linked Tierney to a martial arts school, but it yielded little information other than a basic website with some school and instructor information and a schedule for classes.

He sat back, crossing his arms over his broad chest. His exhaustion had evaporated. His mind was now set on a trail, and he was nothing if not a predator. He'd see this through even if it took him all night.

He snatched his phone off his desk and pulled up Instagram. Typing in Daniella's name yielded more of nothing, but Slate's name pulled him to a page for the martial arts school. *Melisande Martial Arts.*

He scrolled through the feed, finding little of interest. A few pictures of chiselers in their wee uniforms and belts, no more than 5 years old, doing punches and kicks and shite. The page was small, with only a few thousand followers and significantly less than that following. Tier navigated to the "following" tab, searching through accounts *Melisande Martial Arts* found interesting enough to follow.

He glanced at his computer screen and quickly navigated to the *Instructors* page of the website. It was simple, but showed a list of four names as instructors: Slate Melisande, Ronin Konoe, Karisi Meho, and Jian Meho.

He turned back to Instagram and began searching Melisande Martial Arts social media for any of those names. He found one for Jian, *doku_sama*, but it was a private profile.

Tier moved on, scrolling until he found a user with a similar name to Karisi: *foxy_kari_sama*. Tons of images showed up this time, and Tier gaped a little at the sheer following this woman had. Hundreds of thousands of followers.

Not a single picture of her face, though. A bunch of body shots, showing off outfits and bathing suits or posed pictures of tea or gingko trees. She was an absolute ride, he'd give her that. Body for days, that much was certain.

There was a wedding photo near the top of her feed. He clicked on it to enlarge it, and he nearly fell out of his chair.

Two wildly beautiful people—a male with dark hair and bright blue peepers wearing a dark Asian robe of some kind, and a female dressed in a stunning wedding gown, her long red hair in a low ponytail with cascades of red curling over her shoulder, peppered with flowers. Freckles like faerie kisses across the bridge of her nose and her shoulders, and her eyes were wide, happy, and such a true green that summer itself was envious.

The caption underneath said: *I've never seen two more beautiful people in my whole life. Congratulations Slate and Dani!*

There were a lot of comments underneath congratulating the newlyweds.

Tierney couldn't take his eyes off the female. The red hair. The green eyes.

Dani. Daniella. Tanyiel.

A lightest tread of steps sounded outside the office door before the thing pushed in. "Whatchya still doin' up?" a male voice asked.

"Could ask you the same, boyo," Tierney replied, not taking his eyes off his phone. "Aye, come have a look at this…"

The male drifted closer. He was tall and narrow, with the same shock of white hair on his head as Tierney's, but instead of golden eyes, this male had inherited their mam's eyes of a crisp, glacial blue.

The male—Riley—stopped at Tierney's shoulder. He braced a long-fingered hand against the back of Tier's desk chair and leaned over. "What am I lookin' at?" he asked, his Irish brogue softer than Tierney's.

Tier zoomed in on the Instagram picture. "Look at the female there."

"Aye, she's a ride, I reckon. What of it? She's clearly married—"

"Look closer now."

Riley took the phone out of his hands and pinched his fingers on the screen, a frown between his brows. "Alright, well, she looks a bit Irish, I suppose, with that colorin'. Her oul fella's got the bluest peepers though—"

"I think that's Tanyiel Ceallachain."

Riley froze good and still at that. He stared at Tier for a long moment. "Tanyiel Ceallachain is dead."

"Look at what just popped in me email, boyo…"

Tier showed Riley the marriage certificate, the names of the parents, explaining how he came to that picture in Riley's hand.

"Impossible…" Riley breathed. The leather of Tier's chair creaked under Riley's grip. "Folk don't just vanish without a trace. Does she not have a car or a home or nothin'?"

"Could be someone keepin' her records clean… I can't know yet." Tierney plucked his phone out of Riley's hand. "But it'd be nothin' for me to ring up the Alphas in Faerloch, aye, and ask after a *Daniella O'Callaghan*. If she's got the magic, they'd know her."

"If she's got the magic…" There was so much aching hope in Riley's voice. "If she's the blood of the *Tuathe De Danann*…"

"Then we have a lead, boyo."

It was time for Tierney Faolain to make a wee business trip.

To Faerloch, Germany. The City of Wonder.

LET'S CONNECT!

What do you think? A nice, happy ending for Slate and Dani.

Or... *is it* the ending?

Please consider leaving a review on Goodreads and Amazon! Reviews are vital for self-published and indie-published authors. It helps other readers determine if this book is something they're interested in, boosts Amazon's algorithm with increased visibility, and is a great way to support your new favorite books and authors!

You should also join the #SunshineSquad mailing list! I mean, you've made it this far, through two books with intense action, heart-ache, high stakes, and gasping romance. You might as well join the #Squad. It's an exclusive newsletter perfect for casual fans and super fans alike! Be the first to know about new releases, book promotions, sales, deleted scenes, and ARC reader opportunities. There will also be some cat pictures thrown in every now and again.

Be patient with the load time... the website can be a little *dramatic* sometimes and needs a minute to get ready. #Diva

Before you run away, just know that we are endlessly grateful for every page read, every review, every purchase, every recommendation, and every post you share on socials. Thank you so much for taking this journey with us, with Slate and Dani, with this book and this series.

Peace, love, arigatou — Jess and Sierra

INDEX OF TERMS

<u>Definitions:</u>

Aura: Magical output, what others can sense on any magical being. Most magical beings—with skill and practice—can learn to mask their auras either partially or entirely.

Chi: *(Origin: Mystic Magic)* Life energy. Different than magical aura, chi is the amount of life energy in any living thing, magical or non-magical.

Dryad/Nymph: *(Origin: Lore Magic)* Creatures of nature who inhabit a tree or stream, tying them to the land. They are protective of nature, especially of their particular tree or stream, but otherwise nonaggressive. These women are sometimes mistaken for female fae, as both are often lithe and willowy in stature.

Dwarf: *(Origin: Lore Magic)* Lorefolk with strong ties to mountains and the underground, with the unique ability to handle silver and iron, which is harmful to many in Lorekind.

Fae: *(Origin: Lore Magic)* A race of beings prone to magic with a close tie to nature, like most beings in the Lore. They consider themselves the most refined and cultured of Lorefolk. Fae are often distinguished by their pointed ears, sharp, clever faces, large eyes, and uncanny grace. Fae magic is varied but includes such abilities as telekinesis, plant-based magic, portals, warding, empathy magic, and more. Fae react badly to pure iron, making city-dwelling difficult. Fae have an exaggerated life span of up to a thousand years.

- **High Fae:** A term used by the fae to refer to those whose bloodlines stem closely to the original 13 Houses, and has since come to mean fae nobility. It is a contested term by those fae who oppose the idea of classism among their race.

Faeling: *(Origin: Lore Magic)* A fae child, or young faerfolk.

Faeries: *(Origin: Lore Magic)* Tiny winged humanoid beings who stand no higher than three inches. Though they have no gender, their inherent grace is reminiscent of the goddess and so the pronoun "she" or "her" is often used when referring to a faerie. They are drawn to flora and shiny things alike, and are frequently mistaken for dragonflies by mortals. They are well known for their child-like innocence and love of mischief and gossip that sets them beyond the control of even the strongest in Lorekind, though they share a unique relationship with the fae.

Faerloch, Germany: A (fictitious) city set in Western Germany, about two hours north of Zürich, Switzerland. It is a sprawling metropolis with many sub-sections and districts. It is sometimes called the City of Wonder, due to its heavy roots in Lore magic.

Faerish: *(Origin: Lore Magic)* The language of the fae.

Familiar: *(Origin: Lore Magic)* A witch's companion, often a cat or a crow, sometimes a snake or even a fox. Familiars are sentient, capable of mortal speech, and often have extended lives.

Four Gods of Creation: Children to the Mother of the Cosmos, four gods who were given the power to breathe life into the world. They are as follows:

- The Wise Father, who was the first among them and who favored the vast continent of Africa, and created Tribalistic Magic.

- The Jade Emperor, who made his mark in the vast lands to the East, and created Mystic Magic.

- The Goddess of the Wood and Wild, who favored the middle lands of Europe, creator of Lore Magic.

- The Great Spirit, the youngest of them, who favored the Americas and created Shamanistic Magic.

(The) Forest of L'el: A large forest that spans the western border of Germany, sometimes called the Black Forest by mortals. The Forest of L'el runs parallel to Germany's western border, north to south, and bleeds over into parts of France. The trees are ancient, thick, and towering, and magic soaks the land. It has survived when other forests fell to the modern logging industry because of this magic, which makes mortals forget their intentions upon crossing L'el's boundary. Magicfolk believe the Forest is alive and sentient, and it is thought to be the birthplace of the Lore, particularly the fae.

Goddess of the Wood and Wild: *(Origin: Lore Magic)* The mother of the Lore. She created all beings of European magic. She is one of the Four Gods of Creation.

Kitsune: *(Origin: Mystic Magic)* A female-exclusive race of fox spirits. Rare, extremely powerful, and capable of great magic, it is thought that *kitsune* are the right-hand females of the Jade Emperor himself, the Father of Mystic Magic. They are renowned for knowing a great deal about the world due to their innate curiosity and highly observant natures. They can take the form of a fox, mortal, or a combination of both, and are masters of fire, illusions, tricks, and other sleight of hand magicks. Upon reaching a certain age, they are also capable of intense regenerative magic, essentially making them immortal.

Lorefolk: *(Origin: Lore Magic)* A general term for beings all belonging to the magic of Lore—the European branch of magic.

Lorekissed: *(Origin: Lore Magic)* A human with a drop of magic in their blood from some distant Lorefolk ancestor. Some manifest a weak talent for magic, others gain physical advantages, but most never become aware of their ancestry.

Manyeo (witch-doctor): *(Origin: Mystic Magic)* An Eastern witch with the ability to see and manipulate the *chi* in living things in order to create potions, medicines, and healing poultices. Most *manyeo* become witch-doctors by trade, but some prefer to deviate from the art of magical medicine and pursue careers in enchantment work. Enchantment work involves manipulating a being's *chi*, often through tattoos or other permanent markings, to keep an enchantment active. Enchantments can be attached to non-living objects—such as in the creation of wards—but each enchantment still requires a *chi* signature from either the *manyeo* or the client. Manyeo have exaggerated lifespans, upwards of several hundred years. **Manyeo is a fictitious being created for this world/book series.*

Miko: A priestess of a Japanese Shinto Temple. They typically wear a traditional red *hakama* (top) and white *kosode* (pants).

Mysticfolk: *(Origin: Mystic Magic)* A general term for all beings belonging to the magic of the Mystics—Eastern magic.

Shintoism: A Japanese religion in which the core belief revolves around gods (kami) and spirits inhabiting the world around us.

Silver Valley: A large fae city whose location within the Forest of L'el shifts constantly with the magic of the forest. It is considered the seat of power for the fae, and is overseen by the High Fae Council and the *Titania*—the leader of the fae.

Taekwondo: A Korean martial art that developed in the 1950s in Korea, during the Japanese occupation. It takes many of its movements and foundations from Karate, once being called "Korean Karate." It's known for its aerial kicking and recognition in the Olympics for its full-contact and point-based fighting.

Tamashoko *(tama - soul, sho - together, ko - heart) (Origin: Mystic Magic)*: In the Mystics, the idea of a soulmate exists. The red thread of fate binds two people together forever.

Tei Enaid: *(Origin: Lore Magic)* This is what the witches refer to as a soulmate—the person they are meant to be with. Witches often tie their life energies together if they are Tei Enaid. In the case of non-witches, tying life energies together through witchcraft results in the partners sharing the combined lifespans. Because of this, beings with shorter lifespans, including mortals, gain extended life and youth.

Titan's Fen: A small town in the Forest of L'el. It was once the summer retreat for the royal fae family.

Witch: *(Origin: Lore Magic)* A race whose magic favors the females of their lineage, with only rare cases of males born of witches developing magic. Their magic stems from their ability to control one or more elements: water, fire, earth, and air. Witches practice their magic in covens and peddle their enchantments to any with the coin to pay for them. Witches have an exaggerated life span of several hundred years, but also possess the ability to tie the lifespans of two beings together through a blood-tie, allowing species of dissimilar lifespans to mate.

Were (werefolk): *(Origin: Lore Magic)* A race of beings who have two skins, one human and one animal. They can shift between their animal form and human form at will (despite human superstitions involving full moons), and boast the fastest regenerative abilities in the Lore. Their lifespans differ based on the species of their inner beast, from a few hundred years to over a thousand, but all share a weakness to silver, as silver interrupts the regenerative magic.

Vampire: *(Origin: Lore Magic)* Thought to be the first among the Lore created by the Goddess, vampires are creatures of the night. Their solitary nature and low reproductive rates mean they are the rarest beings in the Lore, especially after a bloody civil war decimated their numbers centuries ago. They are the longest-lived, and prone to an arrogant and secretive nature that has done little to bolster their waning numbers. It is unknown if they can die from old age. They consume food as well as blood, and are sensitive to fire, silver, and the sun.

Yokai: *(Origin: Mystic Magic)* A demon from Japanese mythology.

Languages:

Japanese:

Ai: Love

Baka: Stupid, idiot

Domo: Thank you.

Gaijin: Foreigner, or anyone who isn't strictly Japanese.

Happi: A Japanese short sleeved short robe, usually open in the front. Like a short house coat.

Hajimemashite: Nice to meet you.

Inari: Fox deities, often depicted in shrines.

Izakaya: A traditional Japanese bar.

-chan: A Japanese honorific and term of endearment, usually reserved for children or between female friends. It's also a diminutive term, used for anything small and cute.

-kun: A Japanese honorific usually reserved for younger boys and men, added to the end of their name. It has a certain level of familiarity to it, meaning the two people know each other well.

-san: A Japanese honorific which roughly translates to "Mr." or "Miss/Mrs."

Musuko: My son

Ohayo: Good morning

Oyaji/Oto-san: Father.

Ossan: Old man.

Okaa-san: Mother.

Ojii-san/Jii-chan: Grandfather/old man.

Obaa-san/baa-chan: Grandmother/old woman.

Ototo-kun: Little brother

Okaeri: A phrase said in response to *tadaima*, loosely meaning "welcome home".

Oyasuminasai: Good night

Ne: A word that denotes a question or a confirmation. English equivalent of tacking on a "ya?" to the end of a sentence.

Noren: A tapestry.

Kampai: Cheers!

Kami: God/gods. Lowercase *kami* is many gods or minor gods, and uppercase *Kami* is larger deities.

Kotatsu: A low, heated table commonly found in Japanese houses.

Sayonara: Good bye

Senpai: An older student of an organization who mentors younger classmates.

Torii: A red arch that denotes an entrance to a sacred space.

Tadaima: A phrase said when someone returns home from being out.

Faerish:

Mayt: The Faerish term for soulmates. The fae believe that *mayts* are destined to be together, chosen by the Goddess at the inception of magic in the world. *Mayts* are often marked by a scar from a bite, typically found on the neck or shoulder.

Titania: Leader of the fae. This term is not gendered—male and female leaders have used the same term over the centuries.

Tana: Consort to Titania. This term is not gendered. It is simply an honorific reserved for the partner of the Titania.

Tatya: Prince/Princess (non-gendered).

Fayr Dahn: Good morning

Irish:

Iníon: Daughter

German:

Dirndl: A feminine dress native to countries in the Alpine region. A dirndl consists of a close-fitting bodice featuring a low neckline, a blouse worn under the bodice, a wide high-waisted skirt and an apron. It's typically worn by barmaids in Southern Germany.

Herr: Equivalent to "Mister"

Frau: Young woman

ACKNOWLEDGMENTS

Well. We did it again.

Before we get to the individual acknowledgments, we want to take a second to recognize some of the people that helped us get this book palatable for the public.

The Beta Readers: Michael, Liza, Laura, and Amber—your feedback and insight into this book, these characters, and the overarching plot was invaluable. This is a better, more cohesive, more engaging story because of all of you. You cannot even know how important you all are. Thank you for everything.

Stef, our amazing cover artist—you crushed the cover AGAIN. Thank you for all your hard work.

Rachael, our talented map maker—thank you for bringing our map dreams to life.

And of course, to the ARC readers—your early reads and reviews are so incredibly valuable. Thank you for your time and energy in helping get this book in front of hundreds if not thousands of readers.

Lastly, to our fans. Thank you for diving into our world, for following Slate and Dani's story, for all your reviews, and for all the hype. You've helped make our dream come true.

Jess's Acknowledgments:

First, to Sierra. I'll keep them short and sweet this time, I promise. Thank you for reminding me every single day that the opinions of others do not matter whatsoever. Thank you for reminding me that this whole... book publishing and marketing thing is not that deep. Thank you for reminding me to not make it all harder than it's worth.

To my husband Fred—I did it again, and I didn't cry nearly as much this time! There's nothing I can say here that you don't already know. Thank you for your steady love and support.

To all my in-person friends—thank you for celebrating Book 1 with me and being excited for Book 2! It allowed me to feel more confident in talking about this world and these characters.

To all my distant-friends—Nina, Tia, Lindsay, Laura, Amber, Liza, thank you for your steady support through everything. It's such a blessing to have reader and writer friends to lean on when I need them.

Sierra Acknowledgments:

We did it!

Thank you, Jessica, for being the best co-author anyone could possibly dream of. Thank you for all the hard work and dedication you pour into our books; we would never have gotten this far without you.

I'd also like to thank my husband. Michael, you took so much of your time and effort to help make our book the best it can be. Thank you also for all the support and love you have wrapped me up in. I can't imagine my life without you.

Lastly, thank you to everyone else who has supported us, who has read and reviewed and enjoyed our books. Thank you for helping us with our dream, and thank you for loving the world we have built.

ABOUT THE AUTHORS

J.S Alexandria is the dynamic writing duo that comprises of two best friends—Jessica and Sierra. They share a mutual love of fantastical stories and have a 20-year history of writing books together.

Sierra lives in Philadelphia with her husband and guinea pigs. Her favorite part of the writing process is the romance and the delicious angst that comes along with it. When not writing, Sierra can be found playing video games, watching anime, cooking, or listening to audiobooks.

Jessica lives in Vermont with her husband and two cat children—Zelda and Midna. She's a career martial artist and currently holds a 4th degree black belt in traditional Taekwondo. Jess can often be found reading a good book, hunting for Pokémon, playing with tarot cards, or scheming up a new story.

Check out jsalexandriabooks.com for sneak peeks and teasers for upcoming novels.